IMMORTAL PASSION

She hadn't meant to kiss him. The movement of his mouth against hers was highly distracting. The silky probe of his tongue shook her fledgling concentration. With each notch it gave, his responsiveness increased. And she couldn't say she minded so very much being molded by his hands ... tempted by his touch.

She lifted herself up, panting lightly against the invitation of his lips. This wasn't how she'd planned it. But it was so beautiful in its spontaneity.

His eyes were open, their glaze gone. Passion simmered in the darker depths ... desire for her.

"I want to make love with you, Nicole."

She came back down for the luxury of his kiss. His palms were skimming down the curve of her waist. He regarded her somberly while her fingertips fluttered along his cheeks and neck, finally stilling there where his pulse beat hard and relentlessly.

"I love you, Nicole."

"I want you with me, Marchand," she whispered. "Always. *Always.*"

And she bent toward the beckoning bow of his throat, lost to the anticipation of the bite ...

Advance praise for MIDNIGHT TEMPTATION:

"An extraordinary, moving and sensual tale of supernatural love powerful enough to defy death. Nancy Gideon is a bright artistic star of epic proportion in the supernatural galaxy. Five Star!"
AFFAIRE de COEUR

NANCY GIDEON
MIDNIGHT TEMPTATION

PINNACLE BOOKS
WINDSOR PUBLISHING CORP.

PINNACLE BOOKS are published by

Windsor Publishing Corp.
850 Third Ave
New York, NY 10022

First Pinnacle Printing: October, 1994

Printed in the United States of America

Chapter One

A sleek shadow slipped between rocks strewn along the gorge bottom. Sure of foot and just as fleet, the woodland creature made no noise; at least none discernible to the average ear. But to the figure crouched low amid the heather, the animal's passing was heralded by a definite pattern of sound. The soft panting breaths, the steady beckoning of its heartbeat; all the invitation the stalker needed.

Closer the smaller predator came, unaware that the hunter in search of its nightly prey was about to be hunted. And without warning, an agility that could evade the talons of a hawk failed before a more unexpected attack.

Snatched up from the ground and all hopes of escape, the creature squirmed in desperation; then, realizing the futility of its struggle, merely hung limp, its heart pounding, its eyes glassy with terror. And the soothing words of its captor did nothing to lessen its fear.

"It's all right. I won't harm you."

Nicole Radouix held the trembling fox gently, stroking it with a hand both cautious and admiring. How soft its fur, how frantic its respiration. Beneath the silky coat, she could feel the frightened pitter of the animal's pulse, and that beat as much as the creature's warmth charmed her into a mesmerized study.

Though she had caught the fox on a whim, just to see if she could, now that she had it clasped close enough to experience its panic, she couldn't make herself release it. Instinct she didn't understand rose strong and sharp within her and her restraining hand tightened about the delicate rib cage until it felt as though the animal's wild and fragile heart was fluttering in her palm. Sensation stirred, making her own breaths come in quick succession. The fox would have understood the basic urges spiking through her. So would any hunter of the weak and less nimble.

Power. Control. Satisfaction.

Hunger.

But these feelings were not normal for a girl of seventeen and even as she recognized them, Nicole grew afraid.

Mon Dieu! What was she thinking!

Carefully, appalled that she was ready to hurt such a glorious creature, she lowered the fox to the ground and opened her hands. For a moment, the animal stood frozen in uncertainty.

"Go now," she urged. "You're free."

The sound of her voice was all it took to send the fox running. There was a brief flash of dull red color before it darted between the rocks to safety. It realized, as Nicole refused to, how close it had come to dying.

Nicole stood with eyes closed, drawing in deep breaths of the twilight air. Its crispness flushed the strange darkness of her mood and eased her aroused senses into a more relaxed state. It had happened again, that loss of reason to foreign urgency. She didn't know what to do.

She couldn't very well approach her respectable parents with the news that she was helplessly drawn by the desire to kill. They would think her mad. She, herself, was beginning to believe it, for surely it wasn't normal for the human senses to be so razor-sharp and honed to the lure of a heartbeat.

Suddenly agitated to the point of tears, Nicole began to run. She knew there was no way to escape what lay within her, but she'd found there was safety among her own kind. When surrounded by the peasants and the pleasant visitors to their village, her acuity was muted by the confusion of many and she felt as average as any of them. Only when she was alone did isolation provoke her passions into their unnatural state. And here, in this small community, where roads ran through ploughed fields, and houses of grey stone with pale sea-green doors and roofs muffled by moss seemed asleep even until the noon hour, silence and solitude were too often her companions. And with them came the awareness of what was waking inside her.

The streets of Grez were empty of the artists who posed their easels each day behind the row of little houses, capturing the serene beauty of the river Loing and the brooding Fontainebleau forest that bordered the horizon. Many of the cottages had been converted into studios; during the summer months they were packed with painters and musicians who came to soak up the stillness. Many of them were English like her mother, and all of them were a delight to a lonely young girl who'd been no farther from her home than the stands of mammoth oak, beech, and Norway pine. She'd never seen the cities they spoke of. Their words made enticing pictures upon an impressionable mind, until she begged to be allowed to visit at least Paris, which was only forty-some miles to the north. But her parents were adamantly opposed to it. What could she find in Paris that they didn't provide her with here, was their consistent argument. She had an enviable education via an extensive library. She had the frivolous artists to converse with and the local peasant families to care for. And she was greatly loved within the elegant walls of her father's chateau. What more could she wish for?

How could she explain? How would they ever understand that she needed the noise, the distraction, the crowds to hide in. Because she feared if she was left to her own devices much longer, something terrible was going to occur.

She raced along the quiet streets. Sounds of merriment wafted out from behind the closed cottage doors and from the inns that stood side by side with farm buildings. But those excluding sounds did nothing to lessen her sense of separation. So she hurried on toward the home she was raised in, to the family who was devoted to her, hoping that among them, she could find peace. And perhaps on this night, she could find as well the courage to confront them with the truth.

The chateau was some distance from the village, nestled back against the fringe of forest. Its plain stone walls warmed like the sand by the sea in sunlight and its pink brick loggias up above glowed blood red when caught by the setting sun. It was a spacious home made up of Italian-style terraces, a high French roofline, huge chimneys and a courtyard surrounded by arcades and galleries; a study of grace and strength combined, much like the man who'd designed it to be a pleasing blend of Classic and Renaissance. Within, brick walls were hung with tapestries and works of art but held no mirrors to reflect back the scene of wealthy elegance. Within, Nicole would find relief from what troubled her soul.

She was breathing hard when at last she approached the entry door. Unwilling to startle those inside with her rather wild appearance, she took a moment to smooth her skirts and to catch up the long trails of ebony hair that had escaped the coil behind her head, hoping the respite would lessen the flush in her cheeks and the panic in her eyes. Before she could move forward, that great door opened and two figures appeared there in silhouette against the light burning bright within. She recognized them immediately as her parents, and their pose as one of intimate conversation. They stood close together, too involved in one of their many secrets to notice her among the shadows, so she waited and she listened, unashamed. How else would she ever learn of anything that went on within their secluded walls?

"Must you go out tonight?" her mother murmured from where she'd burrowed against his shoulder. Her eyes were closed and her voice caught with an edge of strain.

Very gently, her father's hand stroked down the spill of her hair; hair once as dark as her daughter's but now shot attractively with strands of silver. His words were as soothing as his caress. "I must, little one, not by choice but from necessity. I needn't explain these things to you, my love. You know I would rather spend the evening with you."

"Then stay." Her fingers curled in the folds of his coat, as desperate in effect as the snag in her voice. If he was moved by either plea, he didn't show it.

Instead, he told her, "I love you, Bella. I will not be long," and he began to untangle himself from her grasp.

Before he was completely freed, she reached up to clasp his face between her hands, pulling him down for a scorching kiss. The exchange didn't embarrass their daughter as she watched from the concealing shadows, for they were always candid in their displays of affection. They were a very loving couple, at least in Nicole's romantic mind. Some were puzzled by the bond they shared. Her mother was English. At one and forty, she was still a fine-looking woman. But the man she'd married was obviously of the upper classes; wealthy, cosmopolitan and handsome enough to have any woman of rank he desired. And he'd chosen the daughter of a London physician. A woman who looked old enough to be his mother. He appeared more Nicole's contemporary, with his unlined features and easy grace. But it was ever apparent that the woman he'd married was the woman he adored. At least Nicole had always believed that to be true, in spite of the whispers she'd heard that said opposite.

It was rumored that during his many absences from home, the beautiful Louis Radouix spent his time courting a string of young peasant women who fell easy prey to his cultured charm.

They were just ignorant, Nicole told herself as she staunchly defended her family. Rural minds couldn't comprehend the kind of man her father was. They mistook the innocent captivation of his smile for calculated seduction and his acts of generosity for ones of scheming intent. Had they ever seen her father the way he was now, tenderly framing her mother's face within his palms, they would not cast doubt upon his devotion. Had they ever seen them together, playfully rolling about on the sofa while lost to laughter, or him with his auburn head pillowed upon her lap, murmuring how lucky he was to have her with him, they wouldn't be so quick to gossip that he was bored with her charms. A man as enchanting and mysterious as Louis Radouix was bound to stir up talk. His secluded way of life bred whispering. Even his own daughter was left in the dark about much of his doings and found herself inventing colorful scenarios to explain what he would not. Their lives were wreathed in secrets only man and wife were privy to, so it was no wonder curiosity flourished and blossomed into maligning murmurs and speculation.

Questions about where her father spent his daylight hours never led to any answers. Nicole learned at a young age to merely accept that he was gone and to be glad for his return. When she was a child, she liked to imagine that he was a spy, sometimes for her mother's native England, sometimes for Italy, the country of his birth. He was suave and furtive enough to be cast into that role. But when he was home, he was her loving father, quick to take her up for a tight embrace, always ready with a delightful story about faraway places he'd visited in his youth. He was the buffer to her mother's sheltering.

Had Arabella had her way, Nicole would never step foot outside the surrounding walls of the chateau. Such terrible panic lit her mother's eyes whenever she was a trifle late in returning home. There was a shadow of unmistakable fear that crossed her competent features whenever she heard of a stranger asking about the reclusive owners of the pink-tinged chateau. It had something to do with their rapid flight from England in the year before Nicole's birth. It was somehow connected to the vague responses she got whenever she asked about the past. Arabella lived like a cautious fugitive and would have kept her daughter smotheringly close had her hus-

band not eased the girl away. It was Louis who gently
admonished, "Let her be free, my love. You watch too
close. You worry too much. Let her enjoy life."

So naturally it was her father she thought of when it
became apparent she could no longer contain her troubles. He would listen and he would have some solution
at hand, while her mother would undoubtedly lock her
in her room and dispose of the key. It wasn't that her
mother didn't love her. Not at all. She was a most pampered child. But there had always been an edge of caution to her mother's attention, the feel that she was
being carefully observed. Perhaps it was because
Arabella was English and the English were notoriously
prim and watchful of their children. Nicole was not
about to give her cause to hold any tighter rein than she
already did.

Nicole waited in the darkness until her parents shared
one last long kiss. Then Louis stepped back and her
mother let him go. Nicole was intent upon following
him, yet she saw the look of helpless despair etching
Arabella's features as her mother turned back inside the
house. Saw but didn't understand the cause of her misery. It perplexed her for only a moment, then Nicole focused upon her own problems as she scurried silently
after her father.

There was only the thin slice of a moon overhead.
Nicole was hard-pressed not to lose the dark-garbed fig-
urc ahead amongst the shadows of the wood. As she followed, she kept a careful distance, working on what she
would say to him, working up the needed bravery to
speak the words. She would begin with the dreams;
dreams that were both freeing and frightening. Then
she would tell him of her unusual strength and perceptions. Lastly and most disturbingly, she would have to

confess her developing taste for raw foods. Because he loved her so, he would not be dismayed. He would not turn from her in horror. Or at least, that was what she hoped as she goaded herself on. She was concentrating on this task when he stepped into a small leafy copse where the scent of pine was sharp and sweet and night sounds made a subtle music. He stopped there, head turning slowly as if in search of something. Before she could approach him, she noticed his stance stiffening, then she, too, saw they were not alone.

A woman emerged from the far hedge of pine. She was cloaked for discretion, and the way she came straight toward him told Nicole that this was no chance meeting. Nicole stood, as frozen as the fox had been, paralyzed by what she was sure she was about to witness; the destruction of her secure world.

Louis waited until the woman reached him. Neither spoke. Slowly he unfurled the hood of her cloak to reveal youthful features; as youthful as her own. His fingers worked the fastenings, and the length of coarse wool fell about her feet. Then he began to undo the strings of her peasant blouse, loosening the fabric so that it fell away from the soft white glow of her skin. With a murmur of something too low for Nicole to hear, he bent his head, his mouth moving in a seducing sweep along the young woman's uplifted features, trailing down to the exposed arch of her throat. The woman moaned, a sound rich in rapture.

Nicole clapped her hands over her mouth to contain her cry of distress and outrage. How could he! How could he leave her mother, his wife, to rendezvous with this unworthy creature? How could he so betray she who loved him? How could he so callously destroy her faith in him, her admiration for him, with this illicit moonlit tryst?

She must have made some unconscious sound of protest, for suddenly his burnished head jerked up and the woman in his arms gave a sharp cry akin to pain. Nicole tried to meld back into the shadows, but in her haste and upset, her movements were clumsy and the snap of underbrush gave her away. Her father spun in her direction and for one brief horrifically clear moment, Nicole saw him as he really was. He was no womanizer out to chase a local skirt. He was no coldhearted cheat ready to break the trust of the woman who wed him. What he was, was much worse.

For in that chill ribbon of moonlight, Nicole saw all too plainly the sightless glaze of the woman's eyes and the smear of crimson at her torn throat. A crimson that liberally stained her father's mouth and the sharp teeth he'd bared in a monstrous snarl.

She ran. There was no room for anything in her mind save wild thoughts of flight. She surged through the darkness, losing the path, losing her way in her heedless panic until she heard him behind her.

"Nicole!"

With a sob, she raced onward, feeling the limbs of unseen trees yank at her free-flowing hair and brambles rip at her ankles. Breath came in labored gasps as she staggered through the night, plunging ahead while her senses strained behind for sounds of pursuit. She heard nothing. Seeing the lights ahead as beacons of salvation, she burst out of the forest in a mad scramble across the yard. Inarticulate sounds escaped her. For on this night, she must surely have gone mad to have pictured such a scene.

The familiar sight and welcome of the inside of her

home went by in an unrecognizable blur as Nicole bolted for the stairway rising up majestically through the structure's center. She stumbled upon the carpeted steps and was continuing on all fours when one of her elbows was caught from below. She gave a fearful cry, afraid to look behind her.

"Nicole, wait. Don't run from me."

She risked a glance and saw her father there, his uplifted features stark with despair, his eyes steeped in tragedy. His chin wet with fresh blood.

She gave another incoherent cry and jerked free. Even as she surged forward, his voice followed, so broken, so heavy with pain.

"Nicole . . . please! Let me explain!"

Weeping frantically, she reached the upper hall and darted to the safety of her chambers. She flung the door shut, shot the bolt and leaned back against the sturdy wood, shock rattling through her in fierce teeth-clattering spasms. Then, even before she heard him, she felt his presence on the other side of the door. A whispering chill of something not quite human.

"Nicole, don't be afraid of me. I won't hurt you. Let me explain what you saw."

Her breath caught up in a sob as she watched the knob turn this way and that. And she waited, shaking fitfully, but he made no attempt to force his way in. Not physically, at least.

"Nicole . . . I love you."

She squeezed her eyes shut and shuddered uncontrollably. "My God, what are you?" The question tore from the heart of her confusion.

There was a long beat of silence, then his quiet reply. "Your father."

"No," she moaned in denying misery.

"Let me in. Let me explain. Please."

"No! Stay away! Stay away from me! Demon! Monster! Stay away! You are not my father!"

On the other side of the barring portal, Louis Radman writhed beneath those damning words. And he couldn't deny them. For that was exactly what he was. Demon. Monster. Worse.

"Louis?"

When he turned toward his wife, she gave a soft cry. She'd never seen such devastation in his gaze.

"What's happened? Louis, tell me."

He looked at her through welling eyes and spoke in fractured syllables. "She saw . . . she knows."

Wordlessly, she took him in her arms, sharing his hurt, absorbing his grief and guilt, wishing there was some way to absolve him of it.

"Bella . . . what are we going to do?"

Arabella held him tightly. The day she'd dreaded had come at last.

"We tell her the truth."

Chapter Two

Dawn had warmed the corridor with cheerful pastels when Arabella tried the knob once more and found it turned freely.

"Nicole?"

From where she lay curled upon her bed still wrapped in her cloak against a ceaseless chill, Nicole did not respond. Over the endless night hours, she'd wept a river of tears. Morning left her raw of throat and drained of feeling. For all purposes, she lay lifeless and staring upon the rich gold damask of her coverlet. She couldn't summon enough strength to react to her mother's gentle touch.

"Oh, Nicole, my darling, I'm so sorry you had to discover the truth in such a brutal fashion. Louis wanted to tell you long ago but I begged him not to. I wanted to give you time to know the goodness of the man he is. I was sure if you knew him, you would understand—"

Nicole cut her off with a raspy cry. "How could you let me believe that creature is my father?"

Arabella stroked her tumbled hair and the rigid set of one slender shoulder. She tried to hide the way her heart was breaking. "He is your father."

"No." She gave her head a jerky shake of denial. "No. What I saw was no man at all. How dare you pretend otherwise?"

"Nicole, you have only to look in your mirror to know you are his child. You look at the world through his eyes. You were born of our love."

Those green-gold eyes were now accusing. "Love? How could you love such a—"

"Nicole! I will not allow you to wound him further by saying such awful things." The steel that had always resided beneath her mother's soft facade flexed itself and held strong. But Nicole could be just as stubborn.

"By saying what? The truth? When was the last time anyone spoke the truth in this house?"

Arabella's tone gentled. "Every time we said we loved you."

Nicole swallowed hard, the movement raking her throat with fire. "What is he?" Despite her mother's words, she could no longer think of him as her father.

"A good man cursed to live in darkness off the blood of others. A man my father brought back to a normal life long enough for us to wed and conceive you. He is no monster, no demon. How can you say such things of the man who's loved you all these years? Has he ever harmed you? Has he ever been anything other than a devoted father?"

"I've seen what else he is." She gave a short, half-hysterical laugh. "Oh, how I wish he had been just an unfaithful husband out meeting a lover in the moonlight."

Arabella drew a shallow breath. "Nicole, what he does, he must do. It does not mean he loves us any less."

Then why did her voice waver ever so slightly?

"Where is he now?" For the first time ever, fear inged her voice. As if she thought him a threat.

"He is . . . resting below. As soon as night falls, he will be up to see you. Nicole, I beg you, listen to what he has to say. Give him the chance to make you understand how difficult it has been to live this lie. Will you listen?"

But Nicole wouldn't answer. She rolled away, her arms hugged tightly about herself in a defensive manner.

"Nicole, please. He loves you. We both love you. You must believe that."

Everything Nicole once believed had been shattered beneath that crescent moon. Everything was a lie.

In a soft, stilted voice, she murmured, "I'd like to rest now, Mother. Please go."

And she struggled to keep from stiffening as her mother leaned down to embrace her.

After a time, Nicole let the numbness leave her mind, and unwelcomed thoughts began to turn wildly. The man she'd worshiped and adored was an unholy being. Those same lips that had smiled at her childish triumphs and had pressed to her brow each night as he saw her to bed had feasted in vile abandon upon the blood of innocents. Why had she never suspected? Had her love and their efforts to provide a normal facade completely blinded her to the sham of an acceptable family life? Thinking back, she realized she'd never seen him sit down to a dinner with them. Never. He would drop a kiss atop her head as she breakfasted, saying he was on his way out, or he would arrive just as they were finishing their evening meal, vowing he'd just eaten. Just eaten, indeed! From what unnatural wellspring? How could they have hidden such a horror from her? How could they believe she could accept it now?

And she knew right then she could never look upon her father the same way again. She could never look upon his face without seeing it contorted in that demonic snarl. Or watch him kiss her mother without seeing that unfortunate female swooning in his arms. Nor could she endure his touch or pretend things could remain unchanged between them.

So why remain in this house of lies, where love once betrayed could not be restored?

It took her very little time once she put her mind to it. She took one bag and stuffed it with the things she thought she might need. She had no money of her own but plenty of valuable jewels that could be turned for coin. Those she took as well. And while her mother was below believing her to be asleep, and while her father lay somewhere in his unnatural slumber, Nicole slipped from the house she could no longer think of as her home and fled toward Grez and freedom.

Away from the demon she'd discovered her father to be. Away from the fear that she was becoming just like him.

The slope leading down to the river Loing was already crowded with eager artists, and Nicole wove her way through them. Seeking a familiar face and finding it, she gave a great sigh of relief.

"Camille, are you still leaving for Paris this afternoon?"

"Why good morning, Miss Radouix. Indeed, I am. Daresay you plan to miss me?" The young painter doffed his beret and grinned cheekily.

"Daresay I plan to accompany you."

He blinked as if he'd misunderstood.

"That is, if you have room. You see, a very old and dear friend of mine who lives in the city has recently taken ill and I must get to her side. My father is abroad and I am unable to obtain safe passage. I know I would be safe within your care. Only please say you'll take me with you?"

Overwhelmed by her petition, his chivalrous nature stirred by her confidence, what could he say? "Where are your bags?"

"Just what I'm carrying here. I don't plan to stay. Just long enough to assure myself that she is being cared for. My mother will be joining me at week's end and she is bringing the bulk of our belongings." How quickly that desperate fiction came into her mind, just the right words to put a gentleman at ease. This one smiled with a ready gallantry.

"I depart at noon, fair miss. You may await me at the Loing Inn. I shall be there as soon as I capture the right element of lighting."

She took a moment to admire his canvas. "Your best work," she praised, generous in her relief. He smiled again and daubed at his palette.

Waiting in the common room of the inn was a restless agony. Any moment, she expected her mother or their loyal servant, Takeo, to come bursting in to drag her home. It wasn't her intention to make a scene if they did. But it wasn't her intention to return with them, either. Thankfully, her resolve wasn't tested, for Camille was prompt, arriving to show her the finished landscape; a fine and pretty piece, it was, and to bid her to watch over it while he collected his things and paid for his stay.

Then they were headed north in his poorly sprung carriage. Nicole turned up the collar of her cloak and determinedly refused to look behind her. Her future was ahead in *la ville lumière*. Paris, the city of her dreams. There, she would lose herself and begin a new life, untouched by the dark circumstances she uncovered.

Or so she hoped.

Nicole had always heard that Paris was the most sophisticated city in the world, a place for good food and drink, of men that intrigued and women that fascinated. Her guide could have told her it was also a city of dissipation, pleasure, luxury, extravagance and ruin. A place for men to lose their fortunes, their honor, their manhood and their faith. But Camille remained silent, because the moment they were in sight of the city, Nicole's face began to glow with the animation missing since that morning. And because he also thought it was the most delightful city in the world. If Paris was like a woman, it was a teasing coquette, not to blame if her promises were insincere.

From her seat in her friend's carriage, Nicole felt her level of energy escalate to match the pulse of the city. They wound through a medieval network of streets, culs-de-sac, passages, squares, and boulevards, each leading to another as the whole of Paris spread out before her wondering eyes. The byways were swarming with carriages, sedan chairs and pedestrians. No one walked; they ran to keep up the vigorous pace. The air was alive with the bellowing of coachmen and the coaxing cries of hundreds of small tradesmen shouting: "Oysters in the shell!"; "Chimneys cleaned from top to bottom!"; "Fine cherries, one sou the pound!"; "Flowers, roses and buds for lasses and lads!" All sounds combined in one noisy cacophony of life. And Nicole was charmed into forgetting her troubles as these new surroundings bombarded her senses.

"Where do I take you, Miss Radouix?"

"What?" Nicole tore her gaze from the enchantment of the passing scene reluctantly, then realized what he meant by his question. Where, indeed? "It's not far. Just up ahead. Let me try to remember the name of the street. How foolish of me not to have written it down."

Camille gave her a long look, the beginnings of a frown touching his lips. Nicole could see he was starting to wonder if he'd made a mistake in offering her the ride, wondering if she could be a runaway. The last thing she wanted was for him to suffer a fit of conscience and turn the rig around to pack her back toward Grez.

"Oh, now I remember!" she cried with feigned anticipation. "It's just around the corner, there!" She pointed to a distant street. Between them and it was a veritable clog of vehicles. She could see him trying to plot some way to cross it when she insisted, "You'll never get to that side. Set me down here. I should enjoy the walking. It's such a beautiful day."

"Well I don't know . . ."

"You've been so helpful. How can I thank you?" And she stretched up to touch a kiss upon his reddening cheek. That was all it took.

"Now you be careful. This is not Grez. These ruffians will run a lady down if she makes a misstep."

"I'll be careful." Already she was angling to jump down, her meager bag in hand. Camille stopped the carriage and came around to assist her. He looked most uncomfortable about letting her loose within the rushing mob. In his eyes, she was so fragile, so innocent. Too much so for this place. So he adopted a brotherly air.

"Now, mademoiselle, if you should need any assistance, please come to me and ask. I would be most honored to be of help to you."

She blushed slightly and murmured prettily, "Oh, but you have done so much already."

"Nonsense. I've done nothing. If you should need a . . . *friend,* I have a small flat in the Quartier Latin. Ask for me there, for I am well known." That bit of self-importance was close enough to the truth.

"I do appreciate it. You are most kind."

But seeing the way she was glancing impatiently down the walk, he knew he would not be seeing the lovely lady again. Ah, well . . .

"You've made the journey most enjoyable, Miss Radouix. May I present you with this small token so that you might remember me." And with a grand flourish, he gave her the painting he'd completed that morning.

"Oh, m'sieur! You mustn't. It is too much!"

"Please! I insist. Something to recall you to home."

She took it then, because to protest would be bad form. Something to recall her to home. She glanced at the pastoral scene and felt a sear to the heart. Reminders of home were the last things she desired. But she tucked the painting beneath her arm and shifted her bag to the other while the jaunty artist climbed back aboard and, grinning wide, rejoined the flow of traffic.

Feeling suddenly abandoned amid such strange and unwelcoming surroundings, Nicole took a deep steadying breath. Paris. All of it lay before her. A sense of adventurous freedom overcame her momentary panic. After listening so avidly to tales of the city's many charms, why was she hesitating? Was this not her dream? To break loose from the shackles of her sheltered country life to see something of the world beyond? Of course it was! How she'd come to be here and why were not the issue. She was here! And she would enjoy. She would walk for a while and take in the sights, then she would have plenty of time to decide what to do about money and lodgings. With what her jewelry would bring, she should be able to live comfortably for some months, perhaps longer if she was frugal. Long enough for her to patch together the fraying fabric of her life.

She strolled along the banks of the Seine. It was a delightful exercise, taking in the river's tree-shaded quays and picturesque boats. Her movement was slow, her step a meandering country pace so she wouldn't miss anything. Where she stood at the Pont des Arts was the very center of historic Paris, with the majestic Louvre, which she recognized from books, on the left, and across the river, the *quartier* of the poet and artist where Camille was heading. She paused for a moment to drink it all in. To give her arm ease, she set her bag at her feet. And just like that, it was gone.

It took her a moment to understand the significance of a fleeing figure with all her worldly goods in hand.

"Stop! Thief!"

Her cry blended in with the sounds of the city, swallowed up by the carriage drivers' yells. Clutching the painting to her side, she began to run in pursuit, but the mill of people quickly absorbed the robber. It was obvious he knew exactly where he was going, for he was quickly lost from sight. After running a long block, Nicole slowed, breathing hard and blinking back tears of surprise and despair. Several curious glances touched upon her but no offer of aid came from the indifferent mass pushing to get around her.

All she had was in that bag.
Now what would she do?

Louis Radman took one look at his wife's face upon his waking and he knew all was lost.

"She's gone, Louis."

"Gone?" he echoed in a neutral tone.

"Her bag, some of her clothes, her jewelry. I'm afraid she's fled rather than face the truth."

Arabella stepped back so he could nimbly leap from the silk-lined crate that housed him during his daylight sleep. Within the contoured interior, she had lain beside him to tell him she had conceived a child. It was the same box that had carried him in their flight from London. He'd lain nailed within it on their choppy channel crossing, not so much to keep him inside but to keep the curious out. He kept to it more out of sentiment than comfort, though he claimed it didn't matter where he lay during his twilight slumber as long as it was safe and out of the sun's consuming rays. He preferred a bed with his wife beside him, but that time was a world away, a memory treasured but never returned to.

And now, he would have preferred a way to comfort his wife with a word or touch, but knew of none. Their daughter had run from them—or rather from him—in horror. How could she, and indeed, Arabella herself, not blame him?

Arabella followed wordlessly as he climbed up from the underground caverns into the lamplit spaciousness of their home, his mood composed and pensive. The guilt was not gone, but he was in control of it. One did not live for three hundred years without learning a certain degree of detachment from that kind of pain. But it was new to his wife. He could feel Arabella's watchful eyes upon him, could sense her distress and her impatience. He didn't need to read her thoughts to pick up that message. She was a mother, after all. How else would she react?

"I don't understand her, Louis. Why would she run away?"

"Why?" He gave her a soft, humorless laugh. "She has just found herself to be the offspring of a devil. I would say she acted quite appropriately. We should have expected her to flee and been better prepared."

Arabella blanched. "If I had known she would attempt such a thing, I would not have left her side!"

"I know, my love." He touched her tenderly then, his palms soothing down her forearms until their hands clasped together. His hands were yet cool from below. Cool because he'd been interrupted in his search for inner fire the night before. She clung to him for a moment, then pulled away in agitation.

"After all the love between you, I would have thought she'd stay to hear you out." Arabella paced beyond him to the window, looking out into the darkness, trying not to imagine her child lost somewhere within it. She wasn't sure which emotion to act upon; her worry for Nicole's safety or her anger over the girl's ill-advised flight. She couldn't believe their child had fled out of fear for her own safety. More like a matter of pride. Foolish, dangerous pride in this particular instance. Had she absorbed none of their ceaseless cautionings? Had she taken none of their warnings to heart? But then, Nicole didn't know the true danger. And Arabella prayed she would not find out.

"I don't believe she'd be much interested in anything I have to tell her at the moment. I believe it comes ten years too late. We should have trusted her with the truth long ago, Bella. Now she feels we have betrayed her."

"Hindsight is a marvelous torment. What will we do now?" She was struggling hard not to give way to a wild panic. She was a scientist's daughter, after all. Such a display would do no good. What was needed were a clear head and immediate plans. Still, she could not retain a small sob of anxiousness from escaping when she thought of all that was at stake. Why hadn't she watched the girl more carefully in this most important instance?

Louis came up behind her, his palms gliding over her tense shoulders, kneading them into a state of relaxation. "We'll find her. We'll bring her home."

He made it sound so simple, and she needed that assurance. It helped her get her emotions under control. "Expect a struggle, my love. She is a headstrong girl."

He chuckled and eased a kiss along her temple. "She comes by that quite honestly, I believe."

"Well, it would seem she inherited none of my common sense. What could she be thinking? She is scarcely prepared to meet the world and all its dangers." A shudder shook through her as she imagined the worst, and Louis's arms banded tight, molding her back against him. As always, she took comfort there.

"We will find her. And we will make her listen. Then she can make up her own mind. I will not force her to remain here. I cannot demand that she love what I am when I cannot manage that feat myself."

Moved to think beyond her own fears, Arabella revolved in his embrace, her calm grey eyes lit with concern, a concern with maintaining the close bond of family. That's all she had ever wanted. "Louis, she will come to her senses. She loves you too much not to see the man you are beyond the half-life that you're forced to lead."

"Perhaps." But he looked so uncertain and melancholy. "Right now, she sees only that thing in the woods and she feels she can no longer trust us. It will be hard for her to come back to us. She was raised to believe she was safe here."

"She *was* safe. Were we wrong in thinking we could protect her forever? Oh, Louis, if anything should happen—"

He kissed her furrowed brow gently. "Nothing will. I'll send Mrs. Kampford down to speak to those artists she is so fond of. Someone must have seen her and can tell us her direction. She can't have gotten far. She hasn't the means or the experience to outrun us for long. Perhaps one of them is sheltering her even now. Please do not fret, my love. We will have her back with us and you may delight in scolding her."

Arabella didn't smile at his mild teasing. Her thoughts were much too dark to be shaken loose by light words and a loving assurance.

"She doesn't understand the danger. She doesn't know all that can hurt her. We should have prepared her, Louis. We should have warned her what to watch for. What if others find her first?"

That was the terror that undermined their happy years; the fear that all could be brought to a tragic end. Not at the hands of ignorant and superstitious townspeople but of Louis's own kind. They'd left their London home and prestigious title to sink into the anonymity of the French countryside under an assumed name where Nicole could be raised to a quiet, sheltered life and where, hopefully, Louis's past could not find them. Perhaps those were the naive dreams of two desperate people who were in love and longing to live together in a near to normal existence. But little was normal about Louis Radman other than his devotion to his family. And for seventeen years, they had stood guard over their precious child, protecting her from outside pain, watchful of any signs that would suggest she was following her father's path of the damned.

"If she is your daughter, she will be smart enough to come home." His fingertips soothed over Arabella's worried features. Then his mood deepened into grim reflection. "If she is my daughter, she will be able to take care of herself."

Chapter Three

She spent her first night in Paris huddled in a doorway.

"Here now! Get up from there!"

The firm swat of a stiff-bristled broom sent Nicole rolling off the stone stoop onto the walk.

"Be on your way," shouted the indignant shopkeeper, who brandished the broom like a sword. "The likes of you is bad for business. Go on now. Get, before I call the *gendarmes!*" He gave her another prod to show he was sincere before retreating back into his nice warm building.

She wasn't sure which was harder; forcing her aching muscles to support her after the miserably cramped rest or enduring the fact that she was thought to be a common prostitute. Not certain where she would go but knowing she could not remain where she was, Nicole wobbled to her feet and returned to the cold city streets. This day was more bleak than the former. Grim clouds scudded close to foretell of incoming weather, tinging the Seine the same dreary grey. Pulling her cloak tighter, Nicole tucked her painting beneath her arm and set out at an aimless shuffle. Flavorful scents from the abundant cafés quickened an earnest rumbling, reminding her that she hadn't eaten for an entire day. But food was the last of her worries. Shelter was her immediate concern.

She had few options. If she went to the police to report the robbery, she would be returned home, and that would not do. She would not go back there, regardless of her situation. Her memories of a loving home and caring parents were illusions, lies. She wouldn't think of her palatial rooms and cosseted existence. She wouldn't dwell upon the fact that even now, Mrs. Kampford would have been bringing her a cup of hot chocolate in bed and that a sumptuous feast would be waiting on the buffet below. Because below there rested a nightmare she'd just been wakened to. Since she could not go back, she would go forward. And her first forward move was to find someplace to stay.

Shivering with the night's chill and pinched with hunger, Nicole was not as intrigued with Paris as she had been the previous day. Afoot and adrift, she saw different sights than the grand attractions noted from the comfort of a carriage. She saw the tattered appearance of the populace that pushed by her and the cheerless desperation in their faces. She found herself among a network of stinking alleys, muddly lanes and airless culs-de-sac where poverty was packed in tight amid the monuments of the elite. And it was a scary, unfriendly place to be.

Clutching her painting as she was jostled by the hurrying mass, Nicole had a thought—an inspiration. Camille. He'd said to call on him if she needed anything, and at the moment she as very needy. Perhaps he would be willing to put her up for a few nights and share some bread and a little much-desired warmth of mood. She would have to concoct some tale as to what had happened to her supposed friend and why she couldn't return home, but she could work up that story while she crossed the Seine and entered the bohemian world of the Latin Quarter.

Camille had told her about the colony of artists and students among which he lived. He spoke grandly of *la vie de bohème*, whose borders were poverty and hope, art and illusion, where creativity expressed itself as freedom from responsibility, where odd dress, long hair, living for the moment, radical political enthusiasms, loose sexual mores and an addiction to nightlife ruled. It had sounded wildly romantic to a sheltered girl on the banks of the river Loing. But as that same young woman crossed the Seine to traverse the Boulevard du Monteparnasse, she found not the quaint home of idealism but the glare of ugliness and discontent. Surely there must be more than met the eye or there wouldn't be so many eager to flock to the cold, dirty streets.

After asking for nearly an hour, she found an old woman willing to direct her to Camille Viotti's flat. As she climbed the rickety outside stairs, his painting clutched tight for safety, she tried not to wonder how the *bon vivant* Camille had survived in such a slum. And she refused to look down to see what squished and slid beneath her feet as she continued to ascend. Wishing she had some other alternative but knowing she did not, Nicole knocked upon the partially opened door at the top of the steps.

"*Allo?* Camille?" she called as the door swung inward upon a large shadowed room. She saw movement amid the darkness and a figure started forward in answer to her call. A man, but not Camille. Where the artist was long limbed and reed slender, this man was built sturdy and strong. He was only half dressed, with some sort of military jacket thrown on over a broad, bare chest. That expanse of bronzed musculature was somewhat threatening to the cloistered Nicole. She stood poised to flee, while her uncertain gaze was riveted by that bold strip of manly physique. He paused where dimness cloaked his features. Silence stretched out to an uncomfortable tension, then he asked in a gravelly voice, "What do you want?"

The unwelcoming growl made her take a step back but, remembering her plight, Nicole said steadily, "I'm a friend of Camille Viotti. I was told he lives here."

"He did. He's gone."

The curt reply startled her into arguing. "But he can't be gone. I just came into the city with him yesterday."

"Then you just missed him."

His tone was warped by a searing humor she didn't understand. The quality of it spoke plainly of something very wrong. Alarmed but still insistent, she asked, "Can you tell me where he's gone?"

He laughed, a raw sound without real amusement. "I'm afraid I'm not privy to that information, mademoiselle." He came into the grey-filtered light then. His stride was slightly reeling and the strong scent of drink made the cause apparent. Her first impression was of a brooding face, probably quite handsome when shaven and unmarked by too much drink and the heavy lines of private sorrow. Quietly, with a clarity that was almost cruel, he told her, "Camille is dead. They found his body in Faubourg St. Antoine this morning."

"No," was all she could think to utter. How could that be? Camille with his love of life and carefree philosophies . . . gone. "How?"

"I haven't heard the particulars. I'm not sure I want

to." It was then his bleary gaze fastened upon the landscape she held. He recognized the style but not the work. When he stepped closer, she hugged the painting to her as if fearing he would snatch it away. She was obviously what she said; a friend of Camille's, and just as obviously devastated by the news of his demise. He tried to pull together the rudimentary manners the situation called for but he was too drunk, too stunned by the facts, himself, to do much more than mutter, "Forgive me my rudeness, mademoiselle. I don't know what else I can tell you. If you'd like to wait—"

But she was retreating down the stairs, her movements slow, dazed then brisk with denial. From the doorway, he watched her race down the steps, the canvas banging against her knees, then she disappeared down one of the street's many twists and turns. He leaned back against the weathered frame and closed weary eyes. Just as well she was gone before Bebe returned. The grieving beauty would not be thrilled by the presence of one of Camille's other interests. She would not want to be upstaged in this time of dramatic mourning.

The events had shaken them all, badly. Violence was nothing new to any of them but it had never struck so personally before or taken one so undeserving. Camille had been an innocent soul. He'd never harmed anyone. He'd lived for his art and it seemed he died for nothing. No one could have mistaken him for someone who had anything worth stealing. It was the randomness of the vicious act that shocked his friends. And it was the fact that it could just as easily have been him going down to identify his brother, Frederic, as Frederic going down to identify Camille, that had him halfway down a bottle before breakfast.

He opened his eyes and stared down the street in the direction the young woman had taken. She'd been a pretty little thing, with her big frightened eyes and lush lips. Probably some *grisette* Camille met while in the country, who'd hoped to secure his patronage in exchange for favors. He wondered where she would go now. She'd had a hungry, fearful look about her as if lost. But Paris was full of lost souls. Perhaps she would go home where she belonged. Perhaps on to some other lonely, self-centered bourgeois student looking for an unencumbered liaison. She wasn't his concern. He had enough to do to care for those within these four walls.

He hadn't done a very good job with Camille, had he?

And that would torment him for nights to come. There wasn't enough drink in the world to wash that guilt away.

No, let her be someone else's responsibility. He had no room in his battered heart for another complication.

It began to rain.

Nothing could have been more complimentary to Nicole's mood. By midday, it was dark enough to be twilight. The entire heavens seemed to weep with her over the unfairness of a young artist's death. She wandered the tangle of streets, paying no attention to time or direction. What did it matter, after all? Camille had been her only friend, her only hope. What else was there?

Her drifting indifference was broken by her stomach's demand for food and her body's need for shelter from the pelting cold. She dodged, dripping and shivering, into a small café, where fragrant odors and the warmth of the ovens created an inviting ambiance.

But not so its surly proprietor. He watched her bend down over the display cases, touching the glass with a poignant longing. He knew the look. Half of Paris was hungry. If he gave them all handouts, he couldn't afford to stay in business.

"If you cannot pay be off with you!"

She glanced up with those hopeful, beseeching eyes and he had to harden his heart. That desperate gaze said it all. *Please be generous. I have no money.* She was wet and trembling, but not yet as gaunt as an alleycat. Soon she would be. However, that was not his problem.

"Go on with you. I don't tolerate beggars here."

"I'm no beggar, m'sieur." She announced that with an admirable hauteur.

"Then you have the means to pay?"

She stared at him through thoughtful green eyes. Alleycat eyes.

"I have no money, but I have this painting." Reluctantly, she held out the canvas. Her chin was quivering. "It was done by a friend of mine, a very gifted artist, and it is worth—"

"Nothing. Paris is full of such insipid works. Peddle it elsewhere or try peddling something of real value." As his gaze assessed the way her damp gown clung to the contour of her bosom, she took his meaning. And she became a cat with claws.

"That is not for sale, and I find I am no longer hungry for your pastries. Most likely they are stale anyway." And with that, she stomped back out into the full-blown storm, slender shoulders braced against the chill of the rain and the cut of insult.

Behind the counter, the café owner shook his head

and chuckled. Her indignation would not feed her. She would come to realize the truth of his suggestion soon enough.

And perhaps she would be back.

Nicole was quick to realize pride was a poor umbrella, but she didn't regret her decision. Surely there must be a kind heart somewhere in all of Paris! Somewhere, but obviously nowhere nearby. Shutters closed her out and glowering shopkeepers chased her away from the promising haven of their stores. All seemed to class her as a virtueless creature undeserving of shelter from the elements. Eventually, she took to using Camille's canvas as a buffer. It was a poor tribute to his last work but she was certain he would understand her dilemma. Even partly shielded from the merciless downpour, her feet and stockings were sodden and her cloak was an ineffective insulator from the bite of the wind.

Hoping to escape some of the punishing onslaught, Nicole ducked into an alleyway where ancient buildings towered to cut off the slicing blow and much of the light. She tried not to notice the stink of rotting vegetables or look too closely where she put her feet. Delicacy was a luxury she could not afford.

A whisper of movement distracted her. Immediately, she was alert in every sense. She heard furtive footfalls enter the alley behind her and the pull of rapid breaths. Several men, she determined from what she could hear. Her hope to blend into the shadows and obscurity was a fleeting prayer. She could tell by the way the others closed in with a purpose that she was their prey. Three menacing shapes became unsavory men and there was no misconstruing their intent. Their eyes said it plain.

With a fierce cry, she swung Camille's painting at the man closest to her. The stretcher bars cracked against his thick skull but didn't have the slowing effect she'd desired. She turned to run.

Within three strides, rough hands caught at her skirts, yanking her up and nearly costing her her footing on the slippery cobbles. Instead of struggling to escape, she whirled to confront them with a fiery fury. One of them began to chuckle at her audacity and she knocked the sound down his throat along with several of his front teeth. He gave a wail, staggering back to gurgle, "She broke my jaw!"

"Well, well," rumbled one of the others. "What have we here? Spirited little baggage, aren't you?" And he struck her a hard, will-sapping blow to the cheek. Nicole went down upon the puddled stones and her attacker was quick to straddle her with his knees.

The third man was distracted by a soft whistle from behind him. He turned to take a powerfully flung punch full in the face. He fell, howling, his hands cradling a crushed nose.

"Hey, *poltron*," the newcomer taunted as the remaining man looked up from where he had Nicole pinned to the wet ground. "Can you only beat up on women, or is it just that you fear to face another man?"

A glitter of steel flashed in the dimness as the villain rose up and stepped away from his intended victim. "I enjoy a good fight as much as a quick fondle. Let's get the first over so I can get back to the second."

"Bâtard!" Nicole hissed. She surged up with startling speed to lay open her assailant's cheek with the gouge of her nails. He grunted in pain and hit her again, knocking her against one of the damp brick walls. Then he turned his attention and his knife back to the interloper.

"You should not have interfered," he snarled. "Now you will die."

"I've seen enough death. Run away or I'll make you wish for it," came the low, confident drawl.

The bully hesitated as the figure approached. The man cast a huge shadow along the alleyway. His walk was no arrogant strut but rather an easy swing of powerful grace. A man who knew how to handle himself in a dangerous spot. A man cowards didn't provoke. And all three of the would-be rapists were devout cowards.

Spitting a curse, the bully sheathed his knife and went to drag his docile friends to their feet. The three of them quickly disappeared into the misty nether regions of the premature darkness.

"Mademoiselle, are you all right?"

A soft sound was uttered in response from the woman pressed back against the wall as she faced him as another threat. It wasn't a whimper but rather a low rippling sound, almost like a growl. A trick of light made her eyes gleam golden and her rescuer paused, momentarily taken off guard.

"Mademoiselle, remember me? From this morning. Camille's friend. I mean you no harm."

He heard her breath exhale in a fragile sob and the alarm that had frozen him to the spot abated. For just a second, he could have sworn she was more dangerous than the three roving cutthroats put together.

Abruptly, she seemed to crumple, sliding down the surface of wet brick with a weak bonelessness. He stepped up quickly to catch her in mid-swoon. She was soaked clear through and shivering helplessly. Surely the threatening pose of moment's before had been an illusion, for she was all frail female now.

"Who are you?" she whispered feebly as he wrapped

her up inside the warmth of his coat. She burrowed in against his body heat with an instinctive urgency. He was disturbingly aware of her feminine form through the sodden garments.

"My name is Marchand. I followed you. A good thing, eh?"

"A good thing," she agreed just before pooling into a faint within the circle of his arms.

She was no tigress, only a wet kitten. Shaking his head to scatter the image of her all bristled, with feral eyes glittering, Marchand lifted her easily and began carrying her slight burden back with him.

The tantalizing scent of warming stew coaxed Nicole back to awareness. And instantly, she was wary, uncertain of where she was or of how she'd gotten there. She slit her eyes open to observe her surroundings without betraying the fact that she was awake. It took a moment, but finally she recognized the large one-room flat where she lay upon a corner pallet and the man tending the stove. Marchand. She remembered the name, then the circumstance, and her gasp of recall brought him about to face her.

"Ah, there you are at last. How do you feel, ma'm-'selle?"

She didn't answer right away, for just then, she discovered she was stark naked beneath the woolen blanket draped over her. Her fingers clenched in the stiff folds of the covering, drawing it up beneath her chin as she struggled into a seated position. She saw her clothes to the intimate last detail spread out near the stove's heat. Where he'd put them. After taking them off her.

He noticed the direction of her stare and the depth of

her blushes, treating both with a casual shrug. "You were drenched to the skin. I feared you would take a chill and that could have been fatal. No one has ever perished from embarrassment, to my knowledge. Your things are almost dry and this meal is ready. You look as though you could stand a little something sticking to your ribs."

Nicole sat unmoving in a moment of confused emotion. She was grateful for his intervention. She was so hungry, she would have eaten scraps off the floor. She knew he was right in removing her wet things, yet the thought of a stranger seeing her . . . touching her. Virginal horror clashed with indignation. And then, behind all those proper feelings seeped a seditious disappointment that she'd been unconscious at the time. She hadn't expected the first man to undress her to be someone she didn't know or care about. And what had he meant by his last remark?

Had he found the sight of her displeasing?

And that, quite amazingly, bothered her more than the idea of him disrobing her.

Just then, he placed a bowl upon the table and gestured her toward it with a spoon. Modesty couldn't overcome the savory smell of whatever was in that bowl. She bundled the blanket about her and dragged it to the table, making sure it was tucked in at all the appropriate places as she angled into a chair.

"Eat," he instructed. She didn't wait to be told twice. Breaking off a chunk of crusty bread, she turned her attention to the thick stock and sparse amount of meat and vegetables.

Even famished, she ate with proper manners, Marchand mused as he watched her. Who was she? A beauty, certainly, even half drenched. A woman of the streets? He was beginning to think not. A woman of experience would have viewed her natural state as an opportunity, not with maidenly dismay. Her clothes, though ruined by the mud and rain, were of fine, expensive cloth and made-to-order tailoring. He knew of no *grisettes* who could afford such garments, let alone have the good taste to don them. But what was a young woman of quality doing wandering the streets without enough money to buy bread?

He turned one of the chairs around so he could straddle the seat and lean his forearms upon the high back. She glanced up then, aware of and perhaps nervous under his intense regard. A beauty, certainly! Her features were marvelously cut, like the strong, elegant lines of the crystal his family had once owned. And her eyes—*Mon Dieu!*—eyes a man could sink into like the crisp new green of spring grasses. Her lips, which were pursed now with uncertainty, were full and ripe, too enticing for the innocence the rest of her face projected. He was hardly a stranger to the charms of women, but aligning her winsome loveliness with the perfection of form he'd already admired was a combination a man was not meant to ignore. And he could feel a healthy stir of attraction behind his curiosity. Questions first, he told himself. That was the sensible way to approach things.

His appreciative study narrowed in focus, and he frowned. "I thought you had cut your face."

Her fingertips lifted to one cheekbone. The same one he was sure had been bruised and torn by her attacker's cruelty. But he must have been mistaken. Her skin was smooth and flawless now.

"Perhaps just a trick of the light," she offered, feeling the spot as if she, too, was surprised.

"Perhaps," he agreed. Then, because he could see her growing agitated, he changed the subject. "How did you come to know Camille?"

Her gaze lowered, but not before he saw the return of distress his words evoked. "We became friends while he was painting near—near the school I attended."

"And he brought you to Paris with him from this school you attended?"

"Y-yes." She supposed a little creativity wasn't too sacrilegious. Camille wouldn't have minded, being the chivalrous soul he was. "I have no family, you see, and my funds had run out. Camille was going to let me model for him."

"If you are going to lie to me, do a better job, or simply tell me it's none of my business."

Nicole glanced up in surprise, her wide-eyed gaze confirming his suspicions. "Why would you think I'm lying to you?"

"Because he would never use you for a model."

"And why not? How would you know? You are no artist."

A small smile moved the corners of his mouth. "And why would you think that, ma'm'selle?"

"You don't have the hands of an artist."

He held them out to examine them; big, broad-fingered hands. Hands that had touched her skin. Nicole swallowed convulsively, ashamed of her own guilty pleasure.

"And what's wrong with my hands?"

"They are too clean. No traces of paint in the creases or beneath the nails."

He chuckled softly. "Very observant of you. No, I am no artist."

"Then how can you be so certain Camille would not

want me for a subject? Do you think I am too—
unexceptional?"

"Oh, no. Hardly that. I can imagine you would make
quite a fetching picture garbed as you are now." Then
he chuckled again as she tugged up the edges of the
blanket. "But you see, Camille never painted portraits,
only landscapes. If you were such a good friend of his,
you would have known that, wouldn't you? Now, shall
we try again? Why did he bring you to Paris?"

She met his direct stare without blinking. "That's
none of your business."

He laughed, a full-bodied sound of enjoyment. A
sound that disturbed an odd quiver along the surface of
her exposed flesh. Then he sat and simply looked at her,
an unnerving and unswerving stare as if he was certain
he could learn all her secrets if he looked long and hard
enough. She didn't want to give him the opportunity.

"My things should be dry by now."

He rose up at the same time she did. He was bigger
than she remembered; not terribly tall but very strong
and developed through the body. Not an artist. Something in his steady gaze shifted subtly in purpose and she
could tell as his study took in the drape of the blanket
that he was remembering what she looked like beneath
it. She moved quickly to snatch up her garments, not
caring that they were still slightly damp. They'd dry
quick enough upon the heat of her flushed skin.

A glance about the room told her there was no private place in which to dress.

"We aren't awfully modest here," he told her with a
silkiness of tone that was as inciteful as a caress. And he
waited as if expecting her to garb herself right in front
of him. Her circumstances sank in then, deep and dire.
She was alone in Paris, alone with this powerful stranger

within his flat with little more than a thin blanket between them.

"I'd better get dressed and go.'"

'It's still raining out," he mentioned casually.

"Then I'll get wet."

"There's no need for that. You can stay here." And he moved a step closer, his bold body posture making his intention very clear. Still, she felt none of the disgust that had roiled during her earlier propositioning or attempted violation. His offer woke a strange quiver of anticipation. She stood motionless as his fingertips grazed her cheek and he murmured with smoky appreciation, "You are very beautiful. I think we can work out a beneficial arrangement where you need not get wet or be cold again."

Shaking off the strong enticement of his words, she glided backward, out from under his seducing touch. "I don't think I care to pay in the manner you have in mind."

And there it was again, that cold golden glitter in eyes that had moments before been pools of vulnerability. A warning that she was not as helpless as she appeared.

He wasn't slighted by her refusal. In fact, he'd never planned on making such an offer. He had no use for the kind of women who lived off a man's passions. It turned a private thing into practical purpose. But something about the thought of her wandering the streets of Paris led him to extend his protection. It was a crazy, impulsive thing to do, but once he'd said the words, he knew how deeply he meant them. The idea of having a woman like this one was enough to alter any man's convictions. The idea of having her nightly was enough to alter his breathing pattern.

But she'd said no, and his respect came grudgingly.

"My luck that the first woman I bring home has morals."

Before Nicole could think of a proper retort, the door to the flat opened and they were confronted by a trio of startled faces. Clad in a blanket, with her clothes clutched to her chest, Nicole retreated behind Marchand's solid figure though there could be no escaping what the man and two women were thinking as they beheld her.

Especially when the man drawled with obvious humor, "Marchand, *mon frère*, what have you been hiding from us?"

"I guess it is no secret any longer." He turned and wound his arm about Nicole's rigid shoulders, drawing her up tight against his side. "I've taken your advice and found myself a lover."

Chapter Four

When it was evident that none were as surprised by the news as the lady in question, Marchand hugged Nicole up hard enough to drive any protest from her lungs. And as he nuzzled her ear, his mouth moved against it in a soft whisper.

"Say nothing. Trust me."

Trust him? Nicole didn't even know him!

But when he straightened to regard her with a superbly pretended amorous affection, she didn't dispute it.

"My, my, this is sudden," remarked the taller, darker woman. Her black eyes were red-rimmed by recent tears. She assessed Nicole in an incremental judgement and apparently, was not pleased with the whole.

"That is the way of passion, is it not?" was Marchand's comment.

She made a noncommittal murmur.

The other woman, a petite young redhead, also had the swollen-eyed look of fresh weeping and Nicole deduced that these were friends of Camille's and that she was intruding upon a private moment of mourning. But she was allowed no chance at a dignified retreat, as the redhead gave a somewhat strained smile and scolded, "Marchand, your manners. Introduce us to your *amoureux.*"

Marchand looked momentarily blank, then purred down with an insulting nonchalance, "Forgive me, *mon petit chou,* but in the heat of things, I seem to have forgotten to ask your name."

"It is Nicole," she hissed through gritted teeth.

Without appearing the least bit disgraced, he smiled and announced smoothly, "Nicole, *cher,* may I present my friends Bebe Soulie and Musette Mercier and my brother, Frederic LaValois."

"Enchantée," Frederic murmured with a polite bow, but the black-haired Bebe was not as charmed.

"Is she staying here?"

"I've asked her to," Marchand drawled. "Have you a problem with that, Bebe?"

The challenge was immediate and, Nicole sensed, nothing new. Then the statuesque beauty snapped, "Do what you like, Marchand."

He smiled thinly. "I usually do. Besides, it could be to our good fortune if she knows how to cook and clean. Something the two of you care little about."

"Hah!" the little redhead laughed. She put her arms around Marchand's brother. "Frederic does not love me for my cooking."

Marchand's dry remark of "I should hope not," had her making a face at him.

"I should like to get dressed," Nicole whispered in an urgent undervoice.

His dark gaze swept over her. "Yes, of course." And with his palm against the small of her back, he guided her away from the others. Gripping a curtain she hadn't noticed before, he drew it across the corner of the room to block off a section of privacy. Except it wasn't private, with him standing next to her.

"I can dress myself, m'sieur."

"I'm sure you can." He made no effort to move. So she made no attempt to alter the concealing drape of the sheet.

"Why did you say that?"

"What?"

"That we are lovers. They will think we're sleeping together!"

"What do you care what they think. You don't know them. And besides, if you expect to stay here, you will be sleeping with me. You have no choice. It is your choice, of course, whether or not we will be doing anything more than sleeping."

She sucked a shocked breath. Shocked not because he would mention such a scandalous thing but because she was thinking about staying here with him. And, after a brief summation of his handsome face and form, about what it would be like to do more than just sleep. Morality made her stammer, "I think I'd just better go."

"Where? Back to where I found you? Have you any money? Have you any other friends here in Paris? Or was there just Camille?"

Looking up at him in helpless dismay, she was horrified to feel her eyes well up with tears. He stroked one shimmering droplet away with the pad of his thumb and didn't mock her desperation.

"I thought as much." His tone was low and consoling; just the intonation a frightened young girl in her position longed to hear. "You will be safe here. You can consider us your friends."

"Why?" That had troubled her since he'd stepped into that dark alleyway. "Why did you come after me?"

"Because I was not there to save Camille."

She considered his words a moment, then nodded. But that only answered one of her questions. "Why did you tell the others that we were—intimate? Why not tell them the truth?"

"You haven't told that to me yet." Then he sobered. "Bebe fancied herself Camille's fiancée. To have you arrive at such a time and present yourself as his . . . *friend,* would have hurt her unnecessarily. She is a vain and foolish creature, but I care for her and I would not have her hurt by whatever you and Camille had together."

"We had nothing together. As I said, we were friends."

"As you said," he repeated, not believing her. Not believing any man could just be friends with her.

"Turn your back, please, so that I might dress."

He smiled at her prudishness but did as she requested. He heard the blanket drop and felt his pulse rate rise in response.

"So, who lives here with you?" Her question was muffled by the yards of fabric she was pulling on over her head.

"Frederic and Musette; they are—" He sought a tactful explanation, then said it plain. "They are lovers. Bebe. And up until last night, Camille."

There was silence, then her carefully posed question. "You have no one living with you?"

"No one permanent." A pause. "Unless you agree to stay."

"And how am I expected to pay for the privilege? I have nothing except what you have seen."

That was plenty! But he said, "If you can keep this place from looking like a home for swine, it will be enough. Anything else you wish to do ... would be an appreciated extra."

He let that dangle; a silken temptation that she could not address.

"I would be grateful for the roof over my head and the meals. I was beginning to think there were no kind hearts in Paris."

"There aren't. My motives are purely selfish." He turned to regard her. She was gathering up the heavy cloud of her dark hair and when their eyes met, she went still. It took him a moment to remember to breathe. Camille had been a lucky man. In a slightly thicker tone, he finished, "All you need do is act my lover when we are with the others, and I promise not to act it when we are alone." His gaze darkened into a sultry fire. "Unless you wish me to."

Then he reached up and jerked the curtain open, leaving Nicole to exhale shakily and follow upon legs that went suddenly wobbly.

The others had gathered around glasses of wine at the table. Frederic filled two more mismatched goblets, then somberly lifted a silent toast. To Camille.

Marchand sat. Seeing no other chair, Nicole hesitated until he drew her down to perch upon his knees. His arms curved easily about her waist. Tentatively, she let hers drape along his shoulders. Broad, firm shoulders, she noted nervously. She needn't have worried that anyone would mark her reluctance for such close contact. They were caught up in other thoughts.

"There was no mistake, then?"

Frederic LaValois regarded his brother sadly. "None." He sighed. "Poor Camille. I cannot understand why anyone would do such a thing."

"Do the police know what happened?"

"He had his throat slit. Whoever the vicious animal was that cut him was patient enough to sit around and watch him bleed to death before moving him to where he was found. At least that's what the police surmised, since there was no great deal of blood at the site and he was drained of it."

Nicole gasped softly. No . . . a coincidence, surely. Like the police said; a madman with a knife, not a demon with an unnatural appetite.

Bebe was staring at her closely, suspicious of her pallor. "Did you know my Camille?"

"Yes," she said without thinking, then amended quickly, "Marchand introduced us. He seemed very nice. Too nice to suffer such an awful fate. Please accept my sincere condolences on his loss."

Marchand was staring up at her with a veiled intensity. Was he wondering about the ease with which she lied? She knew he thought there was more to her relationship with Camille than she was saying. Let him believe what he would believe. But she would not be thought heartless at such a time.

"That makes the fifth . . . *body* found in the *quartier* in less than a month," Musette said, shuddering delicately. "I'm frightened to go out alone."

"It's good that you are," Marchand told her. "None of us should go out alone until after this, this maniac is apprehended."

They drank to seal that promise, then drank more until the bottle was gone and the hour late. Then came the moment Nicole had been dreading. Time to bed down for the night with this man who was yet a stranger.

There was one stove in the flat to provide the necessary heat and it was slight at best, so no curtains were drawn to interrupt the even distribution. Frederic and Musette shared the pallet closest to the fire and their silhouettes were cast up in bold relief upon the wall as they embraced and sank down into the covers. Bebe retired to her own empty bed not far from where Marchand marked off his own personal, if not private, space. His clothes were piled high in a basket awaiting a much-needed washing and an odd assortment of serious-looking armaments were laid out carefully beside it within easy reach of the bed.

He sat upon the pallet, stripped off his shirt, levered out of his boots and looked up to where she lingered in an awkward panic.

"Come down here to me, *ma petite,*" he cooed softly—just for effect, she was sure, but that didn't keep her pulse from taking startled flight. He put up his hand and she looked at it, then at him. In the flickering evening light, his face was a subtle dance of shadows, highlighting the tousled dark hair one moment, the refined definition of his mouth the next, then playing upon the passions in his liquid eyes. He was more than handsome. There was a dark fascination to him that appealed to the rebellious streak in her. He was the kind of man her mother would bar from the door in fear for her daughters chastity. And that made being with him both dangerous and exciting. In all her life, she'd never been faced with such an unstable situation. All her decisions had been made for her, all difficulties smoothed before her. This was her first taste of adventure and that taste was bittersweet. She slipped her fingers across his palm and he tugged her down onto the thin ticking. She sat beside him, rigid with anxiety, her heart pounding with an anticipation of the unknown.

"I've promised not to harm you," he reminded softly.

"Do you mean to sleep in all of this?" He fingered the edge of her sleeve and smiled provokingly.

"I could sleep in a suit of full armor at this point," she told him, hoping it was true. But she could see the wisdom of removing her gown. It was the only one she had and not easily replaced. Knowing he'd seen her in much less didn't keep a blush from coloring her cheeks as she shed her dress and carefully folded it away in the cleanest spot she could find. Wearing only her low necked princess-style petticoat, she regarded him with a becoming timidity. He tossed back the covers and gestured for her to recline. When she hesitated again, he mocked, "Do you plan to sleep sitting up?"

Forced to present a brave front, she made a face and dropped down upon her back, determinedly shutting her eyes. She heard him chuckle, then went stiff all over as she felt his weight distribute itself alongside her. The enveloping heat of his nearness was immediate and somehow more inviting than threatening. But wasn't that a threat of a different nature?

"Bonne nuit, cher."

The last thing she expected was to fall instantly and deeply to sleep. But she did, exhausted in body and mind and, regardless of her worries, secure in this room full of strangers on her second night in Paris.

The expression was "Make your own bed, then lie in it," but Marchand had never understood the contradiction until now. Beside him, breathing softly in slumber, was the most desirable creature he'd ever seen. She'd inspired him to act against his every principle. He'd taken her in when he didn't want and couldn't emotionally manage the involvement. He let vital questions go unanswered; like who she was and why she was here. And he let her get close, so close the movement of her chest was rubbing him into a rare state of arousal.

Then he'd done the truly insane. He'd promised not to touch her. He may not have been the best of men, but he prided himself upon being a most honorable one. His word was not lightly given, and never broken. Except the one to Camille. The one in which he swore to keep them all safe.

Movement within the room's shadowed interior jerked him from his troubled thoughts and personal torment. His hand stretched out instinctively for the feel of fine Toledo steel. It was then he recognized the soft pattern of footsteps and heard the first muffled sob.

When he moved up behind her, Bebe turned so quickly into his arms, he had to wonder, somewhat unkindly, if she'd staged the sounds of grieving just to bring him to her. The long lush lines of her barely clad body were familiar to him, but then, she'd been with him briefly before attaching herself to Camille. She used that familiarity and his fondness for her to her best advantage now by angling his face toward hers, by fitting her mouth over his in a hungry kiss. He allowed it for an instant because she was very good at kissing, then he turned his head away.

"Bebe, this is not the kind of comfort I meant to offer you."

"But it's the kind I need tonight. Oh, Marchand, I can't be alone tonight." Her palms were pushing over his bared skin with an impatient eagerness. In his own defense, he caught her wrists and stilled her hands.

"I miss him, too, but this will not make the mourning any easier."

"Yes, it will." And she was leaning into him, sketching the line of his jaw with hurried kisses.

"No, Bebe."

She jerked back and sent a scalding glance across the room. "Because of her? Marchand, it should be us together now."

He gave a harsh laugh. "The proper thing would be to wait until Camille is at least cold before working to replace him. Your grief is very shallow, *cher.*"

"What do you know of my grief? I loved Camille, but he would understand that I have to take care of myself."

"I am not going to be your next lover. Had I wanted things to be that way between us, I wouldn't have let Camille have you."

She spat a low curse at him; he was quick to catch her palm before it reached his cheek. Very gently, he pressed a kiss upon her knuckles while she stood trembling and uncertain.

"We are friends, you and I," he affirmed with a quiet passion. "Nothing more, nothing less. You have a place here with us for as long as you choose. We are like family and this is your home. No one is going to turn you out, Bebe."

He let her hug to him tightly because now her tears were sincere. He held her for a long moment until the tempest of her sorrow seemed to stem. Bebe was a strong woman who was loathe to let true emotion show. She was quick to shore up her composure. He admired her for that.

With a kiss to his bare shoulder, she murmured, "I think I love you, Marchand," but he couldn't tell what she meant by it and didn't ask. It was best he didn't know. He waited until she returned to her blankets and had settled into a restless sleep before seeking his own.

And therein was his other torment, all sweetly displayed in thin white lawn and lace. Who are you, Nicole? What is it about you that makes me willing to concede so much in return for so little? He wondered these things as he watched her sleep, aroused by Bebe's passionate touch, wishing it had been hers. She looked innocent as a child, so weary and frail, but he couldn't forget the tenacious way she'd fought in the alley. Like a tigress, all tawny-eyed and dangerous. A courageous enigma.

And he couldn't forget how soft her skin was. As smooth and flawless as fresh cream. Knowing to let his thoughts trail in that direction was unwise didn't stop him from easing his hand along the gently rising curve of her ribs. He could feel how delicate she was beneath the shift of pristine petticoat. How had someone let such a fragile flower escape them? Didn't they know how harsh the world could be upon such a tender soul?

Just then, she moaned in her sleep and began a feeble thrashing in the throes of an unpleasant dream. How much unpleasantness had she seen in her young life? Nothing compared to his, he was willing to wager. But he didn't like the thought of her in distress, so he gathered her up close against him, hoping to provide a buffer to her troubles, liking very much his role as her protector.

Abruptly, she jerked from his arms to sit bolt upright, the breath sobbing from her in huge gulps. Her eyes were wide open but registered nothing, showing no spark of recognition as he sat up beside her.

"Nicole?" He kept his voice low so as not to disturb the others.

"No, it can't be true. It can't be true!" With that soft wail, she looked to him blindly. At the sight of her tortured, tear-washed face, all the regimented restriction that guided his life fell away. He felt as though his heart was gone.

Her arms flew about his neck in a despairing circle and he was quick to cinch her up tight. The violence of her weeping alarmed him and the notion that she'd loved Camille to the point of such agony woke other feelings not so easily identified. What could he say to lessen her sorrow? Words alone held no charm. This was the second female he'd consoled in one evening; the first out of friendship and this one out of need. He couldn't remember ever wanting to grant peace of mind to another quite so badly, not even his own brother. So he crushed her in his embrace and moved his body to and fro in a soothing rhythm until finally her frantic clutching eased and he could feel her awareness returning. And with it, confusion.

He let her pull away. For a long moment, she simply stared at him, not accusingly, not fearfully, just with a deep bewilderment, as if she couldn't understand why he was being so kind. Then she returned to his arms, pressing up against his chest and snuggling her damp cheek upon his shoulder in a monumental gesture of trust.

He wasn't sure what exactly happened. One moment she was all clinging vulnerability and the next, her purpose shifted to a seduction more aggressive in intensity than even Bebe's had been. Grasping fingers began a hard kneading pressure along the muscles of his back and shoulders while her supple body pressed against him. He almost pulled away; not because he didn't like it but because it was such an unexpected change.

Her breathing stroked along the side of his neck in light, panting whispers. He held his own suspended, then it gusted out in an explosive sigh when he felt the first soft brush of her lips there, just below his ear, followed by the lingering rasp of her tongue. Her fingers had come up to rub along his jaw in a demanding passion, then clamped with a paralyzing sharpness into the cording on the other side of his neck. In a brief spike of surprise, he realized he couldn't move. Then he didn't want to. He forgot about struggle. He wasn't thinking about making love to her, or even of how to respond to what she was doing. He was lost, hypnotized by the seducing caress of her breath upon his throat. Beneath the urgent press of her mouth, his pulse was lulled into a seductive sluggishness. He was aware of his eyes closing, of the world darkening. *Mon Dieu*, was he going to swoon?

Suddenly, Nicole shoved away from him, forcing him to scramble for balance. He shook his head, trying to free his mind from its odd lethargy.

"No," she cried out in anguish. "I won't. I can't."

"Nicole," he slurred as if dragging himself up through a drugging daze. "What—?"

"I'm sorry. I'm so sorry, Marchand."

With that, she curled up in his covers with her back to him. He could see her shoulders shaking with silent weeping, just as he was shaking from a consuming rush of weakness.

What had just happened between them? A moment of impulsive love play? He would never have suspected that she would like such stormy games. He lifted an unsteady hand to the side of his neck. The muscles had gone from numb to a fierce ache. Such strength she had! His skin was warm and wet from her kisses. But they hadn't been kisses of passion or promise.

They hadn't even been kisses for him.

It was Camille. She'd awakened from a nightmare to find it wasn't a dream and that her lover was truly dead. Just as Bebe had tried to do, she had transferred her frustrated longings to him, swamping him with her desire for another until he was helpless to care or resist. Then came her realization that he was not Camille, bringing guilt and remorse and rejection. And to him, an anxiousness he couldn't understand. For a moment, he'd felt powerless in her embrace, and that sensation was both terrifying and exhilarating.

And he found himself wondering desperately what it would take for her to want him for himself. At the same time, he was wondering if it would be wise to find out.

This Nicole of the no last name was no ordinary woman looking for a cozy alliance to see her through the winter.

He wasn't sure what she was.

But Nicole wasn't weeping for a man she'd barely known, nor had she been dreaming about his death. In her nightmare, she'd seen eyes that burned like the fires of hell and had felt the pull of damnation upon her soul.

In Marchand's embrace, she'd known brief comfort. He was so strong, so overwhelmingly male. She'd been captivated by the hard drive of his heartbeats, by the satiny heat of his body. She'd wanted to absorb that warmth, that strength, that beat into herself. She wanted it with an uncontrollable urgency.

And when she'd touched her lips to the vital channels of his throat and had ridden the mystic pulse of his life, what had overcome her senses then, left her quaking with horror now.

For what she'd wanted with an unnatural desperation was to bite.

And to drink.

Chapter Five

It must have been close to the noon hour when Nicole finally roused from a restless sleep. Weak sunshine slanted across the dirty floorboards. A quick look about told her she had the room to herself. She was glad not to have to confront any of her flatmates, for she was groggy and slow to come around to her full senses.

Then she sat up in alarm.

Had it been a dream or part of a waking nightmare?

Had she been within a heartbeat of becoming the same kind of beast her father was? The sensations came back so sudden and strong she could feel the anticipation rise all over again. A desire so dark it seemed obscene in the light of day.

How could she think of harming Marchand, who had shown her only kindness? But then, she hadn't wanted to harm him. She'd wanted to possess him, to swallow down the essence of him, body and soul. And that went far beyond simple malevolence.

She closed her eyes and concentrated on suppressing the feelings. Slowly, her heart returned to its normal cadence and her senses quieted until she felt herself again. She would have to be more careful. She would have to keep things under control. And that meant separating herself from temptation. That meant staying away from Marchand.

She couldn't think of him without tasting the saltiness of his skin upon her tongue, without remembering the enticing throb of his life force, so strong and beckoning. Those were not the things that should have compelled her interest in a man. She wouldn't think of it, of the sweet, hot fire of him just waiting to be shared. Those were not normal desires, and she *would* be normal as long as she didn't act upon them.

She would escape the legacy her father would leave to her.

Desperate to occupy her mind with other thoughts, she decided to rid the dwelling of an eon of neglect. But when she reached for her gown, she was dismayed to find it gone, along with Marchand's basket of laundry. She couldn't spend the day in her underclothes!

Rummaging about through the stacks of questionably clean linens, she uncovered one of his shirts in sore need of starching but presentable for wear. She slipped it on over her petticoat and looped back the cuffs. Its folds engulfed the embroidered cambric of her bodice and the hem hung to the rows of heavy piping that ended just below her knee. Scandalous attire, to be sure, but modest enough to suit her situation.

A home for swine, he'd said, but Nicole couldn't picture any self-respecting hog in her village taking up residence amid the hovel her companions lived in. Camille hadn't mentioned that slovenly neglect was a much-desired state for ones of a bohemian lifestyle. She failed to see the charm. If she was to work for her keep, she had plenty of opportunity for employment. Starting with the dishes. While she heated water, she caught the scent of pan drippings; the heavy odor made her stomach roil. Appetite that had rumbled earlier was quick to abandon her, and a cup of weak tea served as breakfast while she scoured and scrubbed.

She was scraping the evidence of at least a month's worth of meals off the tabletop when the door opened to admit a towering stack of folded clothes.

"Good morning," she heard Musette call from somewhere behind the freshly laundered linens. "I hope you didn't mind that I took your dress to the laundresses. It was my turn to see it done and, well, we all look out for one another. As long as I have a sou to my name, I'd prefer to pay someone else to slave over the wash kettles."

She plopped the basket down so the clean clothes spilled out upon the filthy floor. Apparently thinking nothing of it, she started to sort the collection into six uneven piles. Nicole's was composed of a single item. Camille's made another.

"Here now, you don't need to be doing that." Musette gestured to the tabletop. "Just throw a cloth over it. Good as new. Marchand didn't bring you here to clean his house."

"I promised that I would. And besides, it's my way of looking out for the rest of you."

"Make Marchand happy and it will be enough. For one so *magnifique* not to smile, it is a crime. He is much too serious. He has made himself big brother over all of us and worries like a mother hen. Make him smile. That is work enough." She nodded to herself and went back to sorting linens.

Nicole spent a moment wondering what Marchand would look like with a full-blown smile to warm his dark features. Then she finished the table and moved down to the floor.

"We don't usually eat down there," Musette pointed out.

"It looks as though someone has."

"You are very funny. You will be good for Frederic's brother."

Seeing an opportunity to learn much from the vivacious redhead, Nicole asked, "How long have you been with Frederic?"

"I was very lucky. He was the first one I met when I came into the city. He is so gentle, so smart. He's a writer, you know. He puts such beautiful words to paper. I wish I knew how to read them. He sells pretty pieces of prose to earn enough for bread, but he lives to pen words of revolution. He is not a violent man, so he seeks to use articles instead of swords. He is very brave to take so dangerous a stand." And she sounded proud. That made Nicole like her very much.

"And Marchand? Is he a revolutionary, too?"

Musette laughed. "Marchand? Oh, no, not him. He thinks us fools. He was a soldier of the Fifth Regiment. He believes in order, not ideals."

Nicole paused in her work, bemused. "Then why is he here, living in this colony of students and dreamers?"

"He deserted the army and is considered a criminal by the bourgeois monarchy. He would be shot for treason if they caught him."

That news alarmed her. A criminal? Shot? "But why, if he doesn't believe in your cause—"

"You'll have to ask him."

"Ask him what?"

Nicole was aware of a sudden hard lurch within her chest that made for an odd breathlessness. Cautiously, she lifted her gaze, uncertain of how she would react to the sight of him if just his voice had her quaking. He was standing in the doorway, his impressive figure backlit by late afternoon sun. She couldn't make out his expression with that glare behind him, but she could feel his stare. It left her unsettled.

"Nicole was wondering why a nice bourgeois boy like you was involved with we bohemian rabble."

"Someone must take their head out of the clouds long enough to pay the rent. A thankless job, caring for the lot of you." He strode in and accepted Musette's fond hug with an almost paternal tolerance. As his hand rumpled her red curls, his gaze was fixed on Nicole. "Have you no greeting for me, *cher?*"

Struggling not to balk at that gentle challenge, Nicole rose off her knees, aware that his stare quickly skimmed her shocking garb, then his eyes locked with hers. Patient. Commanding.

She made herself move toward him, all the while terrified that unnatural urges would defile the first blush of attraction his presence stirred within her. When they were toe to toe, she forced her gaze to rise. He must have seen her reluctance, for he handled her like delicate porcelain. His fingertips smoothed back the loose strands of hair that had fallen across her flushed cheek and brow, then his palm came around to cup beneath her chin, holding it secure as he bent down to claim a kiss.

Nicole sucked an anxious breath as his mouth grazed her temple. Then her eyes fluttered shut and her lips parted in awkward anticipation, readying for her first real kiss. It was . . . *magnifique!* He eased over to conquer the soft swells of her mouth, taking them slowly, shaping them sweetly, shaking her completely with his tender mastery. It wasn't what she'd expected his kiss to be. She'd expected rough and hot instead of this sensitive seduction of her will. And as just the tip of his tongue pressed between his lips, the glorious shock to her inexperienced senses had her shuddering in response. When he lifted up, she found her hands clenched in his shirtfront and her gaze helplessly drawn to his in a confusion of uncertainty and surrender. She would have returned to his embrace with a desperate abandon had Musette not spoken up then to remind them of her presence.

"Ah, young love. If you kissed all the ladies just so, you would have a harem at your feet, Marchand, instead of one upon her knees tending your floors."

Marchand canted a quick glimpse to assess what she'd done. "You've worked miracles already, *ma petit.* I thank you."

"Thank her by taking her out and buying her some decent clothes," Musette interrupted. "Where are your things, Nicole?"

Nicole blinked, wading up through the daze of sensations to answer. "I had my bag stolen on my first day in town. All I had brought from the country with me was in it. Everything I had saved while working the farm."

"I thought you said you were in school."

Marchand's smooth observation rattled her. His gaze chided her for her lie.

"I did both," she exclaimed boldly, and worked cramped fingers loose from the fabric of his shirt. Still, she couldn't resist smoothing the white linen over the hard plane of his abdomen. The feel of him was a divine enchantment.

"You are very versatile," he crooned, his disbelief plain. But her reaction to him was pleasing. Her gaze of frustration said she was thinking of him and no other.

And that made him generous. "Come. Let's buy you something pretty. Not that I don't think this is particularly fetching." He fingered the open collar of the shirt swaddling her and grinned wide, displaying even white teeth and a devastating charm.

Oh, yes, thought Nicole in a dreamy appreciation. He should smile more often.

"Have you much money, Marchand?" Musette wanted to know as she wound about his arm in an engaging fashion, batting her eyes up at him.

"Never enough."

"Enough to buy me something pretty, too?"

"Come along then."

"You are so sweet," she squealed in delight, then stretched up to buss his cheek wetly.

"I am too soft," he complained, but he smiled at her excitement, then his eyes took on a lambent glow as they regarded Nicole.

Did he expect squeals and kisses from her, too? Nicole wondered. Perhaps he deserved them, but she made him settle for a slight bow of her head and a soft, "Thank you, Marchand." His shrug accepted her overture but the heat of his gaze said he would have preferred the kisses.

The three of them crossed the Seine and were soon deep in the crush of the city's populace. In order to prevent them from getting separated, Marchand draped an arm about either woman's shoulders and tucked them in close to him, garnering many an envious glance for having such a lovely escort. When they reached Halles Centrales where the ladies of Paris did their marketing for the day, Musette produced a string bag and slipped Marchand's arm to roam about the vegetable stands, returning only to proffer an empty palm for him to fill with coins.

"Are you their banker, m'sieur?" asked Nicole. She was feeling quite content beneath the curl of his arm, though admittedly it was not the wisest thing to allow. However, here in this open, chaotic spot, she felt nothing malignant in her mood, only an enjoyment of the day and of the company.

'They are like children," he remarked with resigned indulgence. "They don't mind getting up in the morning not knowing where or if they will dine that night. Rich one day, poor the next, believing it is a sign of personal freedom to squander for the day in defiance of tomorrow. Me, I like to know my feet will be warm and my stomach full."

"So you are their conscience." She was smiling up at him.

"I am their curse. The curse of common sense. I see the rent is paid on time. I make sure there is enough food and decent wine. And I watch out for their tomorrows."

"Why?"

"Why?" He looked surprised by the question, then nonplused. "Because I love them, I guess. Because for all their grand ideals, they are sheep in a city of wolves and I would not like to see them sheered."

"So you, m'sieur, are a wolf who guards sheep. A thankless occupation for a wolf, I would think."

He crooked a smile in her direction. "Perhaps."

"And are you planning to take me into your flock?"

She'd meant it to be amusing, but his stare was somber and quite complex. "I don't think you are a sheep, mademoiselle. I am not sure what you are. Perhaps a wolf dressed in white fleece. A wolf like me."

She looked away so he wouldn't see how the parallel disturbed her. A wolf, yes. A ruthless predator stalking among innocents.

"Eh! Marchand!"

The gruff cry brought him to a halt as a spindly little man in ill-fitting clothes approached at a wheezing run. Marchand didn't look pleased to see him. "What do you want, Gaston?"

"Sebastien has work for you. He is waiting."

"Now?"

"You have other big plans? Like a post on the council to tend?"

Seeing Nicole's alarm as she accurately judged their interloper's unsavory character, Marchand hesitated. Would she look at him the same way if she knew what he did to pay their rent? Suddenly, he couldn't bear the thought of her distaste when he'd thought himself well beyond the stage of feeling shame. "Tell him no. Another time."

But the ferret-like man insisted. "You know Sebastien. With him, there is only now. You say no, he will ask another. He will see your refusal as disloyalty. You don't want to make M. De Sivry angry with you."

"To hell with De Sivry," Marchand grumbled, but he was looking at Nicole's tattered gown and weighing the lightness in his pocket. Could he afford a prideful gesture when their need was so great? He recanted begrudgingly. "Tell him I'll be there tonight."

"Now, Marchand. It cannot wait."

"All right. I'm coming." Reluctantly, he lowered his arm from Nicole's shoulders. He wouldn't meet her gaze as he said, "I must go. I've some work to do. Musette is right over there. Stay with her. Tell her I will be at the café later. And here——" He tucked a stack of coins into her hand. "Something pretty."

"Marchand, I don't need a new dress." She was looking over his shoulder at the disreputable Gaston, rightly connecting him to no good.

"Yes, you do." And pressed the money upon her. "Be a good girl, now, and do not argue."

Her brows gave a haughty arch that he found quite adorable; he couldn't resist leaning close to take advantage of her pursed mouth. It was a fleeting kiss, snatched from unprepared lips, but she gave a little gasp of surprise and unfeigned delight that charmed him completely. This one was no coquette.

"Something pretty and green like your eyes."

And he was gone before she could protest again.

Raising her fingertips, she touched her mouth, still feeling the warm pulse of his upon it. And what stirred through her then was purely female yearning.

As she started across the walk toward Musette, Nicole found herself intrigued by the other woman's actions. With her bag hanging open from her arm, she would stroll up close behind another shopper, then deftly shift a portion of that unsuspecting marketer's goods into her own bag before moving on. After several such encounters, Musette's string bag was bulging, without its owner having expended a single sou.

"What are you doing?" Nicole whispered as she fell in step with her.

"Shopping. We have to eat."

"But Marchand gave you money."

"Money that can be put to better use buying bullets for the rebellion."

"Musette!"

"Hush! Keep your voice down. And for the love of

God, say nothing to Marchand!" She glanced about quickly to assure no one was listening, then she fixed the shocked woman with a level stare. "You think we are silly wastrels, don't you? But have you never believed in anything with all your heart and soul? That is the way we feel about our cause. Marchand doesn't understand. He was a part of it and he carries the scars of guilt, yet still he refuses to see the right in what we do."

"I'm not sure I understand, either."

"Then come with me and learn." She paused and smiled. "As soon as we find you a dress. One that will make Marchand forget all his grievances."

The school of rebellion was held in a smoky café where students and reactionaries crowded close over the same tabletops to discuss the overthrow of power. Nicole knew little of the country's politics, though she'd been raised her whole life in France. Her father was apolitical and her mother a realist to the extreme, typically and forever English. Nicole had never been exposed to the ideals of these fervid-eyed dreamers who espoused equality and something called free subjectivity. She listened, entranced by their passions, caught up in their sense of creative drama.

Frederic LaValois was right in the middle of it all, with Musette tucked in against his side. Enthusiasm lent an energy to features Nicole had at first thought passive. She could see a bit of his brother's fire in his eyes as he spoke of the article he was writing for *La Liberté, Journal des Arts* which demanded an abolition of official institutions to fulfil the promises made in the 1830s Revolution. In it, he spoke out the popular view that Paris contained two dens of criminals, one of thieves and one of murderers. The den of thieves he likened to the stock exchange; that of the murderers, to the Palais de Justice. Incendiary words to provoke the emotional tide of unrest. Though his recitation won murmurs of appreciation from his peers, Nicole's opinion remained reserved. Perhaps it was due to her political naiveté, perhaps her inbred common sense.

Wine flowed freely and crusty *baguettes* of warm bread were shared until the hour grew late and the sky dark. Frederic rose up at last and waved off his protesting friends by saying, "Another time, brothers. I must be off to meet Marchand. He would not like to know I've been here amongst you rabble-rousers."

That brought a hearty laugh. Nicole was annoyed to think they'd joke at their benefactor's expense.

"That brother of yours needs the bourgeois stuffings kicked out of him," one of the students cried in disgust, and Frederic rounded upon him with a look of cold steel.

"It would take a better man than you, sir. I may not agree with my brother's politics but, by God, I'll defend his right to an opinion down to your last drop of blood."

"Here now, Frederic," Musette soothed, rubbing his forearms gently. "No one wishes Marchand any ill. It's the wine talking."

Mollified, he smiled loosely at his friends, and again wished them good night. He reached out to loop an arm about Musette's shoulders and the other around Nicole's waist. "Come along. We can't afford to lose you two lovely creatures."And they ended up nearly toting him between them as he called good-natured cheer to all they passed.

As they walked toward the bridge across the Seine, all Nicole's senses came jarringly alive. Alarm sizzled through her like a charged current, making the hairs prickle up along her arms and rise at the nape of her neck.

Mon Dieu! What was it?

Still tucked into Frederic's side, she let her gaze fly along the outline of intimate cafés, seeking out the source of danger. She could taste terror in the back of her throat just above where her heart seemed to crowd, beating a frantic tempo.

And then her gaze settled far back in the shadows, upon the figure of a man in stark silhouette. She saw him jerk as if with some shock of recognition, then he took one gliding step forward to the edge of lamplight.

Reflection played an eerie game upon his face, highlighting skin so fair it seemed translucent and hollows so sharp and deep they were like caverns; a face so startling, so unnaturally beautiful she came close to stumbling in her study. Beneath an arch of black brows, eyes of an icy, luminous blue entranced her. And even as she jerked her head away, she caught the impression of his smile; serene and sinister all at once.

Nicole had never seen the Devil but on this night, she was sure he walked abroad. And she was just as certain that he followed safely back amongst the shadows. She could feel him, an essence so powerful, it frightened her. But the moment they crossed the bridge, the sensations faded and she knew he was gone. But the fear lingered, lending a quickness to her heartbeats and an anxious panic to her mind.

"Are you sure?" the woman demanded again as her companion sprawled indolently within one of her chairs so that his legs dangled over one arm and his head hung down over the other. He was smiling most provokingly.

"Of course I am sure." He gave a leisurely stretch, extending his arms over his head and arching like a supple cat. A dark, deadly cat. He continued to smile as he watched her agitation grow. A cautious soul would have been wary, but he had no soul to fear for.

"Where did she go?"

"Across the river to that bastion of young hedonists who call themselves defenders of the poor. Forgive me, but I was unable to follow over the flow of water. A nuisance, but what can one do."

"She was alone?"

He waved a negligent hand. "She was with other mortals."

"But she, alone, sensed you."

"Ummm. Quite an experience that was. I felt her testing me all the way across the square. She's very strong, but I don't think she understands the power. Not yet."

The woman ceased her pacing and regarded him with a pensive smile. "Not yet. Oh, this is too wonderful."

"I thought you would be pleased, *cara*. And how do you plan to reward me for bringing you this news?"

She knelt down beside him, seeing her beauty dazzle in his pale eyes. "You have my eternal devotion."

"Pah!" He laughed at that. "Oh, *mia amora*, I know exactly what that vow is worth. Give me something— new."

She bent down close to the diabolical perfection of his face; the mocking face of her three-century-old lover, and she let her fingertips trail down the taut arch of his throat. His eyes slid down to a glittery half-mast as the muscles moved beneath her touch in a roil of anticipation.

"You, my love," she purred against the cool part of his lips, "shall have the first taste of her innocent blood."

Chapter Six

"Where have you been?"

Marchand glowered up at them from over a nearly emptied bottle of wine when they joined him in the quiet café; quiet for the Latin Quarter, where life didn't truly begin until after sunset.

"We aren't all that late, *mon frère*," Frederic replied, reaching down to rumple his brother's hair. Marchand jerked away with a toss of his head, his mood too dark to be easily dismissed.

"Tomorrow, I go to bury a friend. I'm glad you are amused by my unwillingness to bury another."

"March, you worry too much."

"And you, not at all." He poured himself another glass, nearly missing it with the spill of rich red liquid, making Nicole wonder if this was his first bottle or merely one in a procession. "You were with your romantic-minded friends, plotting revolution as if it was some piece of pretty fiction flowing from your pen, as if you will be able to blot up the blood that spills if you decide it displeases you."

"I don't want to argue this with you tonight. Let's talk of something else," Frederic suggested amiably. He sat the two ladies, then assumed a seat at his brother's elbow.

But Marchand shook his head. "No, I want to talk of it. And I want you to listen."

"All right. I'm listening." Frederic spoke with a resigned sigh, as if he were placating a difficult child. And that hint of patronage angered Marchand all the more. He tossed down the last of his wine and banged the glass upon the table.

"Can't you see what a farce this all it? Why, half of Paris claims to be artists and freethinkers, when all they are are weak individuals following in a common mold. By their outbursts they proclaim their lack of originality. Such theatrics these bohemians display, shunning everything that speaks of comfort or success. They claim to espouse fraternity, equality and freedom from self-interest, but I say if it were a genuine contempt for this bourgeois life, they wouldn't dream of it and cry over its loss. This poverty they worship like some golden calf gives them an excuse to ignore their responsibilities to family and to this nation as a whole. I say they are cowards and fools."

"You have very little respect for me, Marchand," Frederic said softly. "A moment ago, I was ready to fight to protect your views. Will you discard mine as so unimportant? You always have, you know."

"That's not true. You have a marvelous gift for words. All I ask is that you go back and finish your education. Make something of your life. Devote it to a worthy cause."

"I already have." And he reached out to cup his brother's flushed face between his hands, wishing to quietly convey his conviction.

"No!" He pushed Frederic's hands away.

"March, can't you trust me to follow my own conscience?"

"Your conscience? You wail and moan about how your conscience won't permit you to attend school and better yourself. You cry about how it would be a sin against your moral character to support yourself and raise a decent family. You hide behind some romantic notion that it would prostitute your integrity to put food on the table while I—while I sell my principles so you will have that freedom. Here." He slapped a heap of coins upon the table. "That is the cost of my pride. Take it. Squander it on your vain pleasures. Use it to fuel your foolish revolt. But when it's gone, it's gone. See how many of your noble friends remain when you are truly poor."

He stood up, spilling his chair over backward. Frederic surged up to catch his shoulders.

"March, what is wrong with you? Why are you speaking this way?"

He reached up to clasp his brother's forearms, squeezing tight. "You are all I have . . . all I have. I cannot let you risk your life for such a fruitless cause."

Frederic smiled at him. "Ah, but what good is life if it's not spent in a cause worth dying for? You can't weigh that value for me. I alone have that privilege."

"'Please, Frederic . . . please don't involve yourself in this. Don't follow after folly just like—" He broke off, emotions overcoming his power of speech.

"Just like Papa?"

Marchand recoiled as if Frederic had struck him. Realizing his error, Frederic tried to tighten his grasp but Marchand pulled away from it and without a word, stalked from the café into the shadow-drenched streets.

And without thinking, Nicole was up, racing after him.

She fell in step and walked with him in silence, waiting for him to acknowledge she was there. He gave her a quick glance, then focused upon the winding road ahead; a road that seemed to spin into nothingness. Like his father's promises.

"He was a fool, a dreamer. Frederic doesn't remember like I do. Always some cause, always some brave and futile rebellion with the needs of the many more important than the needs of his family. Oh, how he made my mama cry. But she stood by him, letting him sell off all our silver, letting him sell out our futures for his frivolous plots and schemes. Damn him! How we fought, shouting until he'd raise his hand to me in anger. But he never struck me, not until I told him I was going into the military. He threw me down the front steps, called me traitor, told me never to come home again. He didn't understand that I was just trying to provide some sense of security for Mama and Frederic. And him. I needed some order in my life, a sense of stability he would never give us. But he would not listen."

"What happened to him?"

"He lost his head for treason against the state. They wouldn't let me provide him with a decent burial. I went to Mama, to take care of her, and she wouldn't see me. She took her own life a month later. I never got the chance to tell her—anything."

Nicole reached over to touch the back of his hand. Oh, how she knew that feeling of desperate loss! "I'm so sorry."

His fingers spread wide, inviting hers to wend between them as he shrugged eloquently. "But you don't want to hear all this."

"We are friends, aren't we?"

He looked down at her with a fragile smile. "Yes, we are friends."

"Friends listen."

He said nothing, but his fingers squeezed tight around hers as they continued to walk.

"So what happened then?"

"I got Frederic accepted into the university and I devoted myself to my military career. I had hopes that everything would be fine, but Frederic, he got himself involved with these agitators and I found myself caught up in the July Rebellion. We were to scour the town to disperse the gatherings, while citizens threw saucepans and flowerpots down upon our heads. We were ordered to fire upon them in the Rue des Pyramides and the Rue St. Honoré. A baker's workman threw the body of a woman who'd been killed by our fire at our heads, crying, "This is what your comrades do to our women! Will you do the same?" and that night, two companies of the Fifth Regiment went over the side of the revolt. I went with them. It was the only time Frederic and I wore the tricolor cockcades together.

"When Louis-Philippe took power, I was asked to join in his army and I was proud to do so. I believed so strongly in everything I was told. Until the day I found myself with musket drawn, aiming it down the alleyways at my brother's friends. A boy of no more than a half score of years lay dead upon the stones. I put down my gun that day. I could no longer understand my purpose in serving a ruler who would have me shoot down the very people who brought him to power, those he'd had us vow to die to protect."

"And so now you protect Frederic and his friends."

"It's what I've sworn to do, and he fights me as I once

fought our father. We are so far apart in the things we believe and yet the same in what we desire. Why can there never be a balance?"

"I don't know, Marchand."

He drew to a stop then, his expression troubled by more than what he had said. He was kneading her fingers with his, a restless, agitated movement, one he was unaware of.

"March, who is De Sivry?"

He went very still, and for a moment she thought he would refuse to answer. Then he told her in a taut voice, "He is a member of the Paris underworld that preys upon the innocent like my brother. It is his whispering that stirs discontent and coaxes men to believe that violence is the only answer. Fools! If they listen to anyone, it should be to Marat, the villain of the Revolution. But he was a Frenchman and a realist who knew it was impossible to have a revolution without wholesale executions. Rebellion is borne in blood; I'll not have Frederic's spilled in its name. Not when nothing will change in the long run."

"And so you deal with De Sivry to keep him from your brother."

"And because he pays enough for me to support them all."

"Pays you to do what?"

He looked away. "Whatever he asks." She didn't need to ask if those things were illegal. His unspoken anguish said they were. And then he told her in a hush of despair, "I think he may have killed Camille because I said I wanted to quit him."

"Marchand, no—" But she couldn't be sure. She couldn't offer proof. Still, Nicole knew in her heart that no man killed Camille Viotti. No normal man.

"Today, I helped break a man's fingers because he was late in making a loan payment." He glanced at her briefly and she watched the pain fill up in his eyes and liquify with a blink. "I try to hold to the image of Frederic and Bebe and Musette to erase the shame. I tell myself I must do what I must do and stay strong for them because I cannot support them if my conscience falters."

"And who supports you?"

Her gentle question confused him.

"Who is strong for you?"

He stared at her, incomprehensibly.

"I can be," she told him, because she hurt so deeply for his solitary stand. She was beginning to understand how desolate that can be. "You may lean on me, Marchand. I am strong enough to support you."

He didn't move. She could see the uncertainty behind his gaze working to suppress any threads of hope. He'd gone too long alone to believe he could ever share the burden. Until she stepped up and put her arms about his waist and hugged firmly. She felt his startled inhalation and the churn of his inner struggle. Then, at last, his arms came up to curl about her and his cheek pillowed itself atop her head. And as he clutched tight and tremors shivered along his powerful embrace, she vowed she would not fail this man who, in such a short time, had come to mean so very much to her.

She felt his kiss stir her hair and the vibration of his speech.

"You are very brave to align yourself with such a pack of hopeless fools."

"Life has no value if not attached to a cause. You've taken me into your family and I think it only right that I help defend it."

He didn't laugh, because he was picturing her braced against wet brick with eyes flashing fire. He stroked a hand along her hair and whispered, "You make an admirable ally, Mademoiselle Nicole. We will protect our flock together."

It had grown suddenly too comfortable in his arms. Nicole was absorbed by his warmth and solidity. Beneath her cheek, she could hear the strong drum of his heart as it pushed vitality through him. Her senses sharpened as she breathed in his heat, his scent, his energy. And beneath the emotional bond she felt for him rumbled a darker interest. Fearfully, she pushed away from him to begin walking. Though he didn't touch her, she was acutely aware of him beside her. And aware, as well, of the disconcerting changes growling through her.

How could she help him if she couldn't protect him from her own threat?

By the time they reached their flat, she felt in control again. Until they stepped inside and saw Bebe lost to wine and weeping as she studied a newly framed canvas.

Nicole was unprepared for the sweep of longing those familiar fields and forests twisted through her. A pain so poignant and piercing, she reached out without thinking to claim the painting.

"What do you think you're doing?" Bebe demanded, gripping one side of the frame possessively.

"It's mine."

"Yours? What do you mean? It is Camille's."

"He gave it to me. It's mine."

"I've never seen this work. When did he give it to you?"

"On the day he died. After he brought me to Paris."

"You—?" Refusing to relinquish the frame until she

had the truth, she looked to Marchand and he reluctantly gave it.

"The painting is hers, Bebe. Let her have it."

Stunned, she released the canvas as a terrible understanding overtook her. She looked from Marchand, whose features were stoic, to Nicole, who was cradling the painting in her arms. With an anguished cry, Bebe fled the room, stumbling down the outside stairs to disappear into the darkness.

Only then did consequence occur to Nicole. "Oh, Marchand, I'm sorry. I didn't mean—"

"It's my fault," he cut in curtly. "I brought the painting here. I had it restored because I knew how much it meant to you, because it was from Camille."

"No, that's not why—" It had nothing to do with Camille. It was the place he'd captured with his delicate strokes; the place she'd been raised with love and lies and longed for even now. But Marchand wasn't interested in hearing her reasoning.

"I'd better go after her."

"Maybe I should leave—"

"Wait here!" He spoke that command, giving no room for dissension as he strode out the door.

She collapsed upon the pallet she shared with him and hugged the painting until the urge to weep passed over her. Briefly, she considered fleeing the tangle of misunderstanding she'd created, but she was too practical to think of it for long. Where would she go? Where would she find anyone as willing to take her in as these people had been? She'd been gone from home for three days. It felt like a lifetime. She no longer thought of herself as that pampered innocent sequestered from the dark side of existence. That dark side had been brought home to her most cruelly. Pride and panic kept her from returning until she could accept or excuse the facts that had been forced upon her. Until she could understand the changes warping through her own subconscious.

No, she would stay here. She would do her best to fit in among this odd group of friends. She'd make Bebe understand about Camille, and she'd ease the burden crushing down upon Marchand. Because their acceptance felt very good and the sense of safety was wonderfully strong. And her feelings for Marchand stirred all sorts of new sensations. She wouldn't call it love. They were yet strangers. Still, she'd learned to trust him and admired him for his integrity. She enjoyed the hot spark of his wit and the warm flow of his charm and respected his staunch commitment to the welfare of those close to him. He was strong enough to make her feel secure, and yet there was a lonely void in him she could fill and truly belong to. She wanted the chance to repay her gratitude. She wanted the chance to taste more of his kisses.

And as much as she was afraid of the other dark emotions he moved inside her, she was held by the belief that he was a man a woman would be a fool to walk away from.

And so she would stay . . . unless it grew too dangerous to remain beside him. Until she presented too great a threat.

With one last look at the pastoral beauty of Camille's art, she propped the painting up against the wall and stripped down to her wilted petticoat. On second thought, she removed it as well and donned one of Marchand's shirts while she washed the undergarment and hung it by the stove to dry. Then she curled up in his blankets and sought relief from the day's troubles.

Hours later, her rest was disturbed by the feel of

Marchand slipping under the covers next to her. And her peace of mind was shaken when he fit up close behind her, curving against her back to front, his broad palm moving the fabric of his shirt along her thigh, his arm settling over the dip of her waist to secure her to him. Then came the unmistakable stir of his kiss upon her hair. It was nearly dawn before she found sleep again, wondering what it would be like to roll toward him and offer that extra he'd said he'd appreciate.

Frederic and Musette didn't return to the flat that night and their absence had Marchand in a somber morning mood; that along with the fact that he was readying for Camille's funeral. By the time Nicole awoke, he was dressed in dark colors, drinking coffee equally black. He had nothing to say to her, even when she emerged from behind the dressing curtain in the new gown she'd purchased with his coin. She could almost believe from his reserve that she'd merely imagined him cuddling her close throughout the night.

He was gently solicitous of Bebe, which was considerate and appropriate, but Nicole couldn't help the nudge of envy when he bundled the other woman into her coat and escorted her to the door within the circle of his arm.

"Are you coming?" he asked her, as if an afterthought, and she nodded wordlessly. She decided it best if she followed them at a respectful distance, for on this day of grieving, she was an outsider. After they'd walked a block, Marchand looked back over his shoulder, his expression puzzled. And he stretched back his hand for hers, drawing her up on his other side.

If it were possible to love a man in three short days'

time, Nicole could swear she loved Marchand LaValois from that moment on.

It was cold and bleak at the cemetery. Frederic and Musette were already there, standing on the other side of the cheap coffin. A dozen or more fellow artists also crowded around in glum mourning as Camille Viotti was laid to rest.

After a brief, rather indifferent ceremony, Marchand was turning them to leave when Frederic approached. He gave Bebe a tender kiss on the cheek, nodded to Nicole, then caught his brother up in an emotional embrace. Gradually, Marchand returned it.

"March, I'm sorry for the way in which we parted. We must never allow such angry words to pass between us again." He stepped back, still holding Marchand by the shoulders. "I will listen to you. The money you gave me I applied to our rent. I mean to see about going back to school. If you will have patience with me, I will try to become more responsible."

With a gruff cry, Marchand seized Frederic up to place hard kisses on either cheek. It was a touching moment and as Nicole glanced away, feeling like an interloper, she caught sight of Musette's face. And the frown upon it was small and her expression guilty, making Nicole wonder what the two of them were up to.

They dined well and drank much, a Parisian send off for Camille. Marchand and Frederic sat close, arms about each other's shoulders in companionable affection. Musette watched them, her study pensive. Bebe tipped glass after glass until her gaze clouded into a glaze of remembrance and remorse. And Nicole sat in a quiet terror, so hungry her insides ached, yet every time

Nancy Gideon

she tried to partake of her *médaillons de veau,* her stomach knotted up in protest. The scent of the cooked veal was making her positively ill. But the wine was good and she drank more of it than was wise. And as she drank, she watched Musette watching the two brothers. And her suspicious sharpened along with her senses.

Musette was afraid. Nicole could taste her fear. She could smell the salt of her perspiration, could hear the fright in her rapid respirations. She became absorbed by these things to the point of losing her own sense of consciousness. It was as if they'd become one, as if Musette's alarm was her own, moving her blood in that same hurried pulse. Her concentration narrowed, focusing on the other young woman until there was nothing else.

Then suddenly, she heard Marchand call her name. The sound came from a long ways away, a beckoning echo pulling her back into herself. She glanced up at him and she felt his shock as if she was seeing herself through his eyes. Seeing how she was flushed of face and lightly panting, her eyes great, golden orbs, burning with a feverish light.

"Nicole?"

She blinked, and the sensations raveled like brilliant threads of emotion leaving behind the bare cloth of her own mind. And a certain degree of fright over what had just happened. What *had* happened? She was afraid to examine it, and explained it away to him as well as to herself by saying, "I fear I've had too much wine."

Marchand pushed back his chair. "I'll take you home."

Home. Odd feelings rose at the sound of that word. A tangle of images; pink brick and sand-colored stones against a fringe of deep green Norway pines, rickety stairs leading upward, a ragged pallet and a warm man. Home.

She felt Marchand cup her elbow with his palm and lift her. Her blurry gaze scanned those at the table, her friends; her new family. In a moment of unbearable empathy, she bent down to hug Bebe and felt the other's shock, then a grateful acceptance.

"I'm so sorry," she murmured, close to tears. And because she wanted to do something for the other woman, she gave all that she had, a locket on a gold chain that had been a gift from her parents. Bebe looked surprised and touched as she fingered the unexpected offering.

Then Nicole allowed Marchand to guide her away. She felt weightless and was glad for the strong circle of his arm. Glad for the masculine heat of him. She clung to his coat, scarcely aware that they were walking. Impressions flew by her, bright, confusing patterns and sounds so pure, so intense they seemed to pierce her head. The sounds of laughter from a café across the street. Of carriage wheels on the next block. Of a child crying somewhere. And underlying it all was the solid, comforting drum of Marchand's heart. It was that sound she followed, enticed by the beat until it echoed through her own veins.

And with that sound arose a searing emptiness, a pain she couldn't identify, yet instinctively she feared it.

It was hunger.

Bebe wasn't sure what drew her back. Some morbid loneliness awash on a sea of wine. She staggered slightly as she approached the cemetery. Camille was there. She could feel him. If she listened hard enough to the melancholy wind, she could hear his voice.

Bebe . . .

"Oh, Camille, how could you leave me?" she sobbed to herself as she reeled onward through the dragging grief.

As the wind increased, she could see the unhealthy vapors rising from the cemetery. Normally, she had a terror of the graveyard, but on this mournful night it seemed so serene, so inviting to a heart numbed to all but pain. A pain that grew unbearable when she thought of sweet Camille, soon to be lying in the loft of the cemetery cloister, packed in upon the bones of ages. How she wished they could have afforded a nice burial for him, something befitting the sensitive soul that he was, one in which he could forever remain where he was interred. Instead, as soon as the caretakers believed him to be forgotten, his grave would be violated, his remains carried away and he would be stacked with other unfortunates like slices of bacon in one of the large paupers' lofts. Time would dissolve all that was unique, and all that he was would be filtered in amongst indifferent others so that his special plot on sacred ground could be used again by the unsuspecting.

She wept at that image.

Oh, if there was only some way to assure him a decent rest. A sleep like a prince undisturbed and undefiled. She had truly loved him.

Perhaps if Marchand had offered his affection, she could have borne the agony of being alone. Marchand . . . she loved him, too. But Camille had been her hope for a future, Marchand just a glimpse of fleeting pleasure. Without Camille, her days and weeks and years stretched out into an unhappy blur. Why go on?

She'd come to the place where they'd lowered a plain box into warm earth. She stopped, stunned and horrified by what she saw. The ground was savagely disturbed, mounded up on either side of the fresh grave to expose the broken remains of the coffin. The empty coffin. She gave a cry of outrage. They'd taken him! Grave robbers had stolen away her love!

Bebe . . .

His voice whispered upon the midnight breeze. It shivered along her limbs until she was trembling helplessly.

"Camille?"

Could there have been some mistake? She'd heard such things sometimes happened; a poor soul believed to be dead and properly buried, only to find his soul had yet to leave him. Could they have buried her beloved Camille alive?

"Camille? Is that you?"

She saw a shape shifting amongst the mists. A man moving toward her, slowly, somewhat awkwardly. She waited, scarcely breathing, hope crowding out all thoughts of fear.

"Camille?"

She recognized his coat. She herself had picked it out so he might look elegant in his eternal sleep. Only the fabric was caked with earth and torn as if in some terrible struggle. Oh, *mon Dieu!* He'd had to dig himself up out of his grave! She started to rush forward but just then, a pale moon revealed all to her desperate gaze. Camille Viotti as she'd last seen him; his throat viciously torn open, now a huge dark wound. His eyes were open as well, but no sight or sensibility shown in them. There was something burning there in his gaze, a fierce light that held her momentarily mesmerized. But it wasn't human . . .

He reached for her, his movements alarmingly fast,

and Bebe screamed as she realized this was not Camille, her love, returned to her alive. Returned to her, yes, but living, no. The charnel scent of death clung to him. The grave's coloring was upon his face. She would find no warmth within the embrace he offered, because there was no natural life within him.

Shrieking madly, Bebe stumbled from the cemetery. Blindly, she dashed out into the street, screaming . . . screaming.

The carriage never had a chance to stop as her figure hurtled in front of it. And when the medical staff examined the bruised and broken remains, they shook their heads. A suicide, it was decided. And since there was no identification upon the body, nothing except a gold locket, she was callously shelved to await burial in an unmarked tomb.

Chapter Seven

The flat was steeped in darkness, the fire having long since burned down to grey ash. The night air came in with them, filling the room with an invigorating chill, giving them a reason to linger a little longer in each other's arms.

"I'd better see to the stove," Marchand murmured, but he didn't move to do so right away; Nicole was burrowed up against him and she felt so good, he couldn't make himself set her aside. And she seemed in no hurry to have him leave her. She'd pushed her palms inside his coat and was rubbing them up and down the curve of his ribs, continuing the subtle, sensual overtures that had him aroused the entire walk home.

He tried telling himself that she'd had too much wine. That's why she was so cuddly and soft and attentive to him. Too much wine. But knowing that in his head didn't keep his body from responding. She'd quickened a long-suppressed urgency within him, one that tightened and twisted every time they were together. He'd never had a woman confuse him so. He'd never had to rule his passions with such an enormous amount of discipline. When she was near him, he wanted her closer.

When she touched him, he wanted to caress her in return. When she tipped her face up to look at him, he could think of nothing but kissing her. Madness, surely. Because for all her innocent tempting, he wasn't certain of what she wanted from him. Comfort. Safety. Friendship. Passion. Or love. All but the last, he was eager to share. But he feared it was that last emotion that made him hesitate when instinct cried for him to take her as desire dictated.

"Have I told you how fine you look in that new dress?"

"No. Do you really think so?" She sounded shy and insecure. That hint of vulnerability touched off a chord of care inside him that had tenderness overtaking need.

"Yes, I think so." His hand ran over the glossy surface of her hair, catching on the pins that held it confined, working them free so that those glorious dark tresses cascaded halfway down her back. She was leaning into him, her body a bow of willing concession. Want flooded through him, but those softer emotions held it at bay. "You are beautiful and very young, I think, and we are going to be in a great deal of trouble, you and I, if we don't stop this now."

"Do you want to stop?" The words purred from her in calculated innocence. All that was male rumbled to life with an impatient lustiness.

"No," he told her quietly. "I don't want to stop. I want to make love with you, Nicole. But I don't think that would be wise."

He'd expected any number of different responses to that claim; shock, embarrassment, outrage, fright. Any of those would have been consistent with what he'd learned of her. But she expressed none of those things. Instead, she stared up at him steadily with a look that devoured. Her eyes glittered in the darkness, a shimmer of hot gold that woke a quiver of remembered alarm in him. He thought it would be a good idea for him to step away now, but as if she anticipated his sudden reluctance, her fingers balled up in his shirt linen, holding him fast.

"We are wolves, you and I," she whispered with a penetrating fervor. "We survive on instinct, not wisdom." She'd worked his shirt free and her fingertips moved upon bared flesh, creating a tension he couldn't ignore. God, he wanted her! He'd never been so maddened by desire, so blinded by need. Yet still, there was something so disturbing about her and the almost desperate yearning she evoked.

Dangerous. That's what she was. Dangerous. No longer the delicate kitten but a stalking predator. He knew he should break from the intensity of her gaze. He knew he should stop the spiraling desire. Instead, his mouth dropped down upon hers for a wild possessing kiss that shocked as much as it satisfied, for he wasn't one to make rough with the ladies. It was as if she'd woken something powerful and demanding inside him that cried, take her, conquer her! It's your only chance! That made no sense, but then again, it did. Because there was no innocence or reluctance in the way she returned the stabbing thrusts of his tongue or in the raw, hungry sounds she made. Even the way she rose up against him was like a challenge, her fingers spearing into his hair, clenching to lock his head in place. He tasted his own blood as the pressure of her lips mashed his against his teeth hard enough to cut them. Then she made another kind of sound, a low rumbling moan akin to ecstasy as she licked at his torn mouth.

That was enough for him. Something was very wrong with this dark anxious passion. It touched on none of the warm emotions he felt for the woman in his arms. This wasn't how he'd wanted to make love to her; not in a hard, hurtful hurry. He took a hold of her upper arms, intending to lever her away, planning to offer the requisite apology to defuse their direction.

Her snarl of protest was an unexpected shock. And so was the strength she used to throw him down upon the mattress; the impact so sudden and fierce it stunned the breath from him. It occurred to him in an urgent flash that she was intent on his life rather than his prowess as she flung herself down over him, straddling his chest, tearing his shirt collar open, gripping his face between hands that were enormously powerful. It was too dark to see her expression but he could hear the breath rasping from her in quick vicious pulls.

He was startled enough to fling his hand out to grope for his saber. He was frantic enough to look toward the opening of the door as a possible salvation.

How they must have looked to Frederic and Musette as moonlight flooded in and over them; Nicole crouching astride his chest, her eyes all flaring brilliance, his mouth dark with blood.

"Get out!"

The words bellowed from Nicole, so harsh and angry the two instantly retreated and closed the door. The distraction gave Marchand time to heave the clinging figure off him and to roll to a safe distance, sword hilt in hand. And he paused there on hands and knees, panting hard, his heart pounding furiously within his chest.

But Nicole didn't rush at him again. She knelt on the pallet, her face buried in her hands. And the sounds she made were ones of desperate weeping. For a brief second, he considered the blade in his hand, but such a notion so horrified him, Marchand flung the sword aside.

"Nicole?" He started to move toward her.

She edged backward on her knees, trying to keep the separation of space between them. "No, don't!" she cried in a hoarse voice. The tones quivered with a fragile terror. "I don't want to hurt you!"

Her genuine distress was enough to bring him to her. At the touch of his hand, she gave a despairing sob and turned toward him, curling up into a quaking knot of dismay upon his lap.

"Oh, Marchand, hold me! I'm so afraid!"

He was afraid, too.

"Hold me and make me forget," came the pitiful plea that fractured his guard.

He gathered her up into a gentle embrace and rocked her slowly. While he stroked her hair and murmured soft reassurances, his mind was spinning in several directions, each more terrible than the first.

Did she want him to make her forget that she and Camille had indulged in this kind of savage love play?

Or was there something deeper, darker involved?

And he had to wonder as he held her close, if this woman he was falling in love with could have killed his friend Camille.

It was morning when Nicole awoke. She was draped across Marchand's knees and his arms were still snug about her. However, the moment she stirred, he was awake and wary. She couldn't mistake the careful way he eased back away from her as she sat up.

He had good reason to be cautious.

"Good morning," she ventured.

"How are you feeling?" That was asked with a tentative neutrality.

"A little lightheaded. I had nothing to eat yesterday and the wine must have gone straight to it." Would he believe that? That her inhibitions had been destroyed by drink and therein lay the cause of her bizarre behavior? She risked a glance. His expression was shut down tightly. No. He didn't believe it. What was he thinking, then? If he thought her mad, why had he remained? Why wasn't he tossing her out the door? She tried another tack with him. "Things got rather . . . out of control. I didn't mean for them to. I'm sorry." She looked at him beseechingly, seeing the rent she'd ripped in his shirt and the way one side of his mouth was swelling. She reached up to touch that shredded lip but he recoiled with a flicker of uneasiness darkening his gaze. She sat very still, trying to pretend she wasn't wounded to the soul.

"I'm going to make some coffee. Do you want some?"

"Yes, please."

He backed to the stove, never taking his eyes off her. He managed on the third try to get the fire going.

Nicole stood stiffly and brushed the worst of the wrinkles from her skirt. It was then she saw his saber gleaming on the floorboards. He saw the direction of her gaze and met her eyes without blinking. Hers filled up with desolate tears but she didn't speak as she lifted the blade and placed it gingerly alongside his other things where it belonged.

"Why did you come to Paris?" That was asked low and soft but there was no missing the granite-hard meaning. Time for the truth.

"I was running away from my family's chateau in Grez. I've never been to school. I was tutored at home.

The only farms I've ever been on belonged to our tenants."

"Why did you run? Are your parents ogres? Did they mistreat you? Did they try to force you into an unacceptable alliance?" His gaze was penetrating. Was he wondering if she'd escaped from a locked room somewhere; some aristocrat's insane daughter slipping their supervision?

How she wished it was something so easy to explain. She spoke slowly, choosing her words with great care. "I discovered that they'd been lying to me for years, holding back knowledge that changed my life and the way I view them. I couldn't remain there once my trust was destroyed." When he didn't ask what she'd found out, she was vastly relieved. She didn't want to lie to him anymore.

"You're not French."

"But of course I am!"

"Your accent—"

"My mother is English. My father was from Florence—originally."

"Ah, that explains it. Now we are making some progress."

There was a moment of silence with only the coffee water simmering.

"And Camille?"

"I met him in Grez. We'd talk sometimes while he worked. He was very nice to me. I asked him to bring me here . . . I told him a convenient tale." Like the ones she'd told him, he had to be thinking.

But that was not what he was thinking at all.

"Then you and he were not—"

"Not what?" Then her eyes went round. "Oh, no. Never. I let you think that because I was afraid you would put me out if you knew the truth. All my money was stolen, you see, and I had nowhere else to go. Camille offered his aid should I need it. I never thought he'd be d-dead when I came to ask for it." She looked down at the twist of her fingers, forcing out the words. "I am very sorry for deceiving you and for all the inconvenience I've caused. When Bebe arrives, I'll tell her everything. She can keep the painting. Then I'll be on my way. I'll repay you for the cost of this dress as soon as I can find work—"

He crossed to her in two long strides. She looked up at him, lost and oh, so very vulnerable again. His hand cupped her cheek just in time to brush aside the first tear. "No one's asked you to leave. I just wanted to hear the truth. Is that all of it?"

She nodded rapidly, hope brightening in her uplifted gaze.

"If you don't tell me the truth, I can't help you."

"Will you help me, Marchand?"

"If I can."

A great sigh gusted from her and she nestled her cheek into the well of his palm, placing a grateful kiss upon his thumb. He gave her a small smile but the cautious reserve was still there behind the steady fix of his stare. Then he went to make the coffee.

He wasn't going to cast her out! The overwhelming relief of that was knee-weakening. Then her thoughts spun beyond the obvious as she looked to him once more. "Once the truth is known, there is no reason for you to pretend to be my lover." There, she'd given him the chance to back away gracefully. It was the least she could do—after last night.

As he poured, he told her simply, "I have no problem with the arrangements the way they are now. Unless you want them changed." Then he glanced up and she was stunned by the intensity of his dark-eyed gaze. He was afraid of her, or at least justifiably wary, and yet he was willing to let her stay close to him. When the same thing could happen again. Was he foolish? She'd never thought so, and he certainly wasn't a reckless romantic. What, then?

Before she could ask, there was a tap on the door and Frederic peered in cautiously.

"May we come in?" The question was polite. The glance was full of curiosity.

"I was just pouring coffee. I'll get two more cups."

Frederic and Musette came to the table, doing their best to hold their tongues as their stares went from Nicole to Marchand and back again. Finally, her face hot with discomfort, Nicole murmured, "Forgive me for shouting at you last night. I had no right—"

Frederic chuckled. "We're lucky March didn't shoot us—considering how untimely our arrival was. Next time, put a red flag on the door so we'll know it's not safe to come in."

Nicole endured their sly amusement in silence. Marchand distributed the coffee cups and came to stand beside her. When she glanced up, he touched a light kiss upon her lips. If his brother or Musette thought they'd stumbled upon something amiss in the night, that tender gesture put their doubts to rest.

And gave her doubts aplenty.

Why was he so willing to protect her when he had every reason to think her a dangerous lunatic? Because he cared for her? That woke a tug of expectancy within her breast. Or was he simply clever enough to want her where he could watch her? So he could send to Grez and summon her family to come get her in hopes of reward. She knew they would gladly pay him enough to get his little family through the toughest winter months in luxurious style. His steady stare gave no clue. It was watchful, and his expressive dark eyes were carefully veiled.

And where there had been trust, suddenly there was fear. On both sides.

When Bebe had not returned by midmorning, Marchand grew worried enough to ask around the *quartier* to see if anyone had seen her. Frederic left with him, stating he had to turn in some articles he'd written for a respectable journal. They might even bring money, he told his brother with a smile as they closed the door behind them.

The moment they were gone, Musette collapsed in her chair and startled Nicole with her sudden quiet tears.

"Musette, whatever is the matter?" she demanded in concern, kneeling beside the other woman's chair.

"Oh, it's—it's nothing."

"Nonsense! Something was wrong yesterday, too. What is it? Is there something I can do?"

The redhead canted up a suspicious eye. "You won't go to Marchand with what I tell you?"

Nicole took a cautious breath. She was balancing on a thin line with Marchand already, as far as trust went. She didn't want to start deceiving him again. She guessed he wouldn't be so gracious a second time.

Musette was watching the anxious play of her expression and she put a reassuring hand upon Nicole's shoulder. "That's all right, my friend. I should not ask you to betray the confidence of the man you love. Forget I said anything."

The man she loved. It sounded so set and sure when

spoken out loud like that. And so like the truth. However, like family, they all did for each other here, that's what Musette had said, so she covered the other woman's hand with her own.

"It has to do with Frederic, doesn't it?"

"Oh, Nicole, he will be in such desperate trouble if he does what he promised Marchand."

"What do you mean?"

"He's committed his efforts—and a certain amount of money—to a particular political event." Musette was being very evasive, but Nicole had no mind or care for politics. She wanted to know how it affected those she'd come to care for.

"And?"

"And if he doesn't come through, they will hurt him, Nicole. These are not cheerful students he's involved with. They are serious, professional men who would do anything to achieve their end. They have already threatened Marchand—"

"De Sivry."

"How do you know of him?"

"He had Marchand do some . . . work for him the other day. I know he is a bad man to cross."

"Frederic isn't like Marchand. He isn't strong. He isn't a fighter. He can't protect himself."

"Then tell Marchand—"

"No! Frederic would never forgive himself if his brother came to harm over this. Marchand would want to handle it with his fists, and he is no match for the kind of men De Sivry has employed. They would think nothing of killing him."

Nicole's heart went cold. "Then there must be some way to please both Marchand and De Sivry. Would De

Sivry be satisfied if he was paid the money he was promised? Would he leave Frederic alone then?"

"I—I don't know. But how would we come up with the necessary coin? Marchand provides all we survive on."

"Marchand isn't the only one not afraid to take chances."

Musette's gaze flashed over to the mattress ticking and back to her in alarm. "Oh, no! Marchand would never forgive you that. I could not allow you to—"

"I'm not talking about . . . *whoring* for the money." Especially when she couldn't even say the word without turning bright red. "I mean to borrow it."

Musette regarded her for a long moment and then began to smile. "How and from whom?"

"Can you teach me how to do that trick you were doing in the market?"

"Yes, but pinching bread and picking pockets is not the same thing. I'm not quick enough by half—"

"I am. But I need you to tell me whose to pick."

Musette looked as if she might protest, but was too intrigued by the idea. "It is dangerous."

"What did Frederic say about life without risk?"

"You love Marchand that much?"

She could have said yes, but instead she answered, "I owe him that much."

"Then let's hire a rig and go shopping amongst Paris's best."

By late afternoon, Musette may have found annoyance with Nicole's ethics, but she had no complaints about the woman's style. The two of them strolled the posh shopping districts, studying the shoppers, the way the shoppers scanned the shop windows. Nicole would only approach those Musette could name as wealthy, ones who would not miss a few francs and who could be repaid. She carefully noted each name and the amount "borrowed," ignoring the redhead's amusement. Musette didn't ask how Nicole planned to repay them. She was only concerned with obtaining the money.

It was shamefully easy business. Nicole had only to concentrate on the targeted purse, then move past the individual. They might feel a brief brush of air, they might even glance about, but by that time, she was out of sight, their coin safely in her hand. Musette marveled at her, never once able to spot how she managed to lift the purses. Her eyes simply couldn't follow the speed of Nicole's hand. And neither could the unknowing donators to the rebellious cause.

And when Musette presented her love with the day's bounty, he could only stare in disbelief.

"So much! Musette, where did you come by this?" His hands were shaking as they handled the stack of franc notes.

"Nicole. Don't ask how, just accept and pass the money on to De Sivry. Don't worry. Nicole has promised to say nothing to your brother. For all he knows, you are intent upon following the bland bourgeois life he has chosen for you."

"I don't like deceiving him. He's done so much for us—"

She gripped her lover's hands, her tone impassioned, her eyes ablaze with patriotic fervor. "And think of how much we'll be able to do! Within a week's time, we'll be able to fund the coup against Louis-Philippe, who filched our republic for his own profit."

Frederic thought for a moment and his conscience

seemed sufficiently calmed by the right of what he was doing. His father would have approved, and in time, Marchand would know he had done what he'd had to do. Marchand understood duty. "Does Nicole know her efforts go to support the assassination of a king?"

Musette gave him a sly smile that was both clever and cold. "She did not ask, and I thought it best not to enlighten her."

Frederic leaned in to kiss her ardently and to whisper, "You are as brave a soldier as any army of injustice has ever known. And I love you."

"And I, you, Frederic. Let's hurry and meet with De Sivry. He will be overjoyed to learn that our triumph is so close at hand."

And for the rest of the week, Musette and Nicole shadowed the boulevards and shops, adding to the coffer while Frederic worked to allay his brother's suspicions. It was easier since Marchand had found temporary work along the quay and was absent often until midnight. He would come in exhausted, smelling of the docks, taking only enough time to wash up before sliding in beside Nicole. He didn't curl up around her as he once had but rather kept a judicious distance.

Lying beside him, longing for his closeness as much as she feared it, Nicole was awake until the early dawn hours, listening to the sounds of her companions's slumber, listening to the night sounds of the city beyond. She was finding it difficult to sleep at night, her system atuned to those dark hours where energy pulsed in the Paris streets and the cool breeze beckoned to instincts she didn't understand. She lay next to Marchand, watching over him, not daring to touch him, her desire for him growing as severe as the constant sear of hunger threading through her veins.

She couldn't eat from the table like the rest of them. The scents and texture of cooked foods repelled her. She would push them about her plate, and the first moment she had alone, she would devour the raw meats she purchased each day. Even those were getting harder for her to digest. What had begun to attract her appetite was not served upon a plate. It beat, a rich and forbidden temptation through those around her.

She lay there at night remembering the taste of Marchand's blood. That secret contemplation horrified and fascinated. She could feel his heart beating even though they weren't touching, could hear it sending those rivers of delight through his body with every soft thrum. The taste . . . it had been ambrosia, whetting a desire like none she'd known.

The desire for more.

And so, she was satisfied to remain a safe distance from him. She couldn't trust herself with those increasingly violent impulses; to bite, to taste, to feed in bestial abandon.

What was wrong with her? She knew of only one place to get that answer—the one place she would not go. For if she was to accept what he was, she would have to resign herself to being the same. And that, she was not prepared to do. Not while she had a scrap of humanity remaining.

Better to be tortured by the unknown than damned by the certain.

It was dark. The elegant and the well-to-do were bustling to the opera and to their private affairs. Most took carriages, but some enjoyed the night air and a brisk walk. Those were the ones Nicole waited for.

She had no trouble seeing through the shadows. Her night vision was almost equal to that of the day. She stood alone and was a bit uncomfortable without Musette to guide her, but the other woman had gone with Frederic to an important meeting, and Marchand was to be late in getting home. She didn't like lingering in the flat when they weren't there. Too many shadows. Bebe hadn't returned. Camille's clothing lay piled and unclaimed. His portrait seduced with the broken promise of the peaceful greens and blue skies that had once been home. If she stayed in the flat, she thought too much about Marchand. His scent was in the linens of their shared bed and breathing it in brought hunger and frustration. She didn't know how to deal with the conflict he'd created within her. She was in love with him, yet realized that love would bring him harm. Better to deny the one to prevent the other.

So she stalked the dark streets, searching for prey, a sleek hungry wolf hunting those of her kind who were somehow not the same. She channeled her concentration, seeking, finding when she observed a sophisticated figure stepping down from a rig. One gloved hand paid out from a pouch plump with coin.

Nicole fell in behind her victim, pacing her steps to match the other's, moving like a shadow herself until the time was right. Then she picked up her tempo, gliding silently, swiftly past, her fingers darting with an undetectable agility to catch the strings of the purse, confident that she would be blocks away before the theft was discovered.

Then a grip like iron circled her wrist in a cold, unbreakable band, freezing her hand half in, half out of the pocket, the plump prize clutching damningly in her fingers. Her gaze flew up in alarm to meet black eyes and a silky smile.

"*Bon soir.* Do not look so alarmed. I have no plans to call the *gendarmes*. I've been looking forward to meeting you."

Chapter Eight

When Nicole stepped into the sumptuous rooms of the house in the Place Vendôme, it was with an uncertain reluctance. She'd expected to have her attempted thievery reported to the authorities, not to be rewarded by a visit to her intended victim's home.

Her own family lived in quiet elegance, but the splendor of this apartment was grand enough to steal her breath away. She stood in the threshold of the drawing room, taking in the sights. The room was designed to display four large portraits. It was constructed in a Moorish style, its ceiling like that of a Turkish palace: a canopy of trelliswork tied together with ribbons. The borders depicted foliage, flowers and end medallions of peacock feathers all in rich hue above, and beneath their feet were thick Persian carpets. Accent colors were a vivid contrast; a low Eastern-fashioned sofa in deep crimson, walls of sky blue, the ceiling a pale yellow intermixed with azure and sea green. Gold ornamentation relieved and complemented the brightness. Around the room incense urns, cassolettes and flower baskets exuded natural and artificial perfumes. The whole appealed to all the senses in such a way that Nicole was momentarily overwhelmed.

"Please, make yourself comfortable. We must get to know one another better, you and I."

Her hostess stepped in behind her and gave her cloak a careless toss. Nicole found herself admiring one of the most beautiful women she'd ever seen. Glorious blond hair was swept back from perfect porcelain features. A simple sheath artfully displayed a form that was feminine grace and supple strength. Though she was smiling, her eyes were flat black and opaquely staring. Nicole got no sense of warmth or welcome. Power was what the woman exuded. A deep, controlling pulse of power. It was her likeness reflected down from the exquisite oils showcased by the room's splendor; her face rendered by different artists beneath the wimple and veils of the Crusades, beneath the padded roll headress of the Renaissance, set against the wide fanlike collar of Tudor England and beneath the elaborately styled coif à la Pompadour. They must have all been painted within a short span of time, for the exquisite features showed no sign of age.

"Why would you care to know me better, madame? I have just tried to rob you. I would think you would be more interested in calling for the police."

The woman laughed, a light airy sound that struck a slightly discordant key. "Why would I call them? I was hoping to find you. You see, I have been looking for you these last few nights."

Nicole stiffened. "And why is that, madame?"

"You are so like them, you know, so inquisitive, so cautious. What must they think of what you are doing and how you are living?"

"Who, madame?"

"Your parents."

Nicole stared, plainly nonplused. "My parents?"

"Louis and Arabella Radman are the names they used in London. Do they still go by them?"

Nicole ignored the smooth question to ask one of her own. "Did you know them in London?"

"Briefly. I am an old and dear friend of your father's. Perhaps he has spoken of me."

"Your name?"

"Bianca du Maurier."

"I am afraid he has never mentioned you." When the woman's features set into rigid lines of displeasure, Nicole was quick to add, "He doesn't speak of the past at all."

"Ah, how very like him." And she smiled, a silky expression that moved upon her face without affecting the level cut of her stare. "Are they well, your mother and father?"

"When last I saw them, they were." And how would they be now? she wondered. In a panic trying to find her? She had a vivid image of her mother's tears, and quickly blocked it and all other tender memories that tried to seep in with that single recollection.

"So you have been here in Paris for how long?"

Something in the way the woman approached her questions put Nicole on the defensive. Perhaps it was her upbringing of skillful evasion. Answer no queries directly, her father had always said. You never know what the asker is trying to find out. Or why he is doing the asking. Trust no one. She should have applied that sentiment to him as well. "For some time, Madame du Maurier. I am staying with friends."

"Ah, yes. Your friends. The Parisian gypsies. I realize the popular theme is poverty among them, but for this evening, would you humor me as your hostess and spend a few hours upon an elevated plane?"

"I don't—"

"The air of the street hangs upon you. It is not a flattering perfume for one so young and lovely. And those garments befit a pauper, not a princess."

Nicole felt herself flush with unaccustomed humility. No one had ever called her shabby before, and her pride rebelled. "I am sorry if my presence offends you, Madame du Maurier. Perhaps I should go—"

"Oh, no, my child. I was going to offer what luxuries I have at hand. A fragrant bath, a fine linen gown. Would it offend you to enjoy these things while you are my guest?"

A bath. At the thought of it, her skin fairly itched for a decent scrubbing. She washed daily, but it seemed like ages since she'd lingered in a tub.

As if she could read the younger woman's thoughts, Biance smiled generously and gestured to a doorway. "Please. Allow me the pleasure of pampering the daughter of an old friend. You have nothing to fear from me. If you would like, you can leave right now. I just thought you would take advantage of the opportunity to ask me certain things. About your father. About yourself."

Nicole hesitated, caught between alarm and anticipation. What did she know about her father? How could that information be helpful to her now?

"Freshen up," Biance coaxed. "Then when you are feeling better, we will talk for a while and then you can go back to your friends. You may take the contents of my purse. Money means little to me but you . . . mean everything. I consider it a debt of honor owed to Louis."

Again that seamless smile, but Nicole was thinking of

clean water not drawn direct from the murky Seine. She was thinking of what this elusive woman might tell her. The mystery far outweighed the worry.

"I appreciate your hospitality, madame."

"Bianca, please. Enjoy your bath. Take your time. We have until dawn."

Whatever hesitations she might have held to were quickly dispersed when Nicole saw the tub. More a pool, really. Flanked by Grecian pillars, its sleek black tiles were sunken into the floor, creating a rectangle almost large enough for swimming. Candlelight rippled along black satin wall curtains and sparkled across the deep azure ceiling. Low gilt chairs and a chaise lined the walls, offering a comfortable repose. And next to the tub was a stack of plush toweling and a classicially styled muslin gown. All as if just laid out to welcome her.

After glancing about the room and seeing no threat to her privacy, Nicole shed her soiled clothes and stepped down into the water. She gave a slight gasp of surprise, for the bath wasn't warm. Instead, the waters were deliciusly cool and silky, with an application of scented oil. She sank down with a sigh, letting it lap all the way up to her ears, and simply soaked for long minutes until her body went nearly boneless with relaxation. When she opened her eyes, she realized that the luminations on the ceiling had a definite pattern, those of the nocturnal sky in various constellations. Even the ornamental medallions were emblems of the evening, representing the god of sleep and the goddess of night scattered among the stars. It was like bathing under the dome of a twilight heaven. And the sensation was heaven, itself.

Then came a subtle disruption of that tranquil paradise. Nicole sat up slowly, the water falling away from her shoulders, a prickling awareness creeping along her damp skin. She took a soft breath and let her gaze detail the room again. She was not alone.

"*Buòna séra, signorína. Mi scúsi.* I did not mean to disturb you. I was only just told that you were here. Forgive me, but I could not resist."

The warm liquid drawl of his voice directed her gaze. It was no surprise that she hadn't noticed him earlier. All in black, he seemed a part of the lustrous draperies until he stepped forward into the mellow light. He was evcry bit as beautiful as she remembered, his complexion hauntingly fair upon all those intriguing facial angles, his eyes so pale they seemed to glow.

"*Chi stá? Cóme si chiáma?*" Nicole asked languidly.

"Parlá l'italiáno?"

"Poco. Dal mío pádre."

"Of course. From Gino." And he smiled beguilingly, the gesture filling his face with a dark enchantment. "Do you remember me?"

Slowly, he approached. Feelings of modesty or fear never surfaced as Nicole stared up at him. Too many other emotions crowded for her attention, among them a strange quiver of recogniton, a sense of communion she didn't understand. Who was this man? Surely she would remember if she'd ever met him. But she couldn't deny a strong sense of the familiar. It wasn't his looks but rather his voice and the . . . feel of him, the essence of cool strength and dangerous charm.

He'd come to the tiled rim of the tub and knelt down to trail his hand in the water. His movements appeared languid, but she felt power behind them, a power that stirred her like the concentric eddies in the pool. He lifted his hand and shook droplets from long, gracefully shaped fingertips, then eased out to lie upon his side.

She'd never seen a man move with such a feline flow. Except maybe her father.

"I would be surprised if you recalled much of that meeting. We touched so briefly and you were so small, barely a flutter in your mother's womb."

His words held no logic, yet she didn't question them. She was lost in the swirl of his stare, in the sweet brilliance of his smile.

"What is your name, *cara?*"

"Nicole," she heard herself respond.

"Nicole," he repeated, and the sound of her name was a caress. "You are very beautiful, Nicole. I see those I love in your face. I see Gino in your eyes."

"Gino?" When she looked perplexed, he smiled wider.

"Your father. That is the name I knew him by when we were young and like brothers."

Young? But he hardly looked much older than she was. He said he knew her mother before she'd been born. How could that be? She shivered as the water suddenly seemed quite cold. And awareness of her undressed state began to assert itself with a blushing discomfort. But he wasn't ogling her nakedness. He was fixed upon her gaze as if the other was of no importance.

"Don't be afraid. I would not harm you. I only want to express to you the devotion I feel for your father." And he bent to press a cool kiss upon either of her cheeks. And without straightening, he added, "And the fondness I have for your mother." That kiss he planted firmly and passionately upon her lips. An exquisitely explicit kiss.

She was stunned by his intimacy, but he didn't move to touch her with his hands, nor did he close his eyes.

And she didn't push him away. There was something so intensely poignant in that kiss, she was shocked by the suggestion that this gorgeous man had been her mother's lover.

"Gerard!"

The sharp crack of Bianca's voice had Nicole jerking back in alarm, but her elegant seducer merely rolled upon his back to smile languorously up at the seething woman. With one hand, he dropped a towel into the water and Nicole scrambled to cover herself with it. For some reason, she felt much more exposed to the woman's black gaze then she had beneath his.

"Cara, why did you not tell me we had a guest?"

"Get up from there, Gerard. This does not concern you."

"Mía bèlla, how can you say that? She is Gino's child. She is like family! We were just getting acquainted." But he did rise; a fluid gesture that seemed to require no visible effort.

"I did not invite her here so you could indulge in your typical foolishness."

He laughed. It rumbled like the threat of thunder. "Was that what I was doing? I thought I was being quite charming."

"Go away before you ruin everything," Biance hissed, and Gerard sketched a mocking bow toward her.

"As you wish. Shall I step out to find us something to dine upon? What are you hungry for this evening? Some hearty fare or something light and refined? Your taste is so much more . . . particular than mine."

"Go!"

He gave her a sardonic smile, then turned back to Nicole. "We will talk later, signorina. *A più tardi.*"

And he was gone. Nicole but blinked and he had disappeared from the room.

"Please forgive his rudeness." Bianca all but oozed. "He has no manners. Please finish your bath and then join me in the antechamber."

Then she was gone as well. Shivering, Nicole climbed out of the chilled water and quickly dried and dressed. It flirted through her mind to slip away now while she had the chance, but curiosity held her when wisdom urged flight. She realized for the first time that her trip to Paris had been an escape from the inevitable. It was time to find out who . . . and perhaps what she was.

"Ah, there you are," Bianca cooed. She was waiting in a low-ceiled chamber, half reclined upon a chaise. Nicole felt a twinge of foreboding as she observed the menagerie frozen into the furniture. Each table leg, each chair arm, every spool, every spindle was an animal part detailed in smooth mahogany; griffins and Chimeras, leopards' snarls and lions' pads, like some dismembered trophy room. And in the middle of this monstrous fossilization, Bianca du Maurier seemed as inanimate as the wood. Until she stood, and that ripple of sleek strength reminded Nicole to be on her guard.

"Gerard tells me your name is Nicole. A very pretty name."

"Is he your husband?"

Bianca chuckled as if she found that idea greatly amusing. "Gerard? No. He is my companion. He can be quite entertaining when he chooses to be. He introduced me to your father when they were young men in Italy. We've seen and done much since then, Gerardo, Gino and I. I'm sorry, I meant to say Louis."

"Gino what?"

"Luigino Rodmini. He has told you none of this?"

Nicole shook her head, feeling terribly naive under the sophisticate's clucking sympathy.

"He always liked his secrets. But to keep them from his own daughter, shame."

Oh, yes, he liked his secrets. Looking at the other woman, Nicole wondered how many *she* was privy to. "How well do you know my father?"

"Intimately," she purred without a trace of reluctance. Then, with Nicole's stark pallor, she amended that with a cool, "That was before he met your mother, of course. How well do *you* know him?"

"I'm beginning to think I don't know him at all," she admitted softly. "Nor do I understand much of what is happening in my own life."

"What kind of troubles could you possibly have? You are young and lovely—"

"And different. I fear I am very much like the father I do not know." And in spite of her want to sound brave, her voice quavered with uncertainty.

Biance was instantly all gentle reassurance, calming her with just the right words. "You mustn't be afraid of what you are."

"And what am I? Do you know? Can you tell me? Have you a name for it?"

"An old name. A meaningless name. As for what you are, you are special, Nicole."

"I don't feel special," she said almost angrily. She'd held in these feelings for too long to control them now. She stared at the other woman with a fierce intensity. "I don't want to be special or different or—dangerous."

"Only because you are not in control. The powers you possess are like none within the mortal realm." She leaned slightly forward, her eyes glittering, the color in her cheeks growing feverish. "Gerard tells me you have the same gift as your father. Has Louis taught you how to use it?"

"No, madame, he has not." And the hard edge of her voice made the icy blonde smile contemplatively.

"I will show you."

The promise of those words tingled through Nicole. Then, an instant before she heard his voice, she felt Gerard's return.

"And there is much I can teach you as well," came the flow of his accented drawl.

"Back so soon." Bianca was frowning, but there was an odd gleam of anticipation in her flat black eyes.

"Ah, there is no match for Parisian cuisine. Such variety." His piercing gaze settled on Nicole. "Was there anything in particular you had a taste for, *cara?* Forgive me for not asking sooner. As our guest, the choice should be yours."

"I—I'm not hungry."

"Oh, but you look hungry. There's that leanness to your face, that brightness in your eyes. Are you certain you do not care to join us? It would be impolite of me to dine in front of you."

She noticed then that he held an oddly shaped pewter drinking horn. From the wide throat it curved down to an intricately formed griffin's face. "I've seen that before."

He glanced at it and smiled. "This is the mate to the one your father has. We picked them up in the Mediterranean—oh, long ago."

He'd come closer by then, and Nicole was aware of a certain scent intensifying. Her nostrils flared wide to savor it and her lips parted to allow the quickening pants of her breath to pass. Need strung through her veins like fire, and she found herself with stare fixed upon that cup.

Noticing the direction of her gaze, Gerard smiled silkily. "Would you like a sip? I think you'll find it a tolerable bouquet. Not as well aged as I would prefer, but full bodied and quite—satisfying." He dippped his forefinger in, then drew it out, stained in red. Nicole stood motionless, her eyes dilating, shimmering like hot gold as he touched that fingertip to her lips, rubbing it gently along the damp swell. She let her tongue reach out for just a tentative taste.

And then her teeth were snapping together. He jerked his hand back with an indulgent laugh.

"Not hungry. *Bèlla*, you are starving. Here. Enjoy."

And he brought the cup toward her lips.

"What is it? Wine?"

"The nectar of life, my sweet. A good year. Drink."

"Gerardo—"

Bianca's cautioning came a moment too late, for Nicole's hand wrapped around his and guided the horn to her mouth. And she drank.

It was warm, she realized with some surprise, warm and thick and salty. Familiar . . . forbidden . . .

And then she was gulping it down, nearly choking in her haste until he took control of the cup with his other hand and eased it back.

"Slowly. Slowly." Over the rim of the horn, his eyes burned with a clear crystal light.

Then the heat was inside her, streaking down her limbs, flooding her senses, soothing away the ravaging ache of emptiness until she was lightheaded and gasping. She let go of the cup as everything around flared to sudden, brilliant proportions. Her heart was beating so fast, so fast, she couldn't keep up.

"What—?" That pathetic syllable was all she could manage.

"Imbecile!"

She heard Bianca's voice shrill over the thunder in her ears. And then his rumbling reply, "How was I to know?" And then she felt the support of his arms about her and the texture of his coat, so well defined she could differentiate between the threads woven tightly together. And she could feel her heart pounding in her head and his, beneath her cheek. The enormity of everything around her came pressing in, forcing her down as if drowning in sensation. She struggled.

"Help—help me!"

"Shhhh. *Cara, amore di bambino,* don't fight against it. Let go. Enjoy. Don't be afraid."

Her fingers were grappling desperately in his shirt-front as dizziness overcame her. He lifted her easily when consciousness gave way under great, almost drunken swells. And the last thing she heard was his soothing vow: "Don't be frightened. We will care for you."

And very gently, he carried her slack figure over to one of the sofas and stretched her out upon it. He went down on one knee beside her, cradling a limp hand between his.

"Does she still live?" Bianca had come to stand behind him, her mood impatient and angry.

"Oh, yes. Just overcome, I think. I thought she was one of us."

"I wonder what she is." A scheming light came into her eyes, one he didn't like. His posture grew defensive.

"What she is, is mine. As you promised."

"I never did."

"Yes, you promised me the first taste and I will not let

you harm her until I've had it." He rubbed her inner wrist with his mouth. "So warm. So vital." And a glaze of desire covered his stare. Bianca gave him a hard shove.

"Remind yourself to keep her from harm."

He laid the fragile hand upon a slow-rising bosom and knelt there, studying her features with an almost loverlike rapture. "She is so like them."

"But is she more of Gino or of that pallid mortal mother? I wonder."

"I didn't bring her to you so you could vent your revenge upon her."

Bianca glared down at him. "Sentimental fool. Think if you cannot have the mother, the daughter will do?"

His glare frosted for a moment, then he relaxed and laughed with typical negligence. "It would be like coveting my own child."

"You have no children, idiot. You have no heart. Yet you moon away the decades for some silly creature as if you were capable of passions other than those of thirst for the kill."

"And you still hate her because that soft mortal woman was able to capture and hold that which you could not."

She snarled in fury, seizing him by the lapels of his coat, jerking him up and flinging him away so hard he went spinning. He was laughing as he slowed himself in midair, pausing, then spiraling downward with a balletic grace. He might laugh, but he was too wise to rejoin the challenge.

"Come, *mía amora*, our meal grows cold as we argue over meaningless things. Leave her. She will not awake before we do." And he walked away without another glance at the young woman sprawled upon the couch, only to pause in the entrance to the drawing room and give a menacing chuckle. "Where are you going, my love? I thought we were to have dinner together."

And then there came a wretched cry from another woman, a young street woman dragging herself across the tiled floor on shaky hands and knees. She was already too weak to escape, already too close to dying from the slash he'd made in her wrist to drain her blood into the drinking horn. Yet she made a valiant attempt to reach up for the door. Only to have him catch her wrist in a cruel grasp to haul her to her feet. She no longer saw the charming gentleman who'd brought her to his palatial rooms with husky innuendos. But she didn't see what he really was, either. Not yet.

"You cannot leave so soon. We haven't shared the main course."

She was making pitiful noises in her throat, trying to plea for a life he cared nothing about. She might well have been an insect. Though he was smiling, the facade of gentility, of humanity itself, was falling from him. His eyes welled up with a lurid light, gleaming red and silver. She tried to cry out as he drew her up in a mockingly tender embrace.

"Oh, lovely, why do you protest? Did I not promise you a delightful surprise?"

His smile widened to reveal hideous fangs. She was shrieking as he softly hissed, "Surprise"

Chapter Nine

"Marchand?" Nicole moaned his name softly as a gentle sweeping movement rumpled over her hair.

"Who is this Marchand? Is he your lover?"

The soothing accented voice forced her to open reluctant eyes. She felt so heavy, so satiated. So full. The urgent gnaw of hunger was absent for the first time in months. She wanted to do nothing more than sleep. But a vague awareness that she was not among her friends made her struggle against the lethargy. She looked up groggily to see Gerard perched upon the edge of the couch. His smile was small and serene. Her hand was enfolded between his.

"How do you feel, *mío amáte?*"

"I am not his lover. I am not yours either."

He chuckled. "Much better I see. Please forgive me for last night. I didn't know it was your first time."

She considered his statement and all it might mean, then pushed herself upright in an indignant confusion, shoving his hands away. "What first time?"

His features took on an impenetrable cast for some seconds, and she was reminded of Bianca and the inanimate furnishings of the house. Not a flicker of movement was betrayed upon his handsome face. Then he grinned wide and gave a lusty laugh.

"Oh! *Cara,* you flatter me." His fingertips stroked down her bare arm in a gesture that was anything but soothing as he crooned, "Have no fear. I have no designs upon your—virtue. You must think of me like family. I loved your father so, and you are very like him."

Then more of what he'd said earlier became clear in her blurred mind. "Last night?" What had happened to the hours of the night? She had no memory of them.

"You slept the entire day through. The drink quite overwhelmed you."

That she remembered; the wildly satisfying taste, the flame racing through her veins. "W-what was in it?"

His smile grew bland, his eyes amused. "An old recipe. One I was certain you must have tried. As I said, forgive me. Did you—did you like it?"

"I—I don't know." The sensations had been so powerful, so draining and filling all at once. But like it?

Yes. Yes, she had. But she was suddenly afraid to admit that.

"You will get used to it in time and savor the rush of it through you, the quickening of life. But then, you are warm and soft and very—"

"Gerard."

He glanced up and smirked in the face of Bianca's annoyance.

"Shut up, fool."

"Ah, but my love, I was only seeing to our guest's entertainment."

"I do not find you amusing."

He put his hands to his shirtfront in a dramatic pose. "I am crushed to hear you say that. What will Gino's daughter think of us, always fighting? If you are not careful, she will not want to stay with us."

"Stay?" Nicole blurted out in alarm. They both looked at her through flat, inanimate eyes.

"But of course you will stay," Bianca soothed. "We offer you—everything."

"But my friends will be worried. I really must—"

"No." Bianca's smooth white hand rested on her shoulder, pressing there with amazing strength. "You are not like them, Nicole. They do not understand you the way that we do. They cannot help you. Only we can help you."

"Help me what?" She tried not to betray her fright, but they were frightening her. Because she knew they spoke the truth. Somehow, this strange pair who claimed to know her family were the keys to discovering her identity. She sensed a kinship with them just as she felt a separation from those in the flat on Montparnasse. But abruptly she didn't want to recognize that difference. She wanted to leave this bizarre setting and return to the familiar. She stood, easing away from the lounging Gerard, cautiously eyeing the coolly beautiful Bianca. "You said I could go."

"But of course you can go," the woman said with a generous gesture. "You can go back to the confusion, to a world where nothing seems right to you. Where no one can hear and sense the things that you do. Where you have to hide your strength. Where you have to pretend to eat and sleep by night. Where you have to be ever on your guard not to hurt those close to you."

Nicole had gone pale. The breath came trembling from her. "How do you know these things?"

"Because we are like you."

"No."

"Like your father."

"No!"

"Do not be afraid, *mía bèlla*. We want to help you."

She looked from the questionable sincerity of his silky smile to Bianca's unblinking regard. "I don't want your help."

Gerard stood, and she felt the intimidation of both of them pressing in upon her. She had to get away now. Before . . . before they made her believe what they were saying was true. She didn't want it to be true.

"If you go," Gerard began in a softly seductive tone, "what will you do when the hunger returns?"

She shook her head, pretending not to understand. Not wanting to understand.

He pushed up his sleeve, baring a smooth white forearm. Slowly, deliberately, he used his thumbnail to cut a gash across the veins that stood out clearly beneath the pale surface of his skin. A thin line of blood welled up, a bright streak of crimson against that parchment pallor. Nicole stared in a horrified fascination. She felt her pulse quicken. The scent . . . the taste suddenly filled her mouth. Her confusion grew.

"This is what was in the cup you drank from."

Even as she denied it, she knew it was true.

"This is the fuel of our existence. Nicole, you are one of us."

"No!"

"You feel it, don't you? The hunger. The need to grab on to me and feed. Of course you do. It controls you now but you can learn to control it. We can teach you. We can show you how glorious it can be." And he wiped up the blood with his fingertips and leisurely licked them clean. Her own lips parted, watching him, her own tongue moistened them with a nervous, anticipating flicker. As his eyes grew heavy with a languorous delight, she experienced a need for the same rapture.

It was true.

"I have to go . . . I have to think." And she was stumbling backward, away from the two impassive ghouls, finally turning, running from that which she could not escape.

Bianca started forward and Gerard placed a staying hand upon her arm.

"Let me. I am better at this sort of thing than you."

She gave him a suspicious look, then relented with a nod.

Nicole ran, sobbing, panting against the swell of terror constricting about her chest. She raced up the Rue de Castiglione toward the wide Rue de Rivoli and the Tuilleries Gardens and though she heard no sound of pursuit, she felt a sudden whisper of movement at her side and felt a firm grip upon her elbow, pulling her to a stop.

"Nicole, don't be afraid."

She raised her damp face to the unnatural beauty of his and cried, "Don't be afraid? How easy you make that sound."

"It can be easy," he crooned as he brushed the tears from her cheeks. "It can be wonderful. But Nicole, it can also be terrible."

There was a catch to his voice, a tug of anguish so unexpected, her own fears quieted and she listened.

"Before I learned what I was, I committed acts against those I love that will damn me in my own heart forever. Nicole, it is stronger than you know, stronger than your will, stronger than your love. If you don't know how to control it, it will control you. Then you will have an eternity to regret it."

"An eternity," she echoed. She had no real grasp of what he was saying, only of the pain behind the words themselves. And it was a warning that burnt clear to her soul.

"We have all the answers you need. Come to us when you're ready to hear them. We are family, Nicole."

He framed her face with his long, cool fingers and bent to place the tenderest of kisses upon her brow. She'd closed her eyes and when she opened them, he was no longer there with her.

She wasn't sure what she'd expected. So much had changed in the last day. She felt so different, somehow she'd thought all around her would be altered as well.

But the moment she stepped into the crowded little flat and Marchand, Frederic and Musette turned toward her, all felt so familiar and ordinary it was like coming home. The three of them stared at her so long and hard, Nicole wondered if it was readily apparent that she was no longer one of them. That surging sense of separation rose up inside her, bringing a bitter anguish and the sting of tears.

Then Marchand came up from his chair so fast it tumbled to the floor behind him. In four long strides, he'd swept her up in his arms and was crushing her to his chest, tight against the banging thunder of his heart. He kissed her brow, her temple, the top of her head in an earnest, anxious scattering of emotion she didn't understand then, simply held her so close, there was no defineable separation between them.

"You're safe," he cried hoarsely. "Thank God. Thank God."

Then she grew aware of how shivery his breathing had become and of how tremors raced along the length of his strong arms. The depth of his passion alarmed her. She touched the back of his head lightly, then stroked soothingly.

"Marchand?"

She glanced at his brother for a clue to his upset. Frederic's features were unpromisingly grim. Musette was crying.

"What is it? What's happened?"

Since Marchand seemed incapable of speech, Frederic told her.

"One of our friends stopped by this afternoon. We were told that one of the women who lived with us had been buried in a pauper's grave without identification."

"I thought it was you," came Marchand's raw whisper.

"No, I'm fine." She increased the strength of her hold upon him. "I'm sorry if you were worried. I never thought—" Then the significance struck. "Bebe. Oh, no! Was it Bebe, then?"

"We only heard that she was struck by a carriage, that she'd darted out in front of it," Frederic continued somberly. "She had on a locket like the one you always wore, though someone else had already been there to claim it."

"They say it was suicide," Musette moaned, distracting Nicole from an instant of alarm. "Oh, poor Bebe. She must have been more distraught than we realized."

Then, seeing how his brother yet clung to the woman in the doorway, Frederic reached out for Musette's hand. "Come, my love. Let's walk a while. I should like to find a very good bottle of Bordeaux and get very drunk."

The moment the two of them slipped by and into the night, Marchand cupped Nicole's face in his hands. His kisses fell everywhere; upon her cheeks, upon the flutter of her eyelids, on her nose and chin—hot, desperately urgent kisses, tasting of assuaged terror and tears; she wasn't sure whose. Then his mouth sank down on hers and settled there for a lengthy union of hurried breaths and searching tongues. The degree of her reaction matched his, for she was just as glad to be in his arms again, enjoying this particular reunion. He was so solid, so wonderfully male. For a moment, she could believe he had the power to save her from the suspicions quickened in her mind. If she was some unnatural thing, how could this very natural greeting feel so right? And all the right things were tingling through her. He broke off at last, panting hard, resting his forehead against hers as their gazes met and mingled. His eyes were dark, passionate intensity.

"I was so sure I'd driven you away with my uncertainty," came his unplanned confession. "I'm not uncertain any longer. I need you, Nicole. I've been half mad without you. I love you."

He kissed her again, slowly, deeply, but Nicole was too stunned to respond.

He loved her!

A tremendous conflict tore through her; bliss warring with panic. To have her love returned was an unexpected heaven. To have to deny it was a bitter hell. Because after what she'd just learned, deny it she must. Until she knew for sure.

But Marchand didn't know of her decision. He was too overcome by his own relief and revelation to notice her lack of animation. He scooped her up against him and moved them both from the door to the pallet they'd shared for protection and comfort and companionship. He had other ideas now as he drew her down upon it until they were seated close in the gathering shadows. He stroked her loose flowing hair, her soft cheeks still chilled from the night, the gentle slope of her shoulders, with enough persuasion to free them of the muslin gown she wore. And his kisses followed, moving against her hair, adoring the arch of her pale neck, the delicate curve of her collarbone.

Her fingers had risen to mesh in his hair, knotting, kneading in restless spasms. How he made her heart pound with his insistent passion! How he made her youthful body quake with an anticipation of the unknown and arc in hopes of more intimate contact. She gasped softly as his hands eased up to fill with the underswell of her breasts. Slow, sensuous revolutions of his thumbs had her tense and quivering, certain she would die if he didn't continue.

Afraid he might die if he did.

Because she not only wanted him with all her heart, she wanted him with all the hunger in her soul.

She'd recognized the danger the moment he'd gotten near her. Recognized it the way she recognized the luring beat of his blood within his veins. She remembered the taste of him, warm and thick upon her tongue, that vital fluid feeding her the way nothing else could. The way nothing else ever would. And she wanted that from him. As much as she wanted his love and his loving.

She was caressing his throat, feeling the pulse rush through it even as another detached part of her was enjoying the feel of his warm lips grazing the upper curve of her breast. Though she didn't fully understand what she was, she feared what she was capable of. She had incredible strength. She could snap his neck with a slight twist. He was a strong, virile man but she sensed a weakness in him, as she did in all the others. They were different, as Bianca had told her. They were unable to help her even as they were unable to save themselves from her. And she trembled with her first flush of power.

How was it done? Her fingertips rubbed over his neck in agitation as she saw again the horror of her father's face bathed by an innocent's blood. The sharp points of his teeth gleaming with bestial whiteness. But hers were small and even, as if in disobedience to her instinct that said bite . . . drink. That vile thirst rose within her, clutching greedily with its demand to be fed. Just as she was clutching like some ravenous predator, enthralled by the thrum of Marchand's life. Ready to take it, absorb it, destroy it.

"No!"

That small anguished cry ripped from her as she pushed him away. "No, Marchand. We can't do this."

He sat staring at her, his eyes yet dark with desire, his breath laboring with it. Yet he was held by what he observed, by the change in her eyes from green to gold. From the change in her voice to that unnatural growl. He stared at her and she could feel his uncertainty rise up over his passion. She could feel his love, his confusion, his reluctant fear of her. He recognized her as a threat, but he truly hadn't guessed how deadly she was, how close he was to dying when he was courting her with kisses.

"Marchand, I'm sorry. I should not have let you believe that this was what I wanted."

He continued to stare and she watched with a

wretched purpose as an agony of understanding came into those dark devoted eyes. "Sorry?"

"I came here tonight to tell you I would not be back."

The quick, protesting breath he took cut through her like the sharpest steel. "What?"

"I've found some friends of my family. They've asked that I come stay with them. I came only for the painting . . . and to say thank you and goodbye."

She laid the purse of coins that Bianca had given her upon the tangle of linens that might have once held them while passion had its way. His gaze was drawn to it, then back to her in question.

"And to repay you for your kindness."

He blinked hard as if she'd struck him. Then he seized the pouch and hurled it against the wall so that the violence of the gesture made it burst into a clattering gold shower. "I didn't do it for reward." That escaped him in a hiss of fury and frustration. He gripped her forearms and she went tense, fighting the urge to yield to the pleasure of his touch. She was trying to protect him, yet he was pursuing his own destruction with a fierce determination. "I did it for you, Nicole. Because I care for you. I can't explain how much you've come to mean to me—"

"Please don't!" She couldn't listen. The pain of it was too great . . . the words too beautiful to resist. But resist, she must.

"I've spent my whole life alone, doing for others. You are the first to ever want to do for me. Nicole, we are alike, you and I—"

"No." She was almost weeping at the impossibility of that suggestion, yet he continued.

"We are! I feel the same passions in you. The same

strength. You give ease to my soul and put fire to my heart. Nicole, I—"

"Stop!" She pressed her fingertips to his lips, afraid to hear more, fearing if she did, she wouldn't have the strength to walk away. "Stop, Marchand. You misunderstand me. Of course I care for you. And your friends. You've been very kind to me and I wanted to do for you in return. To repay you out of gratitude. But that was all. I don't—I don't love you."

His features went completely blank, as if the devastation of that truth was too much for him. She wanted nothing more at that moment than to hold him close, to comfort him with the real truth that resided so sweetly in her heart—the truth of her love for him. But that very love made her forge on with the painful task of pushing him away. Because that distance meant safety even as it meant heartbreak.

"You are a good man, Marchand, and I admire you for your courage and commitment, but there is nothing for me here. Look around. What can you offer me? These friends of my family have offered a life of comfort and security. I need that now, not this constant threat of danger and upheaval. You must see that."

He did. She could see it in his face, that realization of his own limits, of his poverty, of his failings. It was a stark, angry truth, one he couldn't change if he wanted to. And he wanted to, for her.

But pride kept him still when love would demand more of him. What else could he do? He'd bared his heart and it was rejected. He'd offered his soul and it was denied. A man could stand only so much defeat. Retreat was the only way to salvage the remnants of personal honor. So retreat he did.

"I'm sorry, mademoiselle. I did, indeed, mistake the

situation. No, you have no reason to stay. This inane cause is not yours. You'd be foolish to sacrifice your . . . comfort for something you don't believe in. I applaud your sensibility. If everyone displayed your commendable degree of self-interest, this folly would die out quickly. As for your debt to us for housing you as best we could, consider it paid. You need not look back upon us with anything but . . . fondness."

Fondness? Oh, how pallid a word to describe what beat in her heart. But Nicole forced herself to smile and accept his summation and his thinly guised criticism. She must pretend to be the shallow creature he now believed her to be. She had to pretend she didn't see or didn't care how much she was hurting him. For his own good. She couldn't have him considering her with anything more than . . . fondness. Loving her was too dangerous.

"I really must go now. My new friends will be waiting." She stood and he rose with her. For a moment, she was overwhelmed by his closeness. She could feel the heat and strength of him and the way his kiss still pulsed upon her lips. Her gaze filled up with the sight of his masculine beauty, that brief study enough to hurry her heartbeat. She was crazy to leave him. The temptation to return to his embrace was powerful, but so was her awareness of the luring throb in his throat. Not knowing which of these desires she'd succumb to, she chose to withdraw quickly before she harmed him even more.

Painting in hand, she started for the door. She didn't dare risk another look around the shabby surroundings she'd called home. She'd hoped to slip out without confronting him again but Marchand had other ideas. His hand caught at her elbow. She made herself stare steadily outward into the night.

"If you ever need me—for anything—"

Hadn't Camille said that to her? And see what had happened to Camille.

"Thank you," she said in a hushed voice. "But I don't think I shall."

His hand opened, letting her go. "No, of course not."

She'd reached the door and was almost through it when he said her name.

"Nicole—"

She turned with an anxious reluctance as he fit his hand to her cheek. He'd meant to say, "Don't go," but he couldn't force that further humiliation. She wanted to leave, after all. What was the point in begging?

So he kissed her.

For a moment, she melted into it, her lips parting in needy encouragement, one hand rising to clasp behind his head as if to secure him there forever. She even came up on her toes to meet the urgent pressure more fully. Then she tore away, ducking her head so that he might not see the tears upon her face as she raced down the rickety stairs, the painting precariously clutched beneath one arm.

Marchand leaned back against the doorframe, his eyes closed, his breath chugging against the hard current of regret. *Mon Dieu*, how he'd wanted her to stay. But he was a practical man who was used to applying reason in lieu of emotion and he could understand her choice. But understanding didn't forestall hurt. Nor did it curb his worry, and he wanted to be sure she was safe. He told himself that was his sole motive.

Because even though she didn't return his feelings, he loved her.

So he followed her darting shadow, across the Seine to the luxury of the Place Vendome. And there, before an elegant house, he saw her meet with a man who welcomed her with his embrace. The sight staggered his heart. So, she was going to another's arms. That should have made it easier for him to walk away, but somehow it didn't. He lingered in the darkness, lost to misery, as his successor slipped his arm about Nicole's shoulders to guide her into the palatial home.

And against the glare of the inside light, Marchand saw the man stiffen and turn his way, the intensely blue eyes searching the blackness as if to seek him out amid its impenetrable void. Then it seemed he succeeded, for his gaze fixed on the spot where Marchand was standing and his smile grew wide and taunting in triumph as he led Nicole within and shut the door.

Chapter Ten

"So, you're back," Bianca du Maurier cooed. She was lounging in the private salon where Gerard led her. This room also was opulent in its decoration, draped in various shades of red and highlighted by gilt furnishings and black marble. The effect was a conflict of hot and cold and Nicole realized that these two were very much like that as well.

"I need answers," she stated bluntly. Bianca smiled, not offended by her directness.

"Sit. Ask your questions."

Nicole assumed one of the low stools near Bianca's plush chaise. Gerard slipped up behind her and his hovering there made her uncomfortable. It made her feel vulnerable and she was already well aware that she came to them in a position of weakness.

"I want to know what I am."

Bianca still smiled. "That I can't answer."

"But you said I was like you."

"Yes . . . and no. We are like your father, but you were made between him and his ordinary bride. You are as much a mystery to us as you are to yourself."

Nicole began to rise. "You are playing tricks with me.

You said you knew." Gerard's hands eased over her shoulders, pressing her down firmly. His reply was just as vague.

"We know what you feel. We don't know what you are. Exactly."

"Then tell me what you are. And what my father is."

"Tell her, *cara*."

"We are part of an ancient, powerful race. We are gifted with strengths ordinary men cannot understand. Some would call us gods, others devils. They fear our strength and so we must hide our differences from them or else be destroyed. We are powerful, yet we are also weak in many ways."

This, Nicole believed. She had lived within a house of isolation and fear. She'd been continuously cautioned to act no different than any of those in town and to curb their curiosities as best she could. For suspicion created threat. She was just beginning to understand why.

"We are the victim of superstition and envy," the chill blonde continued. "Our deeds, our very existence is often misunderstood. We must conceal the truth."

"And what is that truth?"

"That we are far superior to the mortals who walk this earth. If they had any idea how much so, we would be mercilessly hunted down and killed. Ours is a secret existence. We live out of need among those who hate us and are forced to pretend to be what we are not."

"What are you?" Nicole asked this with a hush of dread. For what they were, is what she could yet become. "You are human. Aren't you?"

"We are supernatural. We live beyond the realm of the ordinary, outside human time and space. We are not governed by their laws of convention or morality. We are eternal."

Nicole absorbed this for a moment in silence. Then she glanced up at Gerard. "You said that earlier. Eternal. What does that mean?"

"We do not age. We cannot die," he told her with a simple shrug as if this was common knowledge and shouldn't shock her senseless.

"Is that why my mother grows older and my father appears not to?"

"He will never look any older. Neither will we."

"But I age," she murmured more to herself than to them. "Why do I age and for how long?"

Bianca made a helpless gesture. "We don't know. It is because of the human blood you inherited. There may come a time when you will age no more."

"When?"

"When you realize your full potential as one of us."

"And if I don't wish to be one of you?"

Gerard chuckled softly. "I don't think you have a choice."

"You see," Bianca crooned. "You are already changing. You tried to escape it by running away, but you are back here now. Does this mean you are ready to accept your heritage?"

There was more to that question than the silky way it was proposed. Nicole was cautious. "It means I know I am not like them."

"And why would you want to be?" Gerard replied. He bent down so that his smooth cheek rubbed against hers. His skin was cool and she could barely contain her shiver. "We are like gods, Nicole. We can do anything and no one can stop us."

"Gerard," Bianca called with a warning hiss. "Do not overwhelm Nicole. Give her time to adjust, time to decide for herself what she might be."

"She is no mortal," he claimed. "I have felt her power. She could be every bit as strong as we are if she knew—"

"Gerardo!" Black eyes fixed on his with a glittering purpose. After a moment, he relented.

"Forgive me, *cara*. I am too enthusiastic sometimes. I long to share the beauty of what we are with you. It is something your father always denied us."

"Why?" Nicole asked.

It was then Bianca rose. She was smiling, but her gaze cut like the sharp edge of black glass. "Gerard, you should go out and see to your supper while I make Nicole comfortable here with us. There is plenty of time to talk over old times. And if Nicole would tell us where we can find our old friend, perhaps we can get together for a wonderful reunion."

No!

The word struck her subconscious like a heavy blow. She blinked and pressed her fingertips to her temple.

Tell her nothing about your father.

She glanced to Gerard in confusion, for it was his voice she heard so distinctly within her mind just as if he'd been speaking aloud. He only smiled at her in a bland manner, betraying nothing. And Bianca was waiting, unaware of the silent communication that was also a terse warning.

"I should like to be shown my room," Nicole said evasively, and Bianca was forced to nod graciously lest she appear too anxious.

Gerard possessed himself of Nicole's hand and bent over it in a courtly passion. *"Grázie,* signorina," came his drawling whisper. "I will explain later when we are alone."

"Do not mind Gerard," Bianca told her when he had gone. "What he says is of little consequence."

"Are you in love with him?" Nicole asked with a suddenness that surprised the other woman.

"No," she answered at last. "I have never loved him. But then, neither would I ever let another have him. You would be wise to remember that." She let the menace sink in so there'd be no mistake, before gesturing for Nicole to follow her. As they walked, Bianca's mood was restored to a cool congeniality. "We must purchase you some decent clothes. What you have may have been suitable for those bohemians but not for our protégé."

Nicole flushed, humbled by the reminder and at the same time chafed by the woman's haughty snobbery. "They cannot help the way they are forced to live."

"But of course they can. No one need be poor if one is intelligent and willing to do what it requires to be rich."

"And that is?"

"Why anything, my dear. You look shocked. After a while such things will cease to startle you. You were born to privilege and power. Do not disgrace your heritage with sympathy for the less fortunate."

"That is a very cruel observation, madame."

"Is it? Gerard always says I have no heart. Shall I prove its existence? Tell me, my dear, how can I help those who befriended you? Give me the chance to show my generous spirit."

Nicole hesitated. She had no real reason to distrust this woman's motives. She had been unfailingly kind so far. Perhaps the air of reserve was just her way.

"Come, child. Tell me. I caught you picking my pocket. If you were forced to such criminality, their circumstances must be dire indeed."

Nicole thought of Musette's tears and Marchand's frustrations. Yes, perhaps Bianca could help. The woman had given her coin freely enough. Perhaps this was a way in which to validate her love for Marchand without risk. She could gift him with the freedom of his loved ones from De Sivry's influence. She could give him his family's safety ... even if she could not be a part of it. And suddenly, that meant everything to her. She found herself confiding the coil of intrigue De Sivry had snared them in. Bianca listened attentively.

"De Sivry. Sounds like a perfectly beastly man. Someone without a conscience."

"From what I've heard, without a soul."

"Indeed," Bianca mused. "I should like to meet your friends. Perhaps they'd allow me to sponsor their cause. I admire causes. They create such passion, you know." And she smiled in a manner devoid of that feeling, her look completely calculating, and Nicole wondered if she'd made a mistake in saying so much.

However, Bianca was so genuinely thoughtful when showing her to her quarters and bidding her to rest, she believed she wronged the woman with her suspicions.

"Who have we here?"

Gerard had his arms draped about the shoulders of two wide-eyed adolescents, brother and sister from the look of them, barely into their teen years. He was smiling, oozing charm the way he could when he wished to. "Our two young friends got separated from their parents in the Gardens. I told them they could wait in here where it is warm while we sent word where they could be found."

"What a nice gesture," Bianca agreed. "It is late and

not at all safe for youngsters to wander the streets alone. Why, there are all types of dangerous individuals who would prey upon such innocence. You did right to bring them here, Gerard."

"I thought you would be pleased, my love."

"Could we send word right away?" the pretty dark-haired girl piped up. "I hate to think that Mama would be worried."

"Right away," Gerard promised, smiling down as he captured and held the guileless eyes in his. Slowly the awareness began to ebb from her until her gaze was all but sightless and her only focus the hypnotic intensity of his stare.

Meanwhile, her brother was wandering about the room in awe. Bianca trailed behind him, easing ever closer. Her fingertips had just settled upon his shoulders with a paralyzing strength when she heard a soft gasp.

"Excuse me. I thought I heard voices."

"Nicole," Bianca purred. "We have guests. Would you like to help us entertain them?"

Nicole stood frozen. She regarded the helpless children, recognizing the thrall they were in. And she recognized as well the fiery glare of brilliance in the eyes of her host and hostess. There was a sharp scent in the room, a scent she'd come to identify with food. The scent emanated from the two waifs and, realizing what she'd interrupted, sent her stumbling back to the safety of her room.

"How inopportune," Gerard murmured.

"See to her, Gerardo. Calm her fears."

"In a moment, *cara.* She is too fragrant for me to visit until I've fed." His hand stroked over the child's curls. "How pretty you would have been as a woman," he said almost wistfully as the girl continued to stare up in rapt bewitchment. "A pity you did not stay with your parents."

The boy started to turn at the sound of his sister's soft cry but he never completed the revolution. In a minute's time, both brother and sister were drained of their life's vitality.

Gerard released the withered form and paid no mind as it crumpled to the floor when discarded. "Bianca, see to their disposal while I tend our frightened apprentice."

Nicole spun when she heard the whisper of movement behind her. Her eyes were wide and wet with horror as she beheld him.

"What did you do to them?"

"What do you think?"

"You—you killed them, didn't you?" Her words choked on a sob of anguish.

"No, *cara*, they will live forever. Through us. That is how it must be. What did you think we were? What do you think you are?"

She gave a tortured cry and whirled away. She held her body stiff when he embraced her because she didn't have the strength to jerk free. His words whispered seductively against her ear. She could smell the thick odor of blood on his breath and hated the way her senses sharpened in response.

"It's what we must do to survive. It's not something we enjoy."

"Liar! You do! I saw it in your faces."

"Well . . . yes. But we don't think of it as killing. Nothing so crude as that. We absorb what we must to survive and in doing so, oh, Nicole, you cannot imagine the pleasure of it, the power of it."

"It's murder!"

"Do you think of it as murder when you dine upon beef? Is it murder when a hunter brings down a stag in the forest or a bird from the air? No. It is survival. It is instinct. And that's what we are. Creatures of instinct who take the blood of others to survive. You act shocked, but you must know of this already. How else do you explain how you reacted to what you just saw? How else would you know we'd killed them?"

She couldn't contain the terrible agony of it any longer. "I saw him," she wailed in torment. Her head fell back against Gerard's chest and tears flooded down her face. "I saw him with a village girl. I saw her blood on his face."

"Who?"

"My father."

"Oh." How tenderly he said that and how compassionately he held her, as if he truly felt her grief. "And you ran away from him."

She nodded miserably.

"Poor Gino. How that must have broken his heart. He has one, you know, though I can't claim I still do. He didn't tell you what he was."

"No," she whispered.

"Oh, *mío amíca*, what a fool you are." He hugged her gently. "And you never told him what was happening to you."

"No."

"No wonder you were so afraid. I will tell you whatever you need to know. You can trust me, Nicole."

She twisted to look up at him, her features pulled with confusion. "How do I know that?"

"The same way you know me. You did, didn't you,

from the first time you saw me. We are one, Nicole, as your mother and I are one."

"You were her lover?"

He chuckled at her moral astonishment. "No, *cara*. We had a different sort of union. When I took of her blood, I made a bond between us that can never be broken. And, as you were a part of her, you and I share that same bond. Does that appall you?"

"I heard your voice in my mind."

"As I can hear yours once you get used to the power you have."

"Why did you warn me to say nothing to Bianca?"

"Shall we say, she and your mother are not the best of friends."

His tactful amusement gave much away. "Bianca and my father were lovers?"

His tone grew suddenly terse. "That is of no matter now. It was long ago and forgotten. What matters is that you not let her know how to find your parents. She will be kind to you as long as you hold to that secret."

"How is it done?"

He blinked, bewildered by her sudden fervor. "How is what done?"

"How did you take my mother's blood?"

"Here." He stroked his forefinger along the side of her throat. Nicole shuddered but held tight to her courage.

"How?"

"Oh, sweet innocent, you do not wish me to show you that. There is much about you that stirs the hunger in me. You are very mortal for all your power."

"I saw my father's teeth. They were sharp and pointed. But yours aren't like that, nor were his— usually."

He mused over this for a moment. "You've not experienced the change then or you would know."

"What change? Please, I need to know. If I can't change then perhaps I can't feed."

"Cara, the hunger is strong in you. If you don't feed, you will starve."

"But I don't know how!" She couldn't believe she was begging this terrible knowledge from him, but it was all a part of what she was. She had to know. She had to discover all.

"I'll teach you." He was silent for a long beat before saying, "Nicole, there may be no going back from this point on. Once you savor the life force from a mortal, you may lose touch with your own humanity."

"I have to know. Please tell me. What's happening to me?"

He sighed then, resigned. "You know about the strength of ten and the senses of the keenest stalking animal. Your speed of movement is invisible to the average eye. You can smell live blood when you're among mortals and it excites you. It makes you tremble with need. Am I right?"

She looked away, resting her head back against him, nodding once.

"You know the need, the hunger. You crave the taste. Let the urgency overtake you. Let go, Nicole. Imagine it. Hear the pulse of it, so strong and fresh. Smell the richness of that child flowing through me." He curled his forearm up around her head so that his veins were pushed against her mouth, so she couldn't avoid the contact. "Can you hear it, Nicole?"

"Yes." Was that her voice, so strained and raw?

"And you want to take it from me, don't you? You

want to pierce my veins and draw it out. You want to bite, to drink."

"Yesssss."

That hiss of breath was followed by a searing agony through her gums. It shot up to her cheekbones, making her cry out.

"It hurts! It hurts!"

"Oh, but Nicole, it is such an exquisite pain. Relax and let it become rapture."

She quieted then, because it had become just that. When she dared, she touched her tongue to the elongated tips of her incisors and a wild necessity shook her.

"Go ahead," he urged softly. "See what it can be like."

And she bit him. Her teeth punctured the taut flesh of his inner arm and the sense of gratification was like none other. So she did it again. And again, carried away with the act if not understanding the full intention. Until the taste registered in her mind and then there was nothing else. It was everything. But the minute she started to draw upon the wounds she'd made, he shook her off, saying sternly, "No, not from me. Never drink from one of your own kind. It's forbidden."

But she was filled with an insatiable hunger and the aroma of his blood was tantalizing before her. So she grabbed on and drove deep, meaning to begin a frantic suction when she felt the sting of his palm on her cheek and in confusion, she pulled away from seeking satisfaction. She growled in frustration, trembling with the wild desire of her kind and because he understood it better than she, Gerard encased her in strong arms, murmuring quietly for her to relax until the urge subsided.

He held her as a father would a child, as that feeling of bitter anguish cut through gums again and her animal-like teeth receded. When that ordeal was over, she began to notice other things that hadn't been important before. Like how pale he was and how his arm from wrist to elbow was torn savagely open as if some vicious beast had worried it. That beast had been her. She could see the marks of her many bites and she realized now, where she hadn't then, that she'd heard him cry out each time. And she hadn't cared that she was hurting him. Not at all. But now the horror was overwhelming.

"Now you know how it's done," he said with a remarkable calm. He gave her a wry smile as teary eyes rose in abject apology. "You are an apt pupil. Oh, but don't look so upset. You cannot harm me, not for long any way. See, even now they heal."

She gave a reluctant glance toward the butchery of his arm then stared, for all that remained were small red indentations marring his flesh.

"That is the nature of what we are. I think you've learned enough for now."

Chapter Eleven

Nicole couldn't find where they slept during the daylight hours. She looked, wandering about the splendid rooms until her own weariness grew impossibly strong. Everything slowed, her pulse rate, her breathing, her thoughts, until it was inevitable that she seek her own rest. She lay upon her bed in the sumptuous quarters Bianca provided. There, with the drapes drawn tight against the morning, she tried to think of all that had happened. But despite her struggles, awareness slipped from her and she, too, slumbered.

That became the pattern of her life; sleeping through the sunlit hours and rising with her two companions and the moon. They were interesting and, as they promised, founts of knowledge, but after spending several days with them, Nicole began to realize they were careful about what and how much they revealed to her. Just bits and pieces, but never enough for her to get a firm grasp on their existence. If anything, her confusion grew in tandem with her dependence upon them.

Gerard was for the most part a delightful diversion. He played the charming beau or doting father with equal enthusiasm, and his dazzling physical beauty held her spellbound. Though his behavior was often seductive and his embraces were frequent, she sensed no passionate nature within him, no inner warmth. It was as if all emotion was displayed like a carefully chosen gesture, for effect rather than with spontaneity. Occasionally, she would get a glimmer of something stirring beneath the smooth surface of his appeal that would suggest he felt more than he cared to, especially when Bianca tried to draw out of her information about her parents. That subject made him testy and anxious. Those things she intuited more than observed, for Bianca was unaware of the change in him at such times. Perhaps it was the psychic bond between them that had her privy to his moods.

She enjoyed playing games of the mind with him. Her first tentative reaches were frustrating. She could feel him, but couldn't focus enough to find him. His silent voice teased about within her head, making her remember her rusty Italian, coaxing, chiding, challenging her to do better. Then one evening, as they sat listening to Bianca berate the latest fashions, Nicole gathered her energy and sent the call of his name like a bolt from a bow.

Gerard!

He lurched sideways in his chair, tumbling from it to clutch at his temples. When he straightened to gaze at her, there was none of the congratulations or amusement she'd expected to see. His stare was dark and dazed. Shocked. Apprehensive.

"Gerard, whatever is the matter with you?" Bianca demanded in irritation.

It seemed to take him a moment to respond. "Forgive me, *cara*. I wouldn't want you to think your sparkling conversation lulled me into a coma." His reply was barbed enough to make her grumble and ignore him, but his attention was fixed upon Nicole.

I'm sorry. She tried to touch him with that sentiment on a lower scale of intensity, but found herself blocked off from him. She couldn't find his psyche in the cold void of subconsciousness, and she was surprised by how alone that made her feel, as if some vital connection had been severed. He remained withdrawn from her for the rest of the evening, his stare uneasy and remote. He left early to hunt, and that left her with Bianca.

Nicole couldn't summon any liking for the sleek, sophisticated female. Bianca was all poised polish but there was something irrevocably tarnished beneath that glossy sheen. She was kind, even generous with her time and money, providing Nicole with an enviable wardrobe and exposing her to the finest culture Paris had to offer. But Nicole was never allowed close to her. That determined distance bred discomfort; and Nicole was reminded of Gerard's warning. Bianca would be pleasant only as long as she wanted something. And Nicole began to suspect that that something was her father.

Toward a cold aloof dawn, she was brooding in her chamber when she felt Gerard's presence. He glided past her to stand at her balcony window, looking out over a slumbering Paris. His expression was oddly quiet and somehow vulnerable.

"Dawn is such a melancholy time of day," he mused. "We must bid goodbye to the world just as it is waking to life."

She watched him for a moment, steeping in misery because he was holding himself purposefully away when she'd come to enjoy his quixotic company so. It was a kinship she could never feel with Bianca, and the only link she had to this new and deeply frightening life. She couldn't bear to let the barriers stand between them. "I didn't mean to hurt you," she blurted out at last.

His gaze flickered in her direction. A smile moved upon his face, a gesture of forgiveness that never went beyond the outward features. "You caught me with my guard down. It startled me, is all. You are very strong." He fell silent, pondering that with all the wariness of an implicit threat. That was it, she realized at last. Her power scared him. Of the two of them, she'd felt Bianca in control and now he was feeling her intimidation as well and didn't like it.

"I would never harm you, you know."

He continued to smile blandly at her reassurance. "Nicole, I have not lived so long by being trusting."

"But you stay with Bianca. You must care for her."

He gave a snort of laughter. *"Cara,* I am not the fool she thinks me. As for trusting her, I'd as soon place my faith in a desert scorpion."

"Then why stay with her?"

He sighed and looked back out at the city. "You have no notion of how hard it is to live so long. She is the perfect companion for me. The edge in our relationship keeps it fresh, yet we don't pretend to hold great feeling for one another. It is more for the sake of mutual greed than personal need."

"Did you never love her?"

She would have liked for him to look at her when he answered, but then she probably wouldn't have been able to read anything of value in his jewel-like eyes. Not unless he wanted to reveal it.

"I hold to a memory of love, but I don't remember the exact feeling anymore. Amusing how an emotion you are willing to die for becomes an indifferent habit.

Without Bianca, there would be endless mediocrity, and that I could not stand."

"Have you never tried to make friends among the people?"

He glanced at her then as if he thought her suggestion quite astonishing. "Among mortals? Why, that would be like . . . playing with my food, and I was taught as a child that it was impolite. They can be entertaining, for a while. But what they are eventually brings out what I am. Not much future in that type of friendship."

"So you feel nothing for humanity?"

"No. Why should I?"

"What about my mother?"

He didn't move, yet she could feel the sudden flurry of his thoughts, complex in intensity and zealously guarded from her probing. "What about her?"

"She has been with my father for at least eighteen years. He must find her company more than mildly entertaining."

"Your mother is an exceptional creature," he answered with a studied neutrality. "And Gino is not like me. Besides, they made you between them and that creates a different circumstance."

"Then there is a chance that we can coexist without harming one another."

Finally, he took note of her hopeful tone and rightly guessed its cause. "You speak of the one you claim is not your lover."

"I'm speaking hypothetically," she argued.

"Ummm. Of course. Only you can judge that, Nicole. Only you can read your heart and place a value upon his life. Can you be with him night after night, resisting the instinct to take him while he sleeps? Can you exist with the guilt of a momentary lapse of control? My advice to you was learned most painfully, and it is to stay away from those you care for. We are solitary creatures, prone to an independent and territorial nature. We hunt alone, we guard our secrets well. We kill without thought when threatened and we feed to survive. That is my nature and I have accepted it. You would be wise to do the same. Forget this mortal, for you can have no normal life with him. I don't say this to hurt you, but so you don't do something that will cause you unforgivable pain. You are still learning, and you must be careful of consequence."

His words upset her because she was longing for Marchand with an intensity most compelling. She was craving his humanity, his conscience, his basic warmth, all those things she found lacking here. But she feared that consequence Gerard warned of. Because even now, the hunger gnawed through her, streaking a tense agony along starving veins, a hunger that would sooner or later have to be satisfied. A future devoid of any passion or pleasure stretched out before her and she looked to it without anticipation. And for the first time, she damned her parents for so selfishly bringing her into this turmoiled existence.

Gerard had been watching the play of emotion upon her face. For all his glib talk and careless nonchalance, he was far from oblivious to her distress. He stepped up beside her to enfold her in a loose embrace. His kiss was brief and tender against her brow.

Nicole fought against the want to turn into his arms in self-pitying tears. They would solve nothing, and he would despise her weakness. She had to get stronger. She had to know more. That was her only hope of attaining any kind of direction in her life.

So when she spoke at last, her voice was crisp and commanding. "Teach me something new, Gerard."

But he merely rubbed his cheek against her hair and murmured silkily, "But I just have. I've taught you the most important lesson of all."

She drew back to regard him with confusion.

He smiled, sadly she thought, and he touched her chin with his fingertips. "I've shown you what it's like to be alone." Then he left her there to savor that new sensation.

And she hated it.

"How is our guest?" Bianca asked as Gerard joined her in the antechamber.

"I'm not sure what to make of her," he admitted, glancing back from whence he'd come. "She has an ability that quite amazes me, yet she resists her vampiric nature. She hasn't severed her ties to the mortal world and mourns its loss."

"It's loss or *his* loss?"

Gerard gave her an innocuous look. *"Non capisco."*

"Of course you understand, Gerardo, so don't raise those innocent brows to me. She pines for some fool mortal man. She has that same calf look that comes over you when you dream about Arabella Radman."

His expression tightened into a hard mask from out of which pale eyes glittered. "What nonsense you speak."

"Is it?" she taunted.

"You know it is! I have no heart to suffer its breaking. You've often said so yourself."

"If that is true, you won't mind helping me rid our dear Nicole of her foolish sentiments."

His gaze narrowed with suspicion. "How so?"

"I think sweet Nicole needs a harder push to recognize what she is. Do you know who this mortal is?"

Gerard hesitated, then shrugged. "I've seen him."

"And you can bring him here tomorrow night?"

"Sì."

Bianca smiled with divine malevolence and leaned close to press cool lips upon his still ones. "You are right, my love. You have no heart."

And he stood unblinking while she stroked one lean cheek with a careless fingertip.

It was hard to concentrate on anything. Marchand found himself drifting through the days and nights in a glaze of wine-soaked indifference. He had no patience with Frederic, who seemed to be genuinely trying to sever his ties to the rebellion. It was no easy task when revolution teemed about them. More often than he liked, he found himself remembering the old life they'd had, with servants and silver and no worries. But those days were gone and the present was full of danger. He wished for a way to remove them from its temptation, for the means to leave the city and the influences of the revolt, but there was no help in sight. Money was short. He, himself, was finding no legitimate work and it frustrated him to have to depend upon the coins Nicole left behind.

Coins . . . such a cold reminder of what beat so hot within his heart. She'd said she didn't love him, yet how could she have met his last kiss with so much passion if that were true? He could drive himself mad considering it. In fact, he was almost certain he was destined toward that end. He'd wanted to believe her when she said he could count upon her support. That was what he dwelt upon when he wasn't berating himself for lowering his guard to her cruel handling, or totally disgusted with the world in general. His life was miserable and he made sure all around him were aware of it.

They were partaking of an evening meal and he was grumbling unkindly about its quality until Musette fled across the room in tears.

"Enough," Frederic stated, slapping his hands down upon the tabletop, startling him momentarily from his sullen stupor. "Your love life may be a disaster, but you'll not ruin mine. You will apologize to Musette."

"I won't," he growled.

"You will or you will find someplace else to stay."

Marchand stared at him in astonishment. "W-what?" The idea was absurd! He gave a dismissing laugh. "And who will pay the rent, *mon frère?* Who will protect you and your silly strumpet from the ills you seem determined to court?"

Frederic struck him. The blow was hard enough to knock him from his chair, hard enough to rattle his senses. And as he sat on the floor, jaw cradled in hand, Frederic shook a finger down at him.

"Don't look surprised. Did you think I'd forgotten everything I learned from you about brawling when we were boys? You seem to forget all but your sneering contempt these days. It might further surprise you to know I am not a helpless fool led by dreams of utopias in the clouds. I am not a child, Marchand, and you will not treat me as such again. You will not interfere in my life, in my plans. And you will not be insufferably rude to my friends or my fiancée."

"Fiancée?" Both Marchand and Musette, who had turned back toward them, echoed that in mutual shock.

"Yes. We will be married in the spring. If that's all

right with you, my love?" he amended, blushing at his slight oversight. He hadn't asked her first.

"Oh, yes! Yes!" And she crossed to him and her arms flew about Frederic's neck.

Marchand managed to drag himself up to regard their blissful happiness. Aware of it, they stepped apart, uncomfortable with their joy in the face of his pain. But then Marchand embraced them both, placing firm kisses on both their cheeks.

"That is wonderful news. I'm glad for you. Forgive my stupid talk—"

"Oh, March, it's all right," Musette cooed, hugging him tight. "I know Nicole's leaving broke your heart. I'm so sorry for what she did. I could have sworn she cared for you."

"You must forget her, March. Move on."

"Move on," he mumbled, smiling at them crookedly. "To what? You have just cut the ties of fraternity. I must now regard you as a man and not as my little brother who needs my constant care." He fit his palm to Frederic's face, then gave a push away so his brother wouldn't see just how upset he was by this turn of events. He'd had too much wine and he needed to think. "I'm going out to walk awhile."

Already distracted by the way Musette was cozying up to him, Frederic murmured, "Don't fall in the Seine."

His walk was aimless at first, moving him through the Latin Quarter, where the sounds of merriment defied the desperate and despairing mood of the city. It started to rain, which he thought fitting to his own dark humor, and soon the chill downpour was enough to drive conspirators gathered around cheap red wine from the outdoor cafés, leaving their schemes to hatch another night. Marchand didn't seek shelter. Instead, he lifted his face

to the pelting rain, needing its freshness to wash away
the stains of misery from his soul and wake his mind to
the world around him. And when he pushed the damp
strands of hair from out of his eyes, he was seeing things
anew.

Always he'd existed on the surface in this district of
dreamers. He'd held a soldier's contempt for their idealism and believed himself apart from them in his own defensive arrogance. He'd been living in his own dream,
where he made himself responsible for those who didn't
need or want his care. It wasn't for them that he'd done
these things, but rather for himself, because he'd been
afraid to have no purpose. He'd been afraid he'd some-
day realize that he was just like all those around him for
whom he held no respect. He was a member of the bohemian society; the group of young, shiftless and inven-
tive characters who refused or were unable to take on a
stable and useful identity. He lived, like them, within society but outside it, among eccentrics, visionaries, radi-
cals, those rejected by family and the temporary or
permanently poor. Seeing himself there was a terrible
shock to his system and esteem. And he'd been drawn
irrevocably into the underside of the system, into the
shady underworld from necessity, not intention. He
knew violence. That's all he was good at with his background in the military. What he'd become was abhor-
rent to everything he'd stood for. No wonder Nicole
could not love him. He, himself, could not admire what
he was.

The rain eased and mists rose thickly off the surface
of the Seine. He crossed at Pont de la Concorde and the
bridge seemed a murky suspension in time and space.
Rather like his future, he thought wryly. What was a

man who knew nothing but discipline supposed to do with his life?

"Marchand."

He turned at the thin call of his name and scanned the cloudy darkness. Finally the figure of Gaston emerged, and his lips curled in disgust for what the man was and for the part he played in his own moral plunge.

"Amazing the type of vermin scuttling about in the shadows on such a night."

"I didn't come to trade jokes with you, LaValois. Sebastien wants to know why you've been avoiding him."

"Tell De Sivry to go to hell. I'll do no more work for him."

Gaston smiled. "You'll do no more work for anyone, for hell is where he's asked me to send you."

The sound of footsteps on cobbles alerted Marchand to his danger even as a quartet of burly men came forward through the mists to stand ready at Gaston's call. Marchand gave a low curse. He was without the means of defense, not so much as a chip of wood at hand when the others toted lengths of iron and blades that glittered beneath the evenly spaced streetlamps. From Gaston's nasty smile, he knew there was no use trying to bargain for his life. As far as De Sivry's second was concerned, his life was going to end here on this bridge.

Gaston took a step back and gestured to the bulky foursome. "I want nothing left recognizable when you dump him into the water. His brother must never guess our part in it." Then he turned and walked away.

As Marchand ducked the first swing of iron, another caught him with a wind-sapping force against the ribs. He went down to his knees in a daze of pain, managing to shift away from a knifepoint aimed at his throat. The blade snagged on his jacket, tearing a line of agony along his shoulder. He let himself drop to the cobbles, but instead of lying there helpless, he rolled quickly to one side between two of his attackers. Before he could gain his feet, an explosive blow to the back of his head sent him sprawling in the muddy puddles.

"Don't go cuttin' up that jacket," one of the bovine figures muttered. "It looks to be about my size."

Beefy fingers twisted in his hair, dragging him up to his feet. Without a pause, Marchand used that upward momentum to drive forward, butting into an opponent's face. There was a wail of distress, and immediately he lashed back, smashing the back of his head into the other's chin. The fingers meshing in his hair loosened and Marchand bolted, skidding precariously on the slick stones before breaking into a desperate run for the far side of the bridge.

Behind him, he heard fiercely grumbled oaths and the clatter of pursuit. Not knowing if he had the strength left to outrun them, Marchand stumbled along the Quai des Tuileries, seeking some weapon or at least deep shadows of concealment. His legs gave out, spilling him down upon hands and knees. He scuttled around to face his enemies, fingers frantically scrabbling at the stones in hopes of prying one free. A weak defense was better than none at all. And he crouched there, dazed and panting, waiting for his assassins to emerge from the fog.

A moment passed, then two. All he heard was his own ragged breathing. And he was confused. They wouldn't have given up the chase. De Sivry wouldn't condone failure.

Then Marchand saw movement in the mist. A single figure filtered through it. Marchand backed up onto his heels, readying for fight or flight. Then surprise held him immobile.

It wasn't one of De Sivry's men who glided through the dim light pooling at the base of the bridge. But the sharply handsome face was familiar.

"You are Nicole's Marchand?" an accented voice queried.

And that was all Marchand remembered before pitching forward unconscious upon the wet cobbles.

Snarling animals frozen above him.

That sight was so bizarre, it shocked Marchand back to awareness. He stirred, waking all sorts of bodily miseries, to find himself reclined upon a crimson sofa. The fierce bestial faces were carved into the wood of the couch's elaborate arms.

Where was he?

Then he remembered the face of Nicole's chosen lover. He sat up with a groan of effort to see that individual regarding him from across the room. He was lounging indolently upon a stool, his features betraying his mocking amusement.

"So you awake. It would seem I rescued you from a rather nasty situation, yes?"

Chagrined at being in this man's debt, Marchand ignored the reference and muttered, "Who are you?"

"Mi scúsi. I am Gerardo Pasquale."

"And you are Nicole's . . ." He let that dangle so the other man could fill in the degree of his relationship.

Gerardo smiled. "A friend of the family."

Marchand regarded him steadily but sensed no challenge of possession from the man. He relaxed slightly and gave way to the urge to rub the back of his head. The inside of his skull was thundering. "Those men—"

"Met with an end more tragic than they'd planned for you."

He was so nonchalant, Marchand stared. "You killed them?" It seemed impossible. The impeccable lines of his clothing weren't even wrinkled.

"I'm sorry, had you wanted me to invite them here so we could all dine together?"

"No," Marchand said at last. "They were no friends of mine. I don't care what you did with them. But I am grateful for it."

"*Va bène. Prègo.*" At Marchand's blank gaze, he added, "You are welcome." Gerard came up from the chair, his movements all lazy grace and silky strength. He glanced away because Marchand had withdrawn his hand from the wound on his head and his palm was sticky with blood. "I suggest you clean yourself up before meeting with Nicole. It would grieve her to see you so—ill used."

"Is she here?"

"*Sì*. She is attending her—lessons." And he gave a slow, sly smile.

"Perhaps she would rather not see me." Marchand was taking in the heavy luxury of the room around him and the lethal good looks of the smooth Gerardo Pasquale, who claimed to be a friend. He felt very insignificant in comparison.

"Oh, no. She wants to see you very much, I assure you. Please." He made a languid gesture. "The bath is through there. Take a moment to soak away your aches and pains while I find something more appropriate for you to put on. What you are wearing is—soiled." And his narrowing stare lingered along the rent in Marchand's jacket until he pulled his attention away with an effort. By then, his smug smile was rather strained and Marchand sensed an undercurrent that was far from genial. Gerard's dark looks had altered from lazy feline to deadly predator. Yet he was smiling graciously as he bowed out of the room. Marchand never heard the sound of retreating footsteps on marble. He must have walked as light as a cat.

Marchand hauled himself up. His steps were far from graceful. Every inch of him hurt. The thought of a reviving bath scattered his reservations about his host. And no, he didn't want to greet Nicole looking as though he'd been wallowing in a street brawl—and losing.

The sight of the pool awed him but the invitation was irresistible. He shed his dirtied clothes and stepped into water that was surprisingly cool. He sank down, letting it flow over his battered body, easing the ache in his ribs and the burn along his shoulder. He submerged his head for the duration of his lung capacity then came up with a sigh, eyes closed, headache soothed. For a long moment, he let himself drift on a healing tide as a feeling of lassitude overtook him. It rose in languorous waves, pulling him down into a caressing whirlpool. A wonderful sensation, he mused in a mind far detached from weighted limbs. That heaviness drew on him like a sleeping draft, numbing body, stilling mind, until he felt himself floating, unable to move. It never occurred to him to be afraid. The notion that he might drown never formulated within his hazy consciousness.

Then a soft sound provoked his sinking awareness and his eyes fluttered open. At the edge of the tub, he saw Nicole standing still and dreamlike in a silky white robe, but she seemed so detached, so far away. He couldn't manage the complexity of speech, so he smiled, a vague, wandering smile. She advanced a step, one bare foot easing down into the water, then the other. With a whisperlike move, her robe slid down the length of her arms and thighs to pool at the tiled edge and trail like lotus petals atop the water. His gaze had followed, only remotely registering that she wore nothing beneath it.

And then his vacant stare lifted, snared by eyes of molten gold.

Chapter Twelve

Nicole awoke hungry.

Thirst rose in her like a fever, burning along her veins, that need to drink. She couldn't remember the last time she'd taken any food—food other than Gerard had offered in that sacrificial cup. She sat up slowly, her head swimming with lightness, her temples throbbing, urging with every beat that she go out and find a matching pulse to dance alongside hers. Was there any point in resisting, after all? She knew what she was, what she was becoming. The vampire child of a vampire. Did they think she would never figure out the name of her birthright? Her heritage, Bianca called it. Her nature, Gerard seconded. They were right. All that was human within her was growing fainter amid the hugeness of new sensations, feelings that seduced with their power and superiority.

How long could she go on in this ravenous state? She would starve, Gerard told her. Was that true? Could normal food no longer sustain her, or was she being enticed away from it by these stronger cravings? She felt her face. There were no mirrors in the house, but she could feel the hollowness of her cheeks. How soon before that became the gauntness of the doomed? How long before her strength began to fail her? She was afraid of dying. The will to live was as insistent as the beating of her heart. She would do what she had to do to survive. As Marchand had said, as Gerard had said.

A long silken robe had been laid out across the foot of her bed. She slipped it on, enjoying its texture against her skin. She would go to Gerard and, like a babe, ask that he help feed her. He'd been waiting for her to ask, she realized, letting her come to it in her own desperate time. Now, she was ready.

But it was Bianca, not Gerard, who waited for her. At the woman's questioning gaze, Nicole was blunt.

"I'm hungry. Show me what I need to know."

"Bien." The sleek vampiress patted the seat beside her and Nicole eased down upon it, suddenly stiff and reluctant. "What is it, child?"

"Is it terrible for them when we take them? Are they in pain for long?" She didn't notice that she spoke of humans as something other than herself. But the blond demon did.

Bianca restrained her cynical smile. "It can be very pleasant for them, like a dream. They become so dazzled by our unnatural eyes and beauty, they are unaware of fear. It is a bit like falling into slumber, I believe. Unfortunately, it is a dream they do not wake from."

"Does it have to be like that? Do we have to kill?"

"Oh, Nicole, it's not just the taking of blood, it's the sucking of the soul. You'll understand with your first. It's the taking of their life, drawing in their power." Then she nodded to herself as if congratulating herself for putting it so nicely. "Perhaps Gerard can say it better. He fancies himself quite the Renaissance poet. It's the soul's strength that revitalizes our minds, just as the blood restores our bodies. Each of us has our own method. Gerard likes to charm and play. I prefer it more like business."

"And my father? How does he take his meals?"

Bianca pursed her lips pensively. "I do not know. I've never been hunting with him."

But Nicole remembered watching him seduce and destroy. And the image still held pain. She decided she would keep contact at a minimum. Perhaps it would be easier to excuse what she did if she didn't think of them as individual souls whose futures she was devouring.

"For your first few times, Gerard or I will go with you. We can show you how to select, how to overpower, how to dispose of what is left. That is the most important thing. We must be careful never to arouse undo suspicion. It is so much easier in these cosmopolitan cities. Here people are too sophisticated to believe such as we walk about in the night. In the countryside, they have no such doubts. Still, we must disguise what we do. What is it now?" she asked with a tinge of impatience as she took in Nicole's downcast features.

"Such a long and lonely life I'm about to begin."

Bianca's smile was as sweet as too much absinthe, confusing and deadly. "It doesn't have to be that way. You needn't be alone. You can make yourself a companion for eternity as I did with Gerard."

Nicole stared at her, aghast with horror. In her mind, she pictured Gerard as he might have been in life; charming, witty, softened by humanity. Bianca had stolen it from him.

"You look shocked. Don't be. Ask him if he would prefer his shallow mortal's life over what I gave him. I chose him because I didn't want to be alone. I enjoy his pretty face and his pouty dramatics. The world may change around us, but he never will. He will always be mine. Is there one whom you would like to have with you in immortality?"

Marchand. She thought of him immediately, then dismissed the image. To have him would mean to kill him. To take his life.

Then she thought of the centuries of solitude.

"Perhaps," she mouthed faintly. "If I did, how would I go about it?"

"You drink him to the doorway of death, then, before he passes through, you let him drink from you. He will arise reborn, a fledgling to your will, a slave to your desires. The link between you can never be broken."

The notion tantalized. Marchand . . . forever hers. Then another thought came to her. "But what if I don't drink him to the point of death? What happens then? Would he be linked to me like—" She was going to say like she was to Gerard, but caught herself in time.

"There would be a bond between you. As long as it is renewed, he would be powerless to resist your suggestion. He would live to serve you. He would love you above his own life." And the way she said that sounded so seductive, so alluring. So irresistible.

Nicole considered this in the dark quiet of her soul. At one time, her innocent heart would have rebelled against such a manipulative thought, but so much had changed. She had changed. And she was thinking how good it would be to have him with her. She didn't need to kill him . . . not right away. She could have just a taste, just enough to keep him near her. "Would he know what I had done? Would he hate me for it?"

"Not if you do it right."

Never seeing Bianca's smug smile of satisfaction, she asked, "How do I do it right?"

"Reach out to him with your mind, Nicole," Gerard's silky tone instructed. She glanced up in surprise, not having heard him come into the room. He stood before her and cradled her face in his warm hands. "Shut your eyes, *cara*. Think of him. Concentrate on his eyes, on his thoughts. Let yours overtake them, slowly, completely. Like a mist. It is easy to mold mortal thoughts. They are so weak, so fragile, like butterflies, so do not hold on too tightly."

Close your eyes, Marchand. Dream of nothing. And Nicole was surprised by how suddenly near she felt to him.

"Now," Gerard crooned. "Bring on the hunger. Let it flow within you, hot and eager. Reach out and feel the beat of his heart next to yours."

She concentrated and the throbbing tempo whispered through her, growing stronger, clearer.

"When the time comes, you will take him swiftly and he will never know it. He will only remember his need to be with you, to satisfy you." He fell silent, his thumbs stroking over the delicate angles of her face. "Nicole, are you sure—"

"Of course she is," Bianca interjected, shooting him a venomous look. "Nicole, I have a surprise for you waiting in the bath. Go see what it is."

Nicole opened her eyes. She gazed up at her handsome mentor, sensing he was troubled. *Gerard?*

"Go, *cara*. That is how things must be."

She rose up, and as she left the room, Bianca hissed, "You nearly ruined everything, fool."

"Ruined what, Bianca? The death of innocence?"

She gave him a dismissing toss of her head.

"One of us should be with her," he said. "She may

not know how to stop herself from devouring all that he is."

Bianca shrugged. "It doesn't matter. Sometimes it is through such humbling mistakes that one learns the value of humility." And she was looking at him with icy meaning.

"*Il nemico*, would you destroy her as well?"

"That's not your concern, is it?"

He turned away with an angry curse and stalked to his own quarters. And Bianca leaned back upon the sofa, smiling as she thought of Nicole Radman's fall to come.

The perfect revenge.

She stood poised on the cool tiles, unable to believe what she was seeing ... Marchand stretched out in splendid offering before her within that mysterious twilight setting. The perfumed water provided no covering, and her gaze roved down from the exquisite repose of his features along the intriguing terrain left bare to her view. His body was stunning in its virility. She'd sensed the sheer male power of him before, but having it so displayed left her breathless. It made her want to touch him, all of him, to learn each hard swell and taut curve. Her arousal lent a subtle difference to her mood, a different definition of want.

He'd been hurt. She could see the telltale bruising along his ribs and a yet-oozing gash from his collarbone to the cap of one well-developed shoulder. What sympathy she felt was quickly engulfed by the scent of his blood, rich and fragrant in the air. Hunger raged within, a beast long caged and craving freedom. His eyes blinked open and came into a drowsy focus. Patience, she soothed. Slowly. He must not feel afraid. Like a dream. A pleasant dream. She let her robe fall.

She continued to embrace his mind with her own, caressing away the momentary confusion as his gaze was lost in hers. She could feel his pain, and that she blotted out completely. She would not have him suffering, not now. Not ever.

He watched her wade through the water, his expression placid, sleepy, and she was somewhat dissatisfied with that. She eased back on her control until his eyes began an appreciative wandering, pausing at the rounding of her breasts until their peaks tightened in a shy thrill of response, moving lower to where the cool waters stirred against suddenly hot places. She liked the way he looked at her. It brought a shiver of weakness to her sense of power.

She came closer, kneeling over him so that her thighs straddled his and the sensitive pucker of her breasts came into their first contact with his warm, sleek skin. A shudder of expectation made her control over him falter. His hands rose, sweeping gently along her bare arms, and she touched his face, charting the strong contours, seeking the satiny feel of his wet hair between her fingers. Lowering gradually to the damp part of his lips. Finding upon them a lush well of emotions.

She hadn't meant to kiss him. The movement of his mouth against hers was highly distracting. The silky probe of his tongue shook her fledgling concentration. With each notch it gave, his responsiveness increased. And she couldn't say she minded so very much being molded by his hands, being tempted by his touch.

She lifted up, panting lightly against the invitation of his lips. This wasn't how she'd planned it. But it was so beautiful in its spontaneity.

His eyes were open, their glaze gone. Passion simmered in the darker depths, desire for her.

"I want to make love with you, Nicole."

She came back down for the luxury of his kiss, letting it coax the female response in her to trembling heights. His palms were skimming down the curve of her waist, settling possessively at the flare of her hips so he could move her against the ever-increasing proof of his need.

Her need was strong, too. She turned away from his questing lips, letting her own lower to the cruel cut he'd sustained. Her mouth moved gently as if to kiss his wound.

"Marchand, who's hurt you?"

"It doesn't matter now." And his eyes were closing as she exerted the heavy vampire magic so he wouldn't know she was lapping greedily along that wound.

The taste of him was intoxicating. She pressed hard against the tear in his flesh to encourage a fresh flow of blood, licking it up like a hungry kitten when her appetite roared with a lion's strength. Her moan of urgency mingled with his soft mutter of complaint. The thought that she was hurting him made her back away, teased rather than satisfied.

He regarded her somberly while her fingertips fluttered along his cheeks and neck, finally stilling there where his pulse beat hard and relentlessly.

"I love you, Nicole."

"I want you with me, Marchand. Always. Always." And she kissed him so he wouldn't see the sudden glare of bloodlust in her eyes. She pulled away from his mouth as pain shot through her gums. Now, do it now, do it now!

And as she bent toward the beckoning bow of his throat, lost to the anticipation of the bite, his hands lifted her slightly. Even as her lips curled back to expose her teeth, he guided her over him, bringing her down abruptly. That unexpected sear of penetration made her eyes pop open wide and drove a gasp from between suddenly slackened lips. And Nicole forgot everything except the exquisite feel of him lodged deep and hot and full within her, possessing her the way she'd thought to possess him; body and soul.

As she was motionless in a near swooning state of sensory shock, he began to move her in slow gliding strokes up and down upon him. Nicole gave herself up to the sensations; the silky seduction of the cool water sliding between and around them, the fiery ache of him reaching further, stronger within, a scintillating contrast. She rested her head upon his shoulder, afraid to let him see her face in case some trace of unnatural desire remained to distort this glorious mortal union. *Oh, Marchand . . . oh, my love . . .* And she held onto him as he controlled her passions, shaping them with each completing thrust, drawing from her strange panting sounds of pleasure until the intensity was too much to contain.

The strength of her concluding spasms tore a cry from her and brought him to a swift completion. Then she lay contentedly against him while starbursts of sensation more brilliant than those painted heavens above faded upon the horizon of her consciousness. And it was delicious just yielding to his strength in that timeless moment.

Finally, she grew aware that he was shivering in the chill water and Nicole was spurred to reluctant movement. She eased up from him with a voluptuous sigh and whispered against his lips, "Come share my bed with me, Marchand."

She helped him stand, then spent some time drying

him off with a large sheet of toweling. The damp muscular definition of his body demanded exploration and she was held captive by his compelling heat and marvelous humanity. Sated by the sensual peak he'd carried her over, Nicole had no further thoughts of food. It was his physical closeness she desired, his emotional intensity she craved. And when he stilled her hands so that she would look up at him, her cheeks were glistening and her voice unsteady as she told him simply, "Marchand, I love you."

Too bad they didn't share the same degree of stamina, Nicole mused as she watched Marchand sleep beside her. He'd given way to exhaustion almost the moment he settled upon her sheets, while she was left wide awake and restless. She'd wanted to make love with him again. She'd wanted to pursue those breathless delights with him once more, but his mortal form had suffered too much abuse to sustain him. He hadn't said who'd beaten him. She wouldn't allow herself to think it could have been Gerard. No, he wouldn't have had to use something so distasteful as physical force.

They'd brought Marchand here to be her initiation into the vampiric world. How was she to explain why he was yet untouched and her thirst unslacked? Perhaps she hadn't the instinct it took to be a successful predator. That wasn't quite true, because she'd been ready to take him. How was she to have known that he was going to upset her plans so deliciously?

"He is very pretty."

Nicole looked up in surprise to see Bianca at the foot of her bed. Though they were both discreetly covered by the bed sheets, Nicole felt uncomfortably vulnerable to the woman's dark stare.

Bianca eased up until she was standing near Marchand. Her pale fingers took him by the chin, turning his head from side to side. She frowned at the lack of evidence on his neck and Nicole felt herself bristle up in a protective defense.

"Don't wake him."

"He won't awaken." Then more curtly, "He shouldn't awaken at all, at least not in this mortal form. What's wrong with you, Nicole? Is his blood not to your taste? I should think it would be rich and strong in such a man." And her fingertips lingered at the side of his throat. "If you do not want him—"

"I do! He's mine. And you'd best remember that."

Bianca's gaze narrowed. She didn't enjoy having her own threats thrust back at her. "Then take him now. Do not waste what I've brought you by indulging in unnecessary sentiment."

A soft chuckle sounded from the shadowed corner of the room. "Could it be you've made a mistake, Bianca?" Gerard drifted forward, his expression lit with a mocking entertainment. "She is very much like Gino. Perhaps you have chosen unwisely. You should not have made her first one her *innamoráto*. Have you misjudged the power of the human heart in your greed to have all? A consistent failing of yours, I believe."

Fury massed within the sleek vampiress until her image seemed to shimmer without true substance. Gerard stood laughing and unafraid while Nicole eased into a crouch over Marchand, ready to protect him from Bianca's wrath if need be.

"Careful, *cara*," Gerard taunted. "You are close to losing control most unattractively."

Her essence solidified and very calmly, she remarked, "Careful, Gerardo, lest you lose your head. It might amuse me more than your sharp wit to have it upon a pole."

"Oh, *mía amáta,* how could you ever replace me?"

"The world is full of fools. It would not be hard to do."

Then he took a lightning-fast stride forward, seizing Bianca's arms, pulling her up against him so their bodies were flush and their faces inches apart. His eyes were hot and iridescent as they blazed down into hers. And for an instant, the balance of power seemed to shift between them.

"Be careful," he warned in a low, long hiss, "lest I grow bored with you."

Bianca's rigid posture altered, becoming all oozing and sensual. Her silken garments seemed to pour down him as she purred, "Oh, Gerardo, *innamoráto,* it is your Italian temper I love about you. *Un amóre di bambíno.* You can be such a charming child." And she stretched up to kiss him, tugging at his lower lip with her sharp teeth while he stood unmoving and unblinking. She stroked his features and cooed flatteringly, "You are so beautiful. Don't be cruel."

Slowly he smiled, and he *was* beautiful, sleekly, darkly beautiful. "Sometimes I forget just how much I sacrificed for the love of you."

The remark didn't please her, and she searched his expression suspiciously, but it was bland and exquisite, revealing nothing. Until she walked away from him. Nicole saw a glaze of coldness settle over his face, as hard and unreadable as opaque ice. Then with another change that was also mercurial, he seemed to remember

Nicole was there, for he turned to her with a chiding smile.

"Ah, my poor little Nicole. So it's the love sickness you suffer from." He made a *tsk-tsk* sound and settled languidly on the bed next to where Marchand slumbered in unnatural stillness. "He thought I was your lover. Imagine that." And he looked down at the mortal man without a trace of any feeling whatsoever. Never had Gerard looked quite so alien to her as he slowly cocked his head the way spring birds do over damp earth. He was listening to the pulse of Marchand's blood.

"Has my reluctance to take his life disappointed you too?" Her tone was sharper than she intended but Gerard only smiled.

"No, *cara.* You remind me much of your father. Gino, too, was a reluctant apprentice, whereas I took to my new state with a certain—zest."

"Did—did Bianca make my father, too?"

Gerard had lifted Marchand's arm and he was studying the pattern of his veins. *"Sì,* she made us both." Nicole reacted to that news with a slight gasp, but he seemed lost to his reverie. "So long ago. Only she could never keep Gino with her. And he was the one she had wanted." His luminous eyes closed as he rubbed his cheek along Marchand's inner arm. He made a low, purring sound, reminding her deceivingly of an affectionate cat. Until he paused with his mouth pressed to Marchand's wrist.

"Gerard," Nicole called and his eyes slid open dreamily, their color hot and rimmed with red. "Please." Her hand slipped between the caress of his lips and Marchand's vulnerable veins. Gerard chuckled.

"Mi scúsi. I forgot myself." He uncoiled to stand. "I

nearly forgot something else, as well. I have something for you. A moment, please." And in what seemed timed to the blink of an eye, he'd gone and returned to extend the familiar cup to her. "It's no longer warm, but it will sustain you until you're ready to seek out your own next meal."

Her hands were trembling when they reached out. Already the scent was enticing her like some dark perfume. Gerard's face had gone strangely still, all sharp mysterious angles as he watched her drink.

"Slowly, Nicole."

But how could she help her greed for life, for that's what was in the cup—life. She felt it flood through her, plumping withering veins, warming chill flesh, strengthening all her flagging senses until the room seemed to spin about her. She was vaguely aware of Gerard taking the cup from her when it was emptied, of his hand at the back of her head guiding her up against the smooth silk of his waistcoat, where she closed her eyes, lost to the thrall of renewal. She felt his other hand cup beneath her chin, lifting it, then the leisurely movement of his mouth upon hers. It was a slow, sensual pressure, but in no way sexual. He had no human nature to arouse those kinds of feelings within her. He was tasting the blood upon her lips.

"Would that I could be your lover," he murmured wistfully, then straightened and stepped away. Nicole blinked and gradually came around. He was standing over Marchand, looking down at him through those brilliant opaque eyes. "Do not keep him here, *cara.* You cannot keep a chicken amongst wolves and ask that they not be wolves."

Wolves. Marchand hadn't understood the true nature

of the beast when he'd spoken of them being wolves. "I love him, Gerard," she said with an unplanned simplicity.

"Oh, Nicole." How sadly he said that, yet his impassive expression never flickered.

"I want with him the happiness my mother and father have."

He gave a deep sigh. "Then my advice to you is to waste no time in telling him the truth of what you are. If he loves you enough to accept it, *splèndido*."

"And if he can't accept it?" Nicole whispered this, fearing his answer, fearing the possibility.

Gerard shrugged with supreme nonchalance. "Then you will do what you must and kill him quickly."

Chapter Thirteen

For the second time, Marchand awoke without knowing where he was. However, it took him only a scant instant to recognize the sweet figure burrowed up against him upon the comfortable bed.

Nicole.

They'd made marvelous love together.

She'd told him she loved him.

That knowledge was enough to allay all his confusion of time and place as he basked in the pleasure of it. Did anything else really matter to him? He knew that answer was no as he lay upon his side studying the composed loveliness of her features in sleep. She was more beautiful than even he remembered with the dark cloud of hair swirled about soft, pinked skin. Her red-rouged lips were slightly parted and her lashes curved in feathery crescents upon exquisitely sculpted cheeks. About her was an aura of ethereal timelessness that mesmerized, but it was her strength that held him spellbound. Such a strong, compassionate creature with her capacity to love despite flaws, to champion the cause of those she cared for.

She stirred slightly and that shift of movement drew

his attention to the drape of the sheet across the perfection of her form. His recall of the prior night was sketchy at best. What he remembered were sensations rather than details; wonderful, delirious sensations, but now, he wanted to savor the specifics.

He laid his hand upon the sun-warmed sheet wound seductively about her middle. Gradually, he lowered to taste the softness of her lips, shaping them gently to fit his own. He felt her wake beneath his kiss, like the princess in a fairy tale he vaguely recollected his mother reciting to him and Frederic at bedtime. Only he was no rescuing prince, just a man with few sterling qualities and fewer prospects. But as her eyes flickered open and she whispered with husky pleasure, "My love," that ceased to matter. Pride couldn't touch the intensity of feeling this woman woke within him.

Instead of waking completely, Nicole continued to drift upon a languorous cloud of contentment, but she didn't discourage him from touching her as she made soft sounds in the back of her throat and arched to meet the stroke of his palm. To Marchand, she was sleek satin over seductively contoured steel and he couldn't help wondering how such a beautiful young woman had come by the tautly muscled strength of a man. Not that he didn't find it attractive. And puzzling. And frightening. She was not like any woman he'd ever known. He didn't know what to make of the difference, but it was undeniably exciting, that combination of dangerous vulnerability.

And she was all fragile female as he bent to nuzzle a temptingly rounded breast. When he took one pebble-hard peak into his mouth, her quiet gasps became delicate music that deepened in tone and quickened in tempo as his hand adored the concave of her belly and the angle of her hip and the silkiness of her inner thigh.

Nicole had thought nothing could rouse her from her determined daylight sleep, but Marchand LaValois was more than a little arousing. His touch was pure magic, creating tiny ripples of delight wherever he went. And his direction was uncanny, always building sensation upon sensation until she was writhing languidly against him. In her sated state of lethargy, it was wildly erotic the way he provoked a placid form to passion. He didn't seem to mind that she lay still, absorbing rather than participating. In fact, he let her know how much he enjoyed cultivating her response with each lingering caress, with each slow, simmering kiss. And when his touch became its most intimate, rubbing, stroking, parting, until her own moisture became the balm he used to seek a deeper knowledge of her, his name escaped in a throbbing whisper and she let the pleasure take her.

Marchand was bemused by this strangely passive lover. She'd been fiercely aggressive with him before, overwhelming him with her far-from-shy demands. It had been like trying to mate with a jungle cat. Yet here she was, all purring and soft, making him doubt he'd ever felt that threat of violence in her. When she reached up for him, her arms wove about his neck in silken bonds that brought his mouth to hers. One of her hands curled about his nape, stroking there with an amazingly innocent sensuality. All the ardor he'd been so carefully holding in check ran hot and rampant through him now. As he shifted over her, the sweet parting of her thighs invited no further delay. He was trying to go slow, reminding himself that she was still almost virginal, but she was arching up against him, her palms sliding down from his shoulders along his back to taut flanks, clutching there and pulling impatiently to hurry his entrance.

Nicole gave a slight intake of surprise as he pressed his way in, then she released that suspended breath in a shuddering sigh. She'd feared perhaps it was the hunger for his blood that had made all seem so intense and sharply satisfying that first time. It wasn't. It was the way Marchand fit her, immense and powerful, that drove all the fears and isolation away. In this, she could be one with him at last.

He began to move, a gentle plunging designed for her comfort at the risk of his control. Too soon, she was anxious for more and frustrated with his care. But loving him fiercely because of it.

"Marchand, you needn't fear that you'll hurt me. Love me the way you'd like to."

He paused at her quiet plea. Then his mouth was on hers, open and insistent. Her body warped up with the shock of his first hand thrust, then began an undulating welcome for those that followed. And as he continued to take her with those long, commanding strokes, he caught her hands as they clawed at him in helpless abandon and pressed the backs of them into the mattress above her head.

Hot, shivery sensations streaked along her veins; Nicole was stunned to realize it was very much like the ecstasy of feeding and hunger. He was pressing home inside her a massing, churning tension. The pleasure of it kept building, building until the beauty of it had her taking flight.

Marchand felt her body lunge up against him and he reached down to support the arch of her spine. He was stunned to discover that it wasn't only the curve of her back and that had left the mattress. Neither were her shoulders or hips touching upon the tangled sheets.

In fact, no part of her except the glossy dark hair spilling down from the tossing of her head made contact with the bed.

She was floating a good four inches above it.

He was so startled, he would have withdrawn right then. Except at that same instant, she found her fulfillment. The fiery walls of her body clutched around him like a fist, contracting in unbelievably hard, pulling spasms. The response she wrung from him was nothing short of cataclysmic.

Then, as her constrictive passion eased, her body sank languidly back upon the bed. And shaking with the violent force of his release and with the quickening of fear she'd inspired, Marchand rolled away from her onto his back, lying there with eyes squeezed shut and breathing labored.

Mon Dieu, what was she?

"Marchand?"

He fought not to recoil as her hand cupped about the curve of his jaw to turn his head toward her. He was rigid with alarm but she was smiling up at him, not seeing his dismay through eyes of a smoky jade green, all soft with satisfaction.

"I love you, Marchand," she murmured before burrowing close, her head upon his chest and her arms encasing his middle.

He swallowed hard and forced himself to touch her. His hand stroked along her hair in an unsteady movement, but when she sighed sweetly and kissed his bare chest, much of the terror gave way as well.

"I love you, too, Nicole."

And he meant it. God help him, whatever she was, he meant it.

When he awoke, it was dark. The image of Nicole in silhouette seated at his shoulder gave Marchand a violent start, as if there was something unwholesome in the way she watched over him while he slept. If she noticed his reaction, she pretended she hadn't.

"How do you feel, my love?" she asked in a shadow-steeped whisper.

It was then he realized how truly awful he did feel. His head was pounding, his ribs ached. The gash in his shoulder felt like a streak of liquid fire. None of these things had registered earlier and he wondered why. Had she given him some drug? Was that why he'd slept nearly all the day away?

"Marchand, who hurt you?"

Memory came flooding back. "I have to go." He tried to sit up, but Nicole's palm pressed to the center of his chest.

"Who hurt you?"

"I have to leave. I have to make sure Frederic is all right."

"Why? What's happened? Marchand, tell me. Maybe I can help."

"De Sivry ordered me killed because I resisted his offers of work. Several of his men were about to accomplish that goal when your foreign friend interrupted them."

"Gerard?"

"He must have scared them off." He didn't say Gerard had killed them. He didn't want to alarm her. But something in the way she turned her head sharply to one side told him that she already guessed the truth. "He brought me here. He saved my life."

"He saved you for me." There was nothing simple in that multishaded meaning. "Marchand, it's too dangerous for you to stay in the city. I know a place where you'll be safe."

He shook his head. "Frederic—"

"Can come, too. And Musette."

"Just like that? How will we live—"

"We'll go to my home. I am—I am very wealthy. I can see you all well provided for. Let me take care of you for a change."

He became quiet then, studying her. She wasn't sure what she saw in his expression; reluctance or rebellion, but it finally became resignation. "I can't see that I have much choice. I haven't done a very good job of taking care of anyone so far." He was seeing Camille and Bebe. He was seeing the threat of Gaston's smile.

"Yes, you have," Nicole protested. She twisted and came down to him, bringing her face close with her elbows braced on either side of his head. Her fingertips swept the dark hair back from his brow as her gaze delved into his. "You have, Marchand. No man could have done as well under the same circumstances. You don't give yourself half enough credit. But it's a wise man who knows when to ask for help. Ask me, Marchand."

He was stubbornly silent for a long beat and she thought he'd say nothing. Then, his hands rose up to stroke along her shoulders, nudging beneath the spill of her hair to move upon bare flesh. "I would be glad for your help, Nicole. We are kindred spirits, you and I. We need each other."

Her smiled trembled with fragile emotion. Then he

coaxed her down to him, to his expectant kiss, to his warm embrace. And as she lingered there within the circle of his arms, feeling the vibrant pulse of him, remembering the rich taste of him upon her tongue, she strengthened her resolve. She would take him home with her. And there, she could keep him safe from the evils of Paris. And there, she would learn how to keep him safe from the evils within her. If her mother and father could exist together for over seventeen years, they had to know the secret of self-control. She would have it from them. They owed her that much. And she would have Marchand.

"We must go," he said at last. "De Sivry must know by now that I survived. How soon can we leave Paris?"

"As soon as you're ready."

"How? I haven't the kind of money it will take to hire a carriage."

"I'll see to it," she told him with a confidence she didn't feel. Would Gerard help her escape Paris if it meant leaving him and Bianca behind? She had to hope so.

They dressed, and Marchand followed her from the satin-draped bower where they'd confessed and consummated their love. Nicole seemed to have no regrets; his only one was that their exchange of devoted words could not be followed by an exchange of sacred vows. For how could he offer marriage to this woman of privilege? He'd come from an early background of plenty so he knew what he'd be expecting her to surrender. True, she had never complained over what little he'd been able to provide for her and the others, but he knew she deserved better than the furtive life they led. He was a criminal in the eyes of the state. He could never rise above what he was. And what were the chances that her aristocratic family would accept such an alliance for their daughter? It went against every fiber of his moral code to continue as they were, as illicit lovers. He should never have begun with passionate intensity what could only conclude in shame. But how could he now resist the paradise he'd discovered?

Nicole looked up in question when Marchand tugged back upon her hand. His expression was so taut, she was alarmed. But then his fingertips caressed her cheek and the panic faded beneath that tender bliss.

"I love you, Nicole."

Before she could respond, she felt a whisper of movement behind her and turned to find Bianca watching them with a sly smile.

"Nicole, introduce me to your . . . friend."

Waves of hunger emanated from the seductive blonde whose black gaze fixed upon Marchand with a mesmerizing brilliance. Nicole angled in front of him, guarding him from her like a territorial beast of prey. Bianca smiled at her futile attempt to circumvent her power. She held out a languid hand.

"I am Bianca du Maurier, Nicole's temporary guardian."

Inbred manners brought Marchand forward to take her hand and lift it respectfully to his lips. "Madame, I am very grateful to you for seeing to her care. I am Marchand LaValois, at your service."

"How—nice." And her predatory gaze drifted over his handsome features to linger at the clean line of his throat. "Caring for Nicole has been no trouble. I have known her family for—oh, ages. You might say I made her father what he is today." Her glance canted to Nicole, noting how pale and drawn her face became. "I am a very powerful woman, Monsieur LaValois, and fortune follows those in whom I place my patronage. It would please me to have you among the chosen. Nicole is like family now and I would see her happy."

Nicole's gaze darted between the two of them. Bianca was pouring on the charm, lulling him with her dazzling eyes, tempting him with her suggestive words. And Marchand seemed lost. For a moment. Then he blinked rapidly, throwing off her smothering hold. He took a step back, drawing Nicole with him.

"You are very kind, Madame. Nicole's happiness means everything to me, as well. I'll do all I can to see it fulfilled."

Bianca smiled slowly. "I'm sure you will. Nicole, my dear, have you invited M'sieur LaValois to stay with us? You know how I delight in the company of handsome men."

Nicole faced her coolly, her expression carefully impassive. "We were just going to retrieve the rest of his belongings. We will be back shortly."

"Oh, but you needn't go. It would be my pleasure to provide everything he desires."

"We have other matters to attend, as well," Nicole added for extra emphasis.

Just then, Gerard entered the parlor, his arms curled possessively about two voluptuous beauties. His eyes were bright with wicked enjoyment and his smile revealed genuine pleasure when he saw Marchand and Nicole. *"Ah, buòna séra, signóre, signorina. Cóme stá?"*

Gerard, I must talk to you.

He nodded imperceptibly to Nicole to acknowledge her urgent unspoken plea. Then he looked to Bianca and basked in her annoyance. "Bianca, I have brought us guests for dinner."

Her irritation altered swiftly and a flush of anticipation warmed her ivory skin. "How delightful."

"This is Babette, and this lovely"——he paused to nuzzle the other young woman's ear "——is Marie. Ladies, if you would follow Bianca, I will join you in a moment. Don't start without me."

The more than slightly drunk Marie giggled and murmured something slurry like she wouldn't dream of it. He laughed with husky promise as he pressed a lengthy kiss to the inside of her wrist. To Marchand, the scene was somehow askew. He sensed a disturbing current beneath the playful pleasantries. It wasn't a lustful perversion. It was something else. And he was exceedingly eager to leave.

"Come, Nicole. We must go."

But Nicole wouldn't budge until Bianca guided the two women from the room and Gerard approached.

"Now then, *cara*, what did you wish?"

"I need money."

Nicole felt Marchand tense beside her. He wouldn't like her going to another man for aid, but the situation was a dire one. She would not have Bianca preying upon her beloved. She was so concerned about Marchand's response, she completely forgot to be on her guard with Gerard. She felt him probe her mind and frantically threw up a block, but with his superior skill, he peeled back the layers of her defense like skin from a ripe fruit. And he devoured her thoughts.

"You're leaving." And she intuited a surprising sense of sorrow instead of the expected resistance. "That is wise." He reached into his coat and pressed a bulky wad of francs into her hand. *"Stia attènda.* Be careful. Go quickly and leave no trail. Do not come back here." A pause, then his voice lowered to a passionate timbre. "I will miss you."

And with a soft cry, Nicole flung her arms about his neck, hugging tight. She felt Gerard recoil, but she hung on to him and whispered, "Thank you for all you've done. You've been a most patient teacher. I shall never forget."

Gradually, Gerard overcame his reluctance and his hand rose to stroke her hair. *"Va bène.* Remember me to your father." He kissed her cheek. "And your mother." His mouth commanded hers for a long, languorous moment.

"Nicole," Marchand called with a cold hint of impatient jealousy. He tugged at her arm, pulling her back from the handsome Italian's embrace. Gerard responded with a mocking bow and a razor-sharp warning.

"You take care of her."

"Marchand!" Nicole was nearly running to keep up with his long strides as he walked briskly toward the bridge where Gerard had saved his life the night before. He wouldn't look at her, nor would he slow as she hung determinedly onto his arm. "Marchand, he is not my lover. You are!"

His hurried pace broke and she was able to put herself in front of him, forcing him to stop. She cupped his face in her palms and told him earnestly, "I love you. How could you doubt that?"

He took an unsteady breath and exhaled hard with the strength of his rage. It wasn't anger directed at her. "I know you do and I don't doubt it. How can I like the fact that he can give you the help you need and I can only bring you trouble?"

"March," she crooned tenderly. "What you've given me, he could never, ever provide." She leaned into him, rubbing against the hard masculine plane of him. "Gerard was my father's best friend. He's doing this for me out of loyalty to him."

Marchand made a disagreeable noise. "*Cher,* you expect me to believe that? Why, I am older than he is! Did your father befriend him in the cradle?"

"He's older than he looks." She murmured that understatement with a somber face. "Please, can we forget Gerard? We must hurry."

She pulled on both his hands beseechingly and finally he gave in with a resigned nod. Her effervescent smile was reward enough for his concession.

They had crossed the Seine and were winding through the Latin Quarter when Marchand came to an abrupt stop, his attention fixed upon a seedy café, outside of which tables brimmed with patrons drinking *vin ordinaire* and whispering revolution. At one of those tables sat Fredcric LaValois.

Seeing his expression change from the blank of shock to a hot fury, Nicole caught at his arm.

"Marchand—"

He pulled free, unwilling to hear anything she could say in his brother's defense.

Frederic looked up from his glass of wine and froze to see Marchand closing upon him. At his side, Musette clutched his arm, afraid of the confrontation to come.

"March—"

"Get up! Walk away from this nest of traitorous vipers. We're leaving Paris. Now!"

Frederic's features were very calm as he announced,

"I can't go with you, Marchand. I have work to finish here."

Marchand pointed a finger at the indolently lounging Sebastien De Sivry. "Ask him what work he'll be finishing if I let him have his way. Work he sent Gaston to do for him last night."

Frederic glanced at him and De Sivry shrugged in pretended ignorance. It was then Marchand lost all patience. He gripped his brother by the lapels and began to haul him up off his chair.

"We're leaving now."

"No!" Frederic jerked free and restated firmly, "I have things to finish, Marchand."

And Marchand understood with crystal clarity how his brother had deceived him. "And I'm finished with your lies." He snatched up the glass from the table and dashed its contents into Frederic's face before stalking off, shoving his way through the crowd of young bohemians who muttered at his rudeness.

Frederic took out his handkerchief and began to wipe away the wine. His manner was still composed though his eyes betrayed his upset.

"Go after him, Frederic," Nicole urged.

"I can't, Nicole. This time we've gone too far in our own separate ways."

She knelt down beside him in desperate entreaty. "But Frederic, we're leaving the city tonight. Do you want your last words with your brother to be those of anger?" She pressed his hand. "Please. Neither of you will ever forgive yourselves if you don't at least try to make amends."

Frederic stood and addressed his companions. "I'll be right back."

"Frederic, let him go."

"No, Sebastien. He is my brother and I have wronged him. I owe him an explanation at least. Order more wine. On me." That won an agreeable murmur. He gave Musette a quick kiss. "Wait for me, love."

As they hurried after Marchand, Nicole asked tersely, "Was that Sebastien De Sivry?"

Frederic wouldn't meet her glare. "Yes."

"Then Marchand isn't the only one you've played for a fool."

"Nicole, you must try to understand. What we are doing is what's best for France! Marchand accuses me of having no love for my country. That isn't true. My heart breaks for the turmoil in this city. I'm doing what I can to assure a better future for us and for our children."

"And De Sivry has a plan that will do that?"

"You sound so skeptical. Sebastien is not the best of men, true, but he has the means and the contacts to see the deed done. All I need is the money to prove we are sincere."

"Don't you care that the man you partner with ordered your brother killed?"

"Sebastien? No! Why do you say such a thing?"

"Marchand told me."

"Perhaps that is what he believes, but I do not. Sebastien would not jeopardize our alliance that way. Marchand has many enemies in the *Quartier*. He is outspoken in his views and they are not exactly popular. If his life is in danger, then by all means he should not tarry in Paris any longer."

"And if I can get you all the money you need, would you and Musette leave with us? I have a friend, Bianca du Maurier, who has expressed interest in your cause. You could introduce her to De Sivry and she could fund his revolution."

"That is good news, Nicole. But I couldn't leave. I want to be here to see it done before the July Monarchy reconciles with the old regime and all goes back to chaos."

"Frederic—"

"No, Nicole. My mind is made up. I want to see things through."

"You are both so stubborn!"

"But isn't that what you find so irresistible about us?"

And she couldn't resist his smile, for he was right.

About that time, they'd begun to climb the narrow steps to their flat. The light was on, so they knew Marchand had returned. But it was clear to them from the scuffle of sound above that he was not alone.

Nicole bounded up the last few stairs and burst through the doorway, careless in her anxiety. There, she saw Marchand stretched out upon the floor, unconscious, and a man bending over him ready to plunge a knife into his throat.

Chapter Fourteen

Without thought or hesitation, Nicole flung herself at the first assailant with a speed too rapid for him to comprehend. She grabbed the hand holding the knife, crushing fragile bones with a single wrench. Before he knew what had him, she tossed him bodily out the door, past an astonished Frederic and over the rail to the cobbles below. She was upon the other two who stood dumbfounded, seizing the closest and breaking his neck with a twist, then turning to the other with a savage snarl. He screamed in terror at the demon confronting him and ran, colliding briefly with Frederic before tumbling down the stairs. Battered but better off than his two associates, he stumbled up and fled at an awkward limp into the darkness.

Only then did Nicole realize what she'd done. She'd exposed what she was to four others. Two would never tell what they had seen. One would never find anyone to believe his ranting tale. And Frederic LaValois stood too stunned to know what to believe as the creature who had moments before set upon three thugs and had defeated them with an inhuman strength and a display of sharp white fangs and blood-red eyes became again, Nicole, who bent over worriedly at his brother's side.

"Marchand! Marchand!" She was stroking his cheek, cradling his limp hands. A nasty contusion was starting to swell at his temple. Her face was streaked with tears when she lifted it in anguish. "Help me move him to his bed. He's unconscious. Frederic! Help me!"

Numbly, Frederic did as she requested, but once Marchand was lying immobile upon the sheets, his thoughts lost their paralysis.

"My God! What happened to you? What kind of . . . creature are you?"

Nicole fought the overwhelming urge to come apart beneath his terrified scrutiny. Instead, she answered calmly, "I am the woman who loves your brother enough to do anything necessary to save his life. And what are you, sir, who claim to love him yet associate with his would-be murderers?"

That question shocked through his stupor. "You have no proof that these were De Sivry's men. Perhaps the motive was robbery."

"And what would they steal here?" She made a move and Frederic shrank back. Quietly, she said, "I won't hurt you. You've nothing to fear from me."

"I—I don't understand. Am I going mad?"

"I wish the explanation was that simple. Do you trust me, Frederic? Do you believe that I love Marchand?"

"Y-yes." But his gaze was wary.

"What I am is the victim of a cruel, inherited . . . *affliction*. It grants me my strength and allows me to alter my appearance into the fearsome beast you observed. Please accept that and ask no more."

But Frederic wasn't satisfied. Nor was he frightened. He sat beside Nicole at his brother's side and studied her curiously. "But what kind of beast is it that moves so fast it appears invisible?"

"An unnatural one. A creature of the night."

"And your strength. *Mon Dieu,* it's like that of at least ten men. To have power such as this ... Are you the only one or are there others?"

"There are others. The two I lived with in the Place Vendôme, Bianca and Gerard, they are as I am." Then she realized what she'd said; the sacred vow of secrecy that she'd broken with her careless admission. "Frederic, you won't say anything, will you?"

"Marchand told me you had moved there. That mansion, I have seen it. But what of your nature— Marchand does not know?"

"He suspects something is not right, but how could he ever conceive of such a horror?"

But the philosophical Frederic asked, "Is it a horror or a gift? You've harmed no one who did not deserve it. Weren't you afraid you'd come to harm at their hands?"

"With this gift or curse comes the promise of eternity."

"Eternity ... Do you mean immortality?" And a feverish light burned in his gaze as he mused aloud. "Just think of what a difference one could make, living for so long. And what such power could do to aid our revolution."

Nicole grew frightened by his excitement. "Yes, good could come from such strengths, but also evil. Power corrupts, Frederic. It is dangerous, and this gift, as you call it, is not so easily controlled."

"How does one—obtain this gift?"

"You must be mad! It's not something you court. It's something you hope to escape. Believe me, you would not want this particular blessing. Put such thoughts out of your head."

But Frederic was only pretending to listen to her arguments. His mind had seized upon the fantastic, the impossible. But oh, the benefits! If by going beyond the boundaries of humanity, he could help to save it . . . Nicole was like Marchand, worrying too much, giving him no credit for the strength of his convictions. If such incredible power fell to him, he would not be tempted. He'd have the nobleness of his cause to direct him. And think of what he could accomplish!

Marchand gave a soft groan and shifted upon his pallet. Nicole's attention left Frederic to concentrate upon him. But the younger LaValois had made his decision. He stood.

"Take care of him, Nicole."

"Where are you going?" Her gaze darted up, wide with anxiousness and accountability; for it was her words that fired him with this dangerous passion.

"To further the cause of freedom. I will meet with these friends of yours and ask what they are willing to do for our revolution."

"Not you! You must stay away from them. I never intended for it to be you!"

"Who better? This is my hour of glory, Nicole, and I have you to thank for showing me the way."

"No—"

"On this night, the tide will turn in our favor. I only wish Marchand understood and could share in my victory. Tell him how sorry I am to leave him like this, but you must get him to safety outside the city. Ask him to at least forgive me, if he can. If he can't, tell him I learned my strength from him. Tell him I love him and Godspeed. And to you, Nicole."

"But Frederic, Bianca and Gerard are not like me. They have no great love for humanity. They are . . . deadly."

But before she could conclude that phrase in warning, Frederic LaValois was gone.

Bianca du Maurier lounged back upon her chaise, all sensuous grace, a smile curving her seductive mouth as she listened to her unexpected guests. Nicole's friends. An odd lot she chose to associate with. But a very lively bunch, indeed. Passionate. She liked passion. The one talking with such amusing animation was Nicole's pretty lover's brother. She'd already forgotten his name. The one watching through shrewd, greedy eyes was the one to deal with. The other; a weasel, an inconsequential. And there was a young woman, the lover of the poetic orator. Gerard had his eye on the pretty redhead from where he lingered, a motionless sentinel, beside her chaise. Even though his complexion was already ruddy and his pale eyes were still slightly dreamy from having so recently fed, there was the edge of predatory attentiveness in the way he watched her. Gerard; her insatiable lover, the only one she knew as coldly lethal, as amoral as herself. He enjoyed these cat-and-mouse games almost as much as he relished their conclusion.

Bianca continued to smile and listen, secretly entertained by the speaker's professions of love for mankind. Oh, she knew about love. She'd known a love so strong it survived centuries. A love that kept her seated as these fools talked on and on about unimportant things; human things, while her mind spun craftily ahead thinking of how she could use them to her benefit.

And it was to her benefit to find a way to remind her

negligent love that she still remembered how he'd spurned her in his taking of a mortal bride upon whom he'd made an unnatural child.

Some nights she couldn't remember what drove her; her love or her hatred of Luigino Rodmini.

Musette was trying to listen to Frederic. He was in rare form, espousing his view with a fine, vibrant clarity. Who could resist him when he poured so much heart and soul and faith into each word? Usually she was caught up in his fervor, like the newly baptized absorbing the text of a fiery preacher. But tonight, she couldn't shake the chill inside her.

It was this odd pair Frederic called friends of Nicole's. They didn't look like they'd be friends of Nicole's. They looked—unnatural. The woman was pale as moonlight and just as distant and cool. She appeared to be hanging upon every word, but there was the slightest curl—was it of contempt?—to her lips, and the black eyes fixed upon Frederic were empty. Dead eyes. Nonreflective, nonexpressive, flat black eyes. And the man, he was pleasant enough to look upon but he had that same mocking detachment to him, as if he was highly amused at their expense. And the way he looked at her . . . It wasn't just looking, it was consuming, his gaze all cold, icy fire. Like he was ready to reach inside to snatch out her soul.

If it had been just her and Frederic, she would have urged him to leave and he would have listened. But he wouldn't back down, not in front of De Sivry and his sycophant, Gaston, just because she felt uncomfortable around those they hoped would become their benefactors. Too much was at stake to heed one uneasy female's intuition. They might never again have access to such wealthy patrons. So she stayed silent and kept her increasing sense of panic to herself.

Finally, the inner tension grew to be too much. She had to escape the piercing scrutiny else lose all composure. She murmured meekly about needing to refresh herself. It took all her courage to hold back from a run as she left the room with the feel of those iridescent eyes upon her.

Once away from them, Musette felt the roil of distress settle in her belly. She hurried along the marble floor, her footsteps making a nervous patter. What would help her even more than a moment's absence was a good glass of wine, she thought, catching sight of the dining room as she traversed the Egyptian-styled hall. Maybe after several glasses she wouldn't find the twosome quite so disturbing.

She ducked into the dining room, sure her hosts wouldn't miss a glass or two of the good-quality Burgundy she spotted shimmering lustrously in a cut-glass decanter upon the sideboard.

Except when she came further into the room, she saw with a horrifying certainty that it wasn't wine at all.

It was blood.

Blood from the two women seated at the table, their bodies withered white shells drained of all vitality. One had slumped forward, as if resting her head upon her arms. But she wasn't resting. Her eyes were wide open and staring like vacant blue marbles. A gash had been cut around her throat, shining there like a virulent ruby-colored ribbon. The other woman was still sitting upright, her blond head tilted to one side like that of a heavy sunflower on too weak a stem. Her shriveled forearm rested on the table, where crimson stained the white linen.

A scream choked up in Musette's throat, the sound suffocating within the bitter rise of bile. Their hosts had killed these women and now were nonchalantly entertaining guests while the bodies grew ever colder!

De Sivry or no, she was getting Frederic out of there if she had to drag him. She wouldn't waste time with explanations.

Who would believe her?

But before she could take more than two steps down the hall, a terrible cry sounded from the parlor up ahead.

Frederic!

The noise wavered, gurgled and came to an abrupt end. And so, she guessed had Frederic's life.

With hands clapped over her mouth to retain her shrieks, Musette fled the elegant house, running like a madwoman along the dark Paris streets. She had only one thought in her frantic mind. She had to reach Marchand to tell him his brother was dead.

In the end, Bianca simply grew bored. She preferred action to oration, and though the young man was a competent speaker, she got tired of listening to how her money would go to the betterment of mankind.

What did she care about mankind?

She'd planned to wait until the woman returned, but she had no real interest in the female. It was the speaker who mattered, and the clever one, De Sivry.

The young man had come close while lost to the passion of his debate. His features were attractively flushed and she could feel the acceleration of his heartbeat as enthusiasm picked up its tempo. A delightful rhythm. Then she caught some of what he was saying.

"—power. That is the most important thing. Whoever holds that power, holds France. It's not just a matter of money. Tonight Nicole told me something I did not believe at first, a tale about an eternity of strength and youth. Consider what that would do to further our cause! If only there was some way to obtain that power and harness it."

"And if there were a way, would you be willing to embrace it?" she purred softly.

"Oh, yes."

"Then open your arms wide and you shall embrace it as my slave."

And she was upon him, her teeth sinking into his neck even as he flailed and struggled to get free, even as the light was draining from his eyes as fast as the blood was being emptied from his body.

Gerard crossed twenty feet in what seemed to be two steps. He gripped the stunned Gaston by the pointed chin and wrenched his head about one hundred and eighty degrees. He never made a sound. Then Gerard, too, tapped an artery and drank.

De Sivry sat paralyzed with shock. Finally he made a move to rise and Bianca bellowed, "Sit!" One look at the blood-streaked face and he sat.

It took an obscenely short time to deplete the body of its fluids. Once it was done, Gerard collapsed back upon one of the low stools, his head lolling laxly as if he were intoxicated. Bianca fastidiously wiped her face and hands upon Frederic's handkerchief, then she confronted the paralyzed De Sivry with an almost friendly smile.

"Now you and I are going to do business. If you think twice about betraying me, it will be your corpse upon the floor. Do you understand?"

He nodded dumbly.

"Good. I am quite interested in this power of which your companion spoke so eloquently. I care nothing for politics, but the position to rule is intriguing. I think I might like having my own country. Would you care to rule France with me, Sebastien, or would you rather serve in hell like your friends?"

"What do you want me to do?" came his weak question. Already his fear was falling away before greed and self-preservation.

"Tell me more about your plan to kill this king. Who will assume his place and how might I sit as the power behind the throne?" And this time she listened intently, nodding, questioning, scheming. She and the nasty De Sivry would do quite well together. "Return here tomorrow night and I will have the funds you need at your disposal. Cross me and you die. Is that understood?"

"Y-yes."

"Go away. We need to make arrangements for our new friends." She gestured to the bodies upon the floor. "Don't be surprised if you see them tomorrow night, as well." She smiled a slow, wicked smile and De Sivry, who feared nothing, quaked in his chair. Then he fled like the vermin he was into the underworld to see to her bidding. To his thinking, she might be unnatural, but by God, she knew how to wield power. And he wanted to be standing nearby to enjoy the benefits of that power.

"Bianca, *mía amóra,* what are you thinking?" Gerard asked in a slightly slurred voice. "Why do you involve yourself with these creatures? What can they do for us?"

"Fool, they can give me everything I desire."

"You already have that."

"Not quite all."

He regarded her for some time in silent suspicion, then said, "Nicole is gone."

"What?" She whirled upon him in a fury. "What do you mean, gone?"

"She and her lover have run away."

"Is this your doing?" she ranted. "It is, isn't it? All your fine talk about her father. Her father! I will have him, Gerardo. I will! And she is my avenue. How could you let her get away?" She began to pace ferociously, then a cunning look replaced her aggravation. "She will be back. When that silly female finds them, he will come for his brother and I will have them both. And I will have Gino. Then I will have everything."

"And what of Nicole?" Gerard asked smoothly.

Bianca gave him a haughty sneer. "I will get rid of her, of course. She is of no use to me. I believe I promised you that particular pleasure, didn't I? You still want it, don't you?" And she stared at him closely.

Gerard slanted a glance up at her, his eyes all cold, hard brilliance. The eyes of a ruthless killer. "Yes, of course."

"And I will enjoy disposing of her meddlesome mother."

Arabella Radman slept uneasily. Her dreams were dark and troubled, a reflection of her daily reality since they'd learned about Nicole. Everything had changed with that news. She blamed herself, and though she swore it wasn't true, her husband stayed away, certain she felt him the cause behind her misery. Bearing the brunt of grief alone had become the worst possible torment.

It was the cushioning pressure of his mouth moving

upon hers that woke her. A slow, languorous kiss that stirred an immediate and welcoming response and on this very lonely night, a relieved one. Her arms came up to embrace him. His coat was cold, still holding the chill of the night within its fibers, but she found him warm as her fingers messaged his nape and moved up to mesh in his hair, spreading wide to cup the back of his head.

It was then she realized that this man who was claiming her lips with such passion was not her husband.

Her eyes flew open to confront those of luminous blue.

"*Buòna séra, mía ragázza,*" he murmured with loverlike intimacy. When she lay frozen and speechless, he crooned, "What? You are not glad to see me? I would have thought so from your greeting."

Arabella found her voice. "Louis will be here at any moment."

"I do not think so, *mía bèlla.* I waited until he went out to hunt. We have some time to be alone, you and I. We could continue with our reunion." With that husky suggestion, he bent to seek her lips once more, but she turned her head and began to push up against his shoulders. His cheek rubbed against hers as he whispered into her ear. "I could make you want to."

Knowing he could, she went very still. "Don't."

She felt his sigh, then her own relief as he lifted up and stretched out with a comfortable laziness upon his side next to her in her bed. She'd forgotten how breathtakingly beautiful he was with his dark Italian features and startling blue eyes. So unchanged, so smooth and eternally young. And she realized how she must look to him. She began to turn away when his fingertips curled beneath her jaw, angling her back to face him. She felt the caress of his mind flirting with hers, picking up thoughts she would prefer to hide.

"Age has treated you with the adoration due a fine wine," he crooned. "The years have only made you more beautiful."

Refusing to admit how touched she was by his flattering words, Arabella demanded, "What do you want, Gerardo? Why are you here?"

"I've come to see you, Bella. Do you find that so hard to believe?" But his grin was teasing and she couldn't judge his sincerity.

"How did you find us?" And that question was tinged with fear.

"I've always known where you were. All I had to do was reach out for you, here." His fingertips rubbed her temple. "As you could have done with me. But you never did, *cara*. I am wounded by your indifference." Still the playful smile and mocking tone, but his gaze was oddly quiet.

"What about Bianca?" she asked tautly.

"She is—the same. Entertaining, beautiful, dangerous."

"Why isn't she here?"

"Because, *innamoráta*, I don't tell her everything."

It was then that Arabella relaxed.

The door to the bedroom chamber burst open and Arabella was quick to grab onto Gerard as he rolled with a mercurial shift into a defensive pose. He and the Asian in the doorway regarded each other for a long, tense moment.

"Takeo, it's all right," Arabella called as she was trying to distract Gerard from his readiness to attack. "Signor Pasquale is a friend of Louis's."

Takeo's look cast doubt upon her assertion but he

didn't move. Instead, he used his telepathic link to Arabella to ask, *Shall I get Master Louis for you?*

No, it's all right. Really. Signor Pasquale and I have things to discuss.

Gerard was glancing between them, picking up the signals but unable to translate them.

"You may go, Takeo. I'll be fine. Gerardo is not going to hurt me." The Asian bowed and withdrew obediently, closing the door in his wake. Then Arabella asked her unexpected guest, "Are you?"

"No."

She believed him.

"Gino's servant, he talks to you through the mind."

"Through our link with Louis. Takeo can't speak."

"Will he run to Gino and tell him you have taken a lover?" He settled back down upon his elbow, looking arrogantly pleased by the awkwardness of the situation he'd placed her in.

"Takeo will say nothing until he hears my explanation."

"How loyal."

"Don't mock what you don't understand."

He laughed in delight. "Still prickly as ever. You have lost none of your spark, I see. Oh, how I have missed you, *cara*. Say you will leave Gino and run away with me." He tucked her hand up against his heart in a dramatic pose while he grinned irreverently and his pale eyes gleamed with intense fire.

Calmly, she withdrew her hand. "And you have lost none of your conceit. Why are you here, Gerardo?"

He chose to ignore the question. He let his thumb stroke over the curve of her cheek in a surprisingly tender gesture. "There were dried tears upon your face.

Why were you weeping, Bella? Has Gino made you un-happy?"

"No. It's—it's something else."

"Tell me, *cara*. I cannot bear to think of you in pain."

She looked up at him, startled by the passionate words. But his expression was bland and unreadable as if no emotion registered. She wondered which was the illusion and which the reality.

"We've recently lost our daughter."

"Nicole."

She blinked, amazed that he should know her name. But then again, nothing about him should have taken her by surprise. "Yes, Nicole. All our efforts to keep her safe failed. She died in Paris. There was nothing we could do. Takeo brought home the locket she'd been wearing after she'd been buried in a pauper's grave. Apparently, she inherited my mortality." And Arabella turned away, her eyes squeezed shut to conceal her grief, to retain fresh tears.

"Bella, you weep foolish tears."

She looked back at him, her glare wet and furious. "Don't scorn my sorrow, you unfeeling—"

His hand covered her mouth, halting the words. "I understand sorrow. I know the feeling well. But you needn't grieve for Nicole. Not yet. That's what I've come to tell you." And while Arabella stared at him, bewildered, he added, "She is very much Gino's daughter."

Arabella's breath gusted against his fingertips in a desperate rush of hope. "She's alive."

"Alive and in love, but very confused."

"She's alive!"

In her exuberance, Arabella flung her arms about him, heedless of the way he gasped and stiffened at the sudden contact, and she hugged hard, the outpouring of her relief dampening his shoulder. He never made a move until it was to pry her away. His words came gruffly. "All is not well, signora. She is in danger. She's been misled into trusting those she should not. She needs to be here with family, where she can be protected."

The word *danger* brought Arabella back into a cool control. "Do you know where she is? Can you bring her here?"

"Yes . . . and no."

"Why not? Who is threatening her?"

"Shhh!" His thumb slid along the part of her lips. "I cannot tell you everything, either."

She gave him a cautious scrutiny. "If this is some trick, Gerardo—"

"The danger is very real. You must not tarry. I have written two addresses. Send Gino's man and he will find her at one of them. Bring her here by the light of day and then be watchful. I must go. I can't let daylight catch me this far from home."

"Stay," Arabella suggested suddenly. He stared at her through eyes as blue as tranquil ponds. "Leave her, Gerardo. She doesn't care for you."

"Do you, *cara?* Do you care for me?"

"Yes," came her guileless reply. Then she leaned forward and gently kissed his warm cheek. His eyes sank shut and stayed closed even after she moved away. Finally, he exhaled in a sighing whisper and seemed to return quickly to his old mocking self.

"Ah, no, Bella. Bianca and I, we deserve each other. I was not a good man in life, some three hundred years ago. I was vain and foolish, proud and greedy. I brought about my own fall, and the fall of those I loved, and I have not changed in all those years. Eternity has taught me nothing except that I cannot be other than I am. But I thank you for the thought. It is enough." And he stood, his movements a fluid flow. Arabella came up onto her knees.

"Gerardo?"

"*Sì?*"

"Take care."

He sketched a theatrical bow. "And you, *mía ragázza.*"

"Are you sure you can't wait until Louis returns? He would want to see you."

A wry smile touched his lips. "I think not. Not in his wife's bedroom. *Buòna nòtte. Il piacére è státo mío.*"

"No," she disagreed. "The pleasure was mine. Gerardo, if you were not a good man, why did you do this?"

His gaze lowered as he said, "For Gino. Because I loved him."

And then his eyes slowly lifted and she saw another answer in them.

For you.

Chapter Fifteen

Dark eyes flickered open and Nicole was forced to make a soul-wrenching decision. What was she going to tell him? The truth? That she'd sent his brother to make a deal with a demon? That she, herself, was the same kind of monster? He wouldn't believe her.

And if he did, she would lose him.

If he thought Frederic was in danger, he would rush to his aid without hesitation or prudence. And he would die.

Or, she could say nothing and spirit him out of the city to safety. She could continue the pretense as long as possible, and hopefully, by the time it grew necessary to tell him as much of the truth as he could comprehend, he'd be so much in love with her he would never leave.

Or she could take him down, drink him dry and have him forever without fear.

"Nicole?"

"How do you feel, Marchand?" She bent close and blotted a dampened cloth across his brow.

"As if all that exists above my shoulders is a big block of stone that someone is determined to split in two with an even bigger hammer." His gaze sharpened and drifted about, gathering focus. "Someone must have been waiting here inside. I was taken by surprise and—" He broke off and hauled himself up into a sitting position. The effort brought on a dramatic pallor and left him weaving.

"It's all right," Nicole soothed, bracing him with the wrap of her arms about his middle. "Whoever was here was frightened off by my return."

He was disoriented enough to accept her word, and for that she was grateful. While he was unconscious, she'd taken the bodies to an alley off a far-removed street. No connection would ever be made to this flat. Unless someone believed the babbling of the one who escaped her. And no one would, she was sure. Marchand need never know. He let his head sink down upon her shoulder and draped his arm over the other. "My brave Nicole. Are you never cautious?"

"Not when those I love are concerned." And she closed her eyes, holding him tight, absorbing the essence of his strength and vulnerability. How could she face an uncertain future without him? Yet she knew she had to do what was right. She had to tell him. She had to trust him.

He straightened with a weary sigh. "Come. Let's gather our things and go. There's nothing here for either of us any more."

If she said nothing, they'd be at her parents' home by dawn.

"Marchand . . . about Frederic."

"No, Nicole. Say nothing, please. I must let go and now is the time. Frederic must make his own decisions about his life. I regret the way I acted at the café. I'm sorry if I embarrassed you. I was taken by surprise and

I behaved badly, but that's over with. I have my own life to get on to. That life is with you."

"Marchand—"

He cut her words off with a kiss, a deep, descriptive kiss that promised everything she could ever dream of in terms of passion. It weakened her moral resistance and had her selfishly guarding her own tomorrows.

"I love you, Nicole," he murmured as he pulled away. "Now, what was it you were about to say?"

What could she say as he gazed down into her eyes, as his hand stroked tenderly through her hair? He was so handsome, so human in his failings, so honorable in his intentions.

"Oh, March, I—"

The broken clatter of footfalls on the outside steps interrupted. Musette burst through the door. She was gulping for breath through horrible, dry sobs. Her face was etched in stark lines of terror.

"Musette, what's wrong?" Marchand cried as he went to catch her in midswoon. Her fingers snagged his shirt-front, dragging him down close to her.

"They're murderers and they have F-Frederic!"

"What are you talking about? Who? Who has Frederic?"

"That vile couple, the ones Nicole sent us to."

And Marchand looked up, his dark eyes pinning Nicole's. "What is she talking about?"

Courage failed before the accusation in his eyes. Nicole stammered, "I didn't mean for him to go, Marchand. He wasn't supposed to go."

"Where? Go where?"

"To Bianca and Gerard."

Fright settled dark and inexplicable within him. "Why? Why would Frederic go there?"

"To obtain funding for some scheme of theirs. Bianca expressed an interest in causes. I tried to help but I couldn't get enough money together and then they hurt you, Marchand. I wanted to get you both free. I thought if De Sivry was given enough money, he'd let Frederic go, but Frederic—"

"Didn't want to leave," Marchand concluded bitterly. "So you have been involved in this deception all along." He said that with a cold finality, and Nicole saw the hope of her tomorrows extinguished like a snuffed flame.

"Marchand, it was for you, for us."

But he wouldn't listen. He turned his attention back to Musette, who had recovered her wind sufficiently to speak. The terror in her expression alarmed Marchand, as did the fact that she would leave Frederic to come to him. It must have been something terrible to drive her to take flight.

"Musette, can you tell me what happened?"

The gentle strength in his voice gave her the confidence to tell all. Still weeping, she related what she'd seen; the oddness of the two killers, the brazenness of their crime, the two women slaughtered and left in macabre poses as if sitting to a feast. Frederic's awful cries.

"I ran, Marchand. I was so afraid. I was too much a coward to go to him. After what I saw . . . after what they did . . . I just couldn't."

"It's all right, Musette," he soothed as his gaze grew troubled. "You say De Sivry and Gaston were with him."

Her head nodded jerkily.

"Well, they won't be easily taken by surprise." Yet he was thinking of the sleek Gerard coming to him through the parting mists, his clothes not even soiled after killing four would-be assassins. And he wasn't so sure. "You stay here, Musette. I'll go after Frederic."

"No!" That cry tore from Nicole. When he glanced up, she rushed on to say, "March, you can't. You don't know what they are, what they're capable of. It wasn't just the money Frederic was interested in. It was their power. It's too late to save him. You must save yourself. We can still leave the city—"

He shoved her pleading hands away in disgust. "You'd have me abandon my brother to go with you? I cannot believe how badly I misjudged you. You think I would run away?"

"Please," she moaned softly. "I don't want you to die."

"So I should sacrifice Frederic? Is that it?" He set Musette aside so he could stand. Then he went about gathering up his armaments.

Nicole watched him with a mounting dread. "You haven't a chance against them," she mumbled in weak despair. "Marchand, you don't know what they are. You don't know what I am. They are demons."

He whirled to face her, his expression cold. "What you are, mademoiselle, is untrustworthy. You tell me lies, then expect me to believe this, this fairytale."

"You know I'm not lying."

Her levelly spoken words didn't persuade him. "It doesn't matter if you are or if you aren't." He checked the charges for his pistol and buckled his sabre at his waist. He looked competent, dangerous. He looked vulnerably human.

"Your weapons won't do any good against them," she said.

"Next, I suppose you'll be telling me they're some sort of gods."

Nicole didn't blink at his sarcasm. "They are."

His smile was searing. "And that makes you a god, too. You forget I know better."

"Yes, you do know better," she answered quietly. He paused, his gaze locked with hers, and she continued. "You know I'm different. Why won't you listen to me?"

Though he didn't reply, she saw her answer flickering through his eyes. Panic. He was desperately afraid that she was telling him the truth. That his brother was in dreadful danger. That there were such things as demons. That she wasn't what he wanted her to be; a soft, beautiful woman with whom he could spend the rest of his days. But that uncertainty couldn't hold against a lifetime of learned discipline. His training told him to rely on nothing but logic. It taught him to set an established course of action to obtain his goal and to ignore such distractions as instinct and superstition. He was a man of linear direction and he simply could not accept what she was saying.

So he turned away, shut her out, and with her, the confusions of what she told him. "I'll bring him back, Musette," he promised the softly sobbing woman. And he started for the door.

"Marchand!" Nicole caught his arm, pulling him back, but even as she did, she knew she'd lost him. His face was set with purpose, his dark eyes hardened to her pleas. And she saw only one chance to save him. "I'll go with you."

"No." She was so surprised by his objection, she let him push her away. "You go home. You go back to where you belong, away from me and my family. You've stirred up nothing but trouble since I took you in. You've lied and schemed your way into our lives. You've lured me and my brother from the paths we'd chosen, sucking us up into whatever perversions go on in that house in the Place Vendome. Your presence here has seen both Camille and Bebe to their deaths, and I will not lose my brother to whatever darkness moves you. I won't. Had you thought by getting rid of all of them, you would have me to yourself? Is that what this has all been about?"

She was so shocked by his assumptions, she couldn't think of a way to refute them.

"Be gone by the time I get back."

With that, he strode through the doorway and his footsteps pounded down the stairs. And Nicole stood in helpless dismay, knowing he was going to die and that there was no way to prevent it. In desperation, she closed her eyes and concentrated.

Gerard, help me!

And faintly, as if from a long distance away, came his reply.

I'm sorry, cara. I've done all I can.

The air was cold. His breath made frosty plumes upon it. The heels of his boots made a loud resounding echo as he walked down the cavernous hall. The only interior light was moonlight and it streamed down the marble tiles like a silvery runner. As he turned into the antechamber where all those bestial snarls were frozen for eternity, he didn't like the image his mind created; the similarity to a tomb. It wouldn't be his if he could help it.

And he prayed it wasn't already his brother's.

One of the things his military schooling had taught him was how to disassociate fear from his actions. He could make his mind obey regardless of the sense of

threat around him. But he had no control over the way
the hairs at his nape quivered or the way his breathing
increased to a light, fast tempo to match the cautious
quickening of his heart. He knew the feel of death and
it was thick in these cold, quiet rooms. Even so, he
moved boldly through the network of shadows. His
voice rang out clear and steady.

"Frederic?"

It sounded like the hiss of steam escaping, that soft,
whispering reply.

"Marchand."

He stopped. His gaze scanned the dark reaches of the
chamber and the opening that led to rooms beyond.
And as he watched, he efficiently primed his pistol, then
drew his sabre from its sheath.

"Marchand, *mon ami*, how good to see you again."

Marchand turned toward the source of that wet, sib-
ilant noise, bringing up the bore of his pistol. "Who's
there?"

"You don't know my voice?"

"Camille?"

Because he was a soldier who employed reason over
emotion, Marchand's astonishment was manifested only
in his surprised tone. He was a creature of logic, and
logic told him Camille was dead. He held his pistol
steady.

"Come to me, Marchand, and we shall embrace once
more as friends."

There was a beckoning cadence to the words, and
Marchand had to struggle against the pull. He set his
feet in a wide stance as if readying to stand firm in his
resistance. He honed his aim on the dark shape of a
man, lingering in indistinguishable shadow.

"Come forward into the light, Camille, so that I might greet you properly."

His coaxing brought the figure closer. The first thing that struck Marchand was the stench. It was hard not to reel back from the odorous wave of sickly sweet putrefying flesh and stale blood. Marchand locked his knees, refusing to waver.

"That's it. Come closer so I can see you, old friend."

Scuffed and muddied boots poked into the pool of moonlight that edged up soiled trousers and torn jacket, over long, sensitive artist's fingers, now caked with gore instead of oil-base paint. One more step brought him fully into view.

Marchand's breath escaped in a rush. *"Mon Dieu!"* he whispered in distracted horror, but his gun was unfaltering.

Camille Viotti was little more than a rotting corpse held together by tattered garments, leathery strips of skin and exposed sinew. But his eyes gleamed, alive with hunger.

"Camille, you've looked better."

And Marchand fired.

The bullet ripped through Camille's filthy jacket and passed through what was left of his upper chest. His body staggered briefly but didn't fall. Marchand was busy reloading, mentally crossing himself. Just then, a hand clamped down upon his shoulder, fingers pinching so hard his entire arm went numb and his gun fell to the floor. He looked around and gave a small cry.

His first thought was that his brother was dead. The second was that somehow Frederic's body was still obscenely alive.

He acted swiftly before the shock of what he was seeing could settle in. His sword plunged into his brother's belly and abruptly the pressure on his other arm was gone. Marchand stumbled back and watched as Frederic pressed his palm to the wound, then blankly studied the stain upon it. He looked back up and Marchand could see no response to pain, no recognition, no feeling whatsoever. Just that infernal blaze of need. He backed up a few more steps and assumed a defensive *en garde*.

"What are you?" he demanded in a harsh, angry tone of that creature who controlled his brother's remains.

And it was Frederic's voice that answered. "Marchand, we're hungry. Feed us. You've always taken care of us in the past. Feed us now. We need you."

Marchand retreated as the two came closer. They moved with an odd, uncoordinated grace, their movements lumbering yet quick, so quick. From the corner of his eye, he detected the presence of others and he risked a glance behind. There, in another doorway, stood Gaston, his head perched at an unnatural angle upon his shoulders. Behind him were the thugs Gerardo Pasquale had killed at the bridge. He couldn't get past them, so he sought the only other exit and saw it guarded by two beautiful and unholy females. They smiled at him and opened their arms in invitation.

He was going to die.

"M'sieur LaValois, good evening."

He gave a start because the words were spoken right behind him. He whirled upon Bianca du Maurier, swinging his sabre in a deadly arc.

She caught the blade.

He watched her snap it in her hands as if it were made of glass.

"You are impolite for an uninvited guest."

And she struck him. The blow connected with his chin, and the impact sent him sailing across the room. The jarring solidity of the wall broke his flight and he slid to the floor in a daze, the wind knocked from him. He watched the lethal Bianca approach him. She was smiling.

"How brave you are to come alone. And how foolish. What a wonderful companion you would make for me."

"Go to hell," he wheezed with all the defiance he could muster.

Her smile widened and her hand stretched out to him.

"Join me there."

She would not lose him!

That driving conviction broke through the clog of Nicole's misery. If she didn't do something fast, she would never have the chance to win him back. She couldn't let his parting words wound her. She couldn't let his anger shake her confidence. He was hurt and upset. He was afraid. He'd pushed her away because of all those things. He'd said he no longer trusted her, but he'd never claimed to no longer love her.

And he would be dead if she didn't intervene. Bravery and weaponry would not defeat what he'd be facing. His own ignorance of the enemy would be his undoing. If she could get to him in time, she could overpower him and carry him off by force. She was stronger. He might hate her for it, but he'd be alive . . .

Frederic LaValois was beyond needing his help.

She knew it just as surely as she knew her love would be walking into his own doom.

"Musette, we have to leave Paris."

The redhead made a soft moaning sound and refused to stir from where she'd crumpled upon the floor. "I can't leave without Frederic."

"Musette, you know Frederic will not be coming with us, don't you?" She stated that truth as gently as she could and tears welled up anew in the other's eyes. "Marchand will be dead as well if we don't act now. Please. You must help me. He's Frederic's brother. He'd want you to protect him."

A fluttery hand rose to brush the dampness off pale cheeks. In a voice that was strong for all its frailty, Musette asked, "What can I do?"

Nicole embraced her tightly, then sat back, thinking. What could they do? She knew the enemy, but she was no more knowledgeable than Marchand in what it would take to defeat them. She didn't think her own physical and mental skills were developed enough to confront Bianca. And she couldn't count upon Gerard's intervention. But if ignorance was a detriment, hesitation would be fatal.

"We have to hire a rig. Something fast to get us out of the city. Then we have to go after Marchand. If he can survive until dawn, we'll be safe."

Musette didn't pretend to understand what was said to her. She was grateful for the direction. Her own mind was too dazed for clear thought.

"Where can we get horses and a fast carriage?" Nicole asked.

"I-I know a place," Musette stammered. "Let me get my things together."

"Leave them."

"No! Frederic's books, his stories, his words . . . I have to have them."

Seeing there was no swaying her, Nicole nodded and helped her gather all the scattered pages of Frederic LaValois's dreams. With those stuffed into a simple cloth sack, the two women set out to attempt a daring rescue.

It was almost dawn. Nicole could scent it on the last night breeze while the world was yet in shadow. While Musette waited with the nervous driver, Nicole slipped in to the palatial house, where an eerie silence lingered. She didn't call out. She used her senses to reach out, to search. She felt Gerard, but he was already closed away in his daytime hibernation, his thoughts slowed yet guarded, no help at all. Then from one of the rooms, she picked up a definite vibration, one that woke a keen response within her.

A human heartbeat.

She followed that weak inviting pulse, aware at once of her own weakness, of her hunger. She hadn't fed enough. The cup Gerard provided had revived but hadn't satisfied. She found herself tracking down the source of that enticing rhythm like a stalking beast of prey, hungering for the salty warmth of mortal skin and the exquisite taste of life.

She moved like a soundless predator into one of the shadow-drenched rooms, drawn by the frail promise of food, stopped by the sight before her.

Marchand was draped along one of the low benches upon his back. His arms trailed down off either side so that his wrists rested upon cool black marble. His eyes were open. They were as dark and lifeless as those stone tiles.

She was too late.

Chapter Sixteen

"Marchand!"

His name wailed from her, from a grief so deep and desolate it swamped the common sense that told her even now she was hearing his heartbeat. The shock of seeing him there like that was too tremendous to overcome all at once. Until she saw moonlight glitter in his eyes and realized it was a reflection caused by movement. And movement meant life.

She crossed the room in a careless rush, falling to her knees beside the bench and wrapping herself around him. Beneath her damp cheek, a perpetual rhythm throbbed and she spent a long moment worshiping that tempo. Finally, she made herself sit back and take a more realistic look at him. He still seemed to be in some heavy mental fog, unaware of her touch. She eased down the stiff collar of his shirt to scan the unmarked curve of his throat, then performed the same check on either wrist. No puncture marks. She noticed the discoloration on his jaw where a considerable impact must have caught him. Perhaps that was the reason for his daze.

"Marchand," she called in a penetrating whisper as

she lightly slapped his cheeks. Finally his eyes made a slow blink and the cloudy stupor began to lift. "Wake up, my love. We have to get out of here."

He sucked a sudden startled breath as if he'd been shaken from a deep slumber. His arms flew up to ward her off, forming a protective cross over his face. Or was it his neck he was covering?

"Marchand, it's Nicole."

His breathing took on a fast, agitated pattern, a helpless panting that reminded her of the fox she'd snared amid the heather. The sound of a creature expecting an unavoidable death at any second. Her inability to comfort him brought on her own sense of helpless distress. What horror lurked behind the opaque glaze of his eyes? What had he seen when he came in search of demons he didn't believe in? He believed now. Of that she was certain.

She'd bent over him to retrieve one of his limp hands from where it dangled to the floor. One second he was completely unresponsive to his surroundings; the next, he was exploding with motion. The black centers of his eyes enlarged to engulf all color, and with a terrible cry, he seized her and flung her down on the floor beneath him. In that same instant, she saw the broken end of his sabre plunge deep into the bench cushion with a force that would have impaled them both.

Faced with a snarling female ghoul, Nicole shoved Marchand under the bench for safe keeping, then rose up with her own preternatural speed to confront her attacker. She sensed no great intellect in this newly made creature, none of the fluid grace and skill that Bianca and Gerard displayed. But Nicole didn't underestimate the danger. The undead female had incredible strength and the motivating hunger to move the mindless form to violence. She moved away from the bench, trying to draw the creature from Marchand. The ghoul took several uncertain steps, then looked back, lured by the scent of live blood.

"Come on, *chienne,*" Nicole spat. "Come after me. Try making a meal off one who's not defenseless."

The woman turned back, then with an amazing speed had Nicole by the throat, her powerful hands constricting as they struggled. Nicole felt her fangs come down and she let the other see them, hoping she would be intimidated by one of her own kind. She wasn't. She hissed back and throttled all the harder, apparently not caring whom she fed off next, be it vampire heiress or mortal man.

Using all her strength, Nicole struck the other female beneath the breastbone, once, twice, again, until she felt the grip that was darkening her sight relent. Gasping for air, Nicole laced her fingers together to form a double fist and swung them up like she was heaving a length of timber. There was the sound of shattering bone as that blow connected under the woman's chin, flipping her over backward and down to the floor in a motionless crumple. For a moment, Nicole stood *en garde,* rubbing her bruised throat and preparing for another attack. When none came, she bent down for Marchand and gave a cry of surprise when he kicked at her and curled even farther back under the bench.

"Get away from me."

Had that raw and feeble threat come from him?

"Marchand, it's Nicole," she coaxed as she reached for his hand. He struck out again and his hand grazed her cheek. His next words stung worse than the slap.

"Get away! You are one of them!"

"No, Marchand. I'm not one of them. I've come to

take you away from here. To someplace safe. Give me
your hand."

"No!" he growled with the dangerous ferocity of
something cornered and terrified. "I don't believe you.
You lie!"

"Marchand, listen to me. I'm not going to hurt you.
I've come to help you."

"Liar!" And he slapped her hand away. It was like
reaching blindly into a badger hole.

"Marchand, if you truly believed that, why did you
just save me?"

There was a long moment of silence. Then his unsteady hand stretched out to her. With a sigh of relief,
she took it gently in hers and began to draw him out.
Just when she thought she had him, he began to thrash
wildly, pulling back; pulling her with him instead of trying to twist away.

"No. No!"

Then she saw he was staring past her and she turned
to see the female ghoul had regained her feet and had
possession of the broken sabre once again. On her
knees, with Marchand dragging her half underneath the
bench, Nicole wasn't in a position to defend against the
slicing arc of the blade. But abruptly the momentum
stalled and the sword fell from twitching fingers. Nicole
looked up to see the points of a silver throwing star im-
bedded in the creature's forehead just before the ghoul
collapsed. She knew of only two people who used such
a weapon; her father and Takeo, the Oriental servant
who taught him the ancient art of self-defense.

Takeo knelt and clasped his hand to Nicole's shoulder, giving her a half-angry, half-affectionate shake.
Then he beckoned with both hands for her to follow

him. She nodded and said, "Not without Marchand. And Musette. She has a carriage outside."

Takeo gave a sigh of exasperation and nodded tersely. His hand dove beneath the bench, coming out with Marchand's ankle in a firm grip, using it to drag him, scrabbling and kicking, out into the first weak pool of morning light. Marchand rolled onto his back, drawing his fists up into a frantic pose of self-protection. Takeo only stared at him, his delicate brows arched up as if contemptuous of the threat presented.

"It's all right, Marchand," Nicole soothed, rubbing one of his tensed forearms. He flinched away from her, but she pretended not to notice. "Takeo comes from my father. He'll see we get to my home safely. Come on. Musette is outside. She must be frightened to death by now. Come on, Marchand. We have to go now while it's light and they can't follow."

Even as she spoke, the woman's corpse began to smoke upon the floor and finally burst into tiny licks of hot blue flame that totally consumed her. Marchand looked to Nicole in apprehension, as if wondering when she would do the same.

"I'm not like them," she told him quietly.

He continued to stare at her, never blinking.

"Help me with him, Takeo."

Between them, they managed to get Marchand to his feet. He didn't struggle, but he was too weak of body and confused of mind to be much help in their flight. They half dragged him outside to where Musette stood beside a raggedy conveyance. Its driver looked more than a little drunk and more than a trifle impatient with the wait.

"Here now," he bellowed down in disapproval as he watched them haul an insensible figure down the walk.

"I won't be a party to nothing foul." And before they could stop him or explain, he cracked his whip and the horses sped off, leaving Musette spinning, Frederic's jottings clutched to her breast. She looked fearfully to Marchand then behind him, hopefully, searching for another. Not finding him.

Takeo gestured in the air and a second sleek coach pulled up. He opened the door and waved them into the plush interior. As Marchand moved past a tearful Musette, he told her emotionlessly, "Frederic is dead," then he climbed up into the coach. Nicole hurried the weaving woman in behind him, then climbed up herself. Takeo closed the door and thumped upon the roof, putting the vehicle into motion.

"Thank you, Takeo," Nicole sighed, squeezing his hands in hers. He nodded, then glanced curiously at her traveling companions. Musette was huddled against the window, weeping quietly. Marchand sat opposite, his back pressed to the wall of the coach, his legs drawn up until his knees came to his chin. His arms were banded tight about them as if they would provide some sort of barrier between him and Nicole, who shared the same seat. The blank sheen was covering his eyes again, eyes that fixed in wordless horror upon something she couldn't even imagine.

Or then again, maybe she could.

He woke with a start and swiped a trembling hand across his face. His cheeks were feverish and wet. Some dream, he thought, as he tried to quiet his frantic breathing. Then he opened his eyes and the confusion returned.

He was in a luxurious coach heading he knew not

where. Musette was across from him, slumbering fitfully. Next to her was an Asian man he seemed to have a vague recall of seeing once before, also asleep. And at the end of his own seat was Nicole, as beautiful as a Botticelli angel in repose. He started to reach out to her, but something held him back. Something in the repressed darkness of his memory that had his skin crawling and his hair prickling. Something that whispered, *Beware!* He withdrew the gesture and sat in silence, trying to understand what had disturbed him so. His mind was a maddening blank.

He rubbed at an ache in his jaw and was surprised to discover the side of his face was swollen and tender. Someone had struck him. Not someone . . . some*thing*.

He glanced toward Musette and was puzzled by the bundle she held. He could see some sheafs of writing paper protruding. He recognized his brother's angular scribblings. He couldn't seem to pull his attention away from those pages and he wondered why. Why did Musette have Frederic's notes? And just where was—

The knowledge swarmed up so swift and sharp he couldn't help but cry out softly from the pain of it. He stared at those notes until the writing blurred and rippled. Until he felt a gentle touch upon his cheek, turning him away. He looked to Nicole with tears standing in his eyes.

"Is-is Frederic—" The words choked him and it took him a moment to work more of them out. "Frederic's dead, isn't he?"

The last thing he wanted to hear was her soft, "I'm sorry, March."

He made a low, inward sound and ducked his head between updrawn knees. "H-How?"

"I don't know. What do you remember?"

"Nothing. Nothing . . . pieces. Nothing that makes sense. Feelings." And one of them was so overpowering, he canted a look up to ask, "Why am I so afraid of you?"

She didn't move. Her voice was a reassuring lull. "You needn't be, Marchand. You know I love you."

Still, he was troubled. The gaps in his recall were frightening, but not as bad as the terrible emotions roiling underneath them. Emotions that warned, don't ask, don't look, don't find out. But when Nicole reached out to touch him, he shrank back, everything inside him quaking. And he didn't know why. He had to know why.

"Did you see Frederic?" she prompted quietly.

"I—I don't know." Yes, he did know. Awareness was right beneath the surface but, like an image on a clear pond, when he went to touch it, it distorted and broke apart within his grasp. He closed his eyes and absently wiped the cascade of dampness from his cheeks. "I must have seen him." He looked up again. "I know he's dead."

She placed her hand over the top of his; he pulled his back reflexively. She didn't try again. But she did continue the questions. "Did you see him at Bianca and Gerard's?"

He gave a hard shudder as his mind rejected what he would try to remember. The shock was too deep. Instead, he let himself search out small details, ones that skirted the big terrible ones. Those his battered subconscious could contain. The wooden snarls. Shadows shifting across marble tiles. "Yes . . . it was there."

"Was he alive?"

His shaking got worse. His legs shivered. He tried to still them with hands that trembled even more. "No," he told her softly, then, "Yes," then, "No." He tried to concentrate and found himself fixed upon the way his knees quivered. Ridiculous, he told himself sternly. He'd never fallen into hysteria in his entire life. "I hit my head. I must have been delirious. The things I remember are crazy things, like a dream."

"Tell me the dream."

It was like struggling to draw rusted nails from swollen wood. The resistance was fierce, the process awkward and unpredictable. "Frederic. And Camille. They spoke to me."

"Camille?"

A cynical smile braved his lips. "I told you it was crazy."

"What did you see?"

"Camille looking as if he'd stepped from the grave. The smell." He swallowed hard. It was easier if he reminded himself that it wasn't real. Just a dream. "I shot him. The bullet passed through and he never slowed. And Frederic, he was behind me and I could see no soul in his eyes and I—I—"

Words failed.

Nicole gathered him up and he was too weak inside to object when she held him close. It felt good to be in her arms. Real, after all the bizarre things doing jerky puppet dances through his mind. He wanted to lose himself in her embrace but something dark nagged upon the edge of his thoughts. His fingers cramped up in the fabric of her cloak. Tension had him shifting with a helpless agitation. She rocked with him, gently kissing his brow, his temple, his hair. And unbidden rose the cold, cruel belief that it had been no dream at all.

"Oh God, forgive me. Camille . . . Frederic . . . forgive me. I would never hurt you. I would never hurt you. It was a dream! It had to be."

"It wasn't them, Marchand," Nicole whispered as she rocked and stroked his hair.

And suddenly he went very still. Slowly he began to withdraw from her, easing away, edging back until he was plastered up against the wall of the coach, his eyes upon her, huge and staring.

"But it was them," he murmured. "It was them. I saw them . . . And I saw you."

And Nicole saw the horror of what she was reflected back in his gaze.

Just then Musette gave a whimpering cry and came awake. She looked about through bewildered eyes but the minute she saw Marchand, her sorrow returned.

"Oh, Marchand."

He slid off the seat he shared with Nicole, never taking his eyes from her. He nudged in next to Musette and took her up in his arms, cradling her while she wept some more in weary little snatches. And he began to croon to her, the reassuring words ingrained from habit.

"It's all right, Musette. It's all right, *cher*. I'll take care of you. We're family, you and I. We're family." And when his own eyes filled up again, he cried them out silently in the tangle of red hair.

And never had Nicole felt quite so all alone.

Their coach rolled through Grez shortly before sunset. It was its most beautiful at that time of day, and Nicole was pressed to the window, absorbing the sight with nostalgia tugging at her soul. She had to admit, it was homesickness. After the chaos and adventure of Paris, she was straining for her first glimpse of home.

"This is the place from Camille's painting."

"Yes." Nicole looked around, encouraged. Marchand hadn't spoken a word to her since he'd changed seats. "It's Grez. My family lives near here. We should be able to see the house in a few minutes."

But that had satisfied the extent of Marchand's curiosity. He looked away from her, ignoring the yearning in her expression.

"Are you sure it will be all right with your family that we've come with you?"

"Yes, of course," Nicole assured Musette, but she was wishing she could have brought all of them with her; Camille, Bebe, Frederic, instead of just the emotionally fatigued remainders of their once carefree band.

They rode in silence for a time, then Musette came up off her seat, staring in awe. "Nicole, is that your home?"

Eyes welling up at the sight of the crimson-tiled roof and soft sand-colored walls, Nicole murmured, "Yes." Then she glanced at Marchand to find him staring, too. But from his impassive expression, she couldn't know how his heart sank as he took in the immense scale of the chateau, then his own shabby appearance.

The coach whirred in through the open gates and stopped at the front of the house. Twilight bathed the stones with a reflective brightness, giving an almost daytime illumination to the scene Marchand observed. A couple stood waiting. The woman was middle-aged, handsome and teary-eyed. The man was about his age, of striking looks and anxious expression. Even before the step went down, Nicole came flying out of the coach into the woman's arms. They embraced for a long while, both cheerfully weeping. Then the woman, Nicole's mother—he could see the resemblance now—

pushed her back gently and stood away, opening the path to where the aloof gentleman waited.

They eyed one another for a moment, almost like cautious antagonists, then he made a slight gesture, the spreading of his hands, and with a heart-rending cry, Nicole flung herself upon him, burrowing emotionally into the crisp white linen of his shirtfront.

Jealousy spiked high and hot through Marchand as he watched them together. Who was this man? A brother? A betrothed? Then he heard the low caress of Italian endearments and was reminded at once of Gerardo Pasquale. The youthful Gerard who was a re- puted friend of her father's. Who looked the same age as the man who cuddled Nicole on his chest.

And then the man looked up through eyes of a par- ticular shade of green and Marchand knew that some- how, impossibly, this man was her father.

Nicole was loath to step away once she'd bridged the distance between them. The sense of security swept over her as she was hugged to the familiar plane. It wasn't a monster she saw. It wasn't a demon. It was the man who'd loved her all her life and had showered her with her every wish.

"I'm so sorry I hurt you." The words were muffled against him, but she could tell he heard by the way he caught his breath. "Please forgive me, *mío pádre.*"

"It's I who need to beg that of you. But these things we can say between us later. First, introduce us to our guests."

She turned, keeping her arms about her father's lean waist. "Mother, Father, these are my friends, Musette Mercier and Marchand LaValois. They took me in like family while I was in Paris. I would ask you do the same for them now."

"My home is open to you. I am Louis Radouix and this is my wife, Arabella."

Arabella studied her daughter's friends with interest. The girl was pretty, one of those Parisian free spirits, she supposed, and the young man, even slightly battered, bruised and bone weary, was quite impressive to behold. Arabella moved a linking glance between him and the redhead. Then between him and her daughter. Ah, so this was the lover Gerardo spoke of. She extended her hand and smiled.

"Please come in. We owe you a great debt for taking care of our Nicole." And her heart softened as the handsome young man's face took on a warm flush of color and he looked away from her intent gaze. Definitely the lover. "You must be tired after the ride and eager to wash up and have a warm meal. I'll have Mrs. Kampford prepare your rooms. We so seldom have visitors, this will be quite a treat." And she shepherded them inside, pausing to gratefully clasp Takeo's hand and to slip her arm about her husband.

Their daughter was home safe.

His room was huge, bigger than their entire Paris flat, but Marchand noticed nothing beyond the invitingly pulled-back counterpane. He managed the strength to strip down to his worsted drawers, then sank into the sweet oblivion of the bed. All else could wait until he had the rest his body demanded.

Except his mind couldn't rest.

There could be no base of reality to the images tumbling through his head. He was tormented by strange vignettes, snatches befitting some opiate dream or madman's fancy. Over and over, he saw the ragged corpse of Camille Viotti emerging from the shadows. He could feel the resistance and give that met his sword as it impaled his brother's body. The incredulous horror of it. All the reactions denied him at the time returned with chilling consequence. Those dead, empty eyes, burning with bestial fervor. He thrashed upon his sheets, bathed in a sweat of nameless terror. That charnel smell rising up to stir the bile in his belly. The impossibility of it all, the fantastic nature of things that could not be believed or explained.

Shall I make you the companion of my next few centuries?

No! He tossed wildly, fighting the bedcovers as if he was fighting those demons in his dream. His head was full of the sound of his frantic shouts and fierce curses, of the useless thuds of his fists against bodies that felt no pain. He was lifted, his coat and shirt pulled off him. Their touch, so cold upon bared skin. He strained and struggled against the repellant feel of it. Then the insidious purr of a woman's voice.

You were to have been Nicole's first, but since she cannot bring herself to take you . . . ah, well, such strength cannot go untapped.

Then the glare of moonlight upon sharp white teeth. No . . . no . . . no . . . He moaned repeatedly in his restless slumber, his arms outflung as if they were pinned by some greater force, his body warping up, twisting, going abruptly rigid.

With a soft cry, Marchand sat upright in his borrowed bed. The room was dark and he was alone. The only sound was the harsh uneven panting of his breath. He was wet with the stark terror of his dream. A dream. Yes, it was a dream, for even now, the images were unraveling, threads loosening, fraying, parting in the manner of dreams until he was left with no memory other than the disquieting chill. He lay back and brought the knotted covers up to his chin. He was all at once so cold and yet feverishly hot.

With a sigh, he closed his eyes and let a healing slumber overtake him. As it did, he was unconsciously rubbing the inner crook of his elbow where twin indentations throbbed with barely noticeable pain.

Bianca's bite.

Chapter Seventeen

Louis Radman sat on the parlor sofa, his feet stretched out toward the fire, his wife tucked up against his side. The heat from the first was an unnecessary indulgence, for he felt no great influx of hot or cold, but the warmth of the second was vital to his existence: the loving presence of the woman he'd married.

He felt their daughter poised in the hall long before Arabella was aware of her there watching. When his wife would rise up in welcome, he caught her hand in his, kissed it gently and pressed it over his heart.

Let her come to us, my love, was his silent message. Arabella relaxed against him, but he could sense her anticipation. And her anxiety. He shared it.

Finally, Nicole came into the room, approaching them with both haughtiness and humility. There was pride in her ability to escape their rule and survive on her own. There was meekness in her return. It was an uneasy line to walk, and Louis vowed not to upset the balance. He didn't move, continuing to gaze into the flames as she hovered uncertainly at the rolled arm of the sofa. Then she came around in front, settling on the floor at his feet, pillowing her head against his thigh as she'd done since she was a child. It was a submissive gesture then. Now it was one of trust and devotion. He would not mistake the two. Slowly, he stroked his palm along the glossy shimmer of her dark hair and her eyes closed on a sigh.

"Let me tell you a story," he began in a tone as soothing as his touch. "It's about two young friends in Firenze, Italy. One was from a wealthy family. He was a scholar, always thinking deep thoughts, rather shy when it came to life's pleasures. The other was from a modest family. He hungered for those things his friend took for granted. He was full of recklessness and passion. From such different backgrounds, with such different views, they should not have been friends, yet they were almost like brothers in their love for one another. Then a beautiful woman came between them.

"The passionate one was wildly enamored of her air of mystery. The scholar was afraid of her and afraid for his friend. This woman played upon their affection and their fears and soon these friends became bitter rivals without ever intending to be. Through her trickery, she brought them to a point of honor which left the passionate one dying and his somber friend stricken with guilt and grief. The woman whispered that she would spare his life if the other would swear his allegiance to her. The scholar, he was a great fool, and in his ignorance agreed. This woman had no magic. She was no healer. She was a vampire and she drank up their souls, giving them both an eternal death."

"You, Gerard and Bianca," Nicole murmured. And he paused for a moment, wondering how she knew, before answering, "Yes.

"The passionate one, Gerardo, resigned himself to his existence, believing himself damned, but the scholar,

Gino, he would not accept his fate. For centuries he searched for a way to escape his nocturnal curse, until he found a physician in London who was doing experimental work transferring blood. That doctor restored him to life. For a time, he lived as a normal man, falling in love, taking a wife, making a child, but his fortune was not to hold. Now he is once again among the cursed."

He paused in his tale to brush the trail of tears from his daughter's cheek.

"Nicole, you were born of the tremendous love your mother and I have for one another. It was never our intention that you come to any pain because of it. Forgive us our selfishness, but you brought us such joy. Now we must pay for it in your sorrow. It would seem the scholar never learned to think from the head instead of the heart."

Nicole caught his hand and held it against her cheek for a long moment, then she sat up to regard him intently. "I need to know the nature of what I am. I'm not like Bianca and Gerard. I don't think I ever could be. Gerard says I am like you. Tell me what that means."

"I'm not like them, either. I never kill carelessly or for the thrill of the hunt. To me, all human life is sacred. They've forgotten, or pretend not to remember, what it means to be alive. They believe themselves superior, and in their arrogance they hold all else in contempt. We have great powers, great strengths, true, but also huge weaknesses; the light of day, the touch of silver, the scent of garlic, flowing water. We are condemned to darkness, to the vile food of our existence. We are slaves to the hunger. We live in fear of discovery, of being caught when we are helpless to defend ourselves against a sharpened stake or a severing stroke or the simple warmth of dawn."

"But I've seen you during the daylight hours."

"As I said, I'm not a true vampire. The experimentation left me with a trace of humanity. I can bear the daylight for a time. I can see a faint reflection in the glass; the shadow of my soul." He smiled wryly at that. "The hunger no longer consumes me, but I still must yield to it at times."

"So what does that make me?" she asked him.

"I don't know. We've watched you since birth, hoping that you would be a normal child, praying my tainted blood escaped you."

"But it hasn't, has it?" her mother put in quietly.

"No," Nicole answered.

"Tell us the nature of what you are, little one."

She told them everything, about her preference for the night, her acute sensory perceptions, her strength and unnatural speed. It was a relief to unburden her soul to them.

"And upon what do you dine these days?" Louis asked when she hesitated.

"We share the same taste in meals, Father."

"You've killed?" Arabella exclaimed, unable to keep the anguish from her voice.

"No, not for food. Not yet. But the instinct is there. Always. Marchand was to have been my first, but I couldn't—" She broke off and looked away, ashamed, confused, hungry for him even now. "Bianca and Gerard were trying to teach me."

"Them?" Louis scoffed in disgust. "They hunt like savage animals, for the pleasure of the kill. You might as well learn from jackals. How do you know them, these shadows from my past?"

"I've been staying with them in Paris."

"In Paris," Arabella echoed, looking up to her husband in alarm. "So close! Louis!"

He waved off her fright. His gaze was intent upon his daughter. "You lived with them. Explain yourself."

"Bianca discovered what I was. It's a long story." She blushed, unwilling to tell her parents she'd been stealing. "They said they were your friends and that they owed you. Gerard was very kind to me, but I didn't trust Bianca's motives."

"Bianca is a demon and Gerardo is not kind. He is clever and he is dangerous. His affection is unpredictable."

"He saved her life," Arabella murmured.

"What? What do you mean, Bella?"

"He was here the other night to tell me Nicole was in danger. He told me where Takeo could find her."

"Gerardo was here? In my house? And you said nothing to me?"

Arabella glanced uncomfortably at Nicole and rubbed her husband's hand in a placating manner. "We can discuss this later, Louis," she muttered.

"I wish to discuss it now! How did he know where to find us?"

"He—just knew."

"Bella." His voice rumbled impatiently.

"I'm linked to him just as I am to you and Takeo."

Louis stared at her, agog, then he surged up and paced angrily to the fire gate. "Why didn't you tell me?" he demanded of the flames.

"It—it seemed unnecessary. I haven't heard from him since we left London."

"Mama, was he your—Never mind."

"Was he her what? Her lover? No! Never!" And he glared at his wife, commanding her to agree.

"No," Arabella told her. "No, he was not. But regardless of what your father says, I do trust him, and I don't believe he would ever harm you."

Louis snorted. "That's what I thought, too, until he crushed my bones and tore out my—"

"Louis! Nicole doesn't need to hear that. That's past. You and Gerardo have made amends since then."

"An uneasy truce. If he ever puts a hand upon either of you, I will kill him without a qualm." The golden glitter of his eyes attested to his words.

"Bianca is another matter," Arabella continued, ignoring her husband's glower. "She is completely soulless, and there is nothing she would not do to harm us. If she knew where we were, none of us would be safe."

"Gerard warned me not to tell her where you were."

"Did he?" Louis drawled. "How very kind of him."

"Tell us about our guests," Arabella prompted, to turn the subject from Gerardo Pasquale.

"They were friends of the artist who took me to Paris. When he was k-killed, they took me in until I met Bianca. I made the mistake of introducing Marchand's brother, who was also Musette's fiancé, to Bianca. She killed him and would have killed Marchand as well if Takeo hadn't intervened." She didn't mention her own life had been in the balance; a point of pride, perhaps. "I brought them here because it was the only safe place I knew."

"You did the right thing," her mother assured her. Then with extreme tact, she asked, "Your young man, does he know about you?"

"He knows but he doesn't understand."

And Arabella read a world of misery in her daughter's answer. "Then we'll have to show him how to accept the impossible." She patted Nicole's cheek and saw her green eyes fill up with grateful tears. There was more to be said, but it would keep until they could be alone. "Nicole, you need your rest. Sleep well and know that we'll watch over you and your friends."

"There is something you can do for now." Nicole rummaged through her pockets and produced a crumpled paper. Upon it were names and monetary amounts. "Could you see that these sums are delivered to these people?" At her mother's perplexed look, she merely said, "Debts. It would be best if they were sent anonymously."

"I'll see it's taken care of."

Nicole hugged her tight, then went to embrace her father, who murmured softly, "Welcome home, little one."

There was a great sense of comfort in roaming the familiar halls on the way to her room. Nicole relaxed the tense vigilance that had been with her since Paris, but another tension rose in its place. That restlessness drew her to Marchand's door. She could feel him within, could scent him, could hear his heart beating. And she was compelled to open his door.

She stood for a long while upon that threshold, her keen eyes able to penetrate the darkness, to watch him in his uneasy slumber. So handsome, he was. Her heart swelled with a bittersweet love. He was afraid of her now. He wouldn't welcome her approach. Better he rest and recover himself, but she couldn't move away from him. The pulse of him held her hypnotized. Hunger welled inside her in huge dark waves.

Marchand.

He stirred.

He need never know of her visit, came a sinister whisper through her consciousness. Just enough to satisfy. That's all it would have to be. And her lips parted and her eyes grew hot in anticipation.

Then a figure reached past her to pull the door shut.

She stared up at her father, feeling ashamed and helpless in her state of need.

"Would you abuse him after he's placed his trust in you?" Louis asked of her gently.

"I don't want to." Her words came out in a sob. "I don't want to hurt him."

"Come away with me."

But the lure of live blood was strong and her hunger was intense. Nicole hesitated.

"Are you confident in your control, child? Are you sure you could pull away from him in time? Do you know how much becomes too much? You must know these things before taking from a human. Unless you're willing to kill them."

"Teach me," was her desperate plea.

Louis led her from the house. He took her deep into the fragrant forest, where silence hung like the cool mists, draping all in mystery. Then a sound penetrated that veil of quiet, a sound that quickened both their senses and whet an expectant urgency. The rhythm of life. Moving like a swift, deadly panther, Louis brought down a stag, breaking the animal's neck with a powerful wrench of his hands. Then he beckoned for Nicole.

"Quickly. It cools fast."

Not sure she understood, she obeyed his gesture and knelt down beside him. With a slash of his teeth, her father tore into the animal's throat. He hunched there for a moment, crouched like a beast of prey while the aroma of blood rose thick and dizzying in its appeal.

Nicole found herself pushing in close, nudging him aside in her impatience. He guided her head down to where his hand now pinched off the artery. Then he let go and the hot surge filled her mouth and she was swallowing, taking it in as rapidly as she could until her head swirled and her veins swelled, straining to their limit.

Then Louis pulled her away and they sat leaning against one another, panting, replete; unnatural father, unnatural child. Then he cleaned off his face and gave her his handkerchief. While she did the same, he tended the animal's carcass, ripping gashes in the creature's hind quarters. When Nicole questioned him, his answer was cool logic.

"When the animal is found, it will look as though it was brought down by wolves. Always disguise what you do. Leave no evidence that would lead to whispers. We are safe only as long as no one suspects we are other than we pretend. That is your first lesson. You can live off forest creatures for quite some time."

"How long? Indefinitely?"

"No," he told her somewhat sadly. "Eventually you'll feel the need for human blood. When that time comes, I'll teach you lesson two."

Weak sunlight filtered in to sear across Marchand's eyelids. He muttered in complaint and started to roll away, then was perplexed by the presence of a warm human barrier pressed against his side. Thinking it was Nicole brought both pleasure and panic. He wasn't ready to face her with so much confusion reigning in head and heart. Then he glanced over his shoulder and saw red hair peeping above the covers. Musette? She was fully dressed beneath the blanket and her pale cheeks bore the tracks of dried tears. His heart gave a tender twist of melancholy. She must have come in to snuggle up next to him sometime during the night. Could he blame her for wanting to seek out the familiar in such a lonely house amid strangers after sharing a single room for so long in communal companionship? He was her link to the past; a past she couldn't release. Frederic's death had been a terrible shock to her as well.

Though yet weighted with weariness, he had no desire to linger abed with a woman who was not Nicole Radouix. He rolled out carefully so as not to wake Musette, and dressed in his stale clothing. He couldn't remember ever being so thirsty. His throat was tight and achy. When he left his room, he was frustrated by his own lack of direction. He couldn't remember where the stairs were, or, for that matter, even climbing them. He wandered the upper hall on legs that refused to behave reliably until he caught sight of a great sweeping staircase which he all but dragged himself down, so light-headed he feared he'd go tumbling to the bottom at any second. What was wrong with him? His whole body felt watery and weak. Shock, perhaps. Hunger, most likely. He couldn't remember when he'd had his last meal.

The scent of warm bread lured him down one of the corridors, but he drew up outside an open set of doors. Within, he could see the elegantly garbed Madame Radouix sitting down to her midday meal. The table was of banquet-length, all decked in pewter, linen and crystal. Suddenly, he was acutely aware of his appearance; of his soiled and probably offensive clothes, of his own unwashed skin and stubbled face. And he would rather have starved right to bones in the hall than intrude upon the lone diner in such a lowly state.

He was distracted by sounds from deeper in the house

and followed them back to the kitchen in the servants' wing. There he found a tiny woman engaged in bustling activity. She gave a gasp when she saw him.

"Oh! You gave me a start. I wasn't aware you was up and about yet. I be Bessie Kampford." She made a light curtsy, then continued with her English-accented French. "If you'll return to the dining room, sir, I'll fetch you—"

"If you please, I'd rather take my meal in here. If it's no bother, madame."

She blinked in surprise, then shrugged. "Suit yourself, sir. Sit yourself down and I'll dish up some nice hot mutton stew. I myself got no use for your fancy French foods. Good, solid English cooking that'll stick to your ribs. That's what you be needing."

Marchand smiled faintly and let himself plop onto one of the backless stools at the corner table. His eyes closed and he'd almost drifted off when the scent of savory stock beneath his nose brought him around.

"Don't be shy when it comes to seconds."

"Might I have some wine?"

"For lunch?" she muttered disapprovingly under her breath, but added with a proper dignity, "I usually serve tea."

"Mrs. Kampford, if our guest would like wine, bring him wine. Red."

Marchand bolted up off the stool to assume a stiff attention. "Madame Radouix, forgive me if I disturbed you."

Arabella smiled slightly as she watched a deep flush creep up otherwise pale cheeks. "M'sieur LaValois, I'm dining in the other room. Please join me. Bessie, would you bring his plates."

"If you please, madame, I would feel more— comfortable here."

How rigidly that was spoken, as if he were mortified to the soul to be placed in such a position. Arabella gentled her reply. "We don't ask our visitors to dine in the kitchen, m'sieur. If you would—"

"Please, madame," he interrupted. "I could not sit to your table like this. It would be an insult to your hospitality. Nor do I wish to impose upon your sensibilities."

"I see," she murmured, trying to contain her smile. How arrogant he was in his humility. "As you wish."

Marchand swallowed hard after she left the kitchen, so ashamed of his reduced circumstances he didn't know if he could finish his meal. Then, much to his surprise, Arabella returned, carrying her own plates.

"Would you mind very much if I joined you in here? It's been ages since I've had company for my midday meal and eating alone at that big empty table quite depresses my appetite."

He stared at her blankly until aware his mouth was open. Then he moved quickly to relieve her of her dishes and to seat her upon the opposite stool. He settled back before his stew, his eyes downcast, his pride chafing, while a wonderful sense of gratitude blossomed toward Nicole's mother.

"This is not the first kitchen I've ever eaten in, m'sieur. My husband has all the titles behind him. I am but a physician's daughter. I've been known to eat lunch over an autopsy table. I don't mind the surroundings as long as the food is good and the company stimulating."

"And did you find the company stimulating at the autopsy, madame?"

"A dead bore, actually."

And he grinned at that, a wide beaming smile that

overset the pallor and the bruising and the whiskers to give her a glimpse of the man who'd won her daughter's heart.

"You have a very nice smile, Marchand. May I call you that?"

"This is the kitchen, madame. By all means."

"Mrs. Kampford, I would like some wine also. And do not glower at me so. I am old enough to take spirits at a meal if I so choose."

"Yes, ma'am," came the dour reply.

"Please resume your meal, Marchand. Mrs. Kampford may be prickly company but she is an excellent cook."

He was still smiling as if relieved to be enjoying normal conversation in someone's kitchen. Then abruptly his animation faded and she could see his dark eyes fill before he lowered them to his plate, as if he felt he had no right to enjoy this morning when others he loved would not. What an awful time he must have had of it, she thought to herself.

"How is the wine, m'sieur?"

"Very good, thank you," came his hushed reply. And they continued to eat in silence for some time, Marchand trying to focus on his meal, struggling to keep his hands steady; Arabella trying not to act upon her sympathy by pretending not to notice how frequently he was wiping at his eyes.

She studied him, bemused. He wore a pauper's clothes but his actions were crisp and disciplined, his manners and modesty befitting a higher class. She was wondering what kind of man her daughter had fallen in love with.

"What is it you do in Paris, Marchand?"

Again, she saw him stiffen up. "I am currently without work, madame."

Because he was waiting for some negative reaction to that news, she went on smoothly as if it was unimportant. "What is it you used to do?"

"I was in the military."

Ah, that explained his regimented movements and rigid sense of protocol. "A noble pursuit."

"When the cause is noble, madame."

"How unfortunate that so few of them are."

His gaze came up—he had nice eyes, too; dark, intelligent and direct, she noted. She liked that. She liked him.

"And what do you know of causes, madame?" He didn't ask that belligerently, but rather with the challenge of one who liked a good debate.

"Oh, believe me, m'sieur, the medical profession is full of causes, motivated by greed and prestige but rarely by the love of humanity."

"Then they must have much in common, the military and medicine."

"A pity more can't see beyond what is accepted to what is good and right." And he was still for a moment, sensing she was no longer talking theory.

"Limited vision can often be safer."

"And how do you view things, Marchand?"

"Carefully, madame."

She smiled. "Very wise of you."

"If I was so very wise, I'm not sure I would be here."

"More wine?"

"I think not. My head is cloudy enough already."

Arabella stood. "Since I don't care to take all my meals in the kitchen, let me see if I can find something suitable for you and the young lady to wear. I'll have a bath readied so you can clean up. I would prefer you feel comfortable in my house."

His gaze was suddenly very sober. "I don't know if that's possible, Madame Radouix."

Arabella came to stand beside him and slipped her palm beneath his chin, tipping his head up toward the light. He squinted his eyes.

"Look up at me," Arabella instructed.

"What is it?"

"Habit. Always a doctor's daughter. You are very pale, Marchand, and there's a bluish cast to the whites of your eyes. Let me see your hands."

Puzzled, he extended them.

"Your nail beds are very pale as well. Almost as if you'd lost a great deal of blood." Discreetly, she pushed back his cuffs, then examined his neck with her glance.

He pulled his hands back, his look growing guarded. "I hit my head. Could that account for it?"

She probed the back of his skull and found evidence of a wound. It was recent enough for him to wince at her light touch. "That must be it," she murmured. "Drink plenty of fluids. Rest. Recover yourself."

"I don't think that's possible either, madame."

And as she looked down at him, Arabella was wondering if he was right. Because she didn't think his blood loss was due to a bump on the back of his head.

"Marchand, I would like to give you something, a small token to thank you for your care of Nicole."

"Please, madame, nothing is necessary," he began to protest, but she waved him off.

"I insist. Wear this always and know of my gratitude."

And she reached behind her nape to unfasten a light-weight chain, draping the fine link about his neck. Curiously, he reached up to finger it, craning his neck to see what dangled from its end.

It was a small silver cross.

Chapter Eighteen

It was a tense gathering at the Radouix table that night. Musette was the only one animated and Arabella was politely drawn into conversation as the young woman gushed about the beauty of the grounds and the lush vegetable gardens that reminded her of her own rural home. The young Parisian was wearing one of Nicole's gowns and the fit wasn't bad. Cleaned up, she was a very attractive woman. Arabella was aware of a certain sullenness in her daughter's regard of her friend. A sullenness that altered to ill-concealed anguish when directed upon the young man opposite.

Marchand sat coatless at the table and was obviously uncomfortable. He was too broad of body for any of Louis's jackets, so he was relegated to shirtsleeves. His clean-shaven face was nearly as white as the fine linen; and his eyes stood out like large, dark blue-edged bruises. He ate quietly and kept a covert eye on the way Louis and Nicole moved their food about their plates without partaking of any of it.

He was in the process of reaching for his wine when it sounded soft against his ear; a delicate whisper. *Marchand.* He gave a sudden gasp, his hand knocking

the glass over. He stared at the spill stupidly, watching
the deep crimson puddle outward upon the snowy white
linen.

Marchand.

A silky female purr. One he recognized.

He leapt up out of his chair, looking behind him as if
he expected to find Satan at his shoulder.

"Did you hear—" He broke off and glanced at the
others who were gazing at him in blank surprise. Realizing how he must look, he stammered, "Forgive me. It
was nothing. I'm sorry," and he began frantically trying
to blot up the vivid red stain spreading across the table-
cloth.

"It's all right," Louis was saying as he reached to stay
the unsteady hands.

Marchand just stared at Louis's long-fingered hand,
so flawlessly fair and smooth, staring as if it was something alien and awful instead of a casual gesture from
his host. His eyes came up then, round and black, and
he began to back away from the table.

"I'm sorry," he muttered. "I don't feel well. I—I'm
going upstairs." And he practically fled.

Before Nicole could rise, Musette excused herself to
go after him.

By the time he reached the door to his room,
Marchand was drenched in an icy sweet. He was certain
he would hear nothing over the rasp of his own breathing and the loud thunder of his heart, but it came again,
that low seductive whisper.

Marchand.

No, it couldn't be . . .

Marchand, tell me where you are.

The hairs on his arms stirred as the soft command
echoed within his mind. He gripped the doorknob and

in his panic began a desperate pulling instead of pushing inward. Any second, he expected the feel of cold finger-tips and the confusion of helplessness that followed. That helplessness that was like dying.

"Marchand?"

The touch of a hand made him whirl around, his back pressing to the door, his palms flat against the solid wood. But he only saw Musette, her pretty features pinched with concern.

"Oh, Marchand, you are unwell. Let me help you."

She leaned past him to open the door and the tension left his body in a shivery wave. Needing some contact with reality, he caught her up in a tight embrace, hugging her against him, reveling in the feel of warm, well-rounded humanity. After she got over her surprise, Musette put her arms about his middle and hugged back.

"I miss him, too, Marchand. It seems so strange not hearing his voice or seeing him beside me."

Marchand squeezed his eyes shut, "Musette, trust me, do not wish for those things." And he hung on tighter, trying to force out the image of his dead brother looking down at a bloodstained palm, trying to make himself believe it was madness—wishing it was madness.

"What are we going to do, Marchand? I'm at such a loss now that he's gone."

What were they going to do? God, he wished he knew! But then there was one thing he did know, one goal he did hold strong. Marchand took a deep breath. Determination spread like hot steel through his veins. "I'm going to find out what killed him and I'm going to put him properly to rest."

Not understanding the depth of that promise, Musette stepped back, his hands in hers. "Rest is what you need right now. You look terrible, March." She hesitated a moment, then asked, "Would you mind if I lay down with you for a while?"

"Musette—"

"I need to be close to someone who was close to Frederic. I don't mean it in a personal way. It's just that he was everything to me and now—"

"You needn't explain," he murmured. He placed a light kiss upon her brow. "I don't want to be alone with my own company, either." No, he didn't want to be alone. Alone, he was vulnerable. And with his arm about her shoulders, he guided her into his room and shut the door, unaware that Nicole was watching from the top of the shadowed stairs with the same pain-filled expression that had lined her face when she saw Musette exit his room that morning.

They lay together beneath the covers, both completely dressed with the exception of footwear. With Musette's firm little figure pressed against him and her bright head pillowed upon his shoulder, Marchand felt inexplicably better . . . safer. Perhaps her presence would hold the dreams and beckoning voices at bay. It was better that they not be separated. At least here, he could try to protect her from what he'd discovered in this house. He owed it to Frederic, to all of them, to see that one of their number survived unscathed. So he clutched her close, wondering how on earth he was going to see to that vow here in this unnatural fold.

Louis and Nicole Radouix were the same kind of monsters that had stolen Camille and Frederic's souls.

How could he rest while dark questions lingered? He closed his eyes and could see the sleek image of Gerardo Pasquale with his arms about those two soon-to-beghoulish women, purring smugly, "I've brought guests for dinner."

How long before he and Musette were invited to be the main course at the Radouix' table?

Nicole paused outside Marchand's door. Within, she could feel two hearts beating close together. A sudden fierce rage rose up to wipe away her pain. How could he do this to her? How dare he do this to her? She'd saved his life and this was how she was to be repaid? By his fickle treachery? Before his brother's memory was even cold?

Her hands clenched into tight fists where they rested against his door. The rhythm of those two hearts took on a taunting tempo. Didn't he know what she'd offered him? Her love, her strength, her fortune. Yet he chose to discard it. Did he realize how dangerous it could be to slight her? Did he know how powerful she was, how easy it would be for her to tear this feeble door from its frame and simply take what was hers? He was hers, presented to her as her rite of passage. Perhaps she'd been too sentimental in her want to preserve his individuality. If this was how he was going to treat her, he didn't deserve the right to choose. She'd make that choice for him with one swift claim. Then he wouldn't be able to turn away from her in horror or to turn to someone else in her stead. He would be hers to control, hers to command.

She leaned against the door, her pulse pounding, her breath hissing between rapidly altering teeth. How dare he mock her. How dare he dismiss her love when she was like a god! Foolish mortal. She would show him she was not to be trifled with. She would become—

Just like Bianca and Gerard.

That was a sobering shock.

What was she thinking? *Oh, Marchand, forgive me, my love.* She reeled away from his door, racing toward her own room, aghast at how she'd nearly lost her first battle against the pull of power. Now she understood her father's warning. It would be so easy to give way to temptation, so simple to adopt the attitude of contemptuous superiority. So easy to control and kill for reasons less noble than survival.

"Nicole?"

She turned quickly into her mother's arms, letting her tears come and her insecurities flow as freely. "Oh, Mama, what am I to do? He will never love me as I am."

"Is he a strong man, Nicole? A brave one?"

"Oh, yes!"

"Then all is not lost. He's here with you. He hasn't run from you. I'd say that speaks of courage and trust."

"I'm not sure I'm worthy of that trust," she admitted wretchedly.

"You've kept him safe. You've brought him here. I'd say you are. He must love you very much to have come this far."

Nicole sniffled. "He says he does. Or at least he did."

"I like your Marchand. He is a smart, practical man, but his life has just undergone a tremendous upheaval. Give him time to heal, Nicole. Help calm his fears."

"How can I reassure him when I can't convince myself that all will be well?"

"You must work together."

Nicole rested her head upon her mother's shoulder, taking comfort from her confidence. "Mama, were you never afraid?"

"Of your father? No. Not really. There were aspects of him that were truly frightening, but I love the man he is too much to let that part of him scare me away."

"He's never—hurt you?"

"No."

"But he's—he's taken of your blood."

"He takes what I've gladly given."

"But you're not a slave to him."

Arabella laughed. "No, I'm not. He doesn't want me to be. He needs me to be strong for the times when he's not strong. As it should be between man and wife." She led Nicole into her bedroom, sat her down at her dressing table and began to brush out her hair as she'd done since her daughter was a child. Nicole studied her own reflection. Hers was the only mirror in the house. She stared at her face and thought of what her father had said. A shadow of his soul. And she touched her cheek, wondering when her own image would begin to fade.

"What is it like, Mama?" Their eyes met in the glass, Arabella pausing in mid stroke, then continuing the smooth rhythm.

"It's the loss of self, the combining of two into one. It's a perfect union of heart and mind and body. There's no other closeness like it." Then she tipped up her daughter's face to ask her, "Have you initiated Marchand?"

"No." Then her gaze dropped and she murmured, "I've made love with him." When her mother made no comment, she risked a glance upward and was relieved to see no condemnation there. "Oh, Mama, it was so beautiful. Is it like that?"

Arabella caressed her fair cheek, her smile slightly sad at the thought of innocence lost. "Yes, it's like that.

Only—more. It's the ultimate gift of trust, Nicole. It can't be forced. Turn your head and let me finish this."

Nicole pondered her mother's words, then another thought occurred to her, one she hadn't considered before, one that was twice too late to change.

"Mama, you made me while Father was in a human form."

"Yes."

"Marchand is human. What are the chances that he and I—"

"Could you conceive a child between you?" Arabella went still, her expression taking on that cool scientific facade it did whenever she was pensive. "I don't know, Nicole. I suppose it would be possible. But as to what that child would be, I could not guess."

Nicole twisted on the stool, her face lifting in earnest. "Is it wrong of me to want him? To want a child with him?"

"No."

"I do! I do want the things normal women have and I want them with him. I can't bear the way he looks at me now. What am I going to do? How can I convince him not to be afraid?"

"Show him all that you are, Nicole. Then, you must let him decide. It isn't a choice many could make."

"You did!"

"Yes, and I've never regretted it."

"But haven't you ever wanted Father to change you so that you could share eternity together?"

"I thought on it long and hard, my darling, but I couldn't let go of life when I was raised to cherish it. It's that quality Louis loves in me. Yes, it's hard to accept the years when he does not age, but when he tells me it doesn't matter to him, I believe him. He would grow old with me if he could. That is his greatest wish. Alas, he can only grow old through me. Life is sacred, Nicole, not to be taken selfishly or for your own purpose. Believing that is what keeps your father from being a monster."

"I love Marchand, Mama. I can make him want me."

Arabella thought of Gerardo Pasquale and shook her head. "No. It would never be the same. Better to lose him than own him."

Nicole looked as though she might protest, but she didn't. In the end, she nodded, accepting that wisdom with a breaking heart.

"Nicole?"

"Yes?" She looked up alerted by her mother's tone.

"You said you've not taken of his blood."

"No."

"Do you know who might have?"

"What do you mean?"

"What I mean, and I'm saying this strictly from necessity, is that as soon as possible you need to get him into a natural state so you can search for signs of a bite."

"Mother!"

"I don't think he'd be inclined to disrobe for me, physician's daughter or no. And if he is in the thrall of another, he won't be able to volunteer any information on his own. This is important, Nicole, vital to our very safety. You've brought him here and he is the eyes of whomever took him. We could be in terrible danger."

"Then perhaps you should ask Musette to look. She would seem to have a better chance than I."

"Oh, so that's it," Arabella said gently. "I was wondering. I think you're wrong there, Nicole. He doesn't look at her the way he looks at you."

"He looks at me as if I was a demon!"

"He looks at you like a man in love."

And Nicole held to that observation as she paced her room in restless strides through the long hours of the night.

How was she going to go about seducing a man who both loved and loathed her?

When planning a campaign, the first thing one did was find out everything possible about the enemy. His first task was suspending belief long enough to look for that information.

Marchand had slept well and had awakened at first light with his strength restored. And with that energy, came his determination. He'd been helpless and he didn't like it. Knowledge was power, be it battlefield or boulevard, and so far, all he had was a name steeped in superstition.

Vampire.

He chose dawn purposefully. It seemed the time when everything under the Radouix's roof would be resting. leaving Musette abed asleep, he crept down the stairs into the stillness of the lower floor. Then he went quietly and efficiently from room to room, searching for anything that would further his cause. When he opened the doors to an extensive library, he was smiling with a grim satisfaction.

"Were you looking for something in particular?"

The sound of his host's smooth drawl spoken directly behind him gave Marchand a terrible start. He lunged forward, placing a heavy map table between him and whatever Radouix was. There, he waited, tense and *en garde* and frustratingly unarmed. If there was a way to arm against such as him.

Radouix glided in from the darker hall. There was no other way to describe the way he moved. There was something hypnotic in that effortless motion, but Marchand refused to be charmed.

"Might I hazard a guess," Louis continued. "You'll find a surprisingly good section on ancient folklore along that wall. Any subtext you were interested in? Perhaps I could help you. I am rather well learned in the area."

"Vampirism."

Marchand's direct reply brought Louis's dark brows up in a delicate arch. "Ah, I am somewhat of an expert on that topic. Let me save you some time. You may ask me your questions."

Marchand watched his host sink languidly into a leather chair. There was scarcely any give to the cushion, as if a man his size was without weight. Louis crossed his legs and tented long-fingered hands upon one knee and he looked up with an infinite patience.

"Ask your questions."

Marchand tried to speak, but words wouldn't come at first. He wet his lips and assumed an aggressive posture. It seemed his host smiled faintly at that bit of bravado.

"There are such things?"

His smile widened and his green eyes gleamed. "Oh, yes."

"And you are one?"

There was a long silence then a slightly chiding, "Is that what you think?"

"Yes."

"Then you are either very brave or very foolish to be standing there asking such questions of me, are you not?"

He was mad, that's what he was! But Marchand couldn't relent. What did he have to lose, after all? If this elegantly draped creature wanted to kill him, what could he do? Run? How amusing. He'd seen how fast they moved and he'd sampled their strength. He was a babe in his ignorance and here was his chance to learn.

"One of your .... legion, killed my brother and my friend."

"Ah." That was a soft sound, one of infinite understanding. "And what is it you mean to do about it?"

"I'm not sure there is anything I can do."

"Then you mean to accept the fact as it is and go on with your life. Very ... prudent of you."

"I accept nothing about what was done!" he cried out passionately, unaware that he was being gently baited. "He was my brother and now he—he—I don't know what he is." He blinked rapidly to discourage the welling emotions. Now was not the time for grief. He regarded Louis narrowly. "Can you tell me what he is?"

"Not all the victims of a vampire become vampires. A vampire has undergone a ritual of initiation, a rather close-guarded secret among those of my society. It is not casually done, for when we increase our number that way, it is for an eternity."

Marchand swallowed hard because Louis admitted what he had already known. That he was a vampire. "Then what happens to those who are killed ... casually?"

"Whenever blood in any amount is drawn, the victim becomes a pawn to whomever has taken from him. The dominance will last until death—of one or the other. If the victim dies without the initiation, he will rise again in an inferior state, as a *revenant-en-corps*, an animated corpse. Without the transformation of spirit, he is much like a decomposing body wandering at night, killing and making others like himself. It is not an envied state, this mindless existence as a slave to the hunger and to he who made him."

Marchand closed his eyes, overcome by what he heard. *"Mon Dieu.* Oh, *mon frère* . . . Frederic . . ." Then, realizing how far he'd allowed his defenses to drop, his eyes flashed open in alarm. But Louis was still seated, watching him with a century-deep detachment. It was a struggle for Marchand to force down the frailty of heart to ask, "H-How does one put such a creature to permanent rest?"

"There are several ways. A stake through the heart and the severing of the head from the body, consummation by fire and the scattering of ashes, exposure to daylight. They are vulnerable during the day when they are confined to darkness and their unnatural sleep."

Puzzled, Marchand glanced toward the slight gap in the drapes here the world outside was lightening by progressive degrees. Louis smiled blandly, making no effort to lift his confusion. Rather than challenge the truth of what he was hearing, Marchand asked, "Where does one look for these ghouls?"

"At night, they will find you. They'll be drawn to food. During the day, look in dark, secret places where they will not be easily disturbed." He paused and regarded Marchand for a long moment before asking, "And if you find your brother and your friend, will you have the courage it will take to end their existence?"

Marchand thought of those soulless eyes and answered without hesitation, "Yes."

Louis pursed his lips, his gaze leisurely measuring the other man. Then he nodded. "I think you will. And is this your plan, to put them to rest?"

Marchand was silent then, unsure of how much to reveal to the sophisticated demon before him.

Louis smiled. "If I judge you correctly, I would guess revenge figures into your plan as well."

He didn't answer, but instead asked, "How do I protect myself? I've already learned guns and sabres are useless."

"Have you?" Again, that cool arch of his brow. "Steel and lead have no power. Silver is what you must use. Silver and flame purify only second to the sun."

Marchand thought of Arabella Radouix's gift; the silver crucifix even now resting warm against his skin. "And do these same methods hold true when dealing with one of your stature?"

"We are speaking hypothetically, of course."

"Of course."

"Yes. But, be warned. The *revenants* are simple, graceless beasts, easy to catch and destroy. You will not find the same is true of a vampire."

"Oh?" Marchand allowed a haughty lift to his own dark brow. "And why is that, m'sieur?"

One instant Louis was calmly composed in his chair. In the next, his hand was wedged up beneath Marchand's jaw, exerting a paralyzing pressure, as his eyes, now hot and golden, blazed up with a lethal contempt from only inches away.

"Because, m'sieur, you will never see us coming. We will always know you are there even before you get a prickling of intuition. We have had centuries to perfect our skill and you are a novice in the hunt. If you seek to go after Bianca and Gerardo, tell my daughter goodbye, because you will never come back to her. At least, not as a man."

Marchand gasped because the grip was suddenly

gone and Louis Radouix was back in his chair, smiling infinitesimally. His hand shook as he rubbed his throat. He could have easily been killed had that been his host's intention. Humbled by his proven vulnerability, Marchand still did not relent.

"How then can I get to them? How can I see justice done?"

"By surviving once you dispose of their minions. That will be victory enough. Our vanity is monumental. We cannot bear the thought of being outsmarted by a mere . . . mortal. Take from them that which they own, make their lives uncomfortable, force them into hiding, that will hurt them. That's the best you can hope for."

"Are you saying this just to protect them?"

"I am not their guardian. It would sadden me to lose Gerardo, for he was once greatly loved by me, but I would not rush to Paris to save them from you." Again, the faint smile. "I don't think the trip will be necessary."

"You think they'll kill me."

"I *know* they will."

Marchand stared at the motionless features and suddenly he was irritated by the man's almost bored indifference. "And I'm sure that won't sadden you in the least, now, will it?"

Louis's expression shifted from its minimal air to a vibrating intensity and Marchand knew he'd struck on a sensitive spot. His accented voice was low, yet it throbbed with a penetrating power. "Do you think I am without feelings? Do you believe I feel no kinship toward those who walk in light and close their eyes in a final mortal sleep? I feel for your brother and your friend. I feel for your pain of loss, but I simply cannot afford to mourn the acts of the foolish who court their own destruction. I have mourned thousands in my years upon this earth. Do not make me grieve for you, young fool.

"You deal with killers who have ruthlessness refined to an art. They don't care about you or how you feel. They don't care about your brother or your friend. Your existence means nothing—*nothing* to them. I do not wish to console my daughter while she weeps over you."

Marchand said nothing. What could he say? He couldn't give the required assurances. He couldn't swear vengeance was not burning hot within him. And because he didn't, Louis turned away from him with a brusque annoyance.

"What other questions would you ask of me? Ask them quick. I must soon seek my rest. Or should I sleep with one eye open, expecting to see you above me with stake in hand?" The smile curving his generous lips was wry but his gaze was unblinking.

Marchand moved away from the map table, making his steps light and unconcerned even as sweat began to run beneath his collar the minute his back was to the vampire. "I was taught it was impolite to impale your host without due cause."

Louis gave a quiet laugh, then he was silent. When he spoke, his tone was coolly level. "You may find you have due cause if you break my daughter's heart. She believes herself in love with you, you know."

"I know. It was a feeling I returned."

"But no longer?"

Marchand came to a spot in front of the heavy velvet draperies. His fingers plied the sumptuous fabric as he murmured, "I don't know how I feel about her now. I'm not sure what she is."

"She is my child and I would do anything to protect her from harm. Do you understand?"

"Yes. It's not my wish to hurt her, m'sieur."

"It's not your wish to care for her either, is it?"

"She's not—"

"Not what? Loving? Beautiful? Sensitive? Strong? Bright? She is all of those things because she is her mother's child, too. What's not to love?"

"The fact that she's unnatural, m'sieur. She is a vampire, like you, like them. I know what she is. I saw what she is."

And because his voice faltered so painfully, Louis was patient. "Nicole is my child. You misunderstand one thing, my young friend. Someone good does not become evil because evil was done to them. There are as many shades to what we are as there are to what you are. I had not thought you narrow of mind but perhaps I was wrong. Perhaps I will not mind comforting Nicole over your loss after all."

And because there was a soft, subtle threat in those words, Marchand pulled the drapes open and turned to his host, his own figure framed in a halo of sunlight.

Louis gasped and stumbled back into the shadows of the room. His head was averted, his eyes shielded by his upraised hand. Then, surprisingly, came his quiet chuckle.

"You learn fast, *il mio amico*. Perhaps you will come back to her after all."

Chapter Nineteen

He walked so far Nicole began to fear his strength would fail him. He'd been weak and unsure of step the day before, but as he hiked the narrow trails, his stride was long and steady. He didn't seem to be out for the appreciation of the view, for he never paused to gaze upon the finer sights, but rather he was walking for the sake of movement. He was thinking. And she wondered, glumly, how she figured into that somber contemplation.

"Marchand?"

He came about so swiftly, he slipped upon the stones, but as she reached out to steady him, he reared back, skidding several feet off the trail, stumbling for balance. The first thing he did was cast a frantic glance around. And when he realized their isolation, his wariness increased tenfold.

"You followed me." It was an accusation. She tried to smile.

"I was worried about you. And I wanted to talk."

Again, the nervous look around.

"Are you afraid of me, Marchand?"

"No. Of course not," he answered too quickly for it to

be the truth. "I was just—I would rather be alone, is all."

She pretended not to hear that as she walked up near where he was standing and paused to admire the scenery. "It's so beautiful here. So peaceful after Paris. You could go for hours without ever seeing another soul."

She heard the rattle of stones and glanced around to see him on his way back down the trail at a hurried pace. It was no effort at all to catch up to him.

"Going back so soon?"

His gaze canted toward her, then quickly away. She could hear how rapidly his heart was pounding. Its rhythm had been quite calm before her approach, so she knew it wasn't exertion.

"Why are you running from me?"

"I'm not," he claimed tersely. "Why are you tracking me?"

"Tracking you?" She stopped, surprised by his choice of words. Tracking, as in stalking, as in hunting. "For the sport of it, is that what you wanted to hear?"

He gave her a longer look and it was colored with apprehension. Damn him, that *was* what he thought. And she was so incensed, she gave way to a bit of purposeful intimidation.

"How clever of you to have figured that out, that I would follow you to this remote place where no one could possibly hear your cries for help as I leapt upon you like a beast and sucked out your blood."

Immediately, he began to run.

"Marchand!" she called after him, then sighed in exasperation. He couldn't have felt more than a ruffling breeze before she was standing in his path. "Marchand, stop. I was only—"

But he'd braked so fast, he scuffled backward, falling

onto his seat, skinning his palms on the loose rock. He struggled up and was vaulting carelessly over a wall of jagged stone in his haste to escape her. Where did he think he was going to go, she wondered, as her hurt and annoyance grew.

Then she was blocking his way again and this time, he cried out and actually swung at her. She easily evaded his fist, but the thought that he would attempt to harm her made her furious.

"Marchand, I am not a monster!"

But he was already scrambling back down toward the trail.

"You fool, you're going to break your leg!"

Then she held her breath as he tripped and sprawled face first upon the dirt. He seemed momentarily dazed then. As he began to gather himself to continue his flight, Nicole dropped down hard upon the center of his back. His *oof* of surprise kicked up dust, then he was immediately grappling for some loose stone, some weighty stick, anything to wield as a weapon in his own defense. Angry with his persistent fear, she gripped his wrists and pulled them up tight behind his back, forcing his face into the loamy ground, letting him feel her superior strength. He knew struggle was useless, but still he thrashed beneath her.

"Now, you will listen to me," she commanded, bending so her face was close to his. He tossed his head to the other side, away from hers. She gave a frustrated groan. "Marchand, I'm not going to hurt you!"

"No, of course not!" he growled fiercely. "And I'm sure that is what your friends said to Frederic and Camille before they ripped their throats open and made them into—into those killing beasts. Or was that you? You said yourself you were with Camille on the day he

. . . *died*. And you weren't trying to hurt me that night when Frederic and Musette interrupted us on the floor in our flat? What was that? Is that the way your kind mates? Killing when they're through?"

She was so stunned, he was able to fling her off, clawing his way up to his feet, but instead of running, he whirled to confront her and squared off, panting hard, his expression dangerous. She stayed where she was, seated in the crumpled heather, staring up at him in angry anguish.

"I didn't kill Camille or Frederic," she shouted up at him. "And I've never harmed anyone except those trying to harm you!" She rose up so fast, he never saw her move. She had his face between her hands and was kissing him so hard, his senses swam. And when she opened her eyes to find him staring glassily at her, his breathing fast and fearful, she said huskily, "That's how I mate. And I remember that you liked it."

She stretched up again and this time, his eyes slid shut. With the slightest encouragement from her tongue, the seam of his mouth opened, letting her slip inside. In her restless longing for him, she rushed the moment, pressing herself up against him as her hands moved downward, her fingers stroking sensuously along the taut cords of his neck. And his body jerked rigid, his mood of compliance becoming wild resistance.

"No!"

He pushed her away, hard. And as she was tired of fighting with him, she shoved back. Her palms smacked into his shoulders with a force that knocked him flat on his back. She dropped down on him, slowing her descent at the last moment until she was almost floating, settling over him like a gentle breeze. And that agitated him all the more. His hands came up, ready to do battle, but she clasped his wrists and held them down against the earth on either side of his head, her grip gentle yet unbreakable. He tried to throw her off by twisting and tossing, but she made her weight quadruple in mass, pinning him quite efficiently.

"Marchand, don't be afraid." But she could feel his heart pounding against her and the tense shake of his muscles. He'd quit struggling, finally accepting the fact that he couldn't defeat her. He'd closed his eyes, rigidly resigned to his fate. Foolish man. "And what is it you think I have planned for you?" she crooned. "Something terrible, like this?" And her lips brushed over the flutter of his eyelids. "Something vile, like this?" Her tongue traced the whorl of his ear. "Or something truly frightening, like this?"

And her mouth touched his, light as a whisper, flirting along the arcs and swells of his while he took in her breath in hurried little gasps. She wanted so badly for him to respond in the way he once had, for him to be the aggressor, the one to initiate the passionate mood. But first she would have to convince him she meant him no harm. She would have to erase that image of her with fangs out, snarling like the demon she claimed not to be. She had to gain his trust, and to do that, she would have to prove temptation wouldn't sway her.

He moaned anxiously when her mouth pressed below his ear.

"No." His knees began to shift. "No."

"Shhh." Her breath blew warm against his throat. "I won't harm you." And she began to chain soft kisses along that taut curve. Her lips rode his frantic swallowing.

"No . . . please."

"Trust me, my love. I won't take anything from you

that's not freely given." Then she lifted up to whisper against his mouth, "I love you, Marchand."

He opened his eyes slowly.

She released his hands so hers could smooth his hair and stroke his face. His gaze was unblinking, filling up with a gradual awakening.

"Nicole."

A sudden hope shivered through her. Slow, she told herself. Slowly.

She kissed him. Her mouth fit to his with an undeniable familiarity. Let him remember. Let him remember that they'd kissed like this and had gone on to things more pleasant still. That they'd enjoyed each other well and that she'd not harmed him when she'd had the chance. And wouldn't harm him now.

She felt the tentative brush of his hands upon her hair. Soon, his fingers were sinking into the glossy dark waves, tightening, anchoring her above him. And his lips parted to pursue a deeper union. It was everything passion should be and her own heart was racing wildly in response.

"Oh, Marchand, make love with me!"

But even as she said that, she knew it was a mistake. It was too soon to push for intimacy. He broke from her kiss, turning his face away. His hands braced against her shoulders, not actively resisting but rather bidding her to hold back.

"I can't do this, Nicole."

His rejection touched off all the repressed anguish of the past few days, fueled by her own insecurities over who and what she was.

"No, of course you can't," she cried bitterly. "Not when you would take for a lover someone who's not a monster. Someone like Musette."

She was up and off him without registering his look of blank surprise.

"Nicole, what are you talking about?"

But she was marching down the trail, walking away from him as fast as she could without losing more dignity than she already had.

"Nicole? Nicole!"

She could hear him scrambling up, could feel his hesitation, but she didn't alter her brisk pace. He had to jog after her, to catch onto her arm to stop her, then she wouldn't look at him. She couldn't bear for him to see the tears on her face.

"Nicole, what's this about Musette? What would make you think there's anything between us?"

"I—I saw you together. I know she's sleeping with you."

"Oh."

Of course, he couldn't deny it, but the fact that he didn't even try made the tears fall all the faster.

"Nicole." He cupped his hand beneath her chin, but she fought his attempt to turn her face toward him. "Nicole, I have never and will never feel or act as anything but a brother to Musette. She would have been my sister-in-law, Frederic's bride. I could never think of her any other way. As for our sleeping together, that's all it was. Sleeping. Nicole?" He persisted and finally she looked up at him, her eyes melting with misery. "That's all it was."

She believed him. "It doesn't really matter, Marchand. I wish the only thing between us was Musette. But it's not that simple, is it? And it won't ever be as it was for us again."

And she walked away from him.

Marchand followed her with his gaze, and suddenly

he realized just what he might be losing if he let her continue on alone. A lifetime of logic and restraint fell away when he considered the emptiness of a future without her. He had reached out and touched upon a kindred flame. He'd found a spirit attuned to his own. She was the perfect complement and companion . . . except for the fact that she was not quite human. How could he possibly weigh those factors? As he watched her get farther and farther away, he knew he would have no choice but to find a way.

He trotted to catch up with her, then put his arm around her shoulders. Her resistance was meager and soon she was turned against his chest, her damp face buried in his shirtfront, his arms wrapped tightly about her.

"I love you, Nicole."

She made a soft, strangled sound and shook her head.

Marchand stroked her hair back and kissed her brow. "I do. That hasn't changed. Just please, please give me some time to take everything in. I can't rest. I can't make sense of my thoughts. But I know what's in my heart. You are. You are. You're all I have left. I don't want to lose you. Just please give me time."

After an interminable moment, she nodded. When she drew back, he let her go. She didn't look up at him again, but was very aware of him walking at her side as they made their way back down to the chateau. In the foyer, she paused to murmur, "I must rest for a time. Will I see you later?" And then her eyes lifted to engage his in poignant entreaty.

With infinite care, he curled his fingers beneath hers and carried her hand up to press a warm kiss upon it. She fought the urge to squeeze tight or to pursue him further when he released her. Slowly. Let him come to her. Give him time.

She just hoped they had it.

Marchand watched her climb the stairs. How difficult it was to juxtapose the slight feminine figure of Nicole Radouix with the snarling creature he'd seen at Bianca du Maurier's. How hard to accept her kisses and her confessions of love and still wonder if she was going to slay him. It was no longer a matter of love, because he loved her madly. It was an issue of trust. And that, he had yet to resolve.

"It isn't easy accepting what they are."

He turned and sketched a polite bow to Arabella. "No, madame, it is not," he admitted.

"Who they are is not what they do to survive."

"I know."

"But knowing doesn't make it any easier to bear when they go out at night and return filled with that hot flush to the skin and you have to tell yourself not to wonder, not to ask."

"And do you never wonder, madame?"

She gave him a slight smile. "I'm not a saint, m'sieur. I have my failings, too. I deal with them as best I can. Just as you will if you want a life with Nicole." Then she fixed him with an unswerving look. "Do you, Marchand?"

He didn't answer her directly. Instead, he said, "I'm returning to Paris in the morning."

No one needed to tell Arabella the significance of that. She studied his handsome features, reading the determination, the grim nobility of his cause in each line. And she asked, "Have you any idea of what you'll be facing?"

"*Oui*, madame, only too well."

She took up his hand in hers, holding it tight. "Are you strong enough?"

"I will soon find out."

"Do you have what you need?"

"I have your gift." He touched fingertips to his second shirt button, feeling the silver cross beneath it. "The rest I will obtain in Paris."

His confidence gave no comfort. "You will be careful, won't you?"

"I would ask a favor of you, if it's not too much."

"Ask."

"Would you care for Musette while I'm gone? She has no other family. Just me. It would be a great burden off my mind to know she'll be seen to if I—until I return."

"She is welcomed to stay with us for as long as needs be. She'll be good company for Nicole. Marchand . . . they are ruthless."

"I know what they are. And I know what they do."

"Would you let me send Takeo with you? He's had . . . experience . . . in this sort of thing, and he could assist you."

"Madame, this is a personal matter—"

"It won't matter to anyone if you're killed. Honorable causes must be tempered with reasonable caution. I thought you and I agreed on that, Marchand."

He permitted a small smile. "We do, and I thank you. I would be grateful for the help."

"And you will take our coach. It's unmarked so no questions will be raised. You can see to what you must and effect a quick return."

"That is my hope, madame." And he raised her hand up for a respectful kiss.

* * *

After a late lunch, Marchand drew Musette aside to tell her of his journey. She listened with eyes wide and tears gathering, then cried, "Why do you have to go?" not fully understanding the danger but intuiting it just the same.

"I must see to Frederic." And Camille. He didn't add that because she believed their young artist friend already dead and long buried. If only that were true!

"Then I would like to go with you."

"No, *cher,* you cannot. Let me make the arrangements, then I will come for you and we can pray over him together as he's laid to rest. Stay here with Nicole and her family. They've promised to watch out for you in case I—if I am delayed. Now, you be a good girl and give them no trouble."

She blushed and vowed she would not and he kissed her gently on the brow.

"Musette," he broached awkwardly, "I must ask you to keep to your own bed tonight."

"Oh?" She glanced up at him, the first provocative light he'd seen since Frederic's death dancing in her eyes. "You prefer some other company, do you?"

"Perhaps."

"Marchand, you are a great fool if you don't take her to your bed tonight. She is crazy for you and you for her, I think."

"Perhaps." But he was smiling faintly.

"Don't waste time when you could be together. Every opportunity is precious." And her gaze grew cloudy as she thought of her fiancé and the times they would not share. "Love her often and well so she will never have the occasion to feel regret over what might have been.

That is my one consolation. I have no regrets." She stroked his impassive face. "March, don't you have any."

As Marchand stretched out upon his bed in the lazy late-afternoon shadows, he was considering more than just regrets. His earlier outing with Nicole had done more than exhaust what little physical reserves he'd managed to restore. The confrontation had forced him to face what she was and what he'd be without her.

Nicole wasn't human. And without her, he'd be lost.

Perhaps it was his fatigue or the quiet somnolence of the chateau, but as he lay there in the comfort of his shirtsleeves, eyes closed and thoughts adrift, it was somehow simpler to conceive of the impossible and to dream of the unheard of.

Louis Radouix was a vampire, but not of the same sort as Bianca and Gerard. His daughter was some kind of unnatural hybrid, and that daughter firmly held his own heart. The shock of discovering what she was hadn't changed that. Knowing the truth didn't alter what he already loved about her. In fact, knowing what she was only increased his fascination. It was her strength that he admired; her depth of emotion, of commitment, of her resolve to protect those close to her. And most recently, her strength of will. She could have taken his blood any number of times but had refrained. And then there was the unbending belief in justice and common sense they both held to. He couldn't fool himself into believing he'd ever find another woman who possessed these qualities. It wasn't bred into the Parisian women of the day. But in Nicole Radouix he'd discovered everything he needed in a soulmate; he couldn't just give her up because—because she wasn't the average woman. The average woman had never interested him beyond a matter of minutes upon a horizontal plane. In Nicole, he'd found the attraction of a lifetime. Or an eternity.

And as he was thinking these radical thoughts, a seeping awareness came over him that he was not alone. Cautiously, he opened his eyes.

Nicole was standing at the foot of his bed. He hadn't heard the door open or her approach. But he was no longer surprised by either of those things. What did startle him was the dampness glistening in her great green-gold eyes.

"Musette told me you were leaving for Paris in the morning." Her voice was low and rough with poorly checked emotion. "Why, Marchand? Have you so little faith in our happiness?"

He came up on his elbows and told her simply, "I no longer have any doubts there at all." And he extended his hand to her. When she hesitated, appearing unsure, he beckoned with his fingers and called, "Nicole, come here to me."

Still, she held back. "Are you sure you want me to?"

"Very sure."

So she came to him, accepting his outstretched hand in hers rather meekly. And he pushed himself over, inviting, "Join me."

Nicole settled atop the covers. When she lay back, she curled his arm around her, nudging so she was pressed back-to-front against him, with his forearm hugged to her breast. He was bemused by the position and wondered if her intent was not to alarm him with a face-to-face encounter. He slipped his other arm about her, too, and conformed his legs to the curl of hers.

"Comfortable?" he crooned. Her silken hair tickled his nose as she nodded.

They lay like that for several minutes, soaking up the shared heat and sense of closeness until Nicole remembered her question.

"Why are you going to Paris?"

"I must see to Frederic and Camille. I can't let them wander as they are now. I can't."

Her face was turned away from his so he couldn't see her expression. She was quiet for a time and then he felt her trembling. She lifted his hands and began to press frantic little kisses to them. Finally, she said, "It would do no good for me to beg you to stay, would it?"

"I'm afraid not."

"Oh, March, you don't know how strong they are, how cruel they are."

"Yes, I do."

"Then how can you do this? Let me——"

"No. Before you even ask, the answer is no, you can't go with me. I need you here to see to Musette. I need you here where it is safe. Your father has given me the benefit of his knowledge and your mother offered me the company of Takeo, so you see, I won't be going there blind or alone. I'll be going in the daylight hours so the danger is slight and I should be back by tomorrow evening if all goes well."

"And if it doesn't go well? If you don't come back?"

He said nothing.

Her voice was all quivering command as she told him, "Don't you dare leave me to face the future alone, Marchand. Don't you dare!"

"I won't, my love, I won't."

And then he was brushing her hair aside so he could place a string of kisses from her temple to her collarbone. She made a soft sound that was his undoing. She lifted his hand and settled it upon the curve of her breast and sighed at his unhurried fondling. The way her body rubbed against him suggested he move on from there as love and desperate longing encouraged a more fulfilling intimacy. His need for her becoming an urgent thing, Marchand's hands lowered to bunch and gather the volume of her skirt and petticoat upward. She lifted obligingly so he could tug her drawers down, then she gave a tremulous moan at the first warm caress of his hands. It took very little coaxing for her to be wet and ready to receive him. She gave a small cry when he became a part of her and he was amazed anew by the powerful way she welcomed him. Then there were no doubts for either of them that they belonged together.

In no time at all, she'd found that exquisite point of no return. Her back arched away from him as tiny tremors started deep and grew to overwhelming quakes. And with one final thrust, Marchand's seed was planted deep within her receptive female form and there it took tenacious hold without either of them knowing it.

Too replete to do more than pull the counterpane up over them both, Marchand held her close as awareness drifted away on a satisfied tide.

He was somewhere deep in slumber when the first persistent call intruded.

Marchand.

An unpleasant tingling raced along his limbs. In an odd state of suspension, he was aware of Nicole curled against him, of the heaviness of the shadows that foretold of sunset. He tried to open his eyes but found he could not.

Marchand, where are you?

Drowsily, his mind formed a reply. *In bed with Nicole.* He shivered as a current of tension shot through him.

He moaned in his unnatural sleep and tried to twist away from the discomfort.

Where are you?

He continued to shift, not wanting to answer, unable to keep from doing so. *With Nicole's family.*

With Gino.

Gino? Marchand's head shook from side to side. No, he didn't know any Gino. *Want to sleep.*

After you tell me where. Where can I find you? You must tell me. You must answer.

He didn't want to. He grew increasingly agitated. *No.*

You mustn't resist. I'll hurt you if you resist and I'll hurt those you love.

No, don't. "Don't hurt me." He tossed restlessly, eyes squeezing tight. "Don't hurt them."

"Marchand?" Nicole blinked groggily awake.

Tell me where you are?

Chateau.

Where, fool! Tell me where!

"Camille's painting. In Camille's painting."

"Marchand, are you awake?" Nicole stroked his hot cheek and his eyes came open. His gaze was dark and glassy.

"In the painting," he mumbled again, then he gave a sudden jerk, coming fully awake. "Nicole? What is it?"

"You were talking in your sleep."

"I was?" His confusion gave way to the depthless pleasure of seeing her there beside him. He smiled smugly. "Did I say anything I shouldn't have?"

"If you mean did you compromise yourself by crying out 'Fifi' or 'Renee,' no you did not, lucky for you."

"Then it must have been dreams of you that awakened me in such an impatient state." And he drew her up close so she could feel what had stirred to life. He throbbed hard and huge against the tangle of her clothing.

She tipped her face up so that only inches separated them. The desire in his dark eyes excited. She could feel his anticipation in the way his breathing quickened and his heartbeats hurried. She put her hand to his cheek. He didn't shy from her touch. Instead, he leaned into it. Her emotions trembled.

"Then we shall have to do something to make those dreams into reality, won't we?" she suggested with a husky rumble. "How can we do that?"

"We can start here." He began to unbutton her bodice, slipping his hands inside to repeat the process down the length of her corset. Then there was the plain fabric of her chemise, which was easily pushed from her shoulders to expose a wondrously fair bosom. He adored that pale firm flesh with his touch, with his kisses, until she was impatiently yanking his shirt free.

What followed was a sensuous tussle through one another's clothing and then the exquisite feel of skin on skin. Entwined in limb and spirit, they shared a lengthy kiss, then Nicole pushed away.

"Roll over."

"What?"

"Onto your stomach. Go on."

He did so, bemused, then he sighed with sheer delight as her hands plied the tense cording of his shoulders. She bent to place a kiss between them and to murmur, "I love you, Marchand," before moving that penetrating massage downward.

And as she kneaded each swell of dramatically molded man, Nicole was searching his bared surfaces for signs of a vampire's bite.

He was complete putty by the time she ground the

heels of her hands into the small of his back and palmed the tight curve of his buttocks. His legs spasmed in involuntary reflex as she worked his toes, and then she whispered throatily, "Other side now."

Relaxation was the furthest thing from his mind as Nicole eased her way up to his sturdy thighs. He gripped her hand and guided it up a little farther to where the real tension of the moment lay. And the instant her hand closed around him, his eyes closed and the breath began to shudder from him.

She wasn't gentle with him. Her touch was strong, greedy, demanding. She made him so hot and achy he didn't think he could stand another stroke. Gripping her by the upper arms, he hauled her up and then she was plundering his mouth with wild, plunging kisses that were every bit as aggressive as her caress had been. That's when he understood. During the daylight hours, she would be his sweet, responsive lover, but at night, when her more basic instincts growled to life, he was hers.

He had nothing against compromise.

Without relinquishing his mouth, Nicole came up over him, straddling his hips, moving slick and hot above him. And just as she started to drop down onto him, he caught the backs of her thighs, holding her immobile, keeping her from the paradise she pursued until she was panting desperately into his kisses.

"Marchand . . ." It was a plea. It was a command.

He let her down slowly, easing into her so gradually that she was trembling in helpless abandon by the time the fit was complete. And then he held her there so she could feel the strength of him pulsing all the way up to her womb. She lifted off his lips, her eyes seeking his in

an awed daze, then rolling up white from the force of
his first thrust.

From there, it became a rough, sweaty mating punc-
tuated with wet, wide kisses and low, hoarse cries of
pleasure. And when she let go uncontrollably, she had
his fingers meshed between hers, pressing the backs of
his hands down into the mattress as she rode him to a
mutual release of shattering intensity. Then she
stretched out along the hard, bare length of him and
sighed with a blissful contentment.

After a timeless, lazy moment, Nicole shifted back,
wanting to look down upon his handsome face, to smile
at him, to revel in the matching glow of perfect har-
mony shining in his eyes. She did those things and her
heart filled with the marvel of loving him. She saw
about his neck her mother's crucifix, and realized he'd
already won her family's blessing. The moment was perfect.

Until a stray gaze wandered down the muscular curve
of his forearm to the valley of his elbow.

"My God, Marchand, what is that?"

And he followed her horrified stare to the pair of
marks that branded him the possession of another.

Chapter Twenty

Marchand's other hand clapped over the bite and he made the incredible claim, "It's nothing!" There was a growling edge to that, warning her away from further questions. But she couldn't afford to ignore the obvious. She pulled his concealing hand away.

"I know the mark, Marchand. Whose is it?"

So many things paraded across his face in the next half minute; horror, foremost, then anger and fright, frustration, then confusion. And finally, a blank. He just stared at the mark, his eyes empty.

"Marchand?" she persisted gently. "Who did this to you?"

"I—I—" And his voice grew as vague as his expression.

"It happened that night when you went after Frederic, didn't it?"

She saw something shift in his eyes and she didn't like recognizing it as desperate cunning. "No."

"Yes. Who was it? Frederic? Camille?"

"No."

"Gerard?"

"He wasn't there."

"Bianca, then."

And he said nothing. His features took in a belliger-ent, protective opaque. She wanted to shake him, to slap him, to free him from the slavish stupor. But she knew nothing would wake him.

"Get dressed, Marchand. We must go to my parents with this news." She was off the bed, pulling on her clothes while he sat struggling through his daze. Finally, he shook his head slowly.

"No, we can't. They'll think I betrayed them. Nicole, they mustn't know. They won't let us be together."

She looked at him, suddenly suspicious. How much of his concern was for them and how much due to his need to protect the one who'd drunk from him? Know-ing what she did, she couldn't trust him. "They have to know. We could be in terrible danger."

He looked up at her through wide, guileless eyes. "I would never hurt you or them."

Tenderly, she cupped his face in her palms. "I know, my love." And she kissed him with an urgent affirming passion, thinking angrily as she did of Bianca going into the veins of the man she'd claimed for her own. Furious that the other creature could so warp the faith she and Marchand were trying to establish between one another. Now there could be no trust unless she could find some way to free him from Bianca's grasp.

Louis pushed up Marchand's sleeve and with a dis-passionate calm, regarded the marks revealed by the warm glow of their sitting room's fire grate. Marchand stood rigidly at attention, suffering that scrutiny. An un-bidden part of him was demanding that he pull away, that he cover the evidence, that he deny it to his last breath even though it was no longer a secret to be kept. That impulse tortured him while he held himself still, relying on a lifeline of military training for what little dignity he could yet command.

"He'll lead them right to us," Louis stated emotionlessly.

"Is it Bianca?" Arabella asked in a tight, little voice.

Louis forked his hand beneath Marchand's chin and held his head steady so he could delve into the cloudy confusion of his mind. After a long, concentrated moment, Marchand's breath began to labor and his brow broke out in a sweat. When Nicole took an alarmed step forward, her mother caught her arm and held her fast.

"Don't interfere."

"But Father's hurting him!"

"Let him do what he must."

A guttural sound of distress moaned up from Marchand. Louis's eyes had become hot green-gold flares, burning into his, cutting through the torpid layers of his brain to where a wall of unknown resistance stood firm. With his thoughts like great prying hands, Louis worked against that barrier, digging in deep, trying to spread apart those tightly woven links of imprinted defensiveness to get inside, mentally battering, physically rendering until Marchand's knees gave way beneath the pressure. Pushing harder until the force threatened to crush his skull and destroy his mind entirely.

Marchand was clawing at his arm, gasping for air, crying out from the agony that ripped along his veins from those two pulsing points at his elbow that seemed to have grown enormous and alive with pain. Then Louis's hand opened, and freed, Marchand sank to the floor on hands and knees, weaving with a disoriented sickness. He was aware of Nicole's embrace, of her strength supporting him. And he could hear the grim summation Louis made.

"It was done by a master. None but Bianca or Gerardo could have created a bond too strong for me to break."

"Oh, Louis, what are we going to do? I refuse to spend the rest of my life running from that monster! I thought we'd be safe here."

"I didn't tell her anything," Marchand mumbled thickly. He was trying to wedge his feet under him but it was Nicole who had to help set him up on them. "I didn't tell her where you were."

"Yes, you did." That reluctant whisper came from Nicole. He stared at her, bewildered. "Camille's painting. I heard you speaking of it aloud. The painting he gave me. It was of Grez. Any artist would know that. Anyone asking hereabout would know of us."

"I didn't—" But the strength of his protest failed him, because he could remember speaking the words. He pushed away from Nicole, reeling through his own private hell of doubts. What had he done? Had he, with all his high ideals, brought the very devil to their door?

"It's not your fault, Marchand," Arabella told him kindly in spite of her own anxiety. "You can't help what she made you do."

He was rubbing the inside of his elbow with an absent vigor. "How can this power she has over me be broken? What must I do? I will not be a danger to you." Then he saw the way Louis was looking at him and he recalled his words. "Only death," he repeated. "Hers or mine." He drew a slow breath, then said, "Kill me now, quickly."

"Marchand!" Nicole was instantly wrapped around him. "What are you saying? It's madness!"

"Not madness, Nicole. Necessity. Otherwise, it will all be for nothing; Frederic, Camille, and who knows how many others. It has something to do with De Sivry, for I saw Gaston there in her house. Nicole, I will not be a pawn in her plans. I could not bear for her to harm you and your family through me. Your father knows I am right." He was setting her aside firmly. "He will do what must be done, for me, then I beg you, for Frederic and Camille, as well."

Slowly, impressed and grieved, Louis nodded.

"Father, you can't kill him! There must be some other way." Nicole went to him, lifting beseeching eyes.

Louis was unable to reassure her. His solution was not much better. "If I brought him over and made him one of us, he would be my fledgling, not hers. But I don't know if I can, Nicole. I've never done it. I don't know if my blood would be strong enough to carry him back from the veil."

"Then you can't—"

"He must!" Marchand had no time to contemplate the moral nature of his choice. It had to be made. He gripped his collar, jerking it open. "Do it now, before she finds us."

"Oh, *chéri*," purred a lethal voice from behind him. "Such a noble gesture, but alas, it comes too late." And Bianca's hand snaked around to catch him by the throat, compressing to the point of paralysis. Then she smiled at father, mother and daughter with benign malice. "Good evening, my friends. How well you all look. But so surprised! Didn't I tell you I'd return?"

"Get out of my house!" That was growled by Arabella, who alone had no power to withstand the lovely killer's wrath.

Bianca pursed her lips. "Oh, Gino, this one has no breeding at all."

"What do you want, Bianca?" Louis demanded in irritation. "We grow weary of your infantile dramatics. If you've a point, make it and begone."

Her features grew very pinched and pale. Her eyes glittered upon parchment skin like bits of sharp-edged coal. "My point? I believe I made it long ago, just as I made you, Gino. You are mine, just as this pretty one here is mine and Gerard is mine. And what is mine, I keep or I discard at will, but I never, ever share. A minor flaw, perhaps, one I fear I take quite seriously."

And at that moment, Nicole realized how cruelly she'd been used by the lovely blond demon. She, like Marchand, had been Bianca's tool for vengeance, nothing more. Whatever happened within the next few minutes would be entirely upon her conscience.

Arabella stepped closer to her husband and Nicole found her defiant courage nothing short of amazing considering what the vampiress could do. "Nothing here is yours. Louis married me and Nicole is our daughter. That young man is here as our guest. What gives you the right to meddle in our lives?"

"Power. I do because I can and there is nothing you can do to stop me."

"I can stop you, witch," Louis drawled coldly. "Leave my family alone. Let that boy go. Step out into the night with me and we will see who is stronger."

"Louis, no—"

He put his hand over the one Arabella placed upon his sleeve, but he didn't look at her. His attention was fixed upon the deadly vampiress. "I have never liked your games, Bianca. They bore me as you bore me. Be done with them now. You have no power here."

She drew a soft, seething breath. "Oh, you are wrong, Gino. But if you want it ended, so it will end." And from her cloak, she pulled a small pistol.

Nicole and Arabella gasped but Louis sneered at her. "You mean to shoot me?"

Her laugh was discordant. "Oh, no. Not I. I won't have your death on my hands. Gerardo would find out and I don't believe he would be as generous in his vengeance as you have been. For all his truly ruthless points, he can be annoyingly sentimental at the most inconvenient times. No. It won't be by my hand. Take it, Marchand."

And Marchand's hand came up obediently to close about the pistol grip. He was staring straight ahead, his eyes like dark window glass. His aim was true and unwavering as it sighted in upon Louis.

"The bullets are silver," Bianca went on to say. "My young friend's skill should leave no room for error. Goodbye, Gino. I shall miss you."

"Marchand, no!"

But Louis gripped his daughter's arm. "Nicole, stay back. He can't hear you."

"That's right," Bianca chuckled. "Mine is the only voice he recognizes. A bullet through the heart, Marchand. The heart you would not give to me, Gino. Do it now."

Just for an instant, the gun faltered as a dappling of perspiration broke upon Marchand's brow. That hesitation before he squeezed the trigger gave Arabella the time to fling herself in front of her husband, becoming a human shield to save him. The report of the gun was massive within the confines of the room and as the echoes were dying, Arabella sank into Louis's arms, a limp burden.

"Bella!"

He went down to his knees with her, his expression one of anguished disbelief as he regarded the crimson stain upon his palm.

"Bella, no!"

Bianca glared down at them dispassionately, watching the dark fatal flower bloom across the back of Arabella's gown. "It isn't the revenge I came for, but it will do. It is enough to have you on your knees before me once again."

"Marchand . . ."

That moan came from Nicole, distracting Bianca's attention as he raised the pistol again, thrusting the hot barrel up under his own chin and pulling the trigger once, twice. Bianca laughed and wrenched the empty weapon from him.

"Fool! Did you think I would give you more than one chance? Say goodbye to our dear Nicole. You won't be seeing her again." And she jerked him backward through doors she closed and barred behind them, preventing an immediate pursuit.

Marchand remembered none of the trip back to Paris. That the night was cold and damp was all he could recall. Then he was following Bianca into the palatial home she shared with Gerardo Pasquale. Following her with the docile obedience of a puppy because she told him to. Just as he'd fired the gun at her command. Because he was without any will of his own.

However, his mind was not a blissful blank. In fact, it was agonizingly alive to all going on about him. He was aware of what he'd done in that private chamber, that he'd slain Nicole's mother; a woman he admired and respected, that he'd done it with only a token resistance that in the end hadn't been enough. He had seen the horror in his beloved's face as her eyes raised to his in disbelief. And then he'd been unable to do the noble thing to stop the creature Bianca had made him from doing more wrong at her bidding.

For he couldn't stop. That part of his mind that was alive and thinking, reacting with outrage and indescribable dismay, was disassociated from the part that presided over motion. That part of him, Bianca controlled. She moved him about like her living, breathing puppet and, while his mind might shout and scream objections, his body compiled of its own volition.

"Come along, handsome one," Bianca was saying as she walked down the large empty hall with her lithe, soundless step. "You know, you are not very amusing. I thought I might enjoy your spirit but I find it tedious after all. Too much effort to control you. I had considered bringing you over for my companion, but I think not. You would not serve me half as well as Gerard. I don't believe you like me very much, do you, pretty one? No? Ah, well. Too bad.

"And speaking of Gerard, what shall we tell him, eh? We cannot have him angry with us—or rather, with me." She looked back over her shoulder, giving him a cold, calculating stare.

"*Cara*, where have you been?" Gerard's silky voice intruded, and soon Marchand saw him gliding in effortlessly from one of the adjacent rooms. "Why have you brought him here with you?"

"What kind of greeting is that, my love?" Bianca chided. "Only questions? No words of fond welcome?" She slipped her arms over his shoulders, drawing him up close to her. Suspicion immediately flickered in his pale eyes as she pressed several explicit kisses upon his mouth. He caught her wrists and held her away.

"What have you done?"

"Gerardo, what makes you think—"

"Stop simpering. I know you too well." He glanced at Marchand again, then back to his lovely companion of the centuries. "Tell me what you've been up to. Tell me now."

"Really, you force me to hurt you and that was not my plan." She was touching his stern-featured face with light, soothing strokes. "Oh, my heart, I am so sorry to bring you such sad news."

Again he caught her wrists, the compression making her wince. "What news? Has something happened to Nicole?"

"Not . . . directly."

He gave a soft gasp. "Gino?"

"Oh, Gerardo, it's my fault, my fault. I sent this mortal villain to find him. You know how I have longed to see dear Gino again. How was I to know the treacherous creature would decide to do the righteous human thing and end our dear old friend's existence?"

"He killed Gino?" And for the first time, Marchand saw the unfailingly composed Gerardo Pasquale shaken.

Liar! She's lying to you! Those words screamed inside Marchand's head, but all he could do as the vampire's piercing stare turned upon him was stand mute and helpless to defend himself.

Bianca's hands were gently kneading Gerard's forearms. Her voice was honeyed sympathy. "He had a gun with bullets of silver with which to see it done. But when he fired—when he fired, Gino's mortal bride stepped between them. She chose her own death to spare her husband."

Gerard took a step back. There was no change in his expression, no shift in his eyes.

Bella? His mental cry hurtled through space and fell into emptiness as vast as a black sea. He reached again, desperately. *Nicole, what has happened?* But from the vague connection he could make with her mind, he picked up fragmented images rather than coherent words. Marchand with gun in hand. The smoke of it discharging. Arabella sagging in her husband's arms. His friend's stricken face. He closed his eyes, breaking off from that tortuous portrayal.

"I knew how disturbed you would be, my love," Bianca continued with her tender purr of insincerity. "That's why I brought this vile assassin back with me. I brought him for you, Gerardo."

And the iridescent eyes reopened, canting over with glittering intensity to where Marchand stood. "For me?"

She rubbed his prominent cheekbone with her knuckles. "Are you pleased, *caro?* Do you forgive me?"

He turned his head to catch her fingers with a kiss. "A thoughtful gesture. *Mílle grázie.*"

"Because I love you, beautiful one. I don't wish you to be unhappy with me. And Gerardo," she whispered against the cool part of his lips, "don't worry about the mess. I'll clean it up for you."

Marchand watched her walk away. Upon her face, there was a smug smile Gerard couldn't see. *Run,* Marchand instructed his placid body. *Run!* But he continued to stand in place as Gerard approached. Though the sleek vampire's expression was remote and calm, Marchand could sense the violence simmering through him. And when he paused and gradually lifted his pale gaze to fix his own trancelike stare, the century-deep blue of his eyes was ablaze with white-hot sparks.

"So, what shall I do with you, young friend?" came the soft, accented drawl.

Then a tremendous roar tore up through the silvery-eyed Florentine. The back of his hand flew upward, striking a blow that sent Marchand airborne down the thirty-foot length of the hall. He went tumbling in through the doorway of the parlor and Gerard came after him.

From where he lay on the marble tiles, Marchand saw Gerard streak past like the blur of a tornado. Howling like that uncontrollable storm, raging with an unnatural fury that sent him rocketing about the walls and ceiling, he destroyed everything in his path. Priceless artifacts, vases, draperies, furniture; shattered, splintered, ripped assunder as he stirred up an incredible tempest of raging pain.

Move, run, defend yourself or he's going to tear you to pieces! Get up, you fool! He's going to kill you!

But Marchand could do nothing but lie there, body dormant, while his mind shrieked in angry useless warning.

At last Gerard slowed into a recognizable form, one that wandered in wobbling aimless circles, wailing like a wounded animal. Then finally he was still, a low, wet sound seething from him. He turned his face toward Marchand, and there was dying horribly etched in every jutting angle and sunken plane.

Oh God! Run!

"How could you think to do such a thing?" Gerard moaned in abject misery. "Gino, he is the best of our kind and Bella—Bella, she is—she was a most worthy female, one who could move even so hard and black a heart as mine."

It wasn't me! It was my hand but not my deed!

"If only there was a way I could make you live long enough to suffer as I will suffer this through an eternity. But alas, I haven't the patience for torture. I shall have to content myself with ripping you apart and scattering your insides."

And then Gerard came toward him, moving with that slow liquid grace no human being could manage. For all his unchecked fury of moments ago, he was now controlled by an emotionless calm. Only his glittering eyes betrayed any signs of sorrow. He reached down for Marchand, hoisting him easily to his feet, then with one powerful move, tore open his shirt from collar to waist.

And there upon Marchand's broad chest gleamed the silver cross.

Gerard regarded it, not with fear or distaste but with an odd remorse. "That was Bella's. I remember the first time she showed it to me." His lips twitched into a slight smile. Then he was all cold business once again. "She was too brave to be destroyed by one cowardly act. Take it off."

When Marchand didn't move, the vampire roared, "Take it off or I will remove your head from your shoulders, upend you and shake you until it falls off!"

When Marchand didn't move; couldn't move, Gerard reached out to crush the delicate clasp with powerful fingers, snarling in rage as the silver seared him. The chain trickled down from around Marchand's neck, dropping between his feet.

Hit him! Escape while you can! He's going to kill you! But there would be no escape now, even if he could have broken from Bianca's drugging spell. Everything inside him shivered loose as Gerard's cool palm stroked over his cheek and grazed the side of his throat. His heart was beating frantically in contrast to his unnatural outward lethargy and he could tell that hurried rhythm was exciting the vampire's lust for blood, because Gerard was leaning closer, his nostrils flaring, his mouth moistening in anticipation.

Marchand could smell the fine wool of his coat and sense the inhuman chill of his flesh as he was embraced in the other's arms, the way a dear friend would be gathered close and held near. One slender hand was stroking through his hair, petting him in the soothing way one calmed a frightened domestic pet. And then those fingers meshed tight and tugged back hard, pulling his neck into a tautly exposed arch. And Gerard's breath whispered there against the throb of life he was about to lose.

Push him away! Don't go placidly to your death. Strike him. Curse him. Anything! Say something to distract him!

"Nicole."

Her name croaked from the constricted bend in his throat.

"Nicole?"

The hairs all over Marchand's body prickled as the vampire spoke that against his veins.

"Do you think Nicole would save you now?" Then Gerard was still and thoughtful even though his grip on Marchand never slackened. "But perhaps you are right. Perhaps I am being selfish. Nicole should be the one to have the pleasure of the kill." But then his lips were rubbing silkily over the bulge of his carotid artery. "But that's no reason to deny myself for the moment."

Marchand ordered his body to resist. He screamed at

his muscles to jerk back, to pull away, but all he could effect was a tense tremor that shook him from head to toe.

Then came the sudden sharp puncturing pain of Gerard's teeth. And with it, all the shadows fell from his mind. He could remember more than he wanted about Bianca's thirsty kiss, about her softly uttered instructions that clouded memory and morals and made him a devil's pawn. Then with Gerard's first, hard draw, the blood came racing through his arteries, leaving him tingling all over with spots flashing bright before his eyes. His outcry faded to a moan and the involuntary thrust of his palms against the fine wool coat became a helpless flutter and finally, his hands fell limp at his side.

His knees gave and Gerard went with him down to the floor, still feasting greedily from the fount as his throat. A numbing weariness threaded through his veins with each strong pull, but instead of drinking him down into darkness, Gerard lifted up slightly to break the vital connection then leaned for the longest moment with his heated cheek against Marchand's cold one while he gasped for breath and swam with the intoxicating current of blood. Over the fragile thunder of his own heart, Marchand could hear the slurred voice whisper against his ear, "Now, how am I going to hold you until Nicole's return? The dawn is almost upon us."

While he considered that question, his mouth was drawn back to the holes he'd made and Marchand shuddered at the feel of him sucking delicately from them as if he was reluctant to leave the remains of a delicious meal while yet stirred by appetite. Then Gerard was on his feet, dragging Marchand with him across the room to an alcove in the far wall. Marchand felt a breeze of movement against his fevered face and got the impression of the wall yawning open as if to swallow them alive.

His vision was poor. Weakness and shock were seeping though him with a paralyzing chill. He made out a large dark shape but didn't know what it was until Gerard stepped close and opened the top. Then Marchand gave a moan of recognition.

It was Gerard's coffin.

"You'll be safe in here with me. Bianca knows not how to find me and you'll never be able to lift the lid off to escape."

"No!" Horror forced that protest from his lungs.

"Now, don't be squeamish. Get used to the feel and to the darkness. You'll be making your permanent home in one of these quite soon." And he climbed inside, lying back then pulling Marchand in facedown over him. The lid closed, sealing off all light, all life.

Marchand was too weak for full-blown hysteria to take hold, but panic was very much alive within him. The blackness of the interior itself was suffocating, filled as it was with the smell of his own blood and moist frantic breathing. Beneath him, Gerard had gone completely still as the lassitude of daylight overtook him. The thrum of his heartbeat slowed until it was imperceptible and there was no rise-and-fall motion of his chest. It was like resting atop a corpse; except this corpse was hot with the life stolen from him.

He had to get out. The darkness, the cold, the frantic distress compounded by the second until Marchand was panting wildly with it. He pressed his back against the silk-lined lid, pushing up with all his might, but it gave not an inch. He was trapped inside the den of the dead.

Beneath him, he felt the rumbling vibration of Gerard's laugh. "Lay still, fool. Conserve your strength and your air or you'll be dead before Nicole arrives. And I wouldn't want for her to miss the pleasure of ending your miserable life."

Chapter Twenty-One

A pounding upon the chamber door startled father and daughter.

"Master Louis? Mistress Arabella? What's going on in there? I thought I heard a shot!" The knob rattled, then Bessie Kampford's voice sounded more rattled, still. "Break it down, Takeo!"

The heavy portal shuddered and gave inward, admitting the two worried servants who drew up in horror at the sight before them; Louis and Nicole on their knees, Arabella with her pale, still face resting upon her husband's chest. And blood . . . everywhere.

And because it became obvious that her father wasn't going to take control, Nicole did, saying crisply, "Mother's been injured. Mrs. Kampford, we need a doctor, immediately. The one from the village should do for now until we know how bad things are."

"She's—alive?"

"Yes. Hurry!"

And there was the sound of crunching petticoats as the housekeeper fled down the stairs.

Takeo came to kneel down at his friend and master's side, his gaze asking eloquently if there were something he could do. But Louis's look was lost and beyond asking for anything but the seemingly impossible; that the clock could reverse itself to bring him back his vivacious wife.

"We should get her to bed, lie her down," Nicole suggested, but beyond that, she had no answers.

"No, not yet. I would like to hold her a bit longer."

"Father—"

"Just a bit longer."

Takeo rose up, drawing Nicole away with him so that Louis could be alone with his love. He spoke to her softly, unaware of whether he used words or the power of his mind but needing to reach out to her, to touch her any way he could. To make her understand what she meant to him.

"Bella, my love, you cannot do this to me. How will I go on without you? I'm not ready to let go of you yet." He stroked back her hair with stained fingers and tenderly kissed her brow. "You promised you would always be there for me when I awoke. Would you go back on your word now when I need you most? Would you let Bianca have her way? Would you let her have me?"

A soft sound of objection moaned from the figure beginning to stir in his embrace. And a name: "Louis," as fragile fingertips lifted to sketch the dramatic angle of his cheek. He caught that hand and pressed fevered kisses to it.

"Bella, stay with me. Stay with me, little one."

"I would never leave you, my love," came her weak reply, but it was enough to satisfy him. Carefully, he lifted her and bore her to the bed they'd shared in their long and unusual relationship of myth and mortal. She lay upon the covers, white and frail.

"Are you in terrible pain?" Louis asked gently, his eyes reflecting the agony he knew she must feel.

"No," she whispered. "Only a slight discomfort. And I fear for Marchand. Louis, what will happen to him?"

"Shhh. Don't concern yourself over that now. I will see to Marchand. And to Bianca."

"No, Louis. Let her go. If she is satisfied with her revenge, let her have it. I will not lose you to her."

"You must rest now. The doctor is on his way."

"The village charlatan? Louis, do not let him remove anything unnecessarily. I would not like to be a test subject for the local witch doctor."

He chuckled softly and kissed her, murmuring, "I did not know you were a professional snob, my love. I will watch over you for as long as I can."

"Nicole? Where is Nicole?"

"She is here."

"Louis, you must protect her. She will want to go after Marchand. It's what I would do."

He smiled faintly. "I will keep her safe. Now rest. I will be here with you."

And he stayed, even when the doctor arrived and insisted that he leave the room while he gave his examination. Louis fixed him with a cool stare and the man swallowed nervously, agreeing to allow him to remain. Nicole, Musette, Bessie and Takeo hovered in the sitting room, anxiously awaiting news that was pessimistic at best.

"She may not walk again," Louis told the gathering grimly. "If she does, it will be with difficulty. The bullet is lodged near her spine, and few surgeons have the skill needed for such a delicate piece of work. I am sending for one of them, but in the meantime, all we can do is keep her comfortable."

Nicole went to him and hugged him hard. She'd never seen him vulnerable before, not like this, and that frightened her deeply. Morning was upon them and she could tell its brightness was hurting him, but he refused to go below until the doctor had finished and was seen to the door. By then, he was gaunt and distressed.

"Father, you must rest," Nicole urged gently. "Go below and I will see to things here."

He looked as though he might argue, but the advancing daylight was wearing on him, dragging down upon the clarity of his mind even as he struggled to stay alert. "All right, but you must promise to do nothing foolish, Nicole. You are not strong enough. You don't know all that you face. Leave them for me. Your word."

"I will do nothing foolish." And she leaned forward to kiss his hollowed cheek. "I love you, *mío pádre.*"

No, she would do nothing foolish, she told herself as she climbed the stairs alone. She'd already done enough foolish things. Things that endangered her family and her love, nearly costing her mother her life and Marchand his freedom. It was time to do sensible, well-thought-out things.

She glanced in on her mother to find her sleeping peacefully under Bessie's care. Takeo was in the sitting room, his impassive Oriental mein poorly disguising his concern.

"Takeo, I must leave for Paris."

He instantly gripped her wrist and held fast. She patted that imprisoning hand.

"I want you to watch over my father and mother. Keep them safe. I must go for Marchand. He may not survive another nightfall. I am responsible for all that has happened and I will see things to right. I have the advantage of the daylight and I can no longer claim ignorance of my enemy. My mother was willing to make the ultimate sacrifice of her life for my father. Can I do any less for the man I love?"

Takeo continued to stare at her as if he was seeing some strange metamorphosis from child to woman before his very eyes.

"Let me go, Takeo. I should hate to harm you but be warned, you will not stop me."

He smiled blandly and released her wrist, executing a formal bow of acquiescence that humbled her. Winning his acceptance was a monumental feat, especially when it meant going against her father's wishes. It was a sign of faith that he believed her capable of seeing to her quest. She hoped he was right.

Nicole delayed long enough to kiss her mother's still cheek and to reassure Musette that she would be bringing Marchand back with her. As she headed for the door and the destiny that awaited, Takeo sketched another bow and extended an ornate sheath. She took it curiously and, placing a hand upon a finely wound leather hilt, withdrew from it a glittering silver blade approximately a foot in length. He didn't need to explain. It was for the taking of a vampire's head.

In spite of her hurry, Nicole dreaded the return to Paris. She knew what lay ahead; a challenge she wasn't sure she could meet, a man she wasn't sure she could claim.

What if Marchand was already dead? Did she have the kind of strength it would take to use the blade she carried to put him to a decent rest? She couldn't allow him to rise up as a *revenant*. Not a man of Marchand's noble spirit. He would prefer her to end it for him quickly. And she would. She swore by her love for him that she would.

She bid her father's driver to wait along the avenue within a block of Bianca's house. She walked the rest of the way in the warm sunlight, trying to soak up its heat to bolster her inner fire of determination. The closer she got, the more energy she extended, using her fledgling powers to feel the house before actually entering.

Gerard?

Ah, Nicole, cara! Come to me. I have something for you!

No hint of threat, just Gerard's dark humor. For all her hatred and loathing for Bianca, she remembered her mother's implicit trust of Gerard and shared it. She didn't think he would harm her. She walked into the cool-shadowed hall, trying to prepare for anything she might meet.

Where are you?

Come into the parlor.

What she saw there made her hesitate. It looked as though a torrential whirlwind had gutted the room. And then on the dark tiles, she saw blood. Not a lot, but definite splotches leading to what seemed to be a solid wall. Not so solid, apparently, for that trail of crimson was smeared by dragging movement.

How do I get in?

Straight from the horse's mouth.

She frowned and studied the two relief plaster busts adorning either side of the alcove. Horses' heads, sculpted with eyes wide, nostrils flaring and teeth bared. Feeling rather foolish, she gripped the lower jaw of one and tugged. Nothing. But when she pulled upon the other, there was a soft grinding sound and an entire section of the wall swung out, opening the way to a small dim room beyond.

She stepped in warily, not totally convinced it wasn't a trap until she saw Gerard's coffin. She could sense his presence within it. Hooking her fingers under the edge of the lid, she lifted it up and gave a quiet moan of despair.

Gerard was within, his handsome features flushed with high color and composed in his unnatural rest. Not so natural was Marchand sprawled out across him. From the way his dark head was angled upon the sleeping vampire's shoulder, the wounds on his throat were horribly exposed.

Her hand was trembling visibly as she held it before Marchand's nose and mouth. There, faintly, she felt his breath stir.

"Marchand?"

Her penetrating whisper brought a flutter to his lashes, then gradually his eyes opened and immediately squinted up after the complete blackness inside Gerard's tomb.

"Nicole."

His voice was so hoarse and raw, it hurt to hear it.

"Let's get you out of here, my love."

She was assisting him into a seated position when without warning, Gerard's hand fastened about his throat, dragging him back down into the coffin. Nicole tried to pry the fingers loose, for Marchand was rapidly losing color.

"Gerard! Gerard, release him!" And she drew the short sword, steeling herself to use it when Gerard's grasp abruptly slackened and his hand settled gracefully atop his shirtfront once more. Nicole quickly secured a hold under Marchand's arms and hauled him out of the coffin, letting him down easily to the floor.

The moment his breathing returned to normal,

Marchand's arms went about her, hugging her up tightly to him. "Mon Dieu! I'm so glad to see you!" came the painful rasp of his words. She let him cling, enjoying the feel too much to end the contact, but finally having to. She eased back, then leaned forward again to kiss him. His mouth was dry, rough, desperately eager for hers.

"Marchand, I was so worried," she cried, kissing his cheeks, his eyelids, his temples; everywhere but his neck. She was too aware of the jagged punctures there. "Are you all right?"

"No. I fear Pasquale didn't leave much for you after all."

"Gerard did this to you? Why?" Aside from the obvious, of course. Gerard was a vampire, and to him, Marchand meant no more than dining on French cuisine.

Marchand didn't answer. He was slumped back against the polished wood of the coffin, his eyes half closed, his respiration quick and shallow. Seeing him so callously used up put a fury in Nicole that knew no bounds. She stood, sword drawn, and looked dispassionately down upon her mentor. He who vowed never to harm her. Hadn't he realized how such a cruel attack upon her beloved would affect her?

"What are you going to do?" came Marchand's gravelly tone.

"Reduce our enemies by one," was her determined response as she aligned the blade along Gerard's throat. She didn't look up at his face. She couldn't allow herself to look beyond the savage act.

Cara? She felt his confusion as he touched her mind, and reading her anger, his panic.

"You should never have touched him, Gerard."

And she lifted the sword to make ready.

Nicole never expected resistance to come from Marchand. He flung himself across Gerard, crying, "No, don't!" forcing Nicole to refrain.

"Marchand, move aside. It must be done."

"No, you can't. You don't understand!"

"I understand that you're protecting him because you can't help yourself. Marchand, he almost killed you. Your mind will clear after it's done."

But he grabbed onto the sides of the coffin and refused to be moved. "Nicole, listen. It was Bianca. She tricked him into thinking I willfully tried to kill your father. He believes me responsible for your mother's death. He was acting out of love for them and you. He may be the only ally we have!"

"My mother isn't dead."

Marchand looked up. "What?"

Putting the pieces of Bianca's scheme together ended Nicole's anger with her sleeping mentor. She knelt down and touched her palm to Gerard's still cheek. "She's not dead, Gerard. Just wounded through Bianca's treachery. She was behind it all, not Marchand. It was Bianca trying to exact her revenge upon them. Can you hear me? Do you you understand?"

From the corner of one closed eye, a single droplet tracked down into his hairline.

"My mother sends her regards." And she leaned down to press a brief kiss upon his warm, immobile mouth. Then she straightened and closed the lid. "Come, Marchand, we have much to do."

He was weaker than he wanted her to believe, unable to walk without her assistance, barely able to stand under his own power. Nicole guided him into the sumptuous bath and he went down on his knees at the edge of the pool, dippering out handfuls of the cool water to splash upon his face and rinse his neck. Then he drank deeply, trying to replace the depleted fluids drained from him. Nicole watched worriedly, not expressing her concerns. She wouldn't underestimate him. He was a man of phenomenal courage and fortitude. And right now, that was a about all that was sustaining him. She studied the wound at his neck, wondering if it supplanted the power of the matching mark upon his arm. Could she afford to trust him?

"I love you, Marchand."

He glanced up at her, surprised by the sudden, passionate words. Then he looked away. "I've failed you, Nicole. I brought your family harm. I will never forgive myself for what has happened through my arrogance."

She came down to him, slipping her arms about his shoulders, pressing her cheek atop his dark head. "We've both suffered falls from pride. It's time to put the past behind us."

"First, I must find Frederic and Camille. I can't let them wander soullessly."

"Do you know where to look?"

"I think so. I need your help, Nicole. I can't do it alone."

He looked up hopefully, trustingly, and she smiled.

"Then we'll do it together."

Someplace quiet and undisturbed by day, Louis had said.

The Charnel House of the Innocents held eight hundred years of the dead from twenty-two parishes, the Motel Dieu, the Châtelet prison and the Morgue; monks, decapitated nobles, common washerwomen piled in with Merovingian kings. Twelve to fifteen hundred bodies lay stacked in communal graves. In 1785, the Council of State ordered the Cemetery of the Innocents to be abolished and its interred taken by night to the catacombs in a gruesome torchlit procession. Already excavated a half dozen times, still too many bodies remained, contaminating the city's water supply as their gradual decomposition leeched into the great river sump from which its inhabitants drank.

Grimly silent, Nicole and Marchand examined the cemetery cloisters with their century-deep layers of crumbling bone and coffin planks, finding nothing. Unless the *revenants* had gone underground in natural graves, there was no place for them to hide. Both seekers agreed that the rather mindless beasts would not have the patience to conceal themselves well.

From the cemetery they went directly to the catacombs, the great ossuary of Paris. Where better for the undead to rest than beside their indifferent brethren? They walked the silent corridors, the rock-hewn galleries where bones had sifted together in a careless mingling into gleaming white and aged brown heaps almost six-foot high. But no sign that any had been disturbed.

It was midafternoon and they were both weary and discouraged as they sat amid an unsuspecting populace, drinking wine and trying to think like the cunning creatures they stalked. Nicole was doing her best to ignore the ache of hunger threading through her veins and the sweet fragrant scent of the man beside her. She should have fed before leaving the countryside. Her thirst was a distraction. Sharpened senses brought her the torturing sounds of hundreds of beating hearts, all beckoning to her with soft, seductive promise. And there was Marchand, so close, so readily available. She found herself touching the back of his hand, stroking her fingers along warm skin, curling them insidiously to press against the throb in his wrist.

Unaware of her thought's direction, Marchand continued to drink too much wine while he mulled over the seemingly impossible task ahead. He'd turned up his collar to conceal the marks upon his throat, but the aftereffects were as obvious as the remnants of a wasting disease. His complexion was sallow, his eyes slightly sunken and ringed with bruise-like circles and his hands held a noticeable tremble. It wouldn't take much to suck the remaining life from him, and Nicole found her lips moistening at that vile contemplation.

Marchand looked up in surprise as she shoved away from the café table abruptly. He was so handsome, so vulnerably human, it nearly tore her heart in two. Would that she could send him away someplace safe to gather his resources. He was in no shape to go hunting demons. But there was no time left. Sunset was scant hours away, and with it came the creatures of the night to hunt their human prey. And on this night, they were it. How hard would it be for Bianca to find them using the shared beacon of Marchand's blood?

"There's one place left to look," she said gruffly. "Are you strong enough?"

Of course he wasn't. He was too weak to hold a wine glass let alone wield a fearsome retribution, but he pushed back his chair to claim, "I'm ready." Nicole had to turn away lest he see the tears in her eyes.

The great sewer ran from the Bastille to Chaillot, an underground reproduction of the streets above hidden behind great iron grilles. Eight hundred miles this labyrinth ran, carrying streams of water and fetid matter that were swallowed up in vast cesspools which discharged overflow into open drains. These ran into the stream of Menilmontant, which emptied into the Seine water full of mud, dung, rubbish and filth; the same water the city used to wash and cook and drink. Occasionally twenty-two thousand hogshead of water were poured into this giant sump from a reservoir in the Rue des Filles-du-Calvaire to flush away the residue of rottenness, but it quickly became so pestilential again that none but the sewer sweepers who were paid to brave its stench would enter. The perfect place to disguise the stink of decay.

Nicole broke the lock on one of the grilles with her bare hands, then held it open while Marchand slipped inside. The interior was dank and chill and repellent to the senses. The farther they walked, the worse it got. They walked along the cobbled edges, stepping into the sluggish flow of water only when it was unavoidable. Light filtered down in weak streaks from the streets above, but it took torchlight to penetrate the deeper shadows they searched.

"It would be somewhere near the Place Vendôme." Marchand's voice carried down the cavernous tunnel, coming back to them in distorted whispers. "They wouldn't have wandered far from where they were made."

Nicole squinted upward through the overhead metal mesh. "We should be about there now. Look carefully. We haven't time to miss anything."

They separated, each covering a side of the wide-throated drain. Then came Marchand's hoarse call.

"Nicole, here."

She splashed across the fetid stream, holding her light aloft to pierce the dimness. She could make out a recess in the wall, probably a tributary that, from its dry stones, had been blocked off farther back. In that slightly elevated niche were row upon row of boxes.

Coffins.

Dozens of them.

Marchand had his hand on the crude corner of the nearest box, hesitant now that he was faced with the reality of what they must do. Then he seized it by the sides and dragged it with a grim clatter out into the grey fingers of light threading down from above. And he threw off the lid.

They got the fleeting impression of a human form before the spontaneous burst of bright popping flame.

Marchand grabbed onto another crate and hauled it into that puddle of light. Again, the pulsing blaze, this time accompanied by inhuman shrieks that hurt the ears and penetrated the soul. Nicole took hold of a third, putting up the lid before pulling it into the sunlight. She almost wished she hadn't.

She recognized Camille Viotti by the color of his hair and the remains of the jacket he was wearing. Little else was left of the dashing young artist. She couldn't believe this horror of sinew and bone could rise up at dusk, but she knew it would. She also knew that the only kind thing she could do for the man who'd once dwelt within this rotted corpse would be to end its nightly terror.

Using the blade Takeo gave her, she severed tendon and bone first, because she wasn't sure he wouldn't feel the pain of the fire, then she pushed the box into the light and watched Camille ignite. Marchand was watching, too, and those unholy flames reflected in the glitter of his dark eyes.

"Au revoir, mon ami."

Then he wiped his face on his sleeve and went to retrieve another of the coffins.

They had nine of them consecrated by daylight with only the ash of the demons powdering the scorched linings. Marchand counted Camille, Gaston, his four henchmen and the second female ghoul. He grew paler and less steady with each one they revealed to destruction, and Nicole knew it was because he was trying to harden himself for the discovery of his brother. But in the end, he couldn't.

Nicole turned to see him slumped down beside one of the cheap coffins, his knees drawn up and his head hanging between them as if recovering from a swoon. When he lifted up at the call of his name, Nicole was shocked at how pitiful and lost he looked. His features were tight and drawn with defeat, wet with the glimmer of tears. But it was the sight of his pain that was so hard to bear.

She came over to him, saying with a steely calm, "I'll do it for you," because her sympathy at that moment would have broken his incredible bravery down. But he shook his head, speechless for a moment, then with a remarkably strong voice, he told her, "No, I will." Then, "Help me up."

Frederic LaValois lay inside the box, composed as if for burial, but that was the only thing holy about what they saw. He'd started to deteriorate, but not so much that he wasn't easily recognizable as the idealistic young writer who'd been eager to change the world. It should have helped that his shirtfront was stiff and brown with gore and that his face was bloated and his lips rouged from a recent kill. But it didn't. He was still more Frederic than he was monster. Which was why it was so difficult for Marchand to bring the blade up at ready.

Then the eyes of the thing in the box opened. They weren't Frederic's warm, dreamy eyes but bottomless holes of hunger and hate that fixed Marchand's with a viper's hypnotic power. He hesitated.

"Mon frère," came the low wet hiss, and with a terrible cry, Marchand made a fierce slash with the blade, not jumping back in time to avoid the hot jet of blood spraying upward as head and shoulders parted. He dropped the dripping blade to damp stones and with a wail, shoved the coffin into the sunlight.

And as Frederic burned, his brother wrestled out the remaining two boxes for the same consuming end. Then he stood in that weak curtain of light, head back, face uplifted, hands limp at his side. Nicole left him alone for as long as she dared, then she took up one of his slack hands and gently tugged.

"Marchand, it's almost nightfall. We must go."

He nodded and allowed her to lead him up from the stinking hole of death and purification. She bundled his coat close about him, not just because his was shaking fitfully but to hide the terrible bloodstains from those who passed them by. She guided him back to the house in the Place Vendome, the place they would have their final confrontation, where he staggered through the rooms, shedding his soiled clothing as he went until sinking naked into the pool. Revived by the shock of cool water, he began to scrub himself as if vigorous cleansing would wash away the stain of guilt and fear and horror. But of course it wouldn't, Nicole knew as she watched him.

He came up from the water and straight into her arms, letting her hold him, dry him and finally take him to the first bed they'd shared together. There, she wrapped him up in the covers and bid him to stay still while she went to find one of Gerard's clean shirts and retrieved his trousers and boots which, while distastefully dirty, would have to do.

He was lying back with eyes closed when she returned, so Nicole thought at first that he was asleep. Then she saw the movement of his hand beneath the covers. He was rubbing the bite mark in his arm.

"She'll come for me as soon as it's dark."

Nicole shivered at the cold truth of those soft-spoken words.

"When she does, I won't be able to stop myself from doing whatever she commands. We both know that. I'm damned, Nicole. Nothing can save me unless you'll do for me what we did for them down in the sewer."

Nicole stared at him, aghast.

"I beg of you to save my soul. I want you to kill me, Nicole."

Chapter Twenty-Two

"No!"

"Nicole—"

"No!"

"You know I'm right! I could hurt you. I could even kill you and not be able to keep from doing it. I won't be that kind of risk to you. I couldn't live with more of that kind of guilt. I can't stand the thought of that—creature—controlling me! If you don't do it, she will and she won't be as considerate about it. And then what? Then I rise up at night to stalk the unsuspecting? Nicole, don't condemn me to that, I beg you. If you love me, spare me that. Please."

She came to lie beside him, curling up within his embrace, nestling tight against his solid male heat, absorbing his frail human strength. She'd never loved another the way she loved him. She knew he was right in what he said. She knew she had to save him from the horrors Bianca had in store. He couldn't do it from this mortal state. He wasn't strong enough. She couldn't protect him. But how could she end his life and all her hopes of a future?

"I can't lose you, Marchand. You are everything I've

ever wanted in a man, in a mate. I can't just let you go."

"You must, Nicole. And soon. It grows darker by the minute."

He didn't have to tell her that. She could feel her senses sharpening as twilight deepened toward dusk. They had maybe an hour, probably less. And then she would have to kill him. She would have to.

"I love you, Marchand," she cried wretchedly.

"Shhh." And he was kissing her, lavishly, lingeringly, until her heart was pounding madly and her tears were streaming uncontrollably. Then he simply held her close and she savored the scent of him, so potent and powerful and richly flowing. With her head upon his chest, she listened to the steady beat below, wondering how she was going to stop that pulse and continue on, herself.

But would she have to?

"Marchand, there is another way."

"And what is that, my love? To run? To hide? That would be no good for either of us."

"No. To stay and get strong. To fight her on her own terms."

He was silent for a moment, then asked reluctantly, "And how would we manage that?"

She came up on her elbows so she could look down upon his face; such a wonderfully strong and masculine face. He was watching her, curious, cautious, but he wasn't prepared for her suggestion:

"Let me bring you over."

"Over where?" he asked without thinking.

"Over to the night. Where you can be her equal and free of her control. You don't have to die."

The corners of his mouth quirked slightly. "I beg your pardon, but I believe for what you have in mind, I do."

"But you won't stay dead. You will rise up, eternal."

"A vampire."

"Yes."

"And be more damned than I am already? Thank you, no. I'd rather stay in my grave than rise from it nightly."

"But think, Marchand! What good will you serve if I kill you? You'll be dead and I'll be alone. No one will be able to make her pay for Frederic and Camille. Or for my mother. I'm not strong enough by myself. But together—"

"Together we might be," he finished for her. And his expression grew still and pensive as he considered it.

"You don't have to be damned, my love. Good and evil is the choice of the individual. I believe that was what Frederic was trying to tell me."

"That was what your father said, as well."

"Marchand, we could be together forever or we can lose each other now. I will not force this decision upon you. It must be yours."

He was thinking. "Can you do it?"

"I know how it's done, but, like my father, I don't know if I'm powerful enough to see it through."

"I guess that would have to be my risk, wouldn't it?"

"Then you are willing to let me try?"

Marchand was silent for a moment. His mind filled up with images; of Camille as his bullet tore through him without effect, of Bebe sobbing at his graveside, of Frederic and Musette arm in arm drinking wine at a sunny café, of his brother engulfed in unholy flame. Sensations of rage and helplessness overcame him and then were stilled. Because he didn't have to be helpless.

He didn't have to let Bianca win.

"How is it done?"

Nicole took a breath, garnering her courage to tell him, repressing the sudden anticipation rising inside. "I will take your blood, then you will take it back from me. You must listen carefully for my voice. I will call you over and you must use all your strength to come."

"At what point will I be dead?"

"At no point, I hope." She pressed him back down to the pillows with a gentle touch. "Are you ready?"

He drew a breath and shut his eyes. "Go ahead."

She leaned down over him, inhaling the warm saltiness of his skin and letting her appetite rise. She put her hands on his shoulders and felt his body tense. When her breath brushed the uninjured side of his neck, he reacted with an unconscious will for self-preservation. A thick sound of protest escaped him and his clutched fists rose to push her away. She gave easily and settled back to watch him struggle for control. His eyes opened and he looked at her with what could only be shame.

"I'm sorry. I thought I would be braver."

Submitting himself to death? What could be braver, she wondered tenderly. She let her fingertips trail along the damp curve of his face. "Marchand, I don't want your memories of this moment to be ones of fear. I won't hurt. Don't be afraid. My mother assures me that's better than making love."

His smile was wry. "Not to my experience."

"Then we shall make some new experiences for you."

He submitted to her kiss easily enough. At that point, she could have drugged him with the heavy vampire magic, but she consciously chose not to. She wanted him to be aware. She wanted him to be able to say no.

She wanted him to like it.

She kissed him until his mouth softened and opened for her. She lingered there until his tongue was drawn out to fence with hers and his arms came up to enfold her close. Then she was stroking his hair, his face, his shoulders, kissing him on the lips, on the eyelids, in that delicate hollow at the base of his throat. He stiffened up so she moved on, adoring him with her touch, with the trace of wet kisses. And as passion heated, she let her hunger rise.

"I love you, Marchand," she murmured against the tender corner of his mouth. "I've wanted you like this for so long. For so very long." And she came up over him, straddling him with her knees, rubbing over him until his body was moving in response. "Kiss me, Marchand. Tell my you love me and want me, too."

"I love you, Nicole. I've wanted you forever."

She continued to sprinkle kisses upon his face until his eyes had closed and his breathing had stretched out into long, expectant shivers. And she let the taste of him excite her, the scent of him tantalize her, the heat of him promise what she'd never dared hope for. She was massaging his shoulders, rubbing his chest, coaxing his desire, higher, higher, feeding off the emotions until she was sure he was lost to them.

Then her hands stroked up, her thumbs planting beneath his chin to tip his head back and to one side. Exquisite agony lanced through her gums and cheekbones. She moaned uncontrollably and went into his throat. She felt him jerk and heard his soft cry of surprise but then there was nothing but the sound of his heartbeat and the rush of hot blood.

She drank and drank and drank, overcome by the volcanic pleasure, by the vibrating, caressing pulse of his blood as it filled her. And there was nothing like it, absolutely nothing, because this was Marchand and she was taking of his love, of his trust, and it was powerful, humbling all at once. The thirst was so great, time could not contain it. Her senses blurred, her awareness of Marchand with it. Then there was just the thrum of his heart, strong, challenging, vital, like the man she loved. And gradually, that pace began to slow and falter, but she continued to draw hungrily, helplessly, until the rhythm had become faint and hypnotic and impossible to pull from.

Stop Nicole. You must stop before he dies, cara.

She tore away, breathing hard, dizzy, hot, wildly intoxicated from the blood. It took a moment for her to remember where she was and what she was about, then with a gasp, she focused upon Marchand.

He was white against the bed linens, his eyes almost closed, glazing over even as he mouthed the words, "I love you." Dying.

"No Marchand. Don't let go. Hold tight. Hold tight. Be brave. You must be brave."

And she ripped open her wrist with her own sharp teeth, not feeling the pain, not feeling anything but the panic that he might slip away from her. She fed her spouting wrist into his mouth, crying, "Drink from me, Marchand. Take my strength and live. You must live."

She felt a slight draw, then a suction so strong it seemed to core her veins, ripping at them with tongues of fire. She cried out from the pain, yet held his head so he could continue to feed voraciously while she grew ever fainter. She lay against him, her head on his shoulder, a prisoner of his draining grasp. She could feel her life, her strength flow into him and the weakness became all pleasure, a throbbing, overwhelming bliss. Enchantment and ecstasy meant to disguise a darker purpose; the devouring of heart and soul. Even knowing that, it was such a temptation to languish on that wave of swelling rapture, riding it to its black end. But she was forgetting the rest that she must do! Desperate to break from her swoon lest it become her own death, she pulled her arm away and fell back upon the pillows beside him, panting, weeping, weak.

She wasn't sure how much time had passed. Maybe seconds, perhaps full minutes, but finally the faintness left her and she was able to sit up slightly to see what she'd been able to accomplish. Marchand lay motionless beside her, his eyes closed, his slack mouth smeared a bright wet crimson, his respiration nonexistent. He was dead. She knew death and it was all over him.

"Marchand, come to me!" She waited, but no movement followed. "Marchand, you must wake before it becomes the sleep of centuries. Listen to me. Hear my voice. Come to me. You must. You must awaken. Fight hard. For Frederic and Camille. For me. If you love me, don't leave me! Marchand, wake up!"

No response.

She'd killed him.

"What have I done?" she moaned into her trembling hands. She hadn't been strong enough to coax his brave heart from death. She, the product of a vampire father and mortal mother, had not the power to gift eternity. And she'd lost the only man she'd ever love.

A sound from the outer rooms distracted her. Gerard! Perhaps Gerard knew some magic. He'd been with her. He'd called her back from her hunger. He would help. She staggered from the bed, from one last look at Marchand sprawled lifeless upon it. His blood was still churning hot within her veins and it left her lightheaded and giddy, like too much wine. That was all she would ever have of him, that warm, sustaining taste. And she reeled into the parlor, desperate for her mentor's wisdom.

But it wasn't Gerard. It wasn't yet dark.

The rooms were silent and stealthy with shadow. She moved through them with her quiet preternatural step. A glitter of silver caught her eyes and as she bent to pick up her mother's cross, the feel of the metal tingling in her hand, she saw a figure emerge from the conceal-ment.

"Good evening, Mademoiselle Radouix. Are you alone?"

She straightened slowly, alarm making her pulse pound, but an inner calm controlling her movements. She regarded Sebastien De Sivry levelly. "Not for long, m'sieur."

He was holding something in his hand and when he stepped forward she could see it was a pistol. With that kind of bullets, she wondered. Could the regular variety harm her? She didn't know.

"What are you doing here?" He gestured to the chain trickling through her clenched fingers. "Stealing from my friends?"

"Your friends?"

"Don't look so surprised. I've not let politics or reli-gion matter to me. Why be swayed from taking power by particulars in humanity? Why should I care what they are as long as they can get me what I want, eh?"

"You're a fool if you think they'll let you live beyond their use."

His laugh was nasty and a little nervous. "I'm no fool. I saw what they did to Frederic and Gaston and I'll be no easy mark. Now, you haven't answered my question. What are you doing here? Making problems for our hosts? And where is your troublesome lover? Perhaps he would like to be entertained with how his brother died. No? Perhaps I will just kill you now and him later. How would that be?" And his eyes grew chill and hard as he raised the pistol.

A blur of motion pulled De Sivry's attention to one side. He had time to register shock and gave a brief cry in protest of his own fast-descending death. Incredibly strong hands gripped either side of his head, the pressure crushing. Then, with a quick snap, nothingness.

Nicole stood stunned as she watched Marchand ride de Sivry down to the tiled floor, his face buried at the dead man's throat. Marchand's head gave a savage shake and blood fountained up bright, splattering everywhere.

It was the sound that held her. Soft, sinister, unbelievably terrible. Low, panting growls and deeper purrs of rapture.

What manner of beast had she made?

He rose up at last, the movement effortless, powerful, mesmerizing in its fluidity. She'd never seen Marchand move that way. It scared her. He didn't look at her but rather walked in a sideways sort of reel into the next room. She followed. He dropped down on his knees beside the pool, studying its calm, clear surface with a puzzled fascination. He touched it with his hand and was entranced by the spreading ripples. It was as if he'd never seen water before. And Nicole realized he hadn't, not through these new vampire eyes.

He put his hands into the water at last and brought cups of it up to wash his face, letting the pinkish streams run down his shirtfront and back into the pool. And from a distance, Nicole observed him, frightened, uncertain. Overjoyed to see him, yet so very cautious.

"Marchand? Are you all right?"

He turned his head to look at her and she saw the difference right away. It was in his eyes, eyes that had lost their humanity. They were a dark, opaque glitter.

"Surprised the hell out of him, didn't I? That was long past due."

"You killed him," was all she could think to say. And it wasn't the fact, it was the way in which he'd done it. Brutally. Remorselessly. Like an unrepentant monster.

And he smiled, a cold, teeth-baring smile and said, "Let our hostess clean up the mess."

Chapter Twenty-Three

He woke up changed.

It was more than physical. It was perceptual difference so profound Marchand couldn't begin to comprehend it all at once. He no longer felt the pain of Nicole's bite, nor the fear or instantaneous regrets that followed. Those things were dead to him, as dead as his human form. The dark void of dying had been too quickly engulfed by the amazing newness of the world around him. He suffered from no great stress of separation, only from excitement and wonder.

It had begun with that first cautious swallow, then came the hunger for warmth, for life, so keen, so intense, it surpassed all other things. Nicole had shared that rich wondrous vitality with him, had fed it to him on each compelling beat of her heart, as if he'd been a babe suckling at her breast. Now he was the dark child she'd created with that gift. A child just beginning to understand his place in the surrounding universe.

He might have lain there all night enthralled by the beauty of simple sound, astonished by the poetry of movement in his own hands as he held them before his face, like a baby discovering his fingers and toes were a part of him and not of a separate existence. He was fascinated by the feel of the sheets, aware of the woven textures, the variation of colors, the scent of soap and starch, each sensation so intriguing he could barely stand to let go and move on to the next.

He could feel Nicole, could hear the heartbeat she'd shared with him, and a confusion of love and awe overwhelmed him. He didn't understand the enormity of those feelings so he let them slip away, gratified just to know she was near.

But then there was something else; a strong, sharper scent. Harsh liquor, male sweat, gunpowder. Blood. Rich, flowing, beckoning with its tempting beat. A primal craving stirred inside, deep and dark and dangerously basic. The urge to claim that heat, that warmth, that life as his own. It was survival, but he knew it only as hunger. Pangs so strong and provoking, he couldn't not act upon them.

He dressed quickly, distracted for a moment by his own movements as they seemed to flow one into the next with a quick silver liquifaction. Then he allowed the smell to guide him, feeling the urgency rise with each step like no arousal he'd ever known.

He saw De Sivry and recognized his threat to Nicole and the rest came so quick, he had no time for cognitive thought. He acted; swift, sure, deadly. Killing, feeding, letting instinct guide him to De Sivry's throat, where he ripped with as yet undeveloped teeth until he knew once more that euphoric pleasure, learning as he did the first lesson of his vampiric state: It wasn't as good as if they were already dead.

When he'd taken in all he could, Marchand basked in a wonderful lassitude that was like the afterglow of exhaustive sex. Contented and drowsy, he was also aware of a nagging discomfort. It had nothing to do with the moralistic horror he once would have held in view of what he'd just done. He'd done murder—worse—yet he felt not the slightest remorse. Indeed, he was smugly satisfied by the death of Sebastien De Sivry. The man had deserved to come to such a horrific end. That sense of justice done waived all his onetime reservations and he was surprised by how detached he was from any feelings of guilt. More than surprised: Dumbfounded.

He'd just killed a man and drank his blood.

And he didn't care.

Confused, he looked up from the cleansing waters of the pool to Nicole, needing her guidance, her sensibility, her love, and he was met with wariness and fright. That affected him the way nothing else could. How had he displeased her? By being what she'd made him? He didn't understand, and a terrible panic settled inside him. He needed her approval, not just because he was in love with her but because a whole new layer had unfolded in their relationship; a dependence he couldn't yet grasp completely. A devotion so deep, her distance brought desolation. He didn't mind leaving his mortal life behind. He'd had nothing left to hold him there. But in this new realm he'd found upon opening his eyes, there was just Nicole, his one link to self and soul. He crossed over barriers of time and space to be with her and now she would not have him. The sense of isolation was awful, worse even than the realization of his death.

He watched her watching him and saw her in a different way. He could feel her power, her goodness, her control. He could still taste the sweetness of her on his mouth, hear the commanding strength of her voice calling him back from the void of finality into this infinite existence. And he wanted—no, needed—to be close, to feel cherished, to be held, because he was yet new and frail. But her suspicions kept him at bay. She didn't know quite what he was, and he didn't know how to reassure her. What he was was all tangled up in her perception of him. He had no identity unless it was through her eyes. And he was scared even as she was afraid of him.

There was no more time for reflection as Marchand's gaze caught upon a silky movement within the shadows. Gerardo Pasquale. He came to his feet, aware as he did of Bianca's silhouette in the doorway. Quickly, without thought, he put himself between them and Nicole.

"How delightful," Bianca purred. "We have guests, Gerard. Unexpected but not unwelcomed. Good evening, Nicole. How is your dear family?"

"Waiting to hear that I've sent you to hell."

She laughed softly. "How amusing. And how naive."

"I was naive, wasn't I? Enough to be taken in by your twisted schemes, but no more. I see you for what you are now. A vain, pathetic creature who refuses to accept another's happiness. Well, you did your best to make my father miserable, didn't you? I'm glad to say he survived your cruel affections quite nicely. And that galls you, doesn't it?"

"Be careful, girl, lest you end up like your foolish mother."

"And how is that, Bianca? Perhaps Gerard would like to hear you tell it. Or perhaps I should."

Bianca glanced at her sleek, dark lover and frowned. Gerard was regarding her with a half smile. He drawled, "Yes, *cara*, tell me. I do so enjoy a good story. Though I must confess my fondness for clever fiction is fast failing me."

"I've told you the truth of it already," she snapped. Then she looked to Marchand, and a slow, puzzled look came over her. "What have you done to him, Gerardo? Surely you could not have been so big a fool as to—"

"No," Nicole put in coolly. "I did."

"You?" Bianca stared, for once plainly startled. Then she gave a little laugh. "I seem to be always underestimating you. So, you have made your own companion after all. How very sweet."

"How very necessary to keep you from having him," Nicole corrected.

She waved a dismissing hand. "I gave him to Gerard. If you have some grievance, take it up with him, not me."

"And such a generous gift," Gerard purred lethally.

At that point, Bianca honed in on the figure sprawled in the parlor, another surprise she found most unpleasant. "And what have we here?"

"Sorry about the mess," Marchand said with a grim smile.

Bianca went still, reassessing the situation in her cunning mind. She could feel the power from Marchand LaValois. It was new and somewhat undirected, but strong, so strong. Nicole had made him well. Perhaps she'd been wrong to dismiss him from her attention so quickly. Her gaze heated with a sensual speculation. "Perhaps I should thank you. De Sivry was proving quite the nuisance. Good riddance, I say."

"Is that what you said when you killed my brother?"

"Your brother? Oh, yes. The well-spoken one. Would you like to see him again?"

Marchand's smile tightened. "I've already seen him. Several hours ago. He and about a dozen of his friends." He put his hand in his pants pocket and withdrew it, filled. "They send their regrets." And he opened his hand, releasing a filtering of ash.

Bianca stared at the ash. "You destroyed them?"

"No. *You* destroyed them. I put them to rest. And soon I mean to pray over them. Will there be anyone to do the same for you, I wonder?"

Bianca continued to regard the challenging couple. Her black eyes blazed. Her plans, ruined. Her minions, destroyed. She had lost her foothold in Paris because of this one impossibly headstrong girl and her noble-hearted lover. What idiots they were to think they could take a stand against her and then walk away with victory. The two of them with their weak fledgling powers against two who had seen centuries pass!

Then she looked to Gerard and knew a moment of real fear. He was looking back at her, his smile remote, his expression far removed. His eyes glittered like hot silver. What was he thinking, her unpredictable companion?

"Gerard, I have grown weary of our guests. I made you a promise once that the first taste of her would be yours and now you may claim it."

"Mí dispiáce, I am so sorry, but I fear my tastes have changed."

His bland mutiny made her tremble with rage. "Gerard, you fool, we are in danger here!"

"We, my love?"

"Imbecile!" she spat at him. "I could never depend on you. Never. You were weak and treacherous in life and so you are now."

He merely stared at her, unmoved and unmoving.

She turned on Nicole, seething furiously. "So this is how I am repaid for bringing you into my home, nurturing you in the ways of our kind, treating you like family."

"What do you know of family, Madame Viper. You

would kill your own to escape consequences. You know nothing of loyalty or love."

"Loyalty? Love! Bah! Only the frail-minded hold to such pale conceits. Power is the only thing that matters. And I am power. You may think you've won but I shall rise up again. I will always be triumphant. And I will always have my way."

Marchand circled slowly around her, his movements all strong, alien beauty, his smile familiar and at the same time, darkly fiendish. "Perhaps not," he told her softly. He reached up to detach one of the ornate wall lamps, then went to the edge of the pool to pour the scented oil into the water. It spread out across the surface in a thin glistening film. Then he took down one of the torches and touched the flame to it. There was an immediate sheet of fire.

He watched it burn for a moment, then asked, "Have you ever heard them shriek as they burn, these unfortunates casually made by you? It's an awful sound. The sound one imagines from hell." His gaze came up an increment at a time, glimmering with the unholy light he'd seen in his own brother's pyre. "Rise up from this, bitch."

And he grabbed her by her long blond hair, swinging her about, thrusting her toward the blazing pool. Bianca screamed in fright and rage, and before he could shove her over the edge, her feet found purchase on the tiles and her hands clenched in his shirtfront. If she went over, he was going with her.

They grappled on the slick marble, both fueled by inhuman strength and unnatural hate.

"Let me go, you idiot! You will burn with me!"

"I'd rather burn in hell than see you go free!"

"No!"

That cry tore from Nicole. There was no way she was going to lose her love now! She sprang forward, whipping the chain of her mother's necklace around the vicious Bianca's neck, pulling back with all her might. There was the sound of hissing flesh as the delicate silver links tightened and bit deep. Bianca's fingers loosened from Marchand. The instant they did, Nicole used the chain to sling the screeching female into the fire.

She and Marchand stumbled back as a tremendous ball of scarlet flame rocketed to the ceiling, scorching plaster, setting draperies ablaze before falling to the marble floor. What had been Bianca du Maurier writhed and howled with an ear-splitting fury.

"Gerardo! Gerardo, help me!"

But Gerardo Pasquale looked on impassively, making no movement in her defense. *For Gino,* his hard eyes said. *For Bella,* echoed his softer heart.

As the heat grew intense, Nicole gripped Marchand's arm and pulled hard. "Come on! We must get out before the whole house goes up in flame. Marchand! Come on!" And finally he gave, following her through the increasingly thick smoke toward the front hall. She paused only once. It wasn't until they reached the searing freshness of the night air that he saw she held Camille's painting tightly in her arms.

Spotting them, her father's driver angled the coach up before the blazing house. It was then, that Nicole hung back with an anguished cry.

"Gerard! We can't leave him!"

But Marchand had her by the waist and was lifting her into the dim interior. "He can take care of himself."

And inside the elegant inferno, Gerardo Pasquale stripped off his tailored jacket and bent down to wrap it about the charred figure on the floor. He tamped the fabric carefully so as not to ignite his own unnatural flesh and when the tiny popping flames were out, he gathered the crisped bundle in his arms and exclaimed, "Now who is the fool, *cara?*"

The fleet coach closed quickly upon the countryside chateau even as the distance grew ever wider between its two occupants. They sat on opposing seats, not looking at one another but awareness throbbing between them just the same. The tension was palpable, an invisible wall of uncertainty neither could scale until Marchand lost all patience with the awkward mood.

"If you can no longer care for me, I wish you would have let me fall into the fire."

Nicole's eyes went incredulously round. "What?"

"I cannot bear this, Nicole. I'm lost and you refuse me all comfort."

"Marchand, that's not true!"

"Isn't it? Then why are you way over there instead of over here where I need you so desperately?"

Why, indeed? she asked herself, yet still could find no answer. He wasn't Marchand, he wasn't the man she loved. She had only to look at him to know that. Over just the past few hours, he'd taken on that haunting air of gauntness and that pale magnetic beauty that glimmered about her father and Gerard, that vampire luminescence that set them apart from humanity. His eyes were no longer expressive windows to his soul. In fact, his whole facade was one of minimal change, glossy, flawless, unnatural.

Unfeeling.

That was what she feared. What if all that made him

who she loved was no longer in existence? What if she'd killed that wondrous spirit along with his mortal form?

Because she needed to find out, Nicole slipped over onto the same seat. When she didn't move to touch him, he leaned against her, curving his arms loosely about her waist and resting his head upon the soft swell of her bosom. And for the longest time, he didn't move. Gradually, her arms came up to hold him and her hand brushed gently across his brow, soothing back the hair that strayed there in a boyish disarray.

"Are you afraid you've made me into something that you cannot love?"

Yes. That's exactly what she was afraid of. But she couldn't say that to him, not after he'd given up all upon her assurances.

Arabella opened her arms wide to accept her daughter down into them. "Oh, Nicole, oh my dear, we've been so worried!"

"And I've been worried about you. How are you feeling, Mother?"

"Stronger. I'll be fine." Knowing these were the words her daughter needed to hear, she didn't regret the small lie. She looked over Nicole's shoulder to where Marchand hung back at the door, his eyes downcast, his posture uncertain. "Marchand, come in."

And the minute he lifted his gaze, she knew what had happened, what he had become. That didn't stop her from extending a warm embrace for him as well.

"I'm so glad you're safe," she murmured against his smooth cheek.

He caught her hand in his and pressed a grateful kiss to its back. "Your gift, it saved my . . . soul."

"Good. Then I've not become totally useless upon this bed."

Again, his gaze shied away. "I am so sorry—"

She touched her fingertips to his mouth, halting the anguished words. "Enough said."

"You are very generous, madame."

"I am hoping to become a mother-in-law soon." He leaned back, saying nothing, still avoiding her eyes. She looked between him and her daughter, sensing all was not well there. It wasn't the absence of love, it was the presence of tension. The knowledge of their distress lessened her own pain. Her hand cupped under his chin, forcing his gaze up. "Marchand, are you in love with my daughter?"

"*Oui*, madame," came his gruff reply.

"Then nothing else is important to me."

He canted a glance toward Nicole, who was still and distanced by the conversation. "There is nothing else for me either."

"You're back."

Marchand rose to face Louis, uncomfortable with Nicole's remoteness and uncertain of his place here in her home with her family. Then he saw her father take in the significance of the marks on his throat and his recognition of the cool vampiric fire in his eyes.

"I see things have changed."

"Some, m'sieur. Others, thankfully, have stayed the same." And he adored Nicole briefly with his gaze, disheartened when she failed to respond.

"You've come back here. That is good. Tell me of Bianca. Is she responsible for your state?"

Marchand purposefully didn't look to Nicole as he answered, "No, it was your daughter who acted to save me from the hell of her possession. I am forever in her debt. And yours, m'sieur."

"And Bianca?"

"Destroyed."

Louis held to his reservations, then asked more softly, "Gerardo?"

"He survived, as far as I know."

Louis allowed himself a small sigh of relief.

Marchand hesitated and then had to prod himself past his pride. "M'sieur, we've come so we might learn from you how to control what we are. Nicole and I both believe we can do good with the skills we possess just as others seek to do wrong. Teach us how to use them wisely."

He chanced a glimpse at Nicole and saw her regarding him with . . . admiration. It wasn't that he wanted to earn from her. But he supposed it was a start.

"It would be my pleasure," Louis said, and he took Marchand's hand for a firm press.

"They will be good for one another," Arabella stated sagely.

"I think so," her husband agreed as he lounged on the bed beside her. "He has the strength to care for her and the caring to make her happy. That's all I ever wanted for her. A little of what we have." He rearranged her pillows solicitously for the umpteenth time and she slapped at his hands.

"Really, my love, you have a very patronizing bedside manner."

"When you are stronger, I will change that manner to one we'll both enjoy more."

Though her answering smile was edged with doubt, she replied, "I love you, Louis."

"Bella, you will be better."

"Yes, of course."

"You will walk again."

"I plan to."

"I love you so much. I just wish—" He broke off and looked away.

"What do you wish, my lord?"

He faced her directly, his expression moved by passionate feeling. "I wish you would give up this tortured mortal shell and be with me!" The minute he uttered the words, he looked ashamed of them, but Arabella caressed his lean face and kissed him tenderly.

"Oh, Louis, we've been over this so many times. If I had not been so well-decided before this would anchor my choice. Could you guarantee that I would not spend eternity trapped in this motionless prison? Could you assure me that I would rise up on legs that are strong and whole? Or would you be condemning me to being an endless burden upon you?"

"Bella, how could you say that?"

"Not to hurt you, my love. Can you promise me a perfect immortality?"

"No. From what I know of it, bringing one over only changes the circumstance of death. The rest remains as it was."

"So if I am a cripple in life, I would be a cripple forever."

"Bella—"

"Louis, don't be so distressed. Don't you dare pity me. I would gladly give my legs, my arms, my life for you without regret and you know it. I will not complain, not ever! If I had not done what I did, I would not have you now—for as long as you wish to stay."

His features tightened. "What do you mean by that?"

"Only that I am far from the woman you married, while you remain unchanged. I will not hold you any longer than you wish to remain."

He seized her chin and kissed her hard enough to bruise her lips. Against that damp, well-molded mouth, he murmured fiercely, "I will never stray from your side. Never. You will always be the same woman I married, the same woman I love. Always, Bella. And I will love you madly until—"

"Until death us do part."

He said nothing. He was kissing her again.

After a time, when they were comfortably arranged in one another's arms, she said, "I think I should like to see America next. When I'm strong enough to travel."

"America," Louis mused. "I've always been curious about the new world."

What neither of them said was that they would never feel safe again within these warm sand-colored walls. Because neither of them believed the threat of Bianca du Maurier was gone.

"We must make some preparations for you," Nicole was saying as they moved along the dimness of the upper hall. "Your . . . needs . . . are different now. We must see that you're protected."

Marchand said nothing.

"You can rest below with my father. We have some time before dawn to obtain a coffin—"

"No!"

"Marchand—"

"I won't sleep in a box." The memory of being closed in with Gerard rose strong. He could feel that paralyzing terror, the sense of suffocation, of isolation.

"Marchand," Nicole explained brusquely, "you know what you are and what precautions you must take. Don't be ridiculous."

"I won't sleep in a box!"

Nicole repressed her agitation. The situation was difficult for her as well. She didn't want to imagine her love interred below. It was too grim a reminder of his physical death. The death she'd brought him. Her tone was rough when she concluded, "We'll settle on something before sunrise. Perhaps Father can help you become accustomed to your ... fate." For she certainly was doing a poor job of it!

Marchand paused outside one of the closed doors. She saw his head tip slightly as that alien look of concentration came over him. "Musette," he murmured, and his voice was edged with confusion. Nicole knew he was struggling between the fondness his once-human heart held for her and his new awareness of her as a mortal. Nicole too could feel the temptation of live blood stirring on every pulse from within. And she put her hand upon Marchand's arm.

"Musette is sleeping. Come away, Marchand. We don't want to disturb her."

He hesitated, and Nicole could well imagine his distraction. She tugged gently and he finally followed. He drew up again outside his door.

"I'll sleep here."

"I don't think you can. The daylight will be too strong."

But he wasn't listening. He entered the room and went to stretch out upon the bed, his iridescent gaze fixed upon the ceiling. Aside from those glowing eyes, he looked appealingly normal there upon his back. And her response to him was achingly normal. But neither of them were ordinary.

How much had changed? She stood there at the door wondering that, second-guessing her actions that had brought him over into this twilight world. She'd done it because of her love for him, but what of that love remained? She thought of Gerard and his passionless kisses; something remembered but not really enjoyed. Had emotions been bred out of him in the transformation or over time? She didn't want Marchand as her eternal companion. She wanted him as her love, as her lover. But what if what she'd done to him made that no longer possible? What if a lust for blood replaced a need for intimacy? Where would that leave her and her yearning for a future?

She approached him slowly, apprehensively, aware of the way his gaze followed. When she settled on the edge of the bed, he continued to study her in silence.

"How do you feel?" she asked at last.

"The same. Different. I don't know. How am I supposed to feel?"

She touched the back of his hand where it lay on the counterpane beside her. He felt good, at least to her. Warm and strong. "Marchand, I had no choice. I need to hear that you forgive me."

He looked perplexed. "For what?"

"For what I've made you. For the life I've made you abandon."

His smile was small and wry. "It wasn't much of a life. It wouldn't be any kind of a life at all . . . without you."

When she said nothing, he curled his fingers about hers tightly.

"Nicole, I have no regrets over what we did or concerning what was done. The only loss I'll feel is if we can't bridge the distance I feel between us now."

She didn't have to say anything. He could feel her pulling farther and farther away and he didn't know what to do to hang onto her. He sat up, cupping her lovely face between his palms, delving into the lush anguish of her gaze, praying for a response when he told her, "I love you, Nicole. I came back from death to be with you."

And there was so much passionate feeling in those words. All she could ever want or need to hear. But it was the sudden difference in his gaze that convinced her. Gone was that cold vampiric fire. In its place shone a deep light of love, strong enough to overcome the inhuman brilliance of what he was. That familiar warmth was enough to make her believe that all would be well for their future together, because the inner man she loved remained.

"Oh, Marchand!"

She was in his arms, hugging him fiercely, kissing his cheek, his temple and finally his mouth with a wild abandon. He was warm and solid and—the same.

"I was so afraid I'd lost you," she was sobbing softly against the column of his throat where her marks had already faded to faint scarring.

"Nicole, I'm not that same man anymore. I never will be again. I don't know what I am, but I know I will never leave you. I will never stop loving you."

She leaned back just far enough to hold that dear, devoted gaze in hers. She was touching his face, admiring its sleek perfection with the spread of her fingertips.

Love and desire flared hot and urgent. As she kissed him again, deeply, wetly, her hands stroked down his chest and came to rest at his trouser band.

"I love you, Marchand," she whispered hungrily against his mouth. "I want you in every way possible." Then she paused and asked more huskily, "What ways are possible?"

He caught her by the rib cage and lifted her up to straddle his lap. "The old way is always good." And his hands burrowed up beneath her crumpled skirt, touching her, waking her to desires more completely until she was shifting impatiently against him.

"Marchand—" she panted hopefully.

And he continued to kiss her in a hard, plundering fashion while he fumbled with their clothing and finally, fantastically, filled her.

"Oh, Marchand!"

He moved her over him a rough, gratifying rhythm, his strength allowing him to lift her as if she weighed nothing, her strength letting her accept his savage thrusts with soft whimpers of delight. And as a mutual satisfaction sent them both soaring, Marchand was startled by the feeling of weightlessness. He looked down to see they were hovering some dozen or more inches off the bed. As their passions spiraled down, they settled easily upon the covers once more. He raked his fingers back through Nicole's tumbled hair and vowed, "Give me that for an eternity!"

"That, my love, will be my pleasure."

"As my wife."

"That will be my privilege."

They were kissing again and desire was quick to flame and follow.

As Nicole drowsed some time later in her lover's embrace, she felt the need to make peace with the past before moving on to a promising, if unconventional, future. She reached out tentatively with her thoughts.

Gerard?

Ah, la mía ragázza! Cóme stá? The fluid warmth of his voice was like a caress within her mind. She smiled to herself.

I wanted to thank you for what you did for me and Marchand.

You are safe? That's good to know. It was my pleasure, cara. Anything for you.

"Gerardo?"

Reluctant to be drawn from the telepathic communion, Gerardo Pasquale turned from his study out the coach window to the whining creature beside him all draped in the concealing folds of a cloak. "What is it?"

"I am weary and hungry. When can we stop?"

"Presently."

"Gerardo—"

"I grow bored with your constant complaints," he snapped tersely. "Have I not seen to your every wish and demand? Cease your harping or I shall lose all patience and put you out to fend for yourself."

The petulant commands stopped and Gerard canted a glance toward his traveling companion. The burns were still quite horrible. Nothing natural could have survived them.

"We shall stop at the next inn. I find myself hungry for Spanish food." His tone had gentled almost imperceptibly and the hood gave a haughty toss.

"You are too kind, *caro.*"

"I am too selfish to wish to be alone. Now, be quiet and let me have some time with my own thoughts." He could feel her glower upon him, but the threat was an empty one. She was helpless without him and he found he quite liked lording his power over her.

He closed his eyes and leaned back against the comfortable seat of their traveling coach.

Take care of your family, mía amóra.

And you see to yourself.

Give them my regards. And a big, big kiss to your mother. And he smiled, thinking of his old friend's ire. *Until we meet again.*

Please turn the page for an exciting
sneak preview of the next enthralling chapter
in Nancy Gideon's spellbinding vampire romance trilogy
MIDNIGHT SURRENDER
on sale at bookstores everywhere in
May 1995

Chapter One

He was as one with the shadows, steeped in the same darkness, the same deep chill. He moved alone, silent and undetected where the soft glow of street lamps fell short in their conquest of the night. Winter was in the air and crystals of it hung in the rapid plumes of his breathing as he waited. As he watched.

There was a sudden burst of sound overhead, a woman's laughter. He sucked a quick breath of anticipation, beginning to ease from his hiding place. Then a man's voice mingled with her merriment and he darted back into the anonymity of blackness. He pressed back against the cold stones, closing his eyes, calming the shiver of his impatience.

Soon. Soon she will come.

The couple crossed over the bridge oblivious to him and continued on in their late evening stroll, unaware of the evil they brushed past.

A few more minutes went by then he was rewarded.

She approached the bridge with a hurried step, probably tired and cold and eager to gain the warm comforts of her apartment. Her haste made her careless as thoughts focused ahead on those waiting pleasures. Pleasures she would never know again. The tap of her boots made a hollow reverberation as she passed over him. He eased from the shadows just far enough to get a glimpse of her. She was bundled up in her cheap coat, her blonde hair all but hidden under a silly hat. Her arms were laden with paper-bound parcels; articles of clothing she meant to alter that evening so they would be ready for her customers the next day. She didn't sense her danger.

The cold gleam of lamp light glittered in his stare as he turned slightly to follow her progress down the twist of the path as it led to the walk below. To where he waited. She stumbled, uttering a soft, unladylike curse as her packages shifted and threatened to tumble. She juggled them for a precarious moment then continued down the gradual incline with a more confident step once they were under control. She was looking ahead as danger, swift, and certain, moved up from behind.

He struck without warning, muffling her startled cry with the clamp of his hand, silencing it forever with a quick slash across her throat. The packages she held tumbled to the ground and lay scattered, forgotten.

Her blonde head wobbled loosely as he unwound the handknit scarf she wore. A more vivid hue dominated its subtle pattern. He held it up against his cheek, breathing in the fragrance held in its yarns, the floral hint of her perfume, the heavy scent of her blood. His glazed eyes slid closed as if in some dreamy rapture. There was a soft thump at his feet as her body crumpled, purpose served and now discarded without care.

"For you," he whispered in a tender reverie.

Cassie Alexander sat back in her chair, giving her head a slow revolution upon a stiff neck. It was late, much later than she'd realized. The papers spread across her father's desk would have to wait until morning. There was no way to straighten a five year tangle overnight.

Brighton Alexander had been a top notch news man but in business, he'd been a disaster.

Her fingertips stroked along the glossy mahogany surface of the desk and she smiled fondly. She wasn't sure whether to bless or curse her father for the legacy he'd left her. At the moment, it felt like a millstone of incredible tonnage. But tomorrow, when she pushed open the frosted glass doors of the Lexicon, and was heralded by the scent of newsprint and energy, she knew she wouldn't feel that way. This was her dream, all she'd ever wanted.

One didn't abandon a pampered child just because it was teething.

But one didn't get much sleep during that time of upheaval, either.

"Good night, baby," she murmured wryly as she turned down her desktop lamp. The outside offices were already dark, everyone else having gone home to their families at the dinner hour. Cassie had no one to go home to. The Lexicon was the only family she had left.

She collected her long velvet coat, and with a ream of proof pages under her arm, she started through the empty office. She was reaching for the knob of the outside door when a distorted shadow loomed large and threatening on the other side of the glass. She stumbled back with a cry of alarm, her papers flying every which way like an early blizzard.

The door nudged open.

"Miss Alexander?"

Cassie clasped a hand to her laboring bosom. It was just Tim, one of their errand boys. "Oh, Tim, you gave me quite a startle! What are you doing out this late?"

"I'm sorry, ma'am." He blushed hot and bent to help her gather her work into an untidy pile. Once they were all collected and they stood, she gave him a questioning look.

"Well?"

"Ma'am?"

"Did you want to see me for something?"

"Oh! Yes, of course. I was to deliver this package to you." He extended a crudely wrapped brown paper bundle with her name and the office address scrawled across the top. She took it curiously.

"And it couldn't wait until morning?"

"I was slipped an extra note to see that you got it tonight."

"Hmmm." She gave it a rattle. There was a soft shifting.

"Maybe something from an admirer," the boy suggested with a deeper flush of color.

Cassie made a non-committal sound. More like another packet of debts she couldn't afford to pay. "Well, thank you for your diligence, Tim. Go on home now. You shouldn't be out on the streets at this hour."

"Beggin' your pardon, Miss Alexander, but neither should you. Can I have your carriage brought round for you?"

"I didn't use it this morning. I'll just catch the late trolly. It drops me off almost at my door."

The lad lingered a moment, looking uncomfortable then all at once bold. "Maybe I should see you home. It is awful late and you being a lady out alone . . ."

She held to her smile. "How old are you, Tim?"

"Almost fifteen, ma'am." He puffed out his slight chest and stood taller.

"Your parents should be proud. They've raised themselves quite a gentleman. Go home. I'll see you in the morning."

His shoulders fell in disappointment. "Yes, ma'am. "Good night, ma'am. Don't forget to lock up tight behind you."

She did smile then. "I won't." Really. Almost fifteen and all patronizing male already. She waited until the sound of his heavy boots sounded on the stairs leading down to the first floor before she turned to lock up the office. Then she brushed her fingers over the gilded plate on the door claiming in bold letters, *THE LEXI-CON, C. Alexander, Owner and Editor*. Owner and editor and still peach-fuzz faced errand boys felt she needed their protection.

The moment she stepped out onto the front walk and the night wind snatched away her breath, Cassie regretted opting for the street car over her personal carriage. Hunching her shoulders against the chill, she started the two block walk, having to run the last half of it when the illuminated car pulled in ahead of her. It wouldn't do to miss it on such a night.

Gasping slightly, she climbed aboard and paid the fare to an indifferent conductor. As she found a seat close to the front, she scanned the car with a quick glance. A old woman snoring loudly. A dapper gentlemen reading from the evening edition. Two large fellows way in back with feet stretched out and arms folded over massive chests. A lively group. She wondered what they were going home to but her mind was too tired to play its usual game of making up histories to go with their faces. Her father always told her she had too active an imagination to be contained by just the obvious. That's what made her a good writer and reporter. She settled onto her seat and laid her papers and the package beside her. She gave the parcel another curious look. It was light. Too light to contain text from some want-to-be author. Maybe it was from an admirer. Smiling at that unlikelihood, she leaned back and watched the New York city scenery drift by.

She was almost twenty-five, too long out of the social light to be considered anything but a self-proclaimed spinster. She'd been more interested in getting an education than in grabbing up a husband and now, at her ripe old age, a man might look twice but he would think twice about courting someone too obviously difficult to have made a match while yet in her prime. The idea didn't distress her. She, like her father before her, considered herself wed to the world of journalism. He'd once said the front page was his mistress, and now it would be her master as well. And it would prove much more responsive and satisfying than the men of this Victorian age.

Few men or women would share her views. They considered her odd, some even said dangerous, with the way she insisted upon keeping her own home and holding a prominent position in a male dominated field. She cared little for their opinion. She knew hers were not the popular choices but then, they never had been. For a score of years, she'd squared off against tradition and had refused to bend before its stuffy demands. Where was it written that a woman had less intelligence than a man? Where was the proof that a female could not reasonably control her own destiny? She'd posed these questions to her father and he'd been impressed by her vinegar, as he'd called it. Had his wife shown some of that same vinegar, she wouldn't have collapsed under the strain of everyday living and ended her days in an opiate daze in an upstate sanatorium. No one was ever going to fault her for that same debilitating weakness, Cassie had determined at a very young age. She was going to be strong and in control. No one would ever mistake for her feeble-minded and lock her away from the world.

She knew and understood the world she lived in, though much of its philosophies she disagreed with. She saw harsh realities in the pages of the Lexicon every day and never shirked from them. If it was news, its existence could not be denied. If it existed, it would not go away if one pretended not to recognize it. She preferred to be the aggressor at the end of this ever changing century and when the next era dawned, she would be ready for it. And the Lexicon would be her sounding board, taking a forward-looking stand amid a backward-thinking populace.

Hers was a necessarily lonely position, both in the professional and personal sector. Those who worked for her bent before her decision because she paid them to. Those who were not on her payroll, shunned her society as if mere ideas could contaminate. She hoped they could. The people of New York could afford to suffer through an epidemic of new ideas. How could industry rush so vigorously ahead when mankind lagged behind in ignorance?

She missed having her father to argue these points with over evening brandy and cigarette smoke. She'd joined him in both vices, feeling wonderfully independent and decidedly wicked. He'd been gone for almost two months and she hadn't touched a drop or had a taste of tobacco since. Decadence was no fun unless it could be shared. Her father had been fun. He'd been a brilliant writer with the sharpest instincts she'd ever seen. He'd had a caustic wit and a cynical world view that allowed her freedoms no other female could claim. He saw her as an equal and when he died, he'd paid her the ultimate compliment. He'd willed her the Lexicon and paved the way for her eternal independence.

He'd also left her nearly penniless.

But oh, how she'd loved him. And missed him.

And she was so deep in her reverie, she almost missed her stop.

"Oh, wait. This is where I get off," she cried to the conductor. She heard him mutter unflattering epithets as the car shuddered to a halt. She gave him a sweet smile in passing. "You are so kind. Have a pleasant evening."

"Same t'you, ma'am," he growled, not meaning it.

When the lights of the tram disappeared, Cassie found herself swallowed up in the chill midnight fog. Its rising billows cloaked all in a silvery haze and she shivered in spite of herself. It was only three blocks to her huge rambling house. Long, silent, empty blocks. She'd never been timid with her own company. Even so, she set out a brisk pace.

She'd gone the first block when a feeling of unease crept over her. It wasn't a definable sensation. More of a tingle of intuition. She was very female in that sense. Keeping to her rapid pace, she tuned her ears for any untoward sound.

And there it was; the soft echo of her own steps, redoubled.

She refused to glance behind her. She would not be

intimidated. With a casual move, she put a hand to her elaborate hat as if to straighten it and removed a long pin. Clutching it in her hand the way she would a dagger, she dared any cut purse thinking to make a quick score to tangle with Cassie Alexander. He'd find her no easy mark.

But she was wrong on two counts. Her money wasn't the focus. And it was two sets of footsteps, not one.

She'd just rounded the second block. She could see her house, big and dark, looming just up ahead. She considered running, weighing the distance against her own fleetness of foot. She considered it a moment too long for suddenly she was flanked on either side by large, threatening forms.

The two men from the street car.

One grabbed her wrist. Without hesitation, she jabbed her hat pin into his meaty hand. He let her go with a wail. She managed one quick forward stride when the other nabbed her about the waist, whirling her around, thrusting her hard up against the narrow iron fence rails of a neighboring home. Still clutching her armload to her chest, she drew a big breath, preparing to scream but a fierce blow caught her on the jaw, skewing the sound along with her senses.

She didn't remember falling but suddenly the ground was cold beneath her palms and cutting into her knees. She tried to scramble forward, to break free of them. All she had to do was bolt down the nearest front walk to the safety of the family within. All she had to do was loose one cry for help.

But the back of her coat was seized and she was flung head first into the wrought iron bars.

The twilight world grew darker as fog rose in her

Nancy Gideon

mind. She uttered what she'd hoped would be a loud plea for aid. It sounded like a whimper. She groped about rather blindly for the hat pin she'd dropped, for anything she could use against her assailants but she was too disoriented, too dazed by the brutal blows to effect any kind of struggle.

"Stab me, will you," came a low snarl from out of the cresting blackness. A rough hand cuffed her arm, dragging her up to unsteady feet. She got a glimpse of hard features, cruelly drawn in their vicious intent.

"Take my money," she panted, throwing her hand bag out into the misty street, half hoping they would go after it. They didn't.

"It ain't your money we want, missy."

She tried to slap the one closest to her but her hand was intercepted and crushed until she moaned in pain. These men were going to hurt her . . . or worse. And there was nothing she could do to prevent it from happening practically on her own doorstep.

Then, amazingly, her attacker was gone, yanked back into the fog by an incredible force. She staggered, clutching at the fence for balance. A terrible wail came from out of the mist then silence.

The other man lost all interest in her. He'd pulled a knife, a long thin-bladed weapon that he bandied before him with murderous intent. He gave a sudden shout and drove it forward with all his sight. Then he, too, was sucked up into the swirl of evening haze.

Cassie leaned back against the rails, breath rasping from her, panic and pain shaking her knees together. She'd dropped her papers and her slick-soled walking shoes slipped on the spill of them on the walk beneath her. Sobbing softly, she started to pull herself along the fence, afraid to take her eyes from the spot where her assailants had disappeared. She screamed hoarsely as one of them lurched into view. He was stumbling, reeling, his hands up at his neck. Blood gleamed black in the faint reach of the closest street lamp. He made a gurgling sound and reached out for her with one wet hand. She couldn't move. It caught on her sleeve, tugging as he began to fall. Frantically, she jerked back to free herself as he slid down silently into the low curtain of mist.

Movement brought her frightened gaze up from the cloud that had swallowed him. She shrank against the unyielding bars, small sounds of terror escaping her with each labored breath.

A lone figure approached from out of the icy clouds. A face that was familiar yet unlike any she'd seen before. Pale as the wisps of mist. With eyes like fiery coals.

"Do not be afraid."

Yet when he spoke that soothing sentiment, two monstrous teeth were exposed; sharp, animallike fangs all tinged with crimson. Cassie tried to scream but the noise suffocated in her horror-constricted throat.

"I will not harm you."

He reached out a slender hand, the gesture an offer of aid not threat. It cupped beneath her elbow just as the strength in her legs gave way, holding her up without any effort. She was aware of her own fear, of how it fluttered about a heart gone mad but she was helpless to act upon it even as he placed his other hand gently against the tangled disarray of her blonde hair. His touch was cold, so cold it made her tremble.

Then the shock of the situation overcame her. Consciousness gave way before a numbing swoon. And just as she sank into its embrace, she felt his hand pass across her eyes and heard the low croon of his voice.

"Remember nothing."